D0861344

THE ROAD TO HELL

Four Novellas

Edited by Eric S. Beebe

Post Mortem Press
Cincinnati, OH USA

Other Titles from Post Mortem Press

These Trespasses by Kenneth W. Cain
The Lord Said Unto Satan by Hugh Fox
Dellwood by Ginny Gilroy
The Beer Chronicles by Scott Lange
Rabbits in the Garden by Jessica McHugh
Perpetual Night by Georgina Morales

Anthologies of Short Fiction
Uncanny Allegories
Isolation
A Means to an End
Shadowplay

Available at www.postmortem-press.com

Contents

Number Six

by Joseph Williams

Zach Meyer took one look at the railroad tracks and that was all he needed to follow them.

The way was hidden. The ties were overwhelmed with the tangle of weeds so heavily that it was difficult to tell they were part of a track at all and not just sporadic clumps of steel. The bolts were rusted and the wood that formed the ladder over the ground had rotted so much that most of it had already been reclaimed by the wilderness. Zach couldn't remember ever seeing abandoned railroad tracks so deep in that stretch of the woods. They were tantalizing enough to send him wandering.

The small, lakeside town of Oscoda, Michigan was fading fast behind him and he wasn't at all sad to leave it just where it was. As of eleven o'clock that morning, he had no job, no car, and no place to call his own, and with no real plan of action to break from the mess he'd left on the shores of Lake Huron, he'd taken to hitching.

He didn't really care where the driver was going (although he'd say he was headed to Standish if pressed, he'd decided, so as not to scare off any potential rides), he just wanted to find someone to put as many miles between himself and northern Michigan as he possibly could.

So far, hitching hadn't been going so well. He was about six or seven miles down River Road by his own reckoning, and not one of the thirty-four cars that had passed by were willing to pick up someone like him: a rough-looking biker in his thirties with a long scar across his bald head and a perpetual sneer hung from his mouth like a damp cigarette. But Zach knew it wasn't just his looks that kept people away. No one really picked up hitchers anymore at all, not like when he was a kid. There was too much evil in the world to take someone into your front seat and listen to his secrets. You never knew who you'd end up with. He wasn't too discouraged. He kept right on walking.

It was a hot day in early August and he could feel the sun's handprints all over him, worst of all along his back and shoulders. It had seemed perfectly reasonable at the time to take off his tee shirt and stuff it in the

1

front pocket of his khakis during the first mile of road, back before the sun really hit him hard. It didn't seem so smart now.

"Should've grabbed the fucking sunscreen," he cursed aloud.

But he hadn't really had a chance to grab anything when he left. Meghan had locked the door to the little house they'd shared as soon as he'd walked out. They both knew that, this time, there was no going home. They'd had one blow-up fight too many, one too many one-night affairs in someone else's bed, one too many days together behind them. Their course had been run, and it was just the same at Posey's, where Zach had worked as a short order cook for the last five years, the only years he'd been in town. He guessed he'd had it coming, mainly for showing up late almost every day he'd ever worked there. Or maybe it was because he'd fucked the owner's nineteen year-old daughter a few nights before his fight with Meghan. It didn't really matter, anyway.

All that mattered was that he was back on his own again, wandering between earth and sky, destination nowhere. Wherever the old train tracks led him was just exactly where he'd be. He'd climb their wooden ladder across the wilderness as far as it would take him.

For a while, the abandoned railroad just followed along the dirt road that branched off of the main one. There were trees on either side of the brown aisle, but none hung over far enough to allow him the mercy of some shade. He kept expecting to see the AuSable River open up in front of him because the road was running in its direction, but he never reached its banks or even smelled the wet, open air.

It didn't sit right with him.

He'd been down all the dirt roads off of River Road at one time or another over the last five years, but they'd all run straight down to the river on its southern shore. And the river was never too far down the way, either. He was sure he would have seen or smelled it by then.

But he didn't see any water at all, and he grew more and more certain as he walked that he'd never seen this road, either. There wasn't even a sign for it.

Probably someone's driveway or a huntin road or somethin.

The wildlife seemed to swell closer to the road than he'd seen them anywhere else that day, and that alone kept him from daring to wander into the shade.

2

He eyed them all suspiciously.

These weren't normal animals, he could see. They didn't freeze or scamper away when they saw him. They stopped and watched him pass. No matter how close he got to them, they didn't budge. And even considering the mood he was in and how unnerving their presence was, he couldn't bring himself to chuck a rock their way or swing out his sweaty right fist like he normally would. It was more than a code of moral decency that kept him from lashing out. With these odd ones, he was afraid of what their retaliation might be.

He walked another half mile with the railroad tracks always close at his side, and then they veered sharply to the right with such abruptness that he lost them for a while and had to retrace his steps to get them back.

"Fuck," he groaned when he saw the way they slugged into the deepest heart of the forest, away from the road.

He stopped walking and frowned.

There was a decision to make. He wanted to work over his options carefully.

On the one hand, he could follow the train tracks for no other reason than it seemed a romantic notion to be wandering like a true free man, emancipated from all worry and obligation. It would be a fitting proclamation to the world at large that he was finally free to follow any of the billion roads that now lay submissive before him. He could pick whichever one he felt like, and he didn't even need to have rationale for it. He could just go.

But that didn't mean he needed to be completely reckless. It was getting late. Pretty soon the sun would vanish beneath the trees to his left, leaving him out in the wilderness with no food, shelter, or water nearby. If he wanted to get back to the main road and make it to any hotel or motel by sunset, he'd have to leave right then or sometime in the very near future. Besides, the tracks went through thick undergrowth and a significant stretch of poison ivy, and those were just the obstacles in his immediate sight. God only knew what it would look like a little further on, once he lost the road completely.

I am pretty goddamned hungry, he thought.

He didn't have a whole lot of money in his wallet, just the parting check he'd gotten from Posey's and thirty-four dollars in small bills he had

3

leftover from visiting the local pub the night before. Still, it was enough to get a cheap burger and a beer somewhere without completely crippling himself, if he wanted.

But did he?

He sighed, staring at the railroad tracks and imagining them without any of the plant-life built up around them.

In his mind, it was the dead of night and a coldly beautiful passenger car steamed through the forest. He could see the women dressed in the latest fashions of an old world, the men sipping whiskey from tea saucers so their children wouldn't recognize the act, the children themselves concealing thoughts and acts of dangerous impropriety from the eyes of their parents.

Faces.

They were all very clear to Zach, but he wasn't sure why they popped into his head instead of just the train tracks or the train. He wasn't sure why he'd placed the faces and dress to an era (the early 1900s) like all the fools on TV with their lady in white, either. It may have been because the tracks looked about that old, but Zach didn't think that was quite the case. He had a cold sensation in the back of his head, much deeper than the sun could reach.

A feeling of familiarity.

He followed the tracks with his eyes as far as they would take him, trying to decide whether to be practical or daring. The animals still watched him intently. The tracks did too, he thought.

Shit, why not? If I don't do something like this now, I never will.

He shrugged.

What's stopping you?

He thought about it and realized he had no answer. It was a sound enough argument to sway him.

Resolved, he pushed the bushes at the side of the road away and climbed the mild incline into the unknown. The road swelled again behind him and then exhaled and shrank to its normal width.

Once he was in, he felt he couldn't turn back, even as the sun was swallowed behind him and he entertained the first waves of doubt, surging like bubbling lava through his cranium. They were only whispers at first, but they would grow soon enough.

JOSEPH WILLIAMS

It was all right starting out. The air was nice, the shade was welcoming, and in his head, the railroad tracks were still mystical, ambivalent portals to another time.

It felt good to be following them. Damned good. He felt at ease. Back the way he came, there was a whole world of problems clinging to him like hooks in his flesh pulling back his skin and exposing the writhing veins beneath, but in the thick of the trees they were all completely severed. He was cut off. No one knew where he was or what he was doing. No debtors, girlfriends, parents, taxmen, police officers, parole officers, or bosses could get to him there. He was free. Free, and alone.

Completely alone.

Sure, there were still animals all around, now minding their own business like they always should have been, but none of them could scold him, nag him, bitch, moan, or otherwise bring a good man down. Here was the wild, untamed Heaven. Here was God's country, unfolding like a dark and living color beneath his feet.

And the tracks unwound like an ever-lengthening serpent, extending so gracefully and hypnotically that Zach was a slave to its every whim.

Over the next few hours, he followed the tracks like they were the words of Jesus. Never once did he pause or break pace or even wonder where they would take him. He watched them moving like a conveyor belt ushering him along, resigned completely to their guiding hand.

Meghan was behind him.

Posey's was behind him and so was Tom, the owner.

Rent was behind him.

Car Payment was behind him.

Mom-and-Dad was behind him.

IRS was behind him.

Parole was behind him.

With all that behind, it didn't really matter what was ahead.

The evening ran on.

The sun was finally swallowed by a dark demon and night mourned its passing. The forest never relented. He never caught a glimpse of a road or a headlight or someone's home or even a stray piece of metal. There were no beer cans, cigarette butts, or any other sign of civilization. There was

5

only the ladder, leading the blind (but free) man into the heart of a mystery Time and Logic had long abandoned.

Station Number Six.

The In-Between.

The Long Track.

The Freedom Train.

The trees grew thicker. Zach dove headlong into the wilderness passage like a maniac. The stars peppered and salted the night sky above the forest ceiling, and still he didn't stop. The bears and raccoons and owls came out to warn him back, and still he didn't stop. His stomach growled, his throat moaned, his bladder screamed, and still he didn't stop.

The world passed on around him, and still the tracks went on. Ever on. Never ceasing, never conquered, never affording Zach a single moment to question them.

"Why don't you do something with your life, you fucking bum? Are you always gonna be workin in some shit diner on 23? Is that what you want for yourself? Is that what you want for us?"

Strange, Meghan's voice could reach him in the wilderness after all. But she didn't stay long. Thank God for small favors. The night drowned her out. The noises of the forest took over. Their voices. Their songs. Their memories. Their regrets.

They filled Zach.

"All aboard!" he screamed suddenly.

He had no idea where it had come from or why he'd said it, but the words made him laugh hysterically. The forest watched him.

His voice echoed back to him and the sound of it, a lonely sound, sobered him back up quickly.

Another half-hour passed.

It was full dark. The stars were out still but mostly blocked by the forest canopy. He was following the tracks with no other guidance than his naked instinct, completely subconscious, not even bothering to stoop down in the darkness to feel for the cold steel and make sure it was still there. Maybe it was just his imagination, but he thought the tracks were becoming less overgrown as he went. Maybe his feet were just numb.

"Getting close," he muttered to no one in particular.

Already, his lips were cracked with thirst. His stomach roared with Achillean rage. He could barely even feel the burn of poison ivy spreading on his leg, and his sunburn seemed to have somehow been cured by the nighttime tides.

"Almost there."

He didn't know where 'there' was, only he could tell it was nearby. Maybe it was a town. Maybe it was the train. Maybe it was the lake. Maybe it was just the end of the tracks. But no matter where it turned out to be, he'd find it soon enough.

Another half-hour passed.

The moon climbed all the way to the top of the sky where it could begin a slow descent into morning. The wild animals of the forest chose, wisely, to leave Zach be. But they still watched him. They knew what he was stumbling towards and that they were powerless to stop it. A time came when even the flies and mosquitoes stayed away, and Zach would have been grateful for that unexpected blessing if he'd had his wits about him. He didn't. All he could think about was how close he was.

"Almost. Almost," he told himself.

The words were reassuring.

"All aboard!" he yelled again. This time, he didn't laugh.

"Freedom freedom freedom…climb aboard the Freedom Train! Hallelujah!" someone screamed.

His eyes focused gravely on the silhouettes of trees ahead of him.

"Zachary Meyer, are you a Free Man?"

"Yes sir, I am a Free Man."

"You got nothin holding you back?"

"No, sir. Nothin. I'm a Free Man."

"Then climb aboard the Freedom Train!"

"Choo-choo, mother fucker!"

"All aboard!"

He started to run. Adrenaline spurted through his body.

"I'm a Free Man!" he yelled, panting.

The tracks seemed to rise to meet him. The animals watched. The night and the dark rolled on.

Another half-hour passed.

Memories of Meghan filled his thoughts. Their first date. Their beagle. Catching each other in lies. Cheating. Fighting. Drinking. Leaving. Reconciling. Un-reconciling. Vacations. Sick days. Christmases. And all the million moments in between.

None of it worth the time or effort.

But that didn't matter now, because he was free.

A Free Man.

Hallelujah!

"All aboard!"

And what was that Freedom Train called? Just 'Freedom'?

"No," he whispered. "Not Freedom. Something else."

And what could that something be?

What did it really matter?

He remembered Meghan slapping him so hard on New Year's Eve that she broke his nose, making him bleed in front of everyone.

"You want her? Go get her!" he'd screamed at one of her dozen other lovers as he stormed out into the night, his pride more gravely injured than his nose would ever be. "I'm fucking done!"

Zach grinned.

Not so cute when you fight dirty, are you bitch?

A half-hour passed.

He kept running, still not caring where the train tracks ended but knowing that he was very close to where he was supposed to be. So fucking close. He guessed he'd know it when he got there.

Still, the tracks went on, until he knew it wasn't just his imagination that the undergrowth covering them had let up. The ties in this new stretch looked like they'd never stopped being used. They were worn but somehow fresh, too. There were no weeds strangled within the wood anymore.

"Freedom Train's a rollin."

"You gettin on?"

He could picture all of the people again, the train steaming through midnight like Apollo in reverse.

They laughed, they smiled, they screamed, they cried, they bled, they burned. They were anxious, scared, and delighted. They shattered plates and made love in echoing passenger compartments while their children pretended not to notice. They told bedtime stories and smoked cigars. They talked about where they were going.

A Mansion.

A Garden.

A Hospital.

The Conductor stepped into the cabin.

"All right, next stop is Station Number Six. If you're switching over to the Number Six Train, please have your papers ready."

Groaning, laughing, sobbing.

He was a fat man with rosy cheeks, a white beard, and a disapproving furrow in his brow.

"Almost there," Zach told himself.

The faces were gone again and so was the inside of the train, but now he could hear it chugging ahead of him.

It was loud but it seemed to fit in effortlessly with the cool wilderness. The air caught it just right, eased the call of the whistle into the trees and blocked out the chug-a-chug of the engine.

"All aboard!"

"Station Number Six!"

"Freedom Train!"

"Have your papers ready!"

The landscape began to change. For hours, there'd been nothing but trees, bushes, bears, owls, wolves, insects, deer, and a few pockets of water. Now the tracks were cutting through all of it. Now, it was completely on its own, raised above the ground, and propped up by mounds of dirt and stone on each side. The trees kept their distance, which was about ten feet.

There were faces hovering in the compartments.

But what was even more of a shock than the sight of the passengers was the fainter glow somewhere off ahead of him. Not light, but something big, white, and solid. A giant boulder, maybe. Or maybe even a house. All Zach could tell was that it was big.

"Almost there..." the words panted out of him in a rhythm.

He'd been running long enough that his body was beginning to catch up to the surge of adrenaline, but holy hell, he was close. So close...

To what? the question finally registered.

The train, he answered.

He couldn't see it, but he knew he was right on its heels.

Almost...

As if on cue, the train reappeared, only this time he saw it from the outside. None of the people stared back at him from the leather seats like they had before. There was just the black steamer rolling through the wilderness like the boundaries of tree and stone and air didn't even exist.

It seemed to be taunting him from a quarter-mile further up the track, calling out for him to hurry, flipping the bird, telling him he was a slow cocksucker and that his mother had been right about him all along.

Their voices fell on deaf ears.

Zach ran harder, determined to catch up to it before it was too late. After all, this was his chance to hop aboard the Freedom Train and ride it to Hell and back, because in the end he didn't care where he was going. It only mattered that he'd chosen to follow this track for a reason, maybe to find where it went and maybe to see if any trains still climbed it, but here was his opportunity for a payoff. Blind chance, maybe destiny, had brought him to this cleared stretch of track and he'd be damned if he were going to miss out on what he had coming.

In that case, luck was on his side. Maybe blind luck. Maybe fate.

Although it seemed like the train was steaming on as fast as it could possibly go, Zach was bridging the gap between them fast. Too fast. Even if the train had been at a standstill. It was almost as though it were running backwards to meet him, only that couldn't have been right because he could see it moving forward, taking the turns, blocking the trees or slapping a rude high-five to the occasional wayward branch hanging too low over the track.

Zach looked down at his feet to see if they were moving faster than he thought. They weren't. When he looked back at the train, no more than eighty yards away by then, it seemed like he was looking at it through a picture frame or movie screen. Time slowed and inertia picked up, pushing Zach to the train at supernatural speeds and the train to Zach with equal intensity. He peeled his eyes away from the blurring landscape with great difficulty.

Eventually, he slowed and so did the train.

The white object came fully into view.

It was a house. He could tell that much, at least. But why was there a house in the middle of the woods like that? In the middle of the track? How?

As far as he could tell, there was no road, driveway, or even a path where someone could have accessed the home. Nothing but the tracks.

"Number Six on the right!"

"Have your papers ready!"

"Are you getting on?"

Zach panted. He could see the glare of moonlight off of the cabin windows. He could hear the frantic conversations of the passengers, coming to terms with leaving their loved ones behind for a new misery on the Number Six stop.

"All aboard the Freedom Train!"

"Are you a Free Man, Zachary Meyer?"

"You got nothing holding you back?"

Here was the stop. Here was where Zach caught up and either boarded this train or the next. He ran closer.

As he approached, he could read the large, white letters streaming down the black cars.

"What's the name of the Freedom Train?"

"Freedom?"

"No," he said. "The Cannonball."

"Hallelujah!"

"The Cannonball."

"The Lord will bring you to your knees so the Devil can bring you home!"

"Hallelujah!"

"All aboard!"

"Choo-choo, mother fucker!"

He stopped running.

The train gasped and came to a stop in front of a rectangular, wooden building. The whistle blew for no sane reason at all. To Zach, it sounded like a great wailing, a mourning, a gnashing of teeth in a vale of tears.

Everything fell still. Even the forest ceased to move.

And then, the Cannonball came alive.

NUMBER SIX

At first, it was nothing more than a low murmur building up from the passenger compartments. Movement. Goodbyes. Tears. Exclamations.

The train idled, hissing out steam-breath occasionally but mostly just crouched like a panther, ready to explode outward and tear away at the track with its black and yellow claws.

The peace did not hold for long.

Zach reached the last compartment and stopped, acutely aware of the voices in the dark, and the fact that it was dark save for the moonlight. He wasn't much of an authority on traveling by train, but he knew enough to realize the station should have been lit to receive the passengers even at so late an hour…especially when it was so late, in fact. It stood to reason that the cabins should have been, too, but both were completely dark. The train didn't even have a headlight.

"Station Number Six!" the Conductor suddenly screamed.

Zach couldn't see him, only remember the glimpse he'd fancied in his head, but he was sure the man had a yellow grin on his fat face right then. A knowing, shit-eating grin.

"If you're riding Number Six, get the fuck off of this one. The train doesn't wait."

The Conductor laughed.

All at once, the passengers began to move. Zach could feel the rumble of their footsteps even though he couldn't see them.

People screamed. Sobbed. Tried to escape through the windows. But none of them were successful. Only one or two of them seemed indifferent to the new track they were to embark upon.

"Shit…" Zach muttered.

Now that he was right up against the train, waiting for it to unload, he realized he would rather be anywhere else in the world. He couldn't remember for the life of him what maniac urge had convinced him to follow the tracks.

"Freedom Train a-loadin'!" the Conductor yelled.

Zach ducked into the trees at the side of the railroad track.

He could hear the passengers filing off, still screaming and sobbing, but he never did see them. He knew exactly what they looked like and what their names were and how they reacted to this new egregious turmoil, but he never caught the light on them even outside of the train.

Still, he stuck to the seclusion of the trees. He couldn't bear the thought of the Conductor seeing him, but he knew he needed to watch the train all the same. He needed to bear witness to this Freedom Train; his own 'amen' and 'hallelujah', the shoes of the fisherman, with its long black snout, its misery, gravity stretched across its steel sides like an idiot face.

The shuffling, murmuring, crying, screaming, persisted for no less than ten minutes, and then the Conductor's voice boomed through the forest again.

"Number Six! Number Six! Cannonball's leavin' the station!"

"Hallelujah!"

"Devil's on the track!"

"Hallelujah!"

"All aboard!"

"Cannonball's a' rollin!"

The whistle blew. The great train hissed. The world rolled over in derision. And the Cannonball left for some other station, presumably Number Seven, to continue its never-ending, late-night run.

Zach waited until he couldn't see its smoke even when he strained his eyes as hard as he could, and then he waited some more.

"What if they're out there?"

"Who?"

"The passengers."

"You know they're not."

And he did know, but that wasn't the same as believing.

"Something is."

"Well, the train's gone and you missed it."

"The Freedom Train!"

"The Cannonball!"

"Hallelujah!"

"Amen!"

"The Devil rides the Midnight Track!"

"Hallelujah!"

"The Freedom Train!"

"You gettin' on?"

"All aboard!"

13

NUMBER SIX

"Have your papers ready!"

"Choo-choo, mother fucker!"

Zach was frozen in place, staring at the track where the train had been moments before. He strained and found he couldn't picture its interior anymore. It was too far away. But there was still a smell in the air. A rotting. Dried fruit. Spoiled milk. Burnt cinnamon. Fall. Winter. Spring. Summer.

It was a bad smell, mostly.

"Jesus," he cursed, regretting the word even as it left his lips. Only, the more he thought about it, the more he believed he had truly been praying. He was terrified.

For a moment, he would have given anything to have Meghan there with him. For a moment, he would have taken it all back just for some comfort of any kind, some company. For a moment, he wondered what the hell he was doing so far out in the strange, isolated forest on his own with no food and barely any money. For a moment, he wished he'd never found the tracks.

Only for a moment.

Then, the moment passed, and when it was gone, he was filled with the maddening urge to walk the track right up to Station Number Six and see for himself what all of the fuss was about.

The rail felt like it had a current running through it. Zach felt a little buzz radiate from head to toe, and the jolt made him queasy. Feeling unsteady on his feet, he thought of his old life. It had aged quickly. All the relative comfort, though misery, of his daily routine. The way Meghan had looked when they'd first met. The days at Posey's when he'd been able to laugh with the dishwashers and pretty, young waitresses. Cushy. And now, he was living the way he'd always said a real man needed to live: off on his own, adventuring, investigating, following every raw instinct, accountable to no one but himself.

"You'll always be accountable to the train."

No truer words had ever been spoken.

"Yes, sir. The train."

"And the Conductor."

"And the Conductor."

"Do you know who the Conductor is?"

14

"His name?"

"His job."

"Conducting?"

"Hallelujah and Amen!"

Zach grinned. The fever of the track was on him again. He wanted to follow, wanted to be led. He wanted to see everything it had to offer and even some of the things it kept secret. His mind would fill in whatever it had left out.

The old life was gone. He had nothing to lose and Freedom to gain.

"Fuck Meghan. Fuck Posey's. Fuck probation. Fuck car payments and rent and step-kids. Fuck Oscoda. Fuck the world."

"Oh, Lordy! You're a rebellious one!"

"I'm pissed off."

"But are you happy?"

"I'm Free."

"What does Freedom cost?"

"Nothing." He thought some more. "I don't know. The courage to take it, I guess."

"What is Freedom?"

"It's a shape-shifting mother fucker."

"Hallelujah and Amen! Ride the Freedom Train!"

"The Cannonball?"

"The Devil's Chariot!"

His feet were barely touching the track as he climbed the ladder across the land. He could still smell the rancid and sometimes fragrant breath the Cannonball had left in its wake. The further he went, the more he could smell the coal. The trees bent and bowed away from the track as though the consistent surge of energy were physically holding them back, punching them in the stomach, laughing in their wrinkled faces.

He would have sworn that every star there ever was could be seen from the woods that night, and the moon was exceptionally bright.

"We've all been left behind."

"Number Six is on its way."

Zach's feet slowed. He was almost sure that those two voices had spoken aloud, and not far away from him at all.

"The Cannonball."

He listened intently.

"Could we have left it?"

"Some do."

"How?"

"They trap others."

"How do they do that?"

"It's not always good. In fact, it's mostly bad."

"I don't care. We should have done it. I don't want to be here."

"No one ever does."

"Amen…"

"The Devil's riding the Midnight Track."

"Then why is it so cold?"

"Because you're at the end of the line."

Zach quit walking. The voices were dead ahead of him but he couldn't make out their shapes at all. Only the abandoned platform and the glowing white building behind it along the track.

He thought about calling out to them, then thought again. It wouldn't do him any good. The voices sounded on the verge of hysterics, especially the second one, and he didn't think he was ready to meet the sort of people who inhabited abandoned railroad stations at midnight in the middle of the wilderness. Just like a hitcher, they could have been anyone. They could have been killers, and there was no telling what they were capable of doing to him in the dark.

Anyone. He shuddered.

They could have been him.

"Almost there," he whispered to himself.

He waited for any form of reply or continuation from the voices, but they were gone. He wondered whether their train had come to pick them up.

After a good deal of walking, he finally reached the slightly elevated platform where the passengers had presumably let off of the snarling, black steam-locomotive. The smell of coal and tea and whiskey and cigars was strongest there. And there were new scents. Ones like fear, sadness, blood. Others, too, but they were far beyond Zach's sensory palette. Maybe they smelled like rotting flesh, maybe half-eaten corpses still ripe from the plucking. Maybe the dastardly broken hearts of unfathomable generations, passengers doomed to cross over at the Number Six Station.

"For what?"

"For themselves."

There was a heavy fog forming across the landscape. Zach ran his fingers through it, tasted it, pulled it aside and examined the thousands of footprints that had once paced the platform or, in vain, tried to break from it. He couldn't imagine anyone truly getting away. Maybe it was the ever-lessening rumble of the Cannonball as it thundered down the track towards the water, occasionally releasing its whistle on the unsuspecting northern night. Somehow, the sound of it still filled him, even from such a distance and with the rolling earth settling back into decency.

"Choo-choo, mother fucker!"

Zach's legs were numb. He had the sensation of a thousand careless hands passing over his body, through him, brushing over his bare skin and clothing alike.

"This is where the lost are taken down the only road that will still have them, helpless to resist its pull because this is where they're supposed to be. They made it so."

"The lost?"

"The weak. The Freedom Train."

"The Cannonball."

"All aboard!"

He shuddered. The air had turned cold sometime around midnight, but the chills assailing his body owed more to the constant chorus of voices around him than the temperature in the forest. They had slipped so effortlessly into him that he hadn't noticed they were there until they had their hands in every part of him. It took the constant repetition of their hopes, fears, and enticements for Zach to realize they'd been right there with him since he'd first spotted the tracks. Maybe it had even been before that. Maybe they were the reason he'd quit his job. Maybe they were the reason he'd called it quits with Meghan (or, rather, that she'd called it quits with him...though if he were being generous to himself, he could get away with saying they'd split amicably). Maybe that was the reason he'd decided to hitch rather than ask one of his 'friends' for a ride. He didn't have many good ones, none in Oscoda, but if he'd offered his final paycheck from Posey's, he could have persuaded an acquaintance to drive him downstate to his parents, or maybe another member of his extended family. He had a cousin who was a doctor somewhere down in the thumb of the mitten, and while he probably wouldn't lend any money, he would likely offer a place to stay while Zach got on his feet. Maybe the voices were what had convinced him to set out on River Road in the first place instead of down US-23, where civilization made one last desperate stand between the wilderness and the open blue of Lake Huron.

The voices. They were to blame.

If he tried, he could trace back their handiwork through every poor decision in his life.

Yet he couldn't deny the urge he'd felt to have his freedom, to feel the cool air of the wilderness shade all up and down his body. The cool air of Freedom.

But not these careless, groping hands. Not the caress of phantom, maniac voices.

"All aboard the Freedom Train!"

"Have your papers ready!"

"You got nothing holding you back?"

"Amen and Hallelujah!"

"Choo-choo, mother fucker!"

The platform creaked under the weight of his black work-boots. The fog swallowed him whole.

He paced the platform like the million souls had before him, swallowing liters of saliva and anxiety while his body bled out sweat from every pore. His muscles tensed, his back arched, and he felt the groping hands in every part of him.

"Cannonball's a'comin!"

"Lord have mercy!"

"Devil's come to claim the weary!"

"The lost!"

"The forsaken!"

"The Free Men of the Long Track!"

Zach walked to the edge of the platform and put his toe on the track. The current rushed through him, pulsed through his bones and made his hair stand on end from shoulders to toes. He could feel the Cannonball running in the distance and wasn't sure whether it was the Number Six train or not, but it was coming around in the bye and bye. He could see the faces in front of him again, close enough to touch, shattering plates, drinking whiskey from teacups so their children wouldn't know the terrible truth of their addictions, making love in echoing compartments while those same children slept just outside the door in the passenger cabs. They were all watching him while they worked, screaming, sobbing, tearing lines in their skin with their own fingernails until blood pooled through their shirts and stained the leather seats.

"Oh my God…"

He ripped his foot away from the track, breathing heavily.

"Fuck!" he yelled, clutching his boot in both hands and hobbling around the platform on one leg.

The night was quiet again. There was only the fog and the platform. The voices were gone, and though he could run ten yards in the direction the Cannonball had taken when it rode away and smack into the side of the station, he couldn't see it anymore than he could hear the screams coming from the big, white house. As far as he could tell, he was alone with his thoughts.

"Where is this place?" he wondered. "Why am I here?"

Neither the forest nor the track responded. At least, not in any way that he understood.

"What is the Cannonball?"

He fully expected a response. If there was one thing the voices were dying to talk about, he thought, it was the Cannonball. But there was nothing. Not even the chirp of a cricket, which had ever seemed inescapable on a summer night. Time had stopped. Or maybe just he had in his time. Maybe the voices had moved on. He couldn't be sure.

"What now?"

There was nowhere sane for him to go. He could start back the way he'd come on the tracks, but there was no way he could run as fast as he had to reach the platform. And even if he could run like that, he still wouldn't make it back to the dirt road before dawn. He didn't think he could go another minute without food or water, let alone a halfway decent night's sleep. Even a power nap, a granola bar, and some lake (or river) water would have been enough to get by. But to have nothing, no energy

19

or destination, that was a dangerous demon. To have such a hopeless and pride-breaking journey back to River Road and Meghan and Posey's and car payments, that was a dangerous goddamned Devil to be riding shotgun on his shoulders. It was enough to make him content right where he was, and even wonder if there wasn't a pantry and a warm bed inside of the ever-tantalizing and ever-depraved white house.

"Can't hurt," he told himself.

"There's nothing back there for me," he told himself.

"I won't go crawling back to that dumb bitch," he told himself.

"I'm a Free Man," he told himself.

"I got nothing holding me back."

Screams. Laughter. Shattering plates.

"I'm so goddamned hungry."

"Yes you are, Daisy. Why don't you come inside for a bite?"

The voice made him shudder, but the idea seemed sound enough. Why not? He was a Free Man. He had nothing holding him back.

As though a giant were drawing it up in a deep breath, the fog began to lift rapidly. The path from the platform to the house opened like a flower before him, and he realized that it wasn't just the white house, the platform, the track, and the station. There were other buildings, too. Presumably a post-office, general store, saloon, a brothel, and a gambling hole. Maybe even a hotel. The whole little town looked like an abandoned Clint Eastwood set when he'd still been a man without an identity. It was fascinating. Zach had no idea such a place existed so deep in the forests of AuSable and Huron. Part of him still believed it didn't.

He took his first few steps away from the platform, feeling the air instantly warming and the nameless, groping hands relinquishing their hold. The dirt path rose up to meet him and the forest seemed to keep an agreeable distance.

If only Meghan could have seen it, he thought. She never would believe him.

"Never would have believed me," he corrected himself.

"Tell yourself whatever you wanna hear, it don't change a fucking thing."

"Bullshit."

20

"You know you'll be begging for a taste as soon as you get out of here."

"If you get out of here."

There was a church with a bell tower, a town hall, a jail, and a doctor's office. There was an empty graveyard, a corral, and a clothing store. There was an odor of death and one of sweet, coppery blood. There was even a sign with 'Station Number Six' painted sternly across it.

"Finally here," Zach muttered.

Once the dirt path had carried him onto the main street of the small town, he stopped walking and began to spin around and around in the dense air recklessly, completely oblivious to the thousand eyes that watched him.

"What the hell is so special about you? Why did I come all the way out here in the goddamned middle of the night?" he yelled.

There was a crash in the trees followed by movement. He stopped spinning and began to laugh bitterly.

"Where'd you go now? I'm here! Show me something!"

The air grew cold again. Zach's laughter sobered and the night rolled on like a steam locomotive on a brand new track.

As soon as he stopped making noise, he could hear them. Men, women, children, beasts...screaming. All of them. Screaming. Endlessly. And all of their screams like fire over Zach's skin. They were wretched, cracked things more like scraped steel than any human noise he'd ever heard.

"Come on in for a bite!"

"All aboard the Freedom Train!"

"Have your papers ready!"

"Cannonball's a' rollin!"

"Devil's on the track!"

"Choo-choo, mother fucker!"

Zach fell to his knees and covered his ears.

"Shit!"

Another series of screams.

He cried out in response.

"Are you a Free Man, Zachary Meyer?"

"You got nothing holding you back?"

21

The voices. The screams. The goddamned voices. They were everywhere and nowhere all at once. They were the very air he breathed and some distant nebula in the exact same instant. They filled him and emptied him and delighted in their own subtle brand of rape.

Quiet. Everything dead quiet.

He knelt in the dirt, panting, on the verge of tears.

"Meghan…" he moaned.

"That ship has sailed, Daisy."

"But we've got a nice train you can take instead."

"This one's guaranteed not to fuck other men behind your back or tell you to get another job."

"There's only one job on the train now, and that's the Conductor."

Now, he could see the fat Conductor with the yellow teeth standing a few paces ahead of him on the track, grinning, an outrageous and depraved mockery of Santa Claus. Zach's body went completely numb on the left side. His right felt like it was being flayed with razor-hooked whips.

"What are you waiting for, Free Man? Come and see the wonders."

Zach gulped and rose to his feet. His nose was dribbling snot from the new forest cold.

The Conductor pointed at the white house, still grinning.

"Plenty to see in there."

"Why am I here?"

"Why don't you go inside and find out? Train's not due in for a little while. We'll wait for you."

Another series of bloodcurdling screams and sobs erupted from the basement.

"What's down there?"

"You've got your own goddamned eyes. Go find out for yourself."

The grin was gone.

For a moment, the town lit up like it was fully inhabited once more, with the sounds of laughter, clinking glasses, snoring, love-making, church bells, and a lone train whistle blaring out on the horizon. Zach could picture the passengers of the train taking a rest there in some bygone time before it had been laid to ruin and the track kept going, ever on and on. They seemed almost happy, though he could tell even through their smiles that there was some underlying knowledge of the things to come, the

22

tragedies and grotesqueries that would brand them the new faces of nightmares to be reviled for an entire age of the world.

But as the happiness and laughter was fleeting, so too was the image of them. The dark and fog-veiled forest returned around Zach and the lights went out in all the windows around town. Even the Conductor was gone. Zach was alone with the fog and the track and the screams. The town seemed like nothing more than cardboard.

He wiped cold sweat away from his forehead and neck, realizing that his hands had been shaking and his stomach was expanding and contracting faster than his breath.

"What now?" he asked aloud.

The world was too quiet and dark for his liking.

"You know."

He scoffed but rose to his feet. Of course he knew. It couldn't get much clearer.

The front doors of the white house were flung back and open so that it looked like the surprised face of a pale, pimpled monster.

"Into the belly of the beast," Zach thought. He wasn't sure why.

There was a rumble in the distance. He couldn't tell whether it was thunder or the Devil's black, steel carriage.

"Come on in, Zachary Meyer!" a voice called out from the darkness of the house.

Zach leapt backward. A fire had lit through his veins.

"Who's there?"

"You've got your own goddamned eyes. Why don't you go and find out?" the Conductor said from behind him.

He jumped again.

When he turned around, there was nothing but the track.

"Jesus…" he muttered, shivering. The night was getting colder and colder as it grew around him. His tee shirt wasn't holding up very well to the breeze.

A lively chorus of screams shot out of the front doors, making Zach's skin do its own primitive version of the wave. He couldn't imagine the torment…the despair…

"What the hell's happening?" he whispered to the darkness.

"You've got your own goddamned eyes."

"Why don't you come see?"

"Are you a Free Man, Zachary Meyer?"

"You got nothing holding you back?"

The forest came alive around him. An unfathomable number of animals roared and howled loaded threats from the ambiguity of the fog, taunting him to come and inspect how sharp their teeth were, how furious their appetites, how unparalleled their ferocity.

"Come on in!"

The animals pressed forward, continuing to buzz and howl and roar until the forest seemed like a jungle and the path a green mile.

Zach panted and wiped the cold sweat from his face.

"Fuck!"

"Come on in!" the voice repeated.

"HELP!" someone screamed.

Zach was sure it was a trick. Or even worse, it wasn't. Either way, he didn't want to follow it. More than anything in the world, he was sure he didn't want anything to do with the white house in the fog.

"You don't have a choice."

"I thought this was the Freedom Train."

"You don't know what Freedom is."

Zach didn't have a response for that because he knew he could never conceive of True Freedom. There would always be desires enslaving him: whims, pleasures, pains, hunger, thirst, and the taxman. He could live on his own in the wilderness for years and still not have the right to come into the towns and kill a man, whether in warm or cold blood. He couldn't walk to Kmart or Huron Music and start taking items off of the shelves. He was an enslaved man and he'd never known just how much of a slave he truly was until the white house showed it to him.

"No." He wasn't even aware the word had left his lips.

"What are you waiting for?"

"We can show it to you."

"All aboard the Freedom Train!"

"Choo-choo, mother fucker!"

Calm settled over him. His hands weren't shaking anymore and the wind didn't feel so cold. When the next series of screams trailed up from the basement of the white house, he didn't even flinch.

He was ready. His papers had already been checked in, he had no bag, and the train was almost to the station.

"Come on in."

His feet began to move forward and the rest of his body dominoed with them.

The fog surrounding the Number Six stop abated as he walked, but he could still tell it was impossibly thick at the borders of the trees.

The moon shone through even the densest of forest and lit the main street of the sweaty old town. The animals had vacated the area, presumably because they'd realized he wasn't going to stumble back to them for an easy meal, but the low rumbling was ever present in the foggy, mysterious distance.

His legs grew steadier. The wind grew warmer. The electricity of the rail reached out and seized him by the teeth to force down into his body.

"Come on in."

"Come and see."

"The Freedom Train!"

"The Men of the Long Track!"

"The Devil's Carriage!"

"The Conductor's Pleasures!"

A flash of lightning struck the ground in front of him and he saw, by its light, a forest of naked, impaled bodies staked like kebobs in the churchyard, the main street, the cemetery, the stables, and the park. The screams erupted anew with terrifying force, blowing the doors to the white house shut and then bounding them open again. The ground was soaked with blood. Red-masked demons watched him from the windows.

There was no time for a reaction. Zach simply stood still and took it all in. His hands were struck with the most minute of tremors, but only for a moment.

The light fell back away and the bodies disappeared.

His whole body convulsed. He bent over and dry-heaved. The smell of blood and intestines was still ripe in the air.

"It's in my head...all in my fucking head," he pleaded.

"It's not even raining."

"You don't need rain to have lightning."

"And you don't need lightning to have thunder."

When he closed his eyes, the bodies reappeared in foul clarity; their faces twisted in every imaginable snarl with bile dripping from their lips, their bodies ever so slowly sliding down the red, splintered stakes.

"God help me," he shuddered.

"This is the Devil's track."

His feet began to move toward the house without his consent. It didn't much matter whether he resisted or not anymore. He was a slave to its will.

"Oh God…please…" he whimpered.

The voices were around him again, the thousand nameless, groping hands.

The town rolled by like he was on a conveyer belt. The church, the town hall, the saloon, the stables, the brothels, all dark and all empty save the demons his mind manifested within them.

"Are you a Free Man, Zachary Meyer?"

"You got nothing holding you back?"

"Come on in."

"You've got your own goddamned eyes."

"Climb aboard the Freedom Train!"

The red-masked faces watched him from the windows and the alleyways.

"Do you know Freedom?"

There were the steps, falling one by one behind as his feet escorted him to the porch of the white house. He reached out and felt the wet, splintered wood of the railing, and immediately the image of the hours-dead bodies sliding ever so slowly down the stakes flashed like lightning through his brain.

"Forest of the Dead," he thought.

The front doors creaked on their old and rusted hinges. He paused on the rug just outside the door, hardly realizing that the porch-swing had begun to rock back and forth.

"This is it," he said. "Do I really want to go in?"

He thought of Meghan and Posey's and the rest of the life behind him. They were starting to look just fine.

Another series of screams cannoned out of the house, this time so close that Zach could almost smell the rancid, coppery breath of it as it whisked past him. He could hear the whips cracking. He could hear the saws sawing. He could hear the forced exits and incarcerations of souls when the work was done. He knew their fear when the red-masked demons chained them up by their ankles and flayed their bodies. He felt the heat of the iron they used to brand their skins.

He knew them all in one instant, and knew their sufferings, too.

"Fuck...Please, God. Please!"

There was no way he was going inside. No way in Hell.

"Too late for that, Zachary Meyer."

"You're already here."

"Are you a Free Man?"

"You got nothing holding you back?"

The whips cracked again, the screams lit out from the hallways like a bullet through a chamber.

"Come on in, Zach," Meghan beckoned from the darkness. "Quit fooling around. Everything's gonna be all right. We'll work it out."

"Mistakes happen, Zach. I like to forgive and forget," Tom Posey told him.

"You don't have to worry about your car payments for now. We know you're going through hard times and we want you to know that we're here to help in any way we can."

The voices were not enticing individually, they were even a little mocking, but their ideas...the dreams and longings they put in his head...the nostalgia and simplicity of the way things used to be...those were hard to ignore. He missed his old life more than he ever thought he would, especially considering he hadn't even spent a full day on his own yet. Maybe Freedom wasn't the way to go for him. Maybe he liked being enslaved. Freedom certainly hadn't gotten him into much of a situation so far.

"Please! Help me!" a woman screamed.

He could hear children sobbing, crying out as the thud of the whip cracked and pinked their flesh.

He sensed the red-masked wraiths somewhere in that miserable and all-encompassing darkness. They were preparing for his arrival. They would not be ignored.

"Hello?" Zach whispered. He couldn't remember speaking anything but pleas and curses since he'd arrived at Number Six.

More long, agonizing screams staggered up from the basement.

"What do you want me to do?"

He was torn. He wanted to help the victims of such outrageous torture and miserable predicament, but he didn't want to become one of them himself. He was sure his company would be little consolation if he were unable to set the forlorn souls free. At least, he hoped it wouldn't help them to see him captured and bled as well. Some people, he knew, always wanted to bring others down with them. It was one of the devils of humankind.

"You don't know what's in there," he reasoned to himself. "It could be nothing. It could just be voices like the ones you've been hearing all night."

"But you also don't know what's in there. It could be a starved, flesh-eating monster too terrible for your imagination to construct."

"I won't know until I go in and find out. At least then I'll die with dignity."

"That's not dignity."

"My Freedom of Choice."

"Your blind recklessness. Your insistence on optimism, naïveté, in a world that allows neither."

"The Long Track."

"The Freedom Train."

His heart slapped rhythm so viciously against his chest that it was difficult to breathe. The animals were beginning to sense his faltering conviction. He could hear them salivating just beyond the boundary of fog.

"Cannonball's 'a comin!" the Conductor yelled from the platform.

A rolling thunder clapped like the hands of God. There was no lightning.

"I've gotta hurry," Zach told himself.

The words seemed to work their own brand of magic. As soon as he uttered them he was pushing the doors to the white house open and making his way inside. On cue, the screams of the tortured souls echoed through the darkness and hallways with such force that he was nearly driven back out the door.

Lightning struck and he saw bodies hanging from hooks and nails and rope all throughout the foyer and in the front hall, all the way down into the study. They were all fresh and soaked with their own blood and open insides.

Zach cried out in terror, bumped into two of them, and then the lightning faded and the visions went with it.

He was back in the front hall, alone, and with no corpses as far as he could see.

"It's a dark house, though," he thought. "They could be anywhere..."

He panted until he was sure the noise would betray his position and then he stopped, but the visions still resurfaced over and over again in his head. He'd never been a fan of Biology class, especially when he'd had to dissect a frog and a cat, but the bodies hanging in the house were even worse. They were sweating, their insides not even a lifeless gray yet. They were leaking digestive juices, pulsing weakly, right out in the open air. And the looks on their faces...their twisted grimaces...their maniac smiles...their nakedness...it was enough to push Zach to the precipice of vomiting. He looked back over his shoulder every three seconds or so, sure each time that he would see a drop of sweat, blood, or intestines gleaming in the dim light from the doorway. Or, even worse, eyes.

"They're not there. It's all in your head."

But were they? How could he be sure?

"Because they're only there for a second, right when the lightning flashes, and then they're gone."

"That doesn't mean they're not there anymore."

"But they're not. I'd be running into them."

"Is that how you tell what's real and what's not?"

The white house was dead silent again. Its twisted, wooden corridors expanded and contracted, creaked, settled, and reformed in new complexities. They never stayed the same. It was impossible to know his way around them even in broad daylight because they were in a constant swell of motion, shifting but never repeating shapes.

The fog was so thick at the windows that he couldn't see outside at all save for a few steps through the open door, but that began to change soon enough. A mist began to float into the house, creeping around corners and filling each room, until it met with the darkened windows and revealed the wall of fog outside.

The white, ubiquitous glow made the parlor and the study somehow stranger. It was eerie and looming. The sensibly placed books on each shelve along with the bowls of fake, wooden fruit only added to the absurdity of it all.

The screams had stopped and Zach no longer had the feeling that there were others in the house. It had emptied quickly.

"Hello?" he whispered. He was afraid to speak too loudly, not sure who, or what, his voice might wake.

"Hello?" he called a little louder.

There was no answer.

He took a few cautious steps forward, listening closely to make sure he'd catch any approaching footfalls before they reached him. When there were none, he walked a little further down the long corridor.

A shadow passed up ahead of him. It was pitched even darker than the suffocating blackness.

Zach's nerves lit up and he froze.

Now that he'd seen something, he regretted calling out to it. He'd been a fool. Why would he ever have thought of contacting something in this place? This house of horrors? This...hell? He thought he should start heading back in the other direction.

"Is there another way to go, though?"

He couldn't see much of anything beyond the door and the rooms immediately off the front hallway. There looked to be a stairway a little further ahead in the darkness but he couldn't be sure until he moved toward the shadow to investigate it. For the moment, he was in no rush.

From where he stood, he couldn't tell if there was another stairway leading to a basement (he imagined the one ahead went up, not down), either, yet somehow he knew the screams had come from a basement somewhere.

"Where you headed, boy? What's your poison?"

"Welcome to the Devil's House."

It was the first he'd heard from the voices since he'd stepped into the building. They weren't exactly the same. These voices were deeper and talked a little slower, with a drawl.

"Welcome to the Mad House."

Zach, now more accustomed to the strange and the absurd, barely marked them. He was much more concerned with figuring out whether or not the bodies he'd seen in the flash of lightning were truly around him or if he'd just imagined them. It was too easy for the eyes to play tricks in a brief, brilliant flash of light like that one. And even more distressing than the reemergence of the voices or the hanging, mangled bodies was the shadow he'd seen in the hallway. He felt its black eyes watching him and knew it had wanted him to see it move. Just to fuck with him. Just to drive him to the verge of hysterics. Those were the most satisfying catches.

Zach eyed the dark corridor, then the study, the parlor, the kitchen, and finally ended up where he thought the stairs would be.

"Gotta start somewhere," he thought.

He gave one last look back over his shoulder to the front door before continuing. The fog was a complete wall, blocking out even the sight of the floorboards on the wraparound porch.

There were things closing in around the outside of the house. Their breath was the smoldering breath of fog, blood, and avarice, and it was overwhelming to see up close. There was no way for him to turn back without them overtaking him. He'd already made his decision. It was time to shit or get off the pot.

The wood floor groaned beneath him with each step, but he cared less and less the more it protested his arrival. A strange mixture of fear and calm resignation had settled into even the deepest parts of his soul.

"Won't last long, boy," the voice told him from the shadows.

He tried his best to shrug it off and continue moving.

He'd already realized there was nothing else for him to do.

On the walls of the corridor, there hung Romantic paintings arranged in meticulous lines. They were of Greek gods and goddesses mostly. He admired them as he passed.

A few of the paintings eventually turned toward macabre portrayals of death and torment. One of them in particular gave Zach goosebumps but he was helpless to look away. It was done in all gray and black and showed a horribly deformed god chained to a pillar in a meadow, surrounded by dead bodies hanging from the trees by their ankles, just like the corpses Zach had seen in the house. The chains were interwoven with his muscles and bones and had his name carved on them. Zach knew

31

inexplicably that it was a god that needed a blood sacrifice in his name to survive, and that some cruel person or people had invented this clever torture device to imprison him so he would never die but endure only by his own torture. It was no god Zach had ever heard of. At the bottom of the painting were three letters: 'CWH'.

"I think I know that name," Zach thought, but didn't have the time to search through his tunnels of memory and retrieve the face to go with it.

He turned back to the first paintings, the ones he could see almost clearly by the gray-white of the fog at the windows. Those were innocent enough. They showed young lovers in moonlit gardens, or angels visiting prophets, or old green landscapes beneath pre-historic mountains. Those paintings were easy enough to decipher in the light, but the ones further on, the weird and grotesque, he could only see in his mind's eye. Maybe they were even the same, he was just overlaying the grisly on the beautiful. He had a habit of doing that.

He reached the old wooden staircase and paused. It was so dark then that he couldn't see anything but darker shapes protruding from the blackness. His feet found the stairs before his eyes, making him fall to an angled push-up position across the first few steps.

A shadow, maybe the same one, moved a little ways above him and he felt the stairway creak beneath his palms. There was an outburst of laughter from somewhere on the second floor.

Zach slowly made his way to his feet, reaching out all around in the dark to firmly place any obstacles he might encounter. The fall on the stair had been a close one. If he hadn't put his hands out to cushion just before his head smacked into the wood, he would be unconscious, and then it wouldn't have been long before he wound up in the basement with all the other tortured souls.

"I wonder how they got there."

He didn't think it was likely they'd come by the same road he had. There was no evidence anyone had traveled that way before him. The path was hidden, overgrown, and deserted. Even after living in Oscoda along River Road for years, Zach hadn't known about those tracks until he'd started blindly following them that afternoon. He doubted many had, even if they'd spent their entire lives combing through the wilderness for just such a track.

Besides, there were far too many in the basement to have passed through in the last few days. By the sounds of it, they had to have been brought in recently or they wouldn't still be alive.

"Are they alive?"

"Are you a Free Man, Zachary Meyer?"

"You got nothing holding you back?"

One step. Two.

The boards creaked beneath him.

Three. Four.

He walked as softly as he could manage, hoping to get to the second floor unnoticed though he knew deep down that it didn't matter either way. If there was something in the house, and he was fairly certain there was, it already knew he was there.

Five. Six.

There was definite movement on the railing that overlooked the stair. He could feel it as well as hear it.

Seven. Eight.

Voices. They were back again. All over. Everywhere. They hissed and whispered in a broad spectrum of speed and tone.

They whispered about him.

He ignored them, or was maybe just indifferent after all he'd seen and heard, and continued up the stairs. By the direction of the voices and footsteps, he knew he was nearing the top.

"You're late."

"You're not wanted."

"You're in deep."

They whispered in his ear incessantly. He could feel their hot breath breaking inside of him.

Then, Meghan's voice. "You're a goddamned joke! You're worthless! You'll never be nothin more than a piece of shit cook at a piece of shit diner! You're gonna die desperate and alone!"

She laughed the shrill laughter of a witch. Had those been her exact words?

Zach clenched his jaw, barely suppressing the urge to swing blindly in hopes it was truly Meghan out in the darkness.

33

"If I ever make it back, first thing I'm gonna do is kill the bitch," he promised himself.

It was a promise he didn't truly intend on keeping, he didn't think. He'd never been able to muster up the nerve to kill and didn't believe he would in the future any more than he believed there'd be a happy ending to this new, terrible journey.

"Cannonball's a' rollin!" the Conductor yelled from somewhere above him.

The voice was followed by shrill laughter and frantic, troubled whispers.

Zach heard another series of screams from the basement and took the final steps a little faster in spite of himself. He could deal with the voices, not the screams. They were too piercing and mysterious.

The top. He was at the top landing, and all the voices from all of the rooms had stopped. All except Meghan. As usual, she kept droning on and on.

"You fucking slob! You limp-dicked asshole! You never gave me what I need!"

Zach felt his insides trembling like a great volcano was brewing somewhere in the depths of him.

"I had to get it somewhere else, didn't I?" She cackled like a thousand year-old demon. "Didn't like that too much, huh?"

Her voice seemed to assault him from everywhere.

"You're pathetic. A fucking waste. You're mucus and backwash in the pool of life and you'll burn for it."

He could do nothing but take the insults, endure the abuse, until he found her. It seemed impossible in the pitch-darkness.

"I don't ever wanna see your ugly goddamned face again," Tom Posey told him. "I don't need garbage like you in my restaurant. Always comin in late, drunk, or stoned. All three, usually."

He seethed with rage as he continued.

"And if you go anywhere near my daughter again, I'm gon rip your little stump off and shove it down your throat! How's that sound, huh? Make you eat it! Maybe then you'll stop stealing food. 'Course, we both know that won't be enough to fill your belly. Shit, wouldn't even be enough for a goddamned cockroach, you mother fucker!"

Posey howled laughter. Meghan joined him.

Now that there were two voices for Zach to place, each on an opposite end of the hallway, it was much easier for him to get his bearings.

"Your father should take the belt to you for being such a coward and a fool! He had such high hopes for you. For you! Maybe I'll take the belt to you for him," his mother scolded him in her old, rasping voice. "And now look at you! You can't even hold a job as a cook in some hick-town diner! You're a disgrace!"

She paused long enough to spit at him. He felt the splat even though he couldn't see her.

"You didn't get it from my side of the family. The Winchesters don't breed losers like you. You're unnatural."

"Amen!" Tom Posey screamed.

"A mutant!"

"Amen!" Meghan joined.

"An abomination!"

"Hallelujah!" all three of them at once, then they burst into hideous, testicle-shrinking laughter.

"You're…"

"…gonna…"

"…die…"

"…miserable…"

"…and…"

"…alone."

They alternated words like a bad comedy troupe.

It was getting to Zach, making him nauseous with anger, but now he had three voices and the location of the stairs to map the layout of the second floor. He'd find them soon enough, and when he did…

"…I'll kill all of them," he scowled through clenched teeth. "I'll make them suffer."

As soon as the words left his mouth the voices ceased altogether. He was left with his own echo and a dull ache deep-rooted in his head from keeping his jaw so tightly clenched.

He took a step down the hallway to his right. It was the direction Tom's voice had come from.

"Cannonball's a' rollin'!" the Conductor hollered up from downstairs.

"The Freedom Train!"

"Devil's on the Track!"

"Hide your women and children!"

"And yourselves!"

"Amen!"

"Hallelujah!"

"Choo-choo, mother fucker!"

Zach barely noticed them. They were like the chorus of an over-played radio anthem, the congregation at a southern Baptist church. They were animated and enlightened.

He took another two steps along the railing towards Tom's room. Three steps, four, getting more confident in his footing with each inch of wood passing beneath him.

"Where you gonna hide when the Devil comes to take you down?"

"Are you a Free Man, Zachary Meyer?"

"You got nothing holding you back?"

"Cut them, whip them, burn them, skin them, eat them!"

"That's the way of the Long Track!"

"The Devil's Circus!"

"The Free Men!"

"The Way of the Red Mask!"

He walked with his hands held out in front of him for at least twenty feet, then he bumped into a wall. The impact nearly sent him sprawling.

His eyes had grown accustomed enough to the darkness by then that he could see the little pockets of emptiness in the black where the hallway stretched out and the thick shadow where the wall hunkered down. With this keen, new perspective, he was able to eventually find the brass doorknob to Tom's room and turn it.

"Good for nothing, pathetic piece of shit," Tom continued as the knob turned and the door creaked open.

The first thing Zach saw was the gray-white fog pressing against the window.

"Why didn't I see that under the door?" he wondered.

The glow was dull but poignant enough after darkness, just like it had been through the windows on the first floor.

But as he studied the room closer, none of that seemed to matter. He realized where he was.

Ahead of him was the steel rack that had always reminded him of an old erector set. On one side of the rack were dozens of bottles of ketchup, mustard, and relish, and white Styrofoam carry out boxes. On the other were boxes labeled salt, pepper, napkins, jelly, brown sugar, raisins, and soufflé cups. In the middle were empty salad dressing containers and jugs of red wine vinegar, olive oil, and cocktail sauce. Grease-stained aprons hung sloppily over the ends of the racks, looking and smelling like the cooks who'd worn them had bathed in the deep fryer and then dried themselves off with raw hamburger meat.

Beneath the window directly across from Zach was Tom Posey: owner and proprietor of Posey's Restaurant and resident asshole for the Iosco and Alcona counties, respectively. He was tall and thin with acne scars on his cheeks and one missing front tooth from falling out of a speeding boat after a dozen beers. His hair was salt and pepper and he always wore faded blue jeans with a button-up shirt of varying color and pattern. And, perhaps the thing Zach hated most of all, he never was seen without a pair of brown loafers sans socks.

Zach noticed he was smoking a cigarette, something he hadn't been allowed to do in the restaurant for years. Yet it was unmistakably his office. And Zach ought to have recognized it, because it was the very same one where he'd been fired.

"What the hell do you want?" Tom asked him accusingly, leaning forward in his chair so that his elbows rested on the wooden desk and the cigarette smoke clouded his already indiscernible face.

"Well? You gonna say something, you piece of shit? Or are you gonna just stand there and look like an asshole?"

Zach squeezed his hands into fists but said nothing.

"You know, Zach, I always knew you'd end up homeless, I just didn't realize you'd be dumb enough to let it happen in your thirties, while there's still a little bit of life left in you. I mean, Jesus, have some self-respect! No wonder you fucked my daughter, everyone over nineteen sees you for the piece-of-shit dirt-bag that you are!"

Zach took a few cautious steps toward the desk, never once taking his eyes off of Tom.

"Thank God Meghan finally wised up."

He took a few more steps.

"Did she ever tell you about us? About the nights when I made you stay late and then went to your house and fucked your girlfriend in your bed? Bet my sex-sweat felt good to lay in when you came home from a hard day's work," he laughed. "And you know what the best part of it is? I'll bet she was too exhausted from me to give it to you when you got home!"

Tom slapped the table, took a long drag from his cigarette, and allowed the smoke to billow up to the crumbling, mildewed ceiling.

"And I wasn't the only one either, Meyer. Fuck no, I wasn't! We took turns. We each had a night while you were at work. Ever wonder why you were always the closer? Didn't give it too much thought, huh? But you must have smelled the stink when you got home. Or did your own sweat cover it up too much?"

Zach was all the way to the chair directly across from Tom. It was the chair he'd been fired in.

"Let me ask you something, Meyer. Are you a Free Man? You got nothing holding you back?"

Zach stopped in front of the desk and met Tom's stare. There was little self-control left in him to hold back from knocking the shit-eating grin off of Tom's face but he held onto that little bit like a child with his last Halloween candy.

Pretty soon, it wouldn't matter how hard he tried to suppress the rage. It would be beyond his control.

"No, you don't know what it is to be a Free Man, Meyer. You think you're free now, but you got too much bullshit holding you back. You're a pussy! The world jacks you right in your ugly fucking face and you don't swing back! You've never swung back! So what the hell's stopping you, huh? What's holding you back? When are you gonna cut the crap and be a real man? A Free Man?"

"A man of the Long Track!"

"A man of the Red Mask!"

"When are you gonna show the shit-throwers in your life you ain't gonna take their crap no more?"

He was shouting now. He'd dropped his cigarette and all the veins in his forehead stood out.

"You're a pathetic piece of shit, Meyer! You hear me? A pathetic piece of shit! Now what are you gonna do about that, you pussy? Cry? Smoke another fucking joint? A line of blow? Get lit at the Pub?"

Tom stood and walked around the table. He stepped right up to Zach's nose and glared at him so that Zach could smell the tobacco and jerky on his breath.

"What choo gonna do now?"

Zach swallowed. Tom's breath was cold and rancid. It was a living organism.

"I'll ask you one more time, Meyer. What the fuck are you gonna do now?"

Silence.

Zach carefully considered his options for a moment, then reached around Tom and grabbed the lighter from his desk. Tom watched him closely but made no move to stop him. He'd made the challenge and was dead set on seeing it through.

"Got something on your mind, pussy?"

Zach took a cigarette from Tom's front-pocket.

"You got something to say?"

He lit the cigarette, took one drag from it, two, and examined the thing unceremoniously.

"I'm swinging back," he grinned.

He cherished the hard confusion on Tom's face for a few seconds, marveling at how life-like this revenant seemed, and then he thrust the glowing end of the cigarette into Tom's milky eyeball.

"FUCK!"

Tom screamed, struggled, but Zach held him down to the desk, using the fingers of his right hand to keep Tom's eyelid pried open.

The smell and sizzle were terrible, but it only lasted a few seconds before the cigarette went out and cracked into pieces.

Tom fell to the floor, still screaming. Zach wheeled around calmly, ripped the framed high-school diploma off of the wall, and threw it on the floor as hard as he could.

"You wanna see what I'm gonna do, mother fucker? Huh? You wanna see?" he roared, the fury finally exploding out of him from years of oppression under the asshole's tyranny.

He bent over, picked the sharpest shard of glass he could find from the shattered picture frame, and gripped it so hard with his right hand that blood began to run down his palms and squeeze over his knuckles like he was crushing a fruit or a packet of ketchup.

"Here you go, Tommy boy!"

"Fuck you, Meyer!" Tom cried in defiance.

It was nice for Zach to see him on his knees in such utter agony, the tables turned, but it would have been better if he'd begged for his life. No such luck.

"You're still nothing but a pathetic piece of shit. You're gonna die alone."

Was that a tremble in the unshakable hard-ass's voice?

"Every man dies alone," Zach told him, then he sliced through the corner of Tom's lip.

Tom screamed with renewed vigor, so he cut the other side of his lip. Tom screamed again. Zach made twenty-three tiny cuts over his face before he sliced Tom's eyeballs, and then he went to work on his hands, arms, chest, stomach, legs, and thighs.

Tom screamed.

Maniacal, encouraging laughter raged from downstairs. And the voices returned triumphantly with their old favorites.

"Cannonball's a' rollin!"

"All aboard!"

"Have your papers ready!"

"Climb aboard the Freedom Train!"

"The Devil's Carriage!"

"The Long Track!"

"The Way of the Red Mask!"

"Choo-choo, mother fucker!"

Tom screamed.

A train whistle blew in the distance, followed immediately by colossal, rolling thunder.

When Zach finished he looked like the Devil, all glowing eyes and growling mouth, covered in blood from head to toe. When Zach finished, Tom looked like a pile of wet, raw meat torn apart by careless hands, which was essentially the truth.

"Way of the Red Mask," Zach whispered, echoing the voices without even realizing he'd done it.

Slowly, the nuances of Tom Posey's office began to dissolve into an empty room with old, creaking floorboards and cobwebbed ceilings. The racks of condiments and back-stock trembled and shrank into the floor like they were in the undertow of an earthquake. The desk caved in, the chair sucked in with it, and the wall calendar, the weekly schedule, the yellow, gray, and black newspaper clippings from the local rag were absorbed into wood-paneled walls.

All that was left was the glowing, gray-white window to the fog and the mess that had once been Tom Posey: owner and proprietor of Posey's Restaurant.

Zach examined the work he'd done, wiping absently at the red war paint that had splashed over his face and into his mouth.

Seemingly from nowhere, tears of remorse began to form at the corner of his eyelids. He couldn't believe what he'd just done, whether it had been a real person or not, no matter how much he hated Tom Posey and how much the shit-head had been asking for it.

He never would have believed he was capable of something like that and it was difficult to suddenly accept that he was. And the even greater shock than realizing he could do it was knowing that he actually liked it, too.

"Be a man, Meyer," Tom's voice commanded. "Quit crying like a little pussy."

"Be a Free Man!"

"A man of the Red Mask!"

"After all of that, you're still gonna let me win? What the hell did you prove if you're just gonna sit over my body and cry after you gave me my medicine?"

Zach's sniffles eventually subsided. He couldn't remember the last time he'd cried, but he'd never killed a man before and figured that had to be as good an excuse as any. It was enough of an adrenaline rush to make him feel more than a little queasy. Every muscle in his body shook uncontrollably.

But the room was back to normal and the door to the hallway was right behind him.

The train whistle blew again in the distance. To Zach, it sounded like the labored cheer of a mad man.

"Onward and upward!"

"Amen!"

"Hallelujah!"

"Cannonball's a' rollin!"

"Hallelujah!"

He wiped the blood and tears from his eyes and turned back for the hallway.

As soon as he stepped out of the room, the door slammed shut behind him. The noise made him jump forward and he almost lost his balance in the dark.

"Shit..." he muttered belatedly.

The slam echoed twice in the hallway and then the house was silent once more.

It took a moment for Zach to settle his jittering, rubber legs before he could begin to navigate the dark, and when he did, it was only by the least graceful movements he'd ever made. But little by little, he regained his footing and his confidence, then his steps became more resolute. Steady feet wouldn't help him find his next stop, though, unless he had his wits.

"Who was closest to Tom?" he wondered, trying in vain to recall the voices he'd heard form the dark extremes of the second floor.

It was no use. He could very clearly remember what had been said and who'd said it, but not from which direction.

He made his way over to the wall across from the stairway and felt around for a handle or an opening in the dark. It took some trial and error and his hands wandered onto a few unsavory decorations mounted on the wall (a human hand with a nail through the palm, a rusty saw that almost bit through Zach's skin with its tetanus teeth, a spider at least four inches wide with fangs that would make a saber-toothed tiger jealous), but eventually he found another brass doorknob.

He withdrew his hand immediately as though the knob itself had seared his flesh. After all the strange things he'd held that day, he was a little wary when it came to foreign objects coming in contact with his bare skin.

When his fingers closed around it again, the door slid open and the gray-white light of the fogged windows spilled over his face like a burst gallon of milk. It took a moment for his eyes to adjust even to the dulled-down colors of the forest night, and even once his eyes had grown accustomed to the glare, he stood completely still for several minutes, staring at the spectacle before him.

It was Meghan in their garage, her blonde hair and skinny arms flying all over, breaking all of his few and precious belongings with the axe he'd used to chop firewood for her during the cold, northern winters gone by.

"FUCKING SMALL-DICKED COCKSUCKER! FUCKING COWARD! PATHETIC PIECE OF SHIT!"

He watched calmly as she swung the axe into his trophy case with all of the bowling awards he'd won as a child. He tapped his foot and hummed a tune absently when she drove the axe-head through the side of his snowmobile. He cracked his knuckles, still covered in Posey's blood, when she shattered his workbench and splintered the autographed Al Kaline baseball bat his father had handed down to him when he'd left home.

"These are all just things and they aren't mine anymore."

He popped his jaw and strode into the room with his head tilted to the left.

She quit swinging. Zach edged his way further into the room.

At first, he thought she was crying, but as he moved in closer and the sound and fury of her attacks on his former life ceased, he could tell that she was only seething with rage. The sight of her in such a way made him smile. It was even better, he thought, than if she'd been in tears mourning the loss of a man she'd considered her one and only true love. That wouldn't have been like her at all. That wouldn't have been the Meghan that he'd known.

She heard his steps on the cement floor and wheeled around with the axe ready to strike at a moment's notice. There was a dark hatred in her eyes he'd never seen before, not only in her but in anyone.

NUMBER SIX

"You're a waste," she hissed through teeth clenched so tight the enamel peeled off before his very eyes. "A waste of five fucking years and thousands of dollars. You're a waste of a human being and a waste of a lover."

She was grunting demonically with lunatic eyes and her fingers ghost white from gripping the axe. She might have been laughing. In that state, Zach had no way of knowing.

"Small-dicked faggot. Can't even stand up to one of the eleven guys I cheated on you with. They were all better than you, Zach. How's that make you feel, you pathetic piece of shit? All of them! Even Bigfoot, and he's almost retarded!"

Zach popped his jaw again and wiped his hands on his blood-soaked shirt.

"You're a joke, Zach. You don't mean shit to anybody and you never will. Your own parents hate you. Why do you think Dr. Meyer, a fucking shrink, thinks his own son needs therapy so bad? Why do you think he kicked you out? Why couldn't you be smart? You're not even good-looking. I was embarrassed to be seen with you. If we didn't live in such a small goddamned town, I would have fucked a new guy every day."

Zach stood inches away from her face, untroubled, completely oblivious to the flecks of spit sling-shotting out of her mouth and into his face.

"You deserve to die, you pussy," she snarled, raising the axe over her shoulder with a cry of naked rage.

Zach didn't wait to see if it would drop. He wound up and punched her in the nose harder than he'd hit, or wanted to hit, anything in his entire life.

Meghan staggered backwards a few steps before she slipped on a broken piece of glass and fell. Blood immediately began to flow from her nose, and then the back of her head, too, when she made contact with the side of his snowmobile. She was dazed, but not nearly as dazed as she should have been.

"Hitting a fucking woman, huh? No surprise there. You're the worst kind of coward!"

He kicked her in the ribs. Her breath sputtered and stalled like the engine of his broken-down snowmobile.

"I'm too good for you," she managed once some of the air was back in her.

He kicked her in the teeth without flinching. He could feel the little white chiclets giving way, exploding beneath his boot. It was, without a doubt, one of the most satisfying sensations he'd ever felt.

Blood covered Meghan's cheeks and mouth. She spit out one tooth, then two, then four, but she still wouldn't cry.

"You're the biggest goddamned joke this town has ever seen, and the weakest, too…"

Without skipping a beat, he took the axe from her hands and swatted her in the eye with the blunt end.

She could barely form a word anymore. Zach was surprised and impressed when she did.

"Fucking joke…fucking coward…small-dicked asshole with shit for brains. You're pathetic. You're not even man enough to kill me. You don't have any balls."

Zach smirked, the first time he'd shown her any emotion at all during the encounter, and then raised the axe over his head.

"Fuck you," he said blandly.

He would remember the horrified, pleading look in her eyes forever.

The axe fell. The train whistle blew. The distant thunder applauded. Zach struck her again and again until she looked a lot more like Tom Posey, and then he struck her some more for all of the extra pain and worry she'd caused him.

There was no point in wearing clothes anymore, now that he'd been drenched with enough blood, flesh, and bone to fill the graves of Antietam, so he stripped down to his black boxers even as the garage around him dissolved into another forgotten, wooden room.

He could hear the Conductor roaring laughter from the bottom of the stairs.

"Are you a Free Man, Zachary Meyer?"

"You got nothing holding you back?"

"Do you know what Freedom is?"

"All aboard!"

"Cannonball's a' rollin'!"

"Climb aboard the Freedom Train!"

"The Devil's Track!"

"The Way of the Red Mask!"

"Amen!"

"Hallelujah!"

Zach grinned. "Choo-choo, mother fucker!" he yelled, delighting in the far-reaching echo his call had produced.

He turned for the door, thought better of it, spit on Meghan's corpse, and kicked the stringed muscles and sinews that were left of her. Then, he showed his back to her for the last time and went out into the hallway to pay his mother a visit.

This time, he didn't need to hunt for a room. She was waiting for him right out in the hallway with a kitchen knife and a dog-eared copy of Playboy from 1992.

"What in God's name is the matter with you?"

She slapped him across the face.

Her white, curled hair hung down in loose tufts over her forehead. She was sweating so much that her square-framed glasses were fogged over and great pools of perspiration were pulling down her dark blue shirt. She was a thin woman with premature liver-spots and a scar under her right eye that Zach's father had given her.

She was a mess. But, dear God, she was the toughest woman he'd ever seen. More than the Conductor, the voices, Tom Posey, Meghan, or even the screams from downstairs that ravaged his soul, she terrified him. He'd never outgrown his fear of her. It was almost the same as his fear of the Devil with one important difference: she could get him where it hurt.

"You're a disgrace," she snarled. "Why couldn't you have been like your brother?"

Meghan's dead voice chuckled.

"I hate you. Your dad's ashamed of you. You're the seed of the Devil. You could never do anything right, could you? I should've taken a hanger to you when I was pregnant and there was still hope. Before you were even born, I knew you'd be rotten. You're pathetic."

She was spitting out insults faster than he could process them.

"You shouldn't have been born. My life would have been so much better without you. Everyone's lives!"

She waved the Playboy at him. He tried to move his legs but they wouldn't budge. He felt a warm trickle running down the inside of his thigh and realized he'd pissed himself. It was the ultimate shame, the ultimate reversion back into his childhood self. He gasped.

"And what is this? What is this filth? You think these women want to be ogled by you? With your crooked nose and disgusting, hairy chest? You think you could ever get a woman like one of them? You're disgusting. You make me sick. I'm gonna do what I should have done to you before you were even born."

She threw the Playboy in his face and with one graceless movement stuck the knife into his shoulder.

Zach screamed.

"You get what you deserve!" she screamed right back. "You'll rot in Hell where you belong!"

She jabbed the knife into his right bicep and yanked upward. He screamed again, attempting with a flailing arm to swat the knife away to no avail.

"You disgusting, Devil-worshipper! Go where you belong!"

This time, she got him in the calf.

"AAAGGGH!"

Zach fell to one knee. White and red flashes of pain swept over his eyes followed by the black snowflakes of unconsciousness.

"You fucking whore!" he yelled.

She drew the knife back to strike again, and he knew this time he'd get it right in his cheek.

Her flapping arm hurtled through the air.

Just before the blow landed, he braced himself and launched forward with his left shoulder in the lead. He connected at the same moment the knife passed through the vacant air where his throat had been mere seconds before.

"OW!" she cried, startled.

Zach grunted and drove her forward by the strength of his wounded leg until there was nothing left in front of him to push. She'd gripped the railing with one wayward hand, breaking a few fingers by the sound of it, and clung on unsteadily for dear, spiteful life. He nearly flew headlong down the stairs.

47

"You're a disgrace!" his mother screamed. "You're going to Hell!"

Then, she lost her hold on the railing and disappeared into the darkness of the stairway.

Zach heard an authoritative snap that made him cringe, then silence.

He waited.

One. Two. Three. Four.

No other sound. No vile taunts.

He collapsed at the top of the staircase, panting and trying to make sense of his injuries in the dark without much success. There was fire in his shoulder, fire in his bicep, and fire in his calf. It burned so deeply that he could barely breathe. The invisible ceiling spun around and around through a black chasm of nothingness. It took all of his will to remain conscious.

Then, the voices. Much closer than before. Shriller. Accompanied by a wet dragging sound. Zach was not in a good enough frame of mind to reliably pinpoint the movements.

"Cannonball's a' rollin'!" Tom Posey screamed.

Zach rolled onto his left side and saw his old boss crawling down the hall, his body no more than a heap of guts and crushed organs, but his eyes and the tips of his fingers glowed through the entire hallway like a full, idiot moon.

"Are you a Free Man, Zachary Meyer?"

"You got nothing holding you back?" Meghan asked directly behind him.

The shock of hearing her so close made him scream and lunge forward. He dropped off of the landing and down the stairs.

The first impact with the wall seared pain through his arm and shoulder.

"Fuck…" he grunted, trying to reach out with his healthy arm to slow his fall. He remembered his mother tumbling into the dark and the satisfying crunch when she'd hit the bottom. He had no intention of hearing it again.

With the little drops of adrenaline he still had in him, Zach swung his left arm and leg for the railing and straightened them as much as he could when they made impact.

He cried out in agony, but the railing held him and his back came to a grinding halt halfway down the stair. There was little strength left to hold on with, but he did, sure that the jolt of hooking himself by one arm had dislocated his shoulder and crashing into the wooden steps had shattered at least one rib.

At least he was alive.

"Are you?" he heard the Conductor ask playfully from the bottom of the staircase.

Zach was too terrified and exhausted to reply. He had been so sure it was all a dream, but now…he'd never have thought they'd be able to hurt him like that, and he would've acted differently with Tom and Meghan if he'd realized. And didn't he always wake up when he fell in a dream? If you fell in your dream, didn't they say that you died? It seemed likely, but he thought there was no way of knowing for sure. If you fell in your dream and died, you wouldn't be around to relay the news.

Besides, he hadn't fallen all the way down the steps.

Maybe it was still a dream.

The Conductor laughed.

"Cannonball's a' rollin!"

"Train pullin in!"

"Have your papers ready!"

"Climb aboard the Freedom Train!"

"Do you know what Freedom is?"

Zach struggled to a sitting position against the wall. He needed time to catch his breath and reflect. He needed time to stop the bleeding. He needed time for the dragging meat sound in the upstairs hall to stop so he knew they weren't coming after him anymore and it was just his imagination.

He needed time…

"Better hurry," a voice whispered.

Zach didn't recognize it, but he did feel a sudden urgency to get going.

The whistle blew somewhere off in the distance, but this time it was much closer than ever before. Thunder rolled down the track. The Cannonball would be back in the station soon, he was sure of it.

This time, he wouldn't miss it.

The air grew suddenly stifling, like someone had closed the front door and immediately snorted the cool air out with them.

"Time to roll."

"Choo-choo, mother fucker."

Zach clenched his jaw, his neck muscles tightened, and he braced himself down another step by the strength of his good leg.

"That wasn't so bad," he thought.

The next one he took a little faster, too fast, and ended up stepping with his bad leg, too. The deep puncture in his calf gasped and the cries from the basement joined in unison. He'd almost forgotten about them.

"Fuck!" he seethed through locked teeth.

With a nervous glance over his shoulder into the second-floor darkness and a gentle rub of the skin around his wounded calf, he eased down another step. Two. Three. Four. Seven. And then he was at the bottom.

By the gray fog of the study window, he could see his mother's neck and the broken bones in her arms and legs twisted into angles and shapes that seemed geometric impossibilities. They stuck out in red and white ribbons from her skin like grotesque, half-eaten lollipops. The sight nearly forfeited him of his stomach and his nerves. She was staring right at him.

Smiling.

"Time to roll," the voice told him again.

He forced himself to stand, balancing with his arm on the railing to support his bad leg. There were footsteps all around him. Whispers. Phlegm-thick coughs. Screams. Tears. Shattering plates. He couldn't see anyone else in the house.

The light buzzed on in the kitchen. Zach's heart jumped. He tried to hush his breath but it only grew louder the more he focused on it.

"It's gonna find me right now. It's gonna walk through the door and be big and mean and ugly."

"What is 'it'?"

Zach swallowed.

"The Devil."

"Amen!"

"Hallelujah!"

His ears rang with their exaltations. It made him feel dizzy, which made standing a near impossibility given that he was already balancing on one foot.

Heavy, black footsteps thundered toward the doorway.

He could hear its steady, growling breath, feel the weight of it crushing the air, smell its ancient, foul odor like moth balls and vinegar. He could see its misshapen nose, grinning black teeth, the puss squirting from the craters lining its face.

It was almost to the door.

"...no..."

The light turned off.

The footsteps stopped. The weight of the beast evaporated into the smell of a garbage disposal and herbs soaked too long in dishwater.

Zach's heart continued to act as a battering ram against his ribcage. He was too afraid to move, knowing that he would have no chance to run if it were waiting for him to follow before it pounced. In his condition, stealth was a difficult trick to manage.

"Hell's kitchen," he grinned stupidly. "Devil's in the kitchen."

"Devil's in the recipe."

"Devil's on the track!"

"Hi-ho!"

"Choo-choo, mother fucker!"

He let his breath out as quietly as his full lungs would allow and inched along the wall. He couldn't see into the kitchen even with the gray light coming in from the window, but he sensed the presence was gone.

"Will you go in?"

"You've got your own goddamned eyes."

"Why don't you find out?"

Zach edged a little closer to the doorway.

"I'm dead anyway. Might as well get it over with."

He was certain that if the demon were still in there, whatever sort of perversion of his own life it may have been, he was going to his death. He would have thought his mother would be the easiest to bring down, and she'd done a number on him. There was no point in even imagining what something else, something bigger, might do.

With one more unavoidable look at his mother's dead, grinning face, he resolved to go for it, come what may. There was no way he could stand there looking at her like that. He'd be too tempted to try to figure out how the current angle of her neck was possible even with a bad break, and he knew he'd be stuck on that one for a long, long time.

"Then I'll miss the train."

The accompanying chorus, for once, did not take the bait.

The way his calf was burning, it was tough going even for just a few hops through the dining room. He grunted, sweat, groaned, slipped, recovered, and cursed his way along the wall until he was a dark silhouette standing in front of the kitchen.

"So much for stealth," he thought anxiously.

But it didn't matter. Nothing was there but a gas stove and a kitchen table with a checkerboard tablecloth. So far as Zach could see, there was no boogieman.

Still, he proceeded with caution. There was no telling who or what would be waiting for him in the dark.

He made his way to the table slowly and felt around, surprised to find three plates with fresh, half-eaten meals on them. For a moment, he considered tasting the dishes, but just as quickly snapped his hand back in revulsion. It was dark, after all, and those screams from the basement made him think that the meat might not be the kind he wanted to eat.

Right on cue, the screams of misery and depravity sprang up at him like a jack-in-the-box. They were so close that he shifted backwards and almost lost his balance.

"Come on down, Zachary!"

"Come see the Way of the Red Mask!"

"Come see Freedom!"

"Hop aboard the Freedom Train!"

There was laughter, now. A sick sort of glee accompanied by the tearing of flesh, the shattering of bones, the breaking of spirit.

"Come on down," an impossibly deep, chilling voice whispered from directly behind him. Its breath was cold on Zach's neck. He wheeled around instinctively, every flight response in his body far beyond activation, but there was nothing there.

He stood staring into darkness for several seconds, unable to accept that whatever he'd just heard and felt hadn't been real. Eventually, he turned back to the dark stairway to the basement. He still wasn't convinced he was alone in the kitchen (the half-eaten meal was almost as suspicious as the voice and breath that had made every hair on his body stand on end), but whatever was there with him clearly had some greater plan, otherwise, Zach thought, he wouldn't be alive.

"The Devil's got a plan," he thought, so far-gone in hysteria that he almost laughed out loud.

His whole life, his friends and relatives had tried to comfort each other with, "God has a plan for you," or, "everything happens for a reason," or, "this, too, shall pass," and other empty consolations of the same ilk. Now more than ever, Zach realized, he believed them to be true.

There was just one part they always left out: the Devil has his own plan, too. And sometimes, the Devil gets his way, no matter the obstacles.

"You got it, boy," the Conductor giggled. "Now you better get goin or you'll miss your ride."

Zach hesitated only for a moment before he limped over to the basement stairway.

It was pitch-black after the first few steps, but he could somehow see the movement at the bottom. A pale, naked figure. Gray, even. Pacing back and forth. Muttering and sobbing to itself, trying to keep quiet but physically incapable of silence.

Once it had passed the bottom of the staircase three or four more times, it disappeared. Zach waited a few uneasy seconds to make sure it wouldn't return. The sight and sound of the creature had been the thing of nightmares.

The train whistle blew once, twice, three times. It was getting close. He could feel it thundering down the track with a strength and purpose unlike any other machine he'd ever seen.

"Time's almost up!"

"All aboard the Freedom Train!"

"Have your papers ready!"

"Cannonball's a' rollin!"

"Next stop Number Six!"

"Devil's on the track!"

"Hallelujah!"

"Amen!"

"Choo-choo, mother fucker!"

He started down the steps. His feet seemed to grow heavier as he went until he was sweating with the effort of raising them.

He heard the sounds of a thousand peculiar horrors. The screams. The tears. The dripping. The whips. The cuts. The breaks. The sadness. The acceptance and revolt. The grinning. The many deaths. The tortures. The rapes.

It was all stretched out for him there like a macabre picnic blanket, eager to cater to the desires of the wretched and depraved.

In other words, the ones who knew real Freedom.

He made his way down the steps, this time without the aid of a railing. It was difficult work, but he was oblivious to the pain.

The screams intensified.

His steps quickened, and even when he seemed on the verge of plummeting headfirst to the bottom, his balance held.

The whistle blew once, twice, three times.

The Cannonball devoured the track like a rabid dog on raw meat.

The gray-skinned mumbler passed by the bottom of the steps again, its flayed back so acutely visible it would have made the strongest stomachs nauseous. You could see every muscle ripped open.

"Come on down, Zach!"

"Come see the Devil!"

"The Way of the Red Mask!"

"Hallelujah!"

"Amen!"

"Choo-choo, mother fucker!"

The Conductor stepped into the doorway behind him. "Time's almost up, Zachary."

"Better get rollin."

He didn't even look. He knew the stakes. He didn't even think of trying to get to the door, knowing that it was pointless to run out into the fog until he'd done exactly what they wanted of him. In the fog, the world was beyond his control.

The bottom of the steps was almost within reach. His calf was burning, his throat dry, his arms sweating, and he felt on the verge of utter insanity. But it was almost over, one way or another. He could feel it.

He came to the bottom step with a wet thud and almost sprawled out face first onto the concrete floor in exhaustion.

He took a look around, panting.

The room seemed to stretch forever in each direction. An artificial light glowed dimly in the distance, providing just enough illuminationfor Zach to get an eyeful of the horrors around him.

There were bodies. Thousands of them. Some dead, some alive, some that hovered somewhere in between. Some were screaming, some were sobbing, some were completely unconscious. All of them hung upside down by their ankles. All of them were naked and mutilated.

They were arranged in perfectly aligned rows like corn, and in between the crops walked the men of the Red Mask.

They were more terrifying than anything Zach had ever seen or imagined. One look at them flashed their entire wretched history before his eyes.

They were the embodiment of depravity.

"Come on down, Zach," they taunted in deep, numbing voices.

"Come and see the Way of the Red Mask."

"Come and know Freedom."

They all turned to look at him, for the moment too distracted to continue on with their labor. Zach nearly fainted.

Their masks were crude things, carved from wood and painted with thick brush-strokes still clearly visible across the surface. They were darker than the red Zach had imagined in his mind's eye, with crooked grins etched in black and black, woven patterns along their edges. Underneath the masks, covering the rest of their faces and hair, was a black hood like the mask and bib of a medieval executioner. All of them were dressed in black from head to toe. Black button-up shirts with black undershirts, black scarecrow hats which at one time might have been Stetsons from the old west, black boots with black spurs and black pants with black belts and black gloves, holding whips and knives and maces and scythes and rakes and needles and saws and shovels and scalpels and matches and spears.

Zach didn't need his imagination to wander too far to guess what all of those were for. The evidence of their use was all around him.

The silence was so definite that the room seemed to have its own, perpetual ring echoing too far away to bounce back. Every ten seconds or so, one of the damned would cry out in agony, but the men of the Red Mask didn't stir once. They just stared at him.

Zach ventured into the cornrows of the dead.

"You can be free of this," they whispered to him.

He had no way of knowing which one addressed him.

He continued to walk in their direction, too terrified to wait and see what would happen, also terrified to rush to their arms…or more likely, their blades.

His calf burned.

"Come and know Freedom."

The masks followed him. Now that he was standing closer to them, he could see that they each had one yellow, infected eye behind the mask and one with a normal mixture of white and blue.

The bodies swayed as the damned tried to shift their weight or break free or just breathe. Zach could smell them as he walked, all shit and sweat and blood and organs. All fear. All enslaved. He'd limped so far among them that he could no longer see the staircase, yet the landscape never seemed to change.

The Red Masks closed in around him. They stood in a loose circle with Zach as their center.

His knees began to buckle and his breathing beat rapidly from his chest. They were beyond horrifying, absolutely grotesque in their silence and slow, inquisitive movements.

He could give no act of defiance. All he could do was stand there and wait for them to string him up by his ankles, rip out his insides, and shower themselves with his blood and intestines in their absurd, reserved glee.

That was the Way of the Red Mask.

That was the Way of the Long Track.

He understood it all in an instant but not in word or concept. It was somewhere deep in his soul. He'd been called there for a reason, cleansed for servitude. He was damned.

The Red Masks drew ever nearer, their yellow eyes spinning, oozing in every direction. One of them held a mace to him. Zach stared at it, uncomprehending.

"Take it. Know Freedom."

Zach hesitated again, but only for a moment. He had no choice anymore. He swallowed hard and grabbed the mace with both hands. The weight was formidable yet somehow comforting. Like he'd been born to carry it. When he held it, the whine of the world seemed to dissipate. Everything became clearer.

The Red Masks parted, revealing the fresh, unscarred bodies of Meghan, Tom Posey, and his mother, hanging naked from the ceiling by their ankles. When they saw Zach limping their way, they began to scream.

Zach grinned, his face turning a beet red, his left eye beginning to cloud into a milky gray.

"NO, ZACH! PLEASE!" they screamed.

"Cannonball's a' rollin'!"

"Climb aboard the Freedom Train!"

"You got nothing holding you back!"

"Amen!"

"Hallelujah!"

"Choo-choo, mother fucker!"

"NO!"

Zach raised the mace over his head and bludgeoned their bodies, each swing the manifestation of a thousand hurts, disappointments, tears, and inadequacies, until they gargled with their own blood and tears and strangled fury.

He left nothing of them but the remains of their feet, ankles, and shins, chained to a loathsome, gray ceiling forevermore.

The Red Masks watched him silently, extolling every so often in their own quiet gestures.

When he was done with them, he stood over their corpses, panting. Sweat and blood communed over his body so it was impossible to tell which was which. A cornucopia of body parts were riddled over the ground to be collected and boiled.

NUMBER SIX

When he was done, the Red Masks came over, held him down, and routinely carved out his left eye, severing the nerves and skin remorselessly. Zach didn't even groan. The new eye would fuse with his Red Mask when it grew back, bearing witness to the dark mysteries of the alleyways and the Long Tack with keen clarity for a thousand years.

The whistle blew. Outside, the fog rolled away and the Cannonball rolled into the station with all of its whiskey teacups, its shattered plates, its screaming and sobbing and laughing and thundering, its carnal pleasures in empty compartments while children pretended to cover their eyes.

The Cannonball had arrived at Station Number Six.

Hallelujah.

Amen.

Choo-choo, mother fucker.

Zach rose, limped up the stairs to the kitchen, out the front door, and up the platform.

The old Conductor stepped off of the black train, and Zach of the Red Mask stepped on as the new one, where he'd wear a different mask to carry the souls of the dead to their awful eternities. He'd wear the face he'd worn in life to hide the other.

His real one had turned a dark and landscaped red.

About Joseph Williams:

*Joseph Williams is a freelance journalist for **Real Detroit Weekly** where he has interviewed artists ranging from Grammy Award-winners to American Book Award-winners. His fiction has appeared in **The Wayne State University Literary Review, A Fly in Amber Fiction Magazine, The Western Online,** and **Bewildering Stories**.*

Cemetery Tour
by Robert Essig

PART ONE

CHAPTER 1

Their ultimate goal was to take a road trip touring cemeteries beginning in San Diego, California and ending at the St. Louis Cemetery No.1 in New Orleans, Louisiana--reputed to be the most haunted cemetery in America.

But they didn't make it that far.

It was somewhere in Colorado nearing Kansas when they first came upon something strange in an old and seemingly forgotten graveyard. Up to this point Brent, Colin and Jade had been touring the cemeteries during the day electing to sleep in motels or campout in the woods or state parks where permitted to do so. There wasn't a camper amongst the three of them, so they only chose the latter option when unable to find viable lodging.

"Why don't we go to the next cemetery at night?" asked Jade, her big green eyes locked on her boyfriend Colin who was driving the car, she sitting shotgun with a notebook in her lap. "If we're trying to find proof of ghosts and spirits, why are we checking these places out in the daylight?"

Colin darted her a glance of uncertainty. He knew that even though he didn't like the idea, she would probably get her way. The Cemetery tour was for equal parts fun and a paper she was writing for her anthropology course. As much as he liked the exploits of most college students' Spring Break, he couldn't deprive her of her studies.

"I think that's a great idea," Brent said from the back seat munching on a stick of formed greasy beef jerky. "If anything else, it would add great ambiance--maybe have a few beers, tell ghost stories."

"You tell ghost stories around a campfire, Brent, not a cemetery," said Jade. "What you hope for is a ghost story you can eventually tell at a campfire."

"I don't know, Jade," said Colin. "When we get to Louisiana you may find your paper a bit lacking in supernatural phenomenon. People spend their lives looking for ghosts and never find them, and here you think you'll have enough information from a tour of cemeteries during what should be the Spring Break of our lives." Colin looked in the rearview mirror at Brent giving him a big smile, though he was perfectly aware that Brent had as much a similar interest in things that bump in the night as Jade.

Jade gave Colin a sour glance. He just had to shoot down her hopes, didn't he? Sometimes he could be so unsupportive it made her crazy. She had the notion that he didn't like the idea of going into cemeteries after dark. In spite of his discouraging words, she decided to press the point, figuring that seeing the cemeteries at night would be her best chance at real spiritual phenomenon anyway.

Jade said, "I really think we should find a motel, get some sleep, and go out tonight to find the next graveyard. We could get a cooler full of beer--it'd be fun."

"Sounds good to me," said Brent still chewing on a flavored fatty beef stick.

"All right," said Colin, "We'll stop at the next motel, the next <u>cheap</u> motel."

CHAPTER 2

It was difficult to locate graveyards in the dark, especially during a moonless night such as tonight. Fortunately, they decided to stock up on supplies earlier after they checked into their motel (a Budget Inn, though Colin felt it could have been more of a budget).

Jade was excited. She had a spiral bound notebook open upon her lap where she had made minor notes on the cemeteries they had seen thus far. First was the El Camino Memorial Park in San Diego. There wasn't much to see, not as far as anything supernatural. Her notes were vague and unenthusiastic. Next they visited a small cemetery in Alpine in east San Diego. It was equally unsatisfying, as far as her paper went, but more of what they were interested in. It was an older cemetery, yet something about seeing it in the daylight left much to be desired.

There were many such cemeteries from east San Diego and through Arizona where they came upon the famous Boot Hill graveyard in Tombstone. It was a sweltering day under the radiance of the sun, hardly worthy of notes--she <u>did</u> forced herself to write about the eerie quiet disturbed only by the whistling of the wind through the cacti, that and how strange it was to be looking at the grave markers for many of the outlaws Wyatt Earp killed, but then the chatter of tourists killed the moment.

There was a sense of excitement traveling through an unfamiliar countryside in the dark cloak of night, the sky like a shroud over the birdcage called Earth, a time when so many people sleep, a time when graveyards were frightening to even think about much less roam about in search of something supernatural, something spiritual. But graveyards weren't frightening to Jade, nor Brent. As for Colin...

They were on their way out of Colorado and into Kansas where they were destined to visit the Stull Cemetery in Kansas City. It was supposed to be the second most haunted graveyard in the USA, and very desirable for Jade and her hopes at witnessing real phenomenon.

It was difficult to research and map out other cemeteries so they were winging it most of the time, just keeping their eyes peeled. There were plenty of bone yards in America, some of them nothing more than an acre of old graves dating back to the early pioneers who settled in any given region.

"There's one," said Brent. He was now in the front passengers seat, his eyes scanning the landscape for the inevitable graveyard. "Looks good too."

Jade looked up, a smile now replacing the look of dread her prior notes filled her with. "It does look good."

Colin was mute. He still didn't like the idea of touring the graveyards at night. His stomach churned the way it did when he had to do something he wasn't thrilled about, his nerves a bit frayed. He couldn't wait to crack open a beer; take the edge off.

They pulled into the parking lot beneath a tree in hopes of being concealed from view of the main road. Sneaking into graveyards at night and drinking beer was likely illegal in every state of the Union, but this was Spring Break after all, and as twenty-something college students they were entitled to some fun along the way, and with any luck, an innocent fright.

"What do you think?" asked Colin. "Can we be seen from the road?"

Brent and Jade stepped out of the car scanning the surroundings. Brent stuck his head back in the car. "I think we're good, man. It's a dark night." He looked at the sky. "Hell, it's a moonless night. Nobody's gonna see our car unless they're looking for it."

"Good." Colin exited the car. It was a small car, very gas efficient. In the days of four-dollar gas, they had better be driving an efficient ride, their budget being as tight as a drum skin.

"I hope it's not locked," said Colin, "I'm really not looking forward to jumping the fence."

If there was one thing Jade didn't like about Colin it was the fact that he could be a whiney little bitch at times, especially if he wasn't getting his way. It wasn't that he threw tantrums and pouted, but his demeanor was a clear reduction of what she liked about him: his sense of excitement, humor, his practicality--it all went out the door in moods such as this.

"It's just a fence, Colin, not the Great Wall of China," said Jade.

"Very funny."

Brent chuckled as he retrieved their cooler from the trunk along with some flashlights they picked up at the local drug store. "Should have brought lock cutters," he said sarcastically as he slammed the trunk. "Let's go."

The fence around the perimeter was low, easily low enough to jump over, but that wouldn't be necessary considering the open gate practically welcoming them.

"You don't have to worry about the fence, Col," said Jade. "Looks like they were expecting us."

"We should probably go towards the back," said Brent. "That way we won't be seen from the street, you know, by a cop roaming around looking for trouble."

"It's pretty dark back there," said Colin, "Are you sure it's such a good idea?" Colin was the star quarterback in high school, a big guy with six-pack abs and guns only regular weight training could account for, but sometimes his brawn was shadowed by his irrational fears. The guy could probably free climb a vertical mountain or skydive, but when it came to nocturnal activities whether it be clubbing or just walking down the street, he had a very bad disposition.

"What, do you want to get busted by the cops? I'm fairly sure we're not allowed in this graveyard after dark, especially drinking beer, you know?"

"Besides," said Jade, her eyes scanning the crumbling tombstones they passed as they walked from the comforts of the dimly lit parking lot to the darkness of the cemetery. "What fun is it going to be all lit up like that?"

"Real fun," Colin muttered. He couldn't believe he was going through with this.

Jade had been dating Colin for a year now, but she didn't know much about his fear of the dark. He wasn't one to bring the subject up, feeling a bit childish about it. For the star quarterback, he was embarrassed to admit his nyctophobia and would often go out at night with Jade so she wouldn't think he was weak. To him, his fear of darkness was a sign of weakness.

The trio scanned the bone yard with their flashlights--Colin's flashlight was about three times as large as the others. He wanted a good bright beam just in case anything bad happened. For him, light equaled safety.

The tombstones were very old, some of the dates going back a hundred years and more. There were grave markers in the shapes of crosses as well as monumental statues and even a few small mausoleums. This was very much the type of graveyard both Jade and Brent were looking forward to, she for the possibility of supernatural phenomenon, he because of morbid fascination. Colin, on the other hand, wasn't looking forward to any type of graveyard. He was only doing the tour for the sake of his girlfriend. If he had it his way he would be on lake Havasu pounding a beer bong with a bunch of skanky co-eds. He would like Jade to be there too, of course, although that wasn't her scene. They were a strange couple that way, but opposites attract.

"Grab me one of those beers, Brent," said Colin.

Brent was going to give him a wise crack, but there was something in Colin's voice, a twinge as if he were on the verge of tears that was being covered up in a veneer of thick masculinity. Brent has known Colin for many years, and known too of his fear of the dark. It wasn't something Colin talked to him about personally, but Brent made the connections with the nightlights in Colin's bedroom and his reluctance to go out with the boys at night. He always found Colin's affinity for the dark a bit on the strange side, but they were very close friends, and he just dealt with it the best he could.

Though Brent felt Jade was good for Colin--she had a way of getting him to do more at night than he normally would--he still ached for her the way he has since they were in high school. Sometimes he hated Colin for being with her, yet he didn't want her to become a wedge between then, thus he kept his thoughts to himself.

Brent stopped to open the cooler. He handed a beer to Jade, then Colin, noting the weariness in his eyes. He popped the lid on his beer and took a generous pull. "So, where's the ghosts?" asked Brent.

"Maybe they don't come out until the witching hour," said Jade, looking at her wristwatch. "It's only eleven thirty. They're still sleeping."

Colin leaned back holding his beer an inch from his mouth as the amber liquid poured down his gullet in a smooth stream. As the last of the beer left the can he crushed it and tossed it aside a bit too aggressively. Usually he's had several beers before he starts pounding them like that.

"Ho-lee shit, Col!" Jade said.

"How 'bout another?" asked Brent with a crescent grin displaying his pearly whites. He knew Colin was uneasy and wanted to create a fun atmosphere to chill his ass out.

"Don't mind if I do." Colin's voice was regaining its normal demeanor. The beer seemed to be taking the edge off. "So where <u>are</u> the ghosts?"

After a few more beers Colin began to relax a bit. He couldn't truly be comfortable in a dark graveyard, but the alcohol fogged his brain enough for him to begin to forget his irrational fears, to forget the time spent locked in the closet as a child when his mother would lose herself in a drug stupor. Those were the Bad Nights. Those were the nights he thought the dark would never end.

"So what exactly are you doing your paper on?" Brent asked Jade.

"Our road trip. I would like to witness something extraordinary and write about that, but if all else fails I can do the paper on the various cemeteries. That's why I'm making notes of everything even though the ghosts are ignoring us." She gulped her beer. "I've got to pee."

Colin looked at her. "Pick a grave to desecrate."

She frowned at him. "I can't do that. I sure hope no one pisses on me after I'm dead."

"There's some trees over there," he pointed. "You could go there, but I'm afraid you're gonna have to drip dry, 'cause we didn't bring any tee-pee."

"Shit," she muttered as she walked toward the trees. "Aren't you going to come with me so I don't get abducted by a zombie?" she hollered.

"You're not going too far; I can see you from here. Besides, the zombies are ignoring us, remember?"

"Very funny," she said as her flashlight beam disappeared behind the tree.

"Pretty creepy, huh?" said Brent.

"What?"

"This cemetery, man. You sure are pounding those beers fast enough."

Colin glowered at Brent. "What are you saying?"

"Hey, man, I know you weren't looking forward to this trip like Jade and I, and I can tell you're not diggin' it very much. Let me guess," he took a swig of beer, "You'd rather be in TJ or Cancun or something, right?"

Colin grinned. "You know me too well, my friend. You're goddamned right I'd rather be in Cancun, but Jade doesn't go for that shit. I really love her, but she's not into drinking herself into oblivion with a bunch of total strangers in a foreign land. Can't understand why not." He said the last part sarcastically.

Brent wasn't into that either. He didn't say anything though. Sometimes he was dumbfounded that Jade ended up with the jock. Colin wasn't even her type. Brent seemed to have more in common with her than he ever did. If it wasn't for her good looks and nice body, he didn't know what Colin saw in her. Sometimes he was surprised their relationship lasted this long.

"Shhh, here she comes," said Brent loud enough for Jade to hear him. She smiled knowing he was just joking.

"No zombies, huh," said Colin.

"Nothing but mosquitoes and crickets, but I thought I heard something over there." She pointed across the cemetery. "Probably nothing though."

"Make a note of it," said Colin grabbing yet another beer. He was beginning to catch a decent buzz.

Jade couldn't tell by the tone of his voice whether he was being sarcastic or genuine. The fact that she couldn't tell was a bad sign leaning toward sarcasm.

A sound like leaves rustling issued through the still of night, coming from the direction Jade had pointed toward. Everyone heard it, which was apparent by the way they simultaneously looked in that direction.

"See," said Jade, mostly to Colin.

The sound was a good buzz kill.

"Let's check it out," said Brent. "Probably just an animal or something."

Jade looked into Colin's eyes. She knew he wouldn't be interested in investigating the noise, but he surprised her when he said, "Let's go. Could be your first paranormal experience."

Again, she couldn't tell whether he was being genuine or sarcastic, but she figured, based on knowing him intimately for the past two years, he was just being macho so no one would question his fear of the dark. He had always evaded the subject, but she was quite sure he feared the dark. Sometimes it brought out the asshole in him, his way of acting like there was no problem.

They turned their flashlights on, Colin carrying the lantern they had been using for a light source. Jade knew he grabbed the lantern for his own sake, to eliminate whatever it was he so disliked about the dark.

Dry leaves cracked beneath their steps just as the elusive noise had. It was a bit strange that this graveyard was so filled with trees; it seemed like a lot of maintenance, and by the sounds of their steps, it has been a while, a whole season, since the groundskeeper raked the place.

"Do you hear that?" asked Jade.

"Hear what?" said Brent.

"Sounds like footsteps other than ours."

They stopped, Colin almost knocking Jade down as he ran into her. He had been looking around wide-eyed, fear seeping through his inebriate barrier.

"Watch it, Col!"

"Sorry."

All was silent.

"So where exactly are we going?" asked Colin, ready to return to the cooler for a beer. He was just about done with the one in his hand, hardly warmed from his grip he drank it so damn quickly. Should have stuck one in my pocket, he thought.

"There," said Brent, his eyes wide as he stared at a large hole at the base of an old crumbling tombstone.

"Oh my God!" said Jade.

"What? What are you--" came Colin's voice as he took up the rear, awestruck at the sight of an exhumed grave. "What the hell is this?" Colin's voice was nearing panic. He recognized this and grabbed Jade's hand for comfort, to which she gave his a quick questioning look, no more than a fleeting glance, the look on his face assuring her that he was truly scared shitless.

"Don't know," said Brent as he came closer to the hole, his light into its dark depths. "Whoa! There's a fuckin' coffin down there, and it looks like it's been opened."

"Opened!" Colin's voice was so frantic both Jade and Brent looked at him with questioning eyes.

"You all right," asked Jade.

"Yeah. It's just...weird."

"Weird's right, man," said Brent. "This is an old grave. There's no reason it should have been dug up like this." Brent shined his light on the tombstone. "The date here is 1909."

"Damnit!" said Jade. "I left my notebook back with our stuff. I want to document this."

"You think a ghost dug itself out of this grave," said Colin, once again using ill-timed sarcasm to dilute his fears.

"Not a ghost," said Brent, "but a person." He was shining his light on the disheveled ground around the hole where footprints were evident in the soft dirt that had covered the coffin.

From behind them came another rustling in the dry leaves, very faint.

"What was that?" asked Jade, fear now prevalent in her voice.

"Don't know." Colin held his lantern out in the direction of the sound, swallowing his fears for the sake of his girlfriend. Beyond his own fears he could find strength at the quivering in Jade's voice.

"What are you doing there?" came an older man's voice startling the trio. "Who are you? What are you doing out here?"

"Were doing research for a paper, sir," said Brent assuming it was a police officer who had seen their car in the parking lot.

"Kids," said the voice. Brent wanted to shine his light to reveal the man's face, but wasn't about to shine a light in a cop's eyes.

The man came closer and when his appearance was that of a regular man instead of a police officer, Brent wondered what he was doing out here.

"You know there's a killer on the loose?" said the man. He was wearing a trench coat like a detective in a pulp magazine. He was missing the fedora, though. He pulled a drag off his cigarette and blew the smoke into the cold night. The cloud was twice the size it would have been in the day. "You're from out of town. Saw your car in the lot. I'm guessing you haven't heard about the murders."

They were all dumbfounded. Jade spoke up. "No, we just got into town earlier today."

"Where you coming from?" asked the man. His cigarette smoke was blowing with the slight breeze right into Colin's face, irritating him, yet there was something comforting about another's presence.

"Were on a cemetery tour. I'm writing a paper for my anthropology class. We started in San Diego; went though New Mexico and Colorado. We're going to Kansas tomorrow."

"I see."

"This killer," said Brent, "is he a serial killer?"

"People have been disappearing in the past few months."

"Disappearing? How do you know he's a killer?"

"The way they disappear. It's the same thing every time. He's sloppy, but none of the bodies have been found." The old man looked into the dug up grave. "Took my wife a month ago." He looked at the trio one by one. "I'm going to find him. The cops have got their thumbs up their asses. Without Beth I have nothing to look forward to anyhow."

"What makes you think he's killed them?" asked Brent. "Maybe they're alive somewhere."

Colin was itching for another beer. All this talk of serial killers was deflating his alcohol induced comfort bubble.

The old man looked gravely into Brent's eyes. "He's taken two others as well as Beth. Abducted them in the middle of the night. The police can't find the guy, but they did notice a pattern at all three of the abduction sites."

"So what are you doing out here?" asked Colin a bit agitatedly, ready for this strange man to leave them the fuck alone so he could return to the safe end of the cemetery where the beer was.

"Saw your car, decided to check it out. What, may I ask, are you doing with this grave?" The old man's eyes drifted from the tri to the dark chasm at their feet..

"Nothing," replied Jade defensive against the man's accusatory tone. "We heard a nose and came to see what it was. It must have been you."

The man clicked the button on a small flashlight and shone the beam across the shoes of the three before him. "Clean," he muttered. "Shoes would be dirty if you dug it yourself."

"We didn't dig it, man," said Brent. "Whoever did, they dug right down to the coffin." Brent shined his light inside the hole again. "Looks like they might have even opened it. The lid looks a little askew."

The man stepped beside Brent to take a look down the grave. He felt very comfortable in the presence of these three or he wouldn't have put himself in such a precarious position. With just the slightest push Colin or even Jade could send him down six feet to his death.

He looked at the three college students regarding their stature. "You're the tallest," he said to Colin. "Why don't you go down there and see what's in the coffin."

Colin shrank, scared not only of the deep dark hole, but of the fact that a dead person was down there. He could actually feel his testicles retract as if he had jumped into a freezing cold pool. He didn't like that feeling and would have been ashamed for anyone to know about it. His mind screamed: <u>Where's your balls! Don't you have </u>cahones<u>? Don't be a pussy!</u>

Before Colin could make a move, Brent said, "I'll do it." He all but jumped in, ready for the adventure. To him it was a prime opportunity to see a real corpse, as morbid as that sounds. If it was from 1909 it was bound to be a real

68

ugly one. <u>The uglier the better</u>, he thought as he eased himself down. He didn't want to jump in for fear that he would destroy the possibly brittle coffin.

"You all right?" asked the man.

"Yes."

Jade was peering over the edge but not Colin. He was holding on to his lantern very tightly, trying to regain his manhood, fear having paralyzed him once again. This was getting out of hand very quickly.

"Shine some light down here," asked Brent. "I can't see a goddamn thing."

The question suddenly struck Jade: "Why do you want him to look in the coffin?"

The man answered as he gaped upon Brent in the hole. "You didn't dig it up, neither did the groundskeepers--they wouldn't leave an open grave like this. While we're here together I thought it would be a good idea to check it out."

"Ho-lee shit!" came Brent's voice. That was his tag line.

"What is it?" asked the man. "Are you all right?"

"I'm fine, but this corpse isn't."

"What!" said Jade.

Colin was trying his damnedest to keep his composure, pacing back and forth. He could think of little that would be more embarrassing than having an attack induced by his nyctophobia with Jade and Brent there, not to mention the old man. He desperately wanted a beer, or perhaps a shot of tequila to quell his emotional distress.

"The head's missing."

"Dear God!" said the man.

Jade grimaced and wrinkled her brow.

Colin tried to ignore the grim news.

"I can't believe this." Brent had the sudden urge to get out of the grave as if seeing the defiled corpse had somehow placed a curse on him. Irrational thoughts entered his mind. He could see the corpse come to life and reach for him, blaming him for the loss of its head.

"I'm coming up," Brent said a bit frantically. No one could blame him. It wasn't everyday he looked into a hundred year old coffin to see a headless corpse.

"What do we do about this?" asked Jade. She looked to Colin as if he would have an answer.

"I don't know," he said dumbly.

"Nothing," said the old man. "We do nothing, for now. In the morning I'll call in an anonymous tip, but I don't think it's something we should deal with tonight. It may raise unnecessary suspicion."

"I hear that," said Brent as he climbed out of the grave. The old man promptly gave him a hand.

"Yeah," said Colin, "I think maybe we should get out of here." He didn't sound whiney, and that was a good thing.

"My name's Grady, by the way, Harry Grady. If I were you, I'd go right on through to Kansas and leave this part of Colorado alone. It's not safe being out late at night here anymore."

"Yeah," said Colin, "we'll be outta here in the morning."

The old man nodded and turned back toward the parking lot. He was a strange character fueled by the loss of his wife, yet he seemed to be positive that she was dead even though none of the bodies of the abducted have been found. Any way they looked at it, his acquaintance was strange given the circumstances.

"Guy gives me the creeps," said Colin. Everything gave him the creeps.

"Let's get out of here, man," said Brent. "This is more than I signed up for."

They walked back toward the cooler, all thinking about the headless cadaver. There were questions aplenty as to why it was left there minus the head, why it had been dug up. Jewelry would have seemed a criminally just reason to exhume a corpse, but the head! Why would anyone do that?

"I don't get it," said Brent. He was perhaps the most traumatized since he was the one who actually saw the corpse. It was stained in his mind like red wine on a white tapestry. The hands were gooey and crossed above its chest just like in the movies, the suit worm eaten and moldy. The smell wasn't as rank as Brent would have thought--musky, but not like a freshly rotten corpse (as if he knew what that really smelt like).

"It really had no head?" asked Colin, more to break the silence than curiosity.

"I wouldn't lie to you about something like that," Brent responded.

"What'd it look like?" asked Jade, her morbid sensibilities returning as the scene was left behind them, as the reality of what just occurred faded into something that didn't feel quite real.

"He was in a suit, all dirty and chewed up--worms I guess. The hands were like skeleton hands with..." How could he explain the gooey decomposing flesh? "...It was pretty gross." He left it at that and neither of his friends questioned him further.

70

They all cracked open beers and drank them as they walked back to the car. They exited the cemetery and saw Harry Grady pulling out onto the highway in a white 1980s Lincoln Continental. Despite the strange occurrences of the night, Brent had to laugh.

"What are you laughing at, Brent?" asked Colin.

"Could have guessed the old guy would be driving a boat like that."

Jade had been taking a drink when he said that. It caught her as very funny, which was known to all when a spray of foamy beer blew out of her mouth like a horizontal geyser. Even Colin had a good laugh about it.

It was inconsiderate and cruel to crack on the old man like that, but they made a few more jokes at his expense before loading up the car and getting down the road. They had initially decided to drive toward Kansas stopping at every graveyard they passed, but thought better of it after what Harry had told them about the alleged serial killer.

They would be in Kansas in several hours, probably by the early morning. They decided on getting a bite to eat and a motel room after crossing the state line.

CHAPTER 3

"Do we really have to do this at night?" asked Colin. "Is it really necessary?"

"Sure it is," Jade replied. "We've been over this a thousand time, Col. How am we going to witness a ghost or spirit in the daylight?"

"But I thought we agreed to tour the cemeteries during the day and sleep at night, maybe go to a few bars for some drinks. It is Spring break, remember?"

Brent pulled out the cooler and flashlights as his counterparts bickered with one another. He was definitely on Jade's side, but he didn't want to get in the middle of it. It was a stupid idea to visit the cemeteries in the day for obvious reasons, but he left that for Jade to argue.

"Bars? Is that all you think about?"

"Jade, you know that isn't all I think about, but I'm twenty-four, and there's a certain yearning to party and have fun that flows through my veins during Spring Break."

"Well it isn't as if we aren't going to go to any bars, didn't we just go to a bar in New Mexico?"

"I'll be back in a minute," said Brent. "I'm just gonna case the place real quick to find a way in."

Both Colin and Jade nodded, never ceasing in their argument.

"Yeah, but I think we should bar hop tomorrow," said Colin. "It's Spring Break, we have to."

Brent turned around, several yards away. "Kansas City, my friend. We'll hit some bars when we get there."

"Well, we better make some traction tomorrow 'cause I want to do some <u>real</u> Spring Break partying!"

Jade laughed. "Okay, tomorrow's your night, but tonight belongs to me."

Colin smiled and hugged her. He gazed upon the cemetery, another old bone yard with crumbling tombs and a rickety looking iron fence very much in need of a paint job. His smile faded as the thought of walking around in the dark seeped into his mind. He felt all right in Jade's arms, but away from her he was all alone. Even standing a foot away he would be consumed with that terrible feeling that would clench his soul bringing him into a frenzied panic. He seemed to be able to drive the panic away, but it was hard, and as much as he hated his girlfriend and best friend to know about his nyctophobia, the fear tended to show itself like a gift beneath cheap wrapping paper.

"Easy as pie," said Brent returning from checking the place out. "I pushed a section of the iron fence down by accident. Shit's rusted all to hell."

Brent grabbed the cooler, Colin and Jade the flashlights and backpack.

"This place looks great, man," said Brent. "I think it might be older than the last one we went to."

"Old is good," said Jade, "but I can't wait until we get to the Stull Cemetery in Kansas City. It's supposed to be the second most haunted cemetery in all America."

"Kansas City!" griped Colin. "I thought you said we were gonna hit up some bars in Kansas City?"

"We can spend two nights there, Colin."

"We better." Colin's demeanor was on the offensive, a reaction to his fears.

When they began preparing for this Spring Break road trip Colin was under the impression that they would see the spooky sights during the daylight hours and travel by night drinking in a few bars along the way. When Brent and Jade came up with the idea to see the cemeteries at night Colin could feel his heart drop, though he felt, equally, the disability to protest their excitement about seeing the graveyards at night. How could he stand up against the two of them when they were so adamant about how boring the cemeteries were in the daylight? Though he felt a whole lot safer in the daylight, he could understand the thrill of walking around the graveyards at night, thus he kept his mouth shut and decided to face his fears.

It was about time he extinguished his childish fears of the dark, he just wasn't sure he could take much more of this. It wasn't that he relived those monstrous nights when his mother so detested him and locked him in the closet so he'd shit up and allow her to get high in peace. He didn't. It was the lingering effects that trauma had on him, the fear that the darkness would overcome him forever.

They walked through the fallen piece of iron fence and into the cemetery. Colin felt his body tighten up as the dark encapsulated him. Jade was right there, as was Brent, but that mattered nothing. It was only the thought of embarrassment that fueled him toward bravery.

"Yeah," said Jade, "this is an old cemetery. Some of these graves are from the eighteen hundreds."

"Yeah," Brent agreed. "Y'know I should have brought some paper and charcoal for some grave rubbings. This would be the place."

"Sure would," replied Jade.

"What the hell is a grave rubbing?" Colin wasn't into the morbid shit his girlfriend and Brent were into.

Brent regarded Colin curiously, once again wondering how it was the big dumb jock ended up with Jade. "You don't know what a grave rubbing is?" he said sarcastically.

"Why would I?"

They walked between old graves, most from the turn of the twentieth century, Jade more interested in the ambiance of the graveyard than explaining a grave rubbing to her boyfriend.

"You take a piece of paper and put it against a grave, then you rub it with a piece of charcoal showing the face of the grave on the paper."

Colin grimaced, eager to keep talking away his fears. "You like that?"

"It's interesting."

"You done it before?"

"No," Brent confessed, "but I've always wanted to."

73

"Always wanted to! What, do you not have anything better to do with your time?"

"Whoa, look at that!" said Jade, completely removed from their conversation.

The two stopped in their tracks nearly running into Jade who had taken the lead.

"I think this is a good place to stop a while," she said. "Can you believe this?" She was staring at a huge monument of an angel that seemed misplaced with all of the old and crumbling tombstones.

Brent said, "I think they have a lot of these in The St. Louis Cemetery in New Orleans."

"Doesn't fit here," said Jade.

Colin took the opportunity to rip into the cooler for a brewskie. Tonight they had bought cans of Coors Light. Colin sneered at cans. Everyone knew bottles were better, that cans contaminated the beer with undertones of aluminum residue, but he wasn't going to complain, not when the beer was so detrimental to his survival of another moonless night.

"It's pretty cool," said Colin trying to get into the conversation. He didn't give a good goddamn about the angelic monument; he just wanted the shelter of talk, the comfort of words between good friends.

"I've got an idea," said Jade. "I'm going to take a picture of it."

She dug into the backpack for her digital camera. "Sometimes the ghosts appear in the photo's, you know."

"Yeah," said Brent, "I've seen that before. Little glowing orbs or weird fuzzy splotches, shit like that."

She stood back with her camera. "Maybe we'll get lucky." She put the camera to her face and took several pictures of the large monument, some of the pictures with Brent and Colin present.

In the modern day of digital cameras, she could look at her photos immediately, and there didn't appear to be anything unusual.

"Maybe you should snap some shots all over the place," Suggested Colin. "You'd probably have a better chance at seeing a ghost that way."

Jade smiled at him. She liked when he showed interest in something that was so unlike him such as ghost hunting. "I think I'll do that."

Colin crunched his beer and fished another from the frozen world of the ice chest. He tossed one to Brent and one to Jade. There was no reason to drink alone.

The night remained mellow and Colin began to relax after a few brews. Jade was getting a pretty good buzz, as was Brent, which lightened the spirit of their companionship. With any luck, Colin may convince them to cut the tour of the cemetery short and finish the night at one of the local clubs, if there are any. They may have to settle for a bar.

"So you didn't see anything in the pictures, huh?" Brent asked Jade.

"Nope. I think the ghosts are at rest in this place, probably too old to haunt anymore."

"You really think any of that shit is real?" asked Colin.

"Absolutely," replied Jade. "You remember that magazine I showed you, right? There's no way that was a fake."

"Looked fake to me." Colin took a swig of beer.

"No way. You don't know what to look for. It was authentic."

"You're talking about that Japanese zine, right?" asked Brent.

"Yeah."

"But it's a magazine, not a real photo. They doctored it up. It's all bullshit."

Jade grabbed another beer wondering who was going to drive them back to the motel. They were all getting pretty loose.

"It's a reputable magazine, Col," she said popping her can open.

"We'll have a better chance at seeing something weird at the Stull cemetery in a day or two," said Brent. "That one's had a lot of phenomenon reported."

"Great," said Colin, no lack of sarcasm in his voice.

The night was quiet, dark and mysterious. The graves stood like the ends of huge Popsicle sticks stuck in the ground, a great place for something to hide, perhaps a rabid animal or some deranged midget with murder on the mind.

A regular person couldn't hide behind one of those graves, could they?

The thought struck Colin though he wasn't afraid of such a threat. It was the general dark of night that froze his blood so--weirdoes and madmen he could deal with.

"I've gotta pee," said Jade, standing from the sitting position they had held for at least an hour now.

"There's plenty of graves to hide behind," said Colin, "but you forgot the tee-pee again."

She trotted off quite a distance, the beam of her flashlight illuminating random graves.

"Why don't you go with her, see that she's safe out there," asked Brent.

"She's safe, why wouldn't she be?"

"It's a big graveyard, man, anything can happen."

"What's it to you anyway? She can handle herself."

"I'm just saying, if she were my girlfriend I would have escorted her for her safety, that's all."

Colin felt a rising of anger. "Well, I don't think you need to worry about it because she's my girlfriend, and I know she's all right, so shut your fuckin' trap."

Brent put his hands up in surrender. "Don't want to tread on your territory, man, but--"

"But nothing! What's your fucking problem?" Colin's fear of the dark brought out the anger in waves.

"I don't have a problem," Brent retorted. Now he was becoming angry.

"Apparently you do or you wouldn't be harping on me. You think Jade can't take care of herself? Is that it? She can't even take a piss without me holding her hand?"

"Hey, man, I didn't mean to get on you."

"Then shut the fuck up."

There was an uncomfortable silence for several minutes that seemed like small eternities for both parties as they replayed their little argument over and over in one-another's mind. Colin couldn't believe Brent's audacity, and Brent couldn't believe the way Colin treated Jade. If he were Colin he would be right there with her to make sure nothing bad happened, because you can never tell when trouble will strike.

"Where is she?" asked Brent, breaking the silence.

"Taking a piss," said Colin, annoyance clear in voice.

Brent looked at Colin with eyes wide in amazement at how dim his friend could be. "She walked off almost fifteen minutes ago. She should be back by now."

"Fifteen minutes? Are you sure?"

Brent looked at his watch. "Yeah, she took off fifteen minutes ago."

Colin made a face. "What, you're timing my girlfriend now? What's your deal, man?"

Brent sighed. "Colin, chill out. Jade's my friend, has been for along time. I just think she should have been back by now, don't you?"

76

Colin looked through the dense darkness but he couldn't find her, in fact, he couldn't even locate the beam of her flashlight.

"You don't see her, do you?" Colin asked.

"Oh, I'm allowed to look."

"Don't be a smart-ass, I'm serious."

"No, I can't."

"Maybe I should go check it out, make sure she's all right," said Colin only because he knew that's what he should say. The thought of walking out there alone was maddening.

"I think maybe you should."

Colin regarded Brent curiously, wondering if he somehow knew about his nyctophobia. There was scorn in Brent's voice and Colin didn't like it. He also didn't like the way Brent was keeping an eye on his girlfriend, the way he acted as if he cared about her more than Colin did. He was beginning to wonder if Brent was trying to invade his territory. He sure hoped not, because he wasn't looking forward to beating the shit out of his best friend.

Colin realized his beer was drained and tossed it aside with the other empties. Jade came up with the idea of saving them in a bag to recycle, that way they would at least have a few bucks to put toward the next case.

Colin grabbed the lantern they were using for light and stood up, slowly, as if he were trying to hold off as long as he could in hopes that Jade would come back before he had to face the dark.

"You're taking the lantern?" asked Brent. He couldn't believe Colin. They had been friends for nearly ten years now, and he was seeing a side of Colin on this trip he had never really seen before. He wasn't sure what it was, but it sure did seem like Colin was hiding something, or hiding from something. His attitude was like a shield, and Brent didn't like it.

"I've gotta see, don't I?"

"Here," Brent extended a flashlight. "Use this. The lantern should stay here."

"But I like the lantern," Colin protested, sounding like a bratty little boy.

"You can see fine with a flashlight, man, leave that here." Brent looked over Colin's shoulder toward the dark where Jade had gone to use the bathroom. "Where is she anyway? And what's taking you so long? I'd go, but she's your girlfriend and I'd hate to find her squatting down out there takin' a piss." Then a thought occurred to Brent. "Hey, maybe she's waiting for you." He cracked a smile. "You know, for a little romp in the hay."

"Give me a break." Colin had about enough of Brent's bullshit. He set the lantern down on the tombstone where it had been resting, a bit roughly too, nearly shattering the glass.

"Careful with that thing, what did it ever do to you?"

"Very funny." Colin snatched the flashlight from his friend and turned in the direction Jade had walked off in.

"If you're not back in ten minutes," Brent called out after Colin had taken several steps into the darkness, "I'll assume the best. Hey, maybe you'll want a couple of these."

Colin turned around to see Brent running after him with two beers in his hands.

"I'll assume the best?" Colin repeated. "Dude, are you serious?"

"Hey, man," Brent patted Colin on the back, handing over the beers, "You two haven't had a moment away from me and we've been on the road almost a week. I wouldn't be surprised if she's waiting spread eagled for you."

"Don't be crass."

"Crass, that's a big word for a dumb jock."

Colin smiled and shook his head as he walked away. Brent had been calling him a dumb jock ever since he joined the football team when they were freshmen in high school. There isn't a team at the JC they attend, and he was unable to get a scholarship to a university straight out of high school, but when he starts at State next year, he'll try out for the SDSU Aztecs.

The thought of Jade waiting for him all hot and bothered temporarily dissipated his fear of the dark--that and the beer. It sort of made sense, what Brent was telling him, that she may be waiting for him out there. She wouldn't be spread eagled, that was just Brent's foolish fantasy, but she might be hiding behind a tombstone in a patch of nice soft grass.

The dark was immense, as if he were walking into a darkroom like back in his junior year of high school when he took photo shop not knowing that he would have to spend time in utter darkness while the film developed. He changed that class very quickly before there was any chance of him being embarrassed. He could only imagine what kind of scene he would have made had he actually entered the darkroom and had a panic attack. He would have never lived that one down.

The night wasn't quite as stark as that of a darkroom, but to Colin dark was dark. The beers were very cold in his hand--he was holding both of them in one hand, flashlight in the other--and he wanted very badly to set them down. He stepped soft and slow as if he were approaching a sleeping beast.

It didn't take long before the beer and sex buzz wore away the veneer exposing raw fear. He couldn't lose his cool though, couldn't freak out just in case she really <u>was</u> waiting patiently for him. He wouldn't want to ruin the moment.

His steps quickened and he knew he was very close now. She couldn't be much further than these few graves at the very rear of the cemetery, and that's when he saw the glow of her flashlight illuminating behind a large well-preserved tombstone standing tall amongst so many others that have crumbled over the years due to nature's torments.

"Jade, there you are," said Colin as he rounded the tombstone.

She wasn't there. Her flashlight was mounted on a rock shinning directly at the back of the tombstone where a message was written in blood.

PART TWO

CHAPTER 4

Brent watched as Colin walked off rather cautiously, his maiden awaiting him with open arms and open legs. At least that's how Brent envisioned it. He had many visions of Jade over the years, even on this trip, fantasies of Colin leaving to go to the store and she expressing her true feelings for Brent. He knew that would never happen, but he could dream.

He watched Colin and wondered about him. The poor sod was afraid of the dark. It was so obvious it screamed, yet no one ever really questioned him about it, at least not that Brent knew of. He had when they were younger, but it was a subject Colin cleverly averted.

When they were kids and Colin would sleep over at Brent's house, he would insist on a nightlight, and that behavior continued clear into high school, until Colin finally stopped, probably more out of the possibility of being made fun of than anything else.

Colin was just about there, to the rear of the graveyard where Jade would be waiting for him, and Brent envied him. He had half a mind to sneak a peek at them, but didn't want to risk being seen. It would be a long haul back to San Diego hitchhiking and bussing, not to mention losing the two best friends he has ever had, the kind of friends that stick around even after high school.

There was hope reserved, in the back of his heart, that Jade would one day realize she couldn't stand Colin and come running to Brent. He kicked himself for not making a move on her first, but jocks seemed to have more confidence, and Colin had wasted no time in asking her out.

Colin was pretty far off now, too far to see clearly, though it looked like he turned around. Must have found her.

Brent could see her lying there, naked and smiling, her long auburn hair mingling with the soft grass, her tender lips and green eyes yearning for him. He could put himself in Colin's place very easily.

He was actually beginning to turn himself on, so he decided to crack open a beer and forget about his jealousy for a moment, if he could.

I'll be fine just as long as I don't hear them out there all moaning and getting it on.

But he didn't hear anything of the sort. What he did hear was Colin's voice say, "Oh, shit!" His voice was very far off, but the panic and fear were unmistakable.

"Brent! Come here! Quick!" Colin yelled.

Brent made no hesitation before breaking into a full run, fearing the worst. Beyond his lust for Jade she was also a friend he cared very much for, and he was certain of what he was going to find when he reached Colin, certain, as well, had Colin escorted her into the darkness, nothing bad would have happened.

"What is it?" asked Brent as he neared ground zero.

Colin was mortified, speechless, on the verge of tears, staring at the backside of the tombstone, his head shaking from side to side very slightly. Brent knew what he was thinking even before he saw the message on the reverse side of the tombstone.

"What the..." said Brent. He read the dark red words very slowly:

"Meet tomorrow night at the next cemetery.

"She'll be alive only if you don't call authorities.

"If you do, her death will be on your hands.

"Remember, I'm watching you.

"Even now as you read this.

"See you tomorrow at midnight."

Brent didn't want to look around, but he couldn't help himself. He wondered how quick he would suffer a heart attack if he were to see eyes staring back at him from the woods surrounding the cemetery.

"She's dead," said Colin, staring glassy eyed at the words on the gravestone.

"You don't know that."

"What do we do?"

Brent surveyed their surroundings, suddenly finding the courage to shine his flashlight into the woods looking for the person who wrote the cryptic message.

"See anything?" asked Colin who longed for his lantern.

"Nothing."

"We gotta call the cops," said Colin pulling his cell phone out of his pocket. He flipped it open.

"No cops! Didn't you read the message? He'll kill her."

Colin closed his cell phone, eyes re-reading the message as if he had previously overlooked the line about not contacting the authorities.

"Then what do we do?" asked Colin as if Brent had all the answers.

"Go to the next cemetery tomorrow. What else can we do?"

"What the fuck!" There was a growing unease within Colin, not only from the darkness, but from the situation, from the sudden loss of Jade. He couldn't fathom how she could have been abducted right before their eyes.

"Who are you!" Colin yelled into the silent moonless night. "Show yourself, you asshole!"

"Calm down, man, he might be out there."

"If he's out there," Colin said loudly, "Then I want him to show himself. You hear that?" Colin looked into the forest shinning his light in search of Jade's abductor.

"He's out there, I'm sure of it," said Brent, "but where, I don't know. He's watching. We should probably go."

"Go?" Colin turned to Brent, his face red with fury, the wrath he wanted to unleash on the spineless piece of shit that robbed Jade away from him. "I'm gonna find the son-of-a-bitch and I'm going to kill him."

"Out there." Brent pointed toward the thick forest, the density of it enough to leave it dark even in the middle of the day. "Do you really want to go out there by yourself?"

Colin didn't. In his fit of anger he had forgotten all about his nyctophobia, and now it seemed childish in comparison to Jade's kidnapping.

"You'll get lost out there, Colin. We have to get out of here. We'll go to the next graveyard tomorrow. We'll bring all the cash we can scrape up and maybe he'll give her back for a ransom."

81

"A ransom? What kind of cockamamie shit is that? He's fucking with us, that's what he's doing." Colin turned walking back toward the lantern, ice chest and Jade's Backpack. Brent followed.

"You're right," said Brent. He probably doesn't want a ransom, but he wants one thing, and that's for us to meet him there at midnight. We have to do this for Jade. Maybe we can overpower him and get her back."

"And maybe she's all ready dead. The message was written in blood, you know."

"A person can bleed without dying."

They gathered up their things, Colin throwing Jade's backpack over his shoulder, Brent picking up the ice chest. They had guzzled a beer each in record time before gathering up the gear, both silently pondering the new direction of their cemetery tour, weary eyes shifting toward even the slightest noise.

Colin hadn't been a fan of touring cemeteries from the get go, and he never imagined it would end like this, but was it over? Not if they were going to a graveyard tomorrow night. Now it wasn't a cemetery tour so much as a cemetery game, his game, whoever he is. Colin could only assume it wasn't going to be easy getting Jade back, and he truly believed that she was already dead. If it wasn't for Brent, he would have called the cops to be done with whole charade. Of course he wanted Jade back, but the blood was a very bad sign, one that spelt murder.

The night was more silent than ever, only the sounds of crickets chirping and the occasional bird. It was hard to believe someone was watching them, and for all they knew it was a bluff.

The kidnapping wasn't a bluff.

Jade was out there somewhere, perhaps in the trunk of a car already on the road, maybe just beyond the first layer of the woods, unable to scream with a silver strip of duct tape across her mouth.

Then again, she may be dead, may have even been raped, her body left in a madman's wake, tangled in the underbrush to be discovered after Brent and Colin break down and contact the authorities. Perhaps the message in blood was a means to buy time for the murderer to make a getaway.

"I think we should call the cops," said Colin. As his mind wrapped around the situation, he kept coming back to that solution.

"Can't," said Brent, as if they were physically unable to dial 911.

Both Brent and Colin shone their lights all around as they walked through the fallen section of fence to the parking lot where their car awaited them, looking for any sign of Jade's abductor. There was a feeling of defeat as if they were wounded warriors retreating from a lost battle shamefully. Colin felt this way never having a chance to face the scumbag who abducted Jade. That feeling of taking action in some way was gnawing at him further reinforcing his feeling of hopelessness and his want to contact the police.

Brent popped the trunk, set the ice chest inside, opened it and grabbed two beers. "For the road," he said, handing one to Colin.

They weren't in the habit of drinking and driving, but on this night they were dealing with very unusual circumstances for which only alcohol could help.

On the way back to the motel they stopped at a liquor store for a pint of rum. Brent went inside, all the while wondering if the bastard was out there, following, watching them. There weren't any cars in the parking lot, and that was probably because they were just about to close up for the night.

"Register's all ready counted, sorry," said the man behind the counter. He looked like a backwoods vigilante, salt and pepper beard and worn out ball cap that said 'don't tread on me' on it with a coiled rattlesnake.

"I just want a pint of Morgan's rum, that's all. How much is it?" Brent squinted looking at the array of liquor behind the vigilante. "Say's three ninety-nine, I'll give you a five for it."

"Oooo, wow, a whole fifty cents over the price plus tax for my trouble re-opening the fucking register to sell you a fucking bottle of booze. You should have come in earlier. The store closed about a minute ago."

"But I came in here about three minutes ago." Brent's voice had a twinge of mockery in it.

"I don't give a shit when you came in." The vigilante pointed to a sign behind the register. "You see that, see what is says?"

"Yeah, I get it, you can refuse the right to serve anyone you want to. Yeah, I understand that, I just have to get a pint of liquor, man. If you knew what happened to my friends and I tonight, you'd probably give us a fifth for free."

This piqued the clerk's interest. He nodded, "What happened to you and yer friends?" The clerk stretched for a look at the car outside. "I only see one person in your car."

"Yeah, well, there were three of us before."

"What happened to the third party?" The clerk's eyes were all seriousness as if this longhaired punk was about to tell him some grizzly story of murder and a quick escape.

"Can't say. If I talk, she'll be killed."

The vigilante squinted his eyes to read Brent's true intentions, trying hard to believe his story. "You wouldn't be trying to pull a fast one on me, now would you? I really wouldn't take very kindly to that."

"I wouldn't joke around about this, sir."

"She's in the trunk?"

"No, we don't have her, she was abducted." Brent looked around nervously, realizing he was giving this stranger far too much information.

The clerk nodded. "Can't go to the police, can you?"

Brent shook his head. "We're dealing with it tomorrow," he said. "Do you think maybe I could get that bottle, we just want to get back to our motel and take the edge off, you know. We've got a lot of shit to sort out before tomorrow."

The vigilante looking clerk turned facing the wall of liquor, running his fingers through his beard, the long ponytail tied with several hair ties looking more silver than gray. He grabbed a bottle, but it wasn't the rum.

"Here," he handed the bottle over. "Take this. You won't be able to take the edge off with some cheap pussy-shit rum."

"This is one hundred and one proof Wild Turkey. I don't have enough cash for this, man."

"It's on me." The clerk could see the way Brent trembled, the way he looked over his shoulder as if afraid he was being watched, the quivering of his voice. The clerk knew he was good for his word.

"Thanks, we can use it."

The clerk extended his hand for a shake. "The name's Brisko."

Brent shook his hand. "Brent, nice to meet you."

"If you need anything, Brent, you know where to find me. This is my place, I'm always working the last shift."

"Good to know." Brent looked outside again, paranoid that the abductor was somehow watching them, wondering what was taking him so long. "I'd better go. We've got a lot to figure out."

Brisko nodded. "Here," he reached for something in the clutter of lighters and energy pills that littered the counter. He produced a shot glass with a skull and crossbones on it. "Take this, for the whiskey."

Brent wanted to smile at the generous offer, but couldn't. He merely took the shot glass, thanked Brisko, and left the store, the neon lights flicking off as he entered the car.

"Took long enough," said Colin. His eyes were panicky and wild.

"He gave us a free bottle of Wild Turkey and a shot glass."

"What?"

"Let's just get out of here, okay. The faster we get to the motel, the better."

Colin put the car into gear and headed east, toward the motel.

Toward the next cemetery on their route.

CHAPTER 5

The Wild Turkey went down like Drano settling in their empty stomachs like red-hot coals. It took a few half shots before they were used to the stuff enough to attempt a full shot. It was climbing on top of them too, a high beer could only dream of.

"What do we do?" asked Colin. He seemed to be asking that question a lot, when the answer was written in blood on the back of the grave.

"There's really nothing we can do, man, not until tomorrow, but there's something we could have done, something you could have done."

Colin was seated at the little stationary table, doodling on a piece of paper. He looked up at Brent who was stretched out on one of the beds. "What're you talking about?"

The whiskey was really loosening Brent's lips. He didn't want to make a big deal about it, but why not? If it wasn't for Colin, Jade would be here.

"You should have gone with her," said Brent.

"You think I haven't though about that! It's been ripping at my mind, and you're gonna sit there and make me feel like shit?"

"Why shouldn't I? You should have been there. You talk about how much you want to kick this guy's ass, but you missed your chance. You could have protected her, but you decided to be a pussy."

"A pussy?"

"I don't know what's gonna happen tomorrow, but I'm a little worried about you. I don't think you always make the right decisions. All this bullshit could have been avoided if you would have walked out there with her like a man who knows how to treat a woman right."

Colin was speechless. Where had all this been hiding? Brent and he have been friends for almost a lifetime, all through their schooling, staying over at each other's house on the weekends, and not once had Brent ever laid into him like this.

Brent threw back another shot of whiskey, his eyes watering as he tried to be a man and ignore the Pepsi chaser. "Don't know what she sees in you anyhow," he said, his voice gruff from the liquor.

Colin grabbed the bottle from the nightstand beside Brent. "I think maybe you've had too much." Colin was a bit surprised at his ability to keep cool. This kind of friendship rivalry, especially over a girl, could easily turn mean and nasty.

Brent said nothing, just stared to the ceiling with a look on his face Colin could do without.

"I don't mean to put all the blame on you," said Brent, "but I just don't think you care about her enough, and that's why she was abducted. Any other guy would have been more than happy to walk out there with her to make sure she was all right."

Now Colin's temper was brimming. He had hoped Brent would nix the subject. "Maybe you should have gone out there with her!"

"Maybe I should have."

They mad-dogged one another, heartbeats pumping as adrenalin levels rose. The last thing either of them wanted was to fight, especially when they were both involved, to some extent, in Jade's kidnapping.

Colin sighed. "We shouldn't be fighting like this. My girlfriend--your friend--is out there somewhere, and I can only imagine how scared she is or what may be happening to her. We need to come together or we're never going to get her back."

Brent thought about Colin's words, the threat of saying something he would regret lingering in his mind like dense fog he was unable to see through. He had to swallow his pride, forgive his friend and forget his feelings for Jade. He could blame Colin to his grave and it wouldn't change a thing.

Brent sat up and reached his hand out much like Brisko had at the liquor store. "Deal."

Colin didn't just shake his hand; he gave Brent a hug.

It was late, around three in the morning, but they both knew sleep would elude them. Likely it would be the whiskey that would act as the sandman and finally drag their eyelids closed. In the mean time, Brent used the remote control and turned on the television. Colin grabbed Jade's backpack for her camera. He wasn't sure why he wanted to see the pictures she had taken at the cemetery, but when he unzipped the backpack, there was something else inside that took his breath away causing him, in reflex, to drop the bag on the floor as if it contained a poisonous snake.

CHAPTER 6

The room was hot and stuffy, but that could also have been from the sack wrapped around her head. It was a rustic sack that smelt gritty and dirty, perhaps an old potato sack.

Screaming and crying did nothing but get a piece of duct tape slapped over her mouth. Her nose was draining down her face like an infant, her eyes raw from so many tears--she wondered how many tears a pair of eyes could cry in such a short period of time.

The room was silent, but she couldn't tell if he had gone out. He could be watching her, quietly sitting across the room, watching to see if she would assume him gone and try to wriggle out of her bindings.

She had heard the door shut some time ago, what seemed like hours ago, but he could have done that to fool her. If he was in the room, he was one sadistic bastard to be able to keep such quiet for the sake of watching a tortured woman. She could see him in her mind, standing there motionless, breathlessly waiting for her to relax at the thought that he has gone.

It wasn't physical, her torture, at least not yet, but mental. She knew he was going to kill her, he has already told her this, but the man wasn't a sexual deviant, he also made sure and told her that, "just a homicidal maniac" as he put it.

She hoped it was fast, that he would use a gun and it would be nothing more than turning the lights off, but she knew that was just wishful thinking. Likely he would use a knife and relish in her pain. She would feel the stabs as the blade split her flesh, and she would pray for the end.

It was hard to think of anything else when you knew your days were numbered, hard to try an escape when he told her that he would be watching her, very silently, at all times. He told her that he would prolong her death were she to attempt escape, that mere torture would be a pleasantry compared to what he would do to her.

It was a head game, and it was working horrors on her mind.

He's gone, I know he is.

But what if he isn't?

She heard sounds from outside. She didn't know just exactly where she was, but from the sounds she assumed it was a motel or hotel. Cars would pull up, doors open and close, children laughing, trunks opening, the sound of large bags being hauled out of the trunk grudgingly and slapped onto the ground like so much weight, the small wheels of luggage rolling down the hallway to another room.

Time was the real mystery. She knew it must have been hours, but when you're left with your face concealed from light, the darkness acts as a sort of deprivation, thoughts mingling with one another into mild hallucinations. She had even wondered if the human sounds from outside were nothing more than her mind creating comforting images.

If he's sitting there watching me, he must be having a blast. Sick bastard.

A car pulled into the parking lot, parking very near the room she sat silently in--at least that's what she thought it was. So many cars have come and gone that she could have programmed that sound and been replaying it in her mind just to add a little reality to such a surreal situation.

The trunk popped, she was sure of that, and then it was closed. Steps echoed very briefly in the hallway and seemed to stop suddenly. There was a sound like the swiping of a credit card, and then the door to her Hell was opened.

The door shut.

"Doesn't look like you've moved much," said a very ordinary voice she was becoming used to. The voice could have been a pastor, a father, a teacher--anything but a madman.

"I brought you a little friend," he said, "but I've got different plans for her."

The woman sat silently, breathing heavier now from her congested nose.

"She's bait for the people who ruined our rendezvous."

Neither of the women could see her captor, nor each other, both of them trembling and fragile, counterparts in this shared nightmare.

As the woman listened, her captor tied Jade to the other bed the same way he had tied her: sitting up against the headboard wrapped in rope and duct tape, her arms tied to the headboard, very secure.

"I'll be watching the both of you, and if you move or try to free yourself from your bondage, I will be here to make you regret it. I have a fairly dull knife that rips through the flesh rather than cuts it. Just remember that."

And then there was a lengthy silence.

Eventually the door opened and closed, but it could be a bluff.

Both women sat there, identical captives, both wondering if their captor was still in the room; both too fearful to risk escape or even so much as speak to one another.

CHAPTER 7

"What is it?" said Brent in response to the look of shock on Colin's face.

"There's..." he couldn't say it, couldn't believe it.

"There's what?"

"There's a hand in her backpack."

"What!" Brent jumped up from the bed knocking over a half a shot-glass of Wild Turkey as he did so, clumsy in his drunkenness.

"A fucking hand!"

Brent knelt beside Colin on the floor, opened the bag and recoiled. He had never seen a real severed hand before, and though it could be a fake, there was something about it that was undeniably real.

"No way," whispered Brent. It was very pale, the veins purple beneath waxen flesh, the stub black and crusted with dried blood, a shard of broken bone protruding from the end. He had thought it would be neat to see a real severed appendage, but now faced with the hand, he actually felt sick to his stomach, a feeling very similar to that of seeing the rotted corpse at the graveyard.

"Where'd it come from?" asked Colin.

"Don't know." Brent grabbed the backpack.

"What are you doing?"

"I'm gonna empty the bag, get a better look at the hand."

Colin whispered, "What the hell's it doing in there?"

Brent emptied the contents of the bag over the floor. There wasn't much inside: a makeup case, spiral bound notebook, a small pencil pouch. The hand.

"Now we have to go to the police," said Colin, but Brent's strong feelings about involving the cops were even more evident.

"Nope. Can't do that. He'll kill her."

Colin lost it. "Kill her! That's probably her fucking hand in there! I told you, she's all ready dead!"

"Get a hold of yourself, man! That's not her hand!"

"How do you know?"

Their voices were hitting questionable decibels for three o' clock in the morning at a motel.

"Because," said Brent in a calm voice, "there's a wedding ring on it."

Colin examined the hand further without touching it, and, indeed, there was a wedding ring. "Then whose hand is that?"

"Don't know, but he must have put it there while we were looking at the message he left us. He's trying to scare us into calling the cops."

"How will he know we called the cops? He can't see into our room."

"Not that you know."

There was an eerie silence between them as they both scanned the walls, eyes drifting over the typical pictures of flowers and landscapes, mirrors, the intricate pattern on the wallpaper. They supposed eyes could watch from anywhere.

"What's that supposed to mean?"

Brent wanted to pick up the hand to examine it better now having gotten used to it, but was wary about actually touching it. Looking at it was one thing, but feeling the texture of it was another altogether.

Brent said, "This guy may have been following us. Maybe he tapped the room after we left earlier."

"Then how did he know where we went?"

"I don't know, I'm just speculating here."

Colin sighed. He couldn't believe what was happening, couldn't believe Jade had been kidnapped, and now this. The normal thing to do was call the police, it was sensible, but Brent was so adamantly against it.

He did say--write--that he would kill her if we contacted the authorities, thought Colin.

"What do we do?" asked Colin.

Brent was beginning to wonder if the big dumb jock could think for himself.

"We put the hand in the freezer so it doesn't rot. It must be evidence from some other crime, maybe someone else this freak killed, I don't know, but it'll decompose out here and that's really going to stink."

Colin opened his mouth to speak, but Brent spoke first.

"No cops, got it?"

"A fucking hand in the freezer? Are you kidding me?"

"When it's all done we'll call the cops and turn over the hand. We'll show them the tombstone with the message and they'll have to understand why we didn't call them in the first place."

Colin still didn't like the idea of not calling the cops.

"Look, Colin, Jade's life is in our hands. I know you think calling the police is the right thing, but I'm telling you, it's not. If this freak sees a cop show up at the next cemetery, he's going to kill her right there. If we show up, there's a chance she'll live."

"How do you know? He might kill her any way, and then come after us."

Brent was appalled at what he heard. He stood, leaving the hand on the floor in a litter of Jade's things, and walked to the stationary table where he grabbed the bottle of liquor and took a generous swig.

"You don't even care about her, do you?" said Brent.

"Not this shit again."

"No! You're more worried about your own ass, that's what it is. You know that if you call the police, you'll be safe, and maybe, if you're lucky, they'll get the guy and Jade will be safe and she'll come running to you and everything will be peachy-keen, but that's not what'll happen."

"That isn't it."

"Bullshit! Don't fuck with me, Colin. You're just a big dumb jock, man, just a pussy. All muscles and no mind. I hate to say it, and I never really saw this part of you, but it's true."

Colin went to say something, but was cut off by Brent.

"If you really cared for Jade, you'd risk life and limb for her." Brent stepped forward, getting into Colin's face. "If you really cared for her, Colin, you would be thinking about how you're going to get her back rather than jeopardize her life for the safety of your own. You're a pussy! And if you don't get that idea of calling the cops out of your head, you're gonna be the death of her."

Colin listened to his best friend's rant, his blood boiling as his heartbeat accelerated, fists clenched in balls. He wasn't one for words, so he used his fist to speak instead.

Brent was furious, yet not expecting Colin to lay him out the way he did. He gave him a good punch to the nose; Brent fell like a slab of beef, his face landing in the open severed hand like some twisted comedy act.

Colin cursed his friend, took a pull from the bottle, and left the room.

He wasn't sure what he was going to do, where he would go or whether to call the police or not. In his state of drunkenness sitting in the car wasn't against the law, however driving was out of the question.

After about a half an hour, at four in the morning, a man approached the car.

CHAPTER 8

Shortly after Colin's disappearance from the room, Brent passed out with the television on, salad shooters, chef's knives and golden oldies serenading his dreams as infomercials carried on until the beginning of the morning news, and it was what was on the news that woke Brent to the realization and pain of his throbbing head.

"Well, the police aren't doing their job," said the voice on the TV. "So I have been out every night tracking him down. I think I'm getting close, but really, it's very hard work."

Brent patted his aching head looking at the image on the television through slits for eyelids. The light from the window was like acid seeping into his brain via his eyes, but when he realized why the voice was so familiar he opened them wide letting the brain-burning acid in.

It was the man from the other night, the old man whose wife had been abducted back in Colorado, and that's what he was talking about. The reporter asked him if it was right to become a vigilante in cases such as this one.

"Right? Is it right that this man goes around abducting people and killing them? The police do nothing. They ignore that it's happening, won't do a damn thing until there's a body. Well, now there is, and I hope they get off their asses and do something to get this guy, and until they do, I hope others like me take initiative and track this bastard down, give him what he deserves."

"O-kay," said the reporter as if Harry Grady were a self-proclaimed masochist. His type of grit and passion for the murderer's demise was shocking for a liberal news reporter. "Back to you in the studio."

"That was Diana Schlomec reporting live from Mr. Grady's home after the news of his wife's body being found in a shallow grave at the Sunnyside Cemetery on old highway 25," said a male anchor's voice. "The body was found yesterday by mourners at the cemetery. Though details are vague, there aren't many leads as to who did this, though Harry Grady, the deceased's husband, has not yet been ruled out as a suspect."

ROBERT ESSIG

"There is one thing about this murder that is causing the police to wonder about a possible serial killer," said the female co-anchor. "The body was found intact, cause of death: multiple stab wounds, but with the left hand missing. A detailed search for the hand has turned up nothing."

Brent's eyes traveled across the motel room fixated on the little mini fridge, specifically the freezer. They said it was a left hand, that of Harry Grady's wife, and if he remembered correctly there was a wedding ring on the hand in the freezer.

But he didn't want to look.

Not after knowing where the hand came from, or at least suspecting where.

And even if it did have a ring on it, that didn't mean it was hers.

But that was very likely.

Almost undeniably so.

Brent wondered where Colin went last night and if he would be back. Now they really couldn't go to the police. There was no way of explaining how they acquired the hand, and if it turned out not to be the hand of Grady's wife, there would be even more explaining to do.

Then the thought struck Brent that Colin might have taken the car, maybe sobered up and drove down to the police station to report Jade's disappearance.

"Shit!"

Brent leapt off the bed and over to the window that faced the parking lot, and to his relief the car was still there.

Maybe he slept in the car.

Brent opened the door, approached the car and looked in. Colin was not asleep in the car; however, Brent could see the keys in the ignition, which meant Colin had entered the car last night, but left and forgot his keys.

Maybe that's why he couldn't get back into the room. Couldn't find his keys.

But that wasn't why at all.

CHAPTER 9

Colin was frightened not only because of the bandanna or cloth, or whatever was wrapped around his head blotting out his vision, but because of the smell as well. He knew the smell of blood, but only from personal experience, cuts and scrapes, minor things. He knew the coppery scent of blood, rich like liquid minerals, but never has he been in a room so full of the heavy odor that he could taste it.

CEMETERY TOUR

He was sitting in a chair, in a cold room, dark only because of his covered eyes, body wrapped tightly in Teflon like a kitchen mummy, all but his right arm, though he dare not try anything hasty with the freedom of that one arm.

He wasn't one to fall victim of claustrophobia. Though commonly mistaken, nyctophobia and claustrophobia are two very different afflictions. The darkness was tolerable. It was the rich odor of the room, and the fact that he had been knocked unconscious at some point in the night only to wake up in this state of restriction like a fish wrapped up to be placed in a freezer that was so bad.

"Reach out," said a voice that came from nowhere. Colin was beginning to think he was alone, but the voice came without prior noise indicating the silent presence of a man who has been there all along.

"Reach your hand out. Touch."

Colin didn't want to touch. He was afraid of what he may feel, and if it was as bad as what he could smell he may not be able to take it, yet there was something in the voice that swayed his arm out in front of him, ever so gently in the uncertainty of his surroundings.

"Yes, feel around you."

The voice was now behind him, startling him with the low, cool words. He placed his hand on the chair, the wooden arm, then reached out tentatively, still fearing the source of the blood perfuming the room. As his hand hit a surface, he recoiled slightly, returning his fingers to the surface, certain it was dry. Any wetness he felt would have to be presumed as blood. The surface was dry; felt like wood. On it, he felt an object that was a phone. Next to that something small and rectangular that felt like a remote control. He wanted to pick up the remote and press the buttons to turn on whatever it goes to, but knew that could jeopardize his situation.

"Here," said the man, now close enough for Colin to feel warm breath against his ear. The man grabbed his free arm from the back directing it straight ahead of Colin.

"Now, grab," said the man, his breath like curdled milk overpowering the coppery blood smell when he spoke, like small puffs of pungency.

Again, Colin's hand retracted a bit at the feel of something. It wasn't wet, so he tapped at it with his fingers trying to get a feel for the object. It was completely different from the wooden table he had been feeling before. The object had some play to it, some movement, and it was relatively small in comparison. He grabbed the object feeling the contours in wonder.

94

It's a handle.

But a handle to what?

The man let go of Colin's hand. "Good," said the man, "very good."

The man then grabbed the bandanna that was wrapped around Colin's head and removed it. Colin's eyes squinted at the brilliance of the light in the room until he focused them on his hand gripped tightly around the handle of a knife that was lodged into the chest of a gutted woman on the bed he was seated before.

He pulled his hand from the knife so hard his whole wrapped up body tipped backward in the chair toppling him onto the ground, his head taking a nasty crack on the thin carpet that felt very much like the foundation beneath.

His vision now skewed, Colin could see the man who had guided his hand to the knife. He looked very tall, though that could have been a result of Colin being flat on his back looking up. He was thin, in his thirties, clean-shaven and severely balding. White shirt and blue jeans, very average, but a murderer nonetheless.

"I have Jade in the trunk waiting for the big show tonight. She'll survive in there as long as it doesn't get too hot outside. I can't let her out, of course, not in the middle of the day. Can't risk being seen."

Colin tried to protest, but as his screams were at the sight of the corpse, all he could do was muffle nonsense into the gag around his mouth.

"I saw you out there, sitting in the car. I think you were contemplating calling the cops. Maybe not, but I couldn't take that chance." The man looked at the body on the glistening blood soaked bed. "Couldn't take a chance with her, either. They're your prints on the knife. The room's under her name."

Colin couldn't believe what he was hearing.

"But that's not all. You'll be there tonight, but you're going to be playing a different role than that of your valiant friend. I'll have to be leaving you, but I'll return before we leave for the cemetery."

It was then that Colin realized he was tied to the chair, but apparently that wasn't enough because the man pushed Colin against the bed and used a pair of handcuffs to cuff Colin's free hand to the bedpost.

The man left the room with Colin agonizing over the cooling sticky blood that was beginning to mat in his hair as he was forcibly pressed up against the bed with the slaughtered woman on it.

Colin thought of Jade in the trunk and couldn't help but wonder how it came to this.

PART THREE

CHAPTER 10

Brent sat in the motel wondering where his so-called friend was. He didn't like the idea of being left alone in the room with the hand. Not because of an irrational fear of the hand, but because of the terrible possibilities had Colin to told the police about what happened.

He wasn't sure what to do with the hand anyway. He wouldn't have to worry about the maid discovering it since he planned to be there all day, but it was unsettling knowing it was in the freezer, especially when he knew who it belonged to yet was unable to tell the cops about it.

There was also the realization of whom he was dealing with, of just what kind of monster had abducted Jade. He was a murderer, a psycho who killed a woman several days ago and held onto her severed hand as if he knew he would need it later to plant in their backpack.

Just how much of this was planned, and for how long?

It wasn't as if they lived in Colorado and this serial murderer, as Harold Grady put it--though there has only been one body discovered--has been stalking them and waiting for the right moment to pounce. There was no way he had been stalking out-of-towners, especially if he had abducted Grady's wife a month ago, so they must have been a random target.

What luck.

The day was long; the news of Beth's body small apples compared to the slaughter in the Middle East, and Brent's mind was yearning to know what happened to Colin. Why hasn't he come back yet? Where the hell is he? Big dumb jock.

Brent had decided, somewhere around four in the afternoon after becoming as comfortable as he could with the notion that Colin wasn't coming back, that he would continue on to the graveyard at midnight with or without him. He had to. Being that they were the only two who knew about Jade's disappearance, he was obligated to do whatever he could to save her, which didn't include calling the police.

Brent was afraid that Colin would disregard that caveat on the tombstone, but there hasn't been the pounding of police fists on his door, and nothing on the news that would indicate that the police have been tipped off about Jade's abduction.

If so, she's already dead.

Why it was Colin couldn't see this, and why he was so stubborn and unwilling to rescue his girlfriend, Brent could not understand. He thought it was because Colin was selfish, because it would be far too much work and plain out easier to just call the police and hope her captor didn't harm her, but Brent wouldn't rely on hope, not when he could hold destiny in his hands, not when he could possibly be the one to take the bastard down, the murderer, and save the woman he so longs for, even if she didn't reciprocate those feelings.

Perhaps saving her would change the way she sees Brent. That was something he had been thinking about now that he and Colin were no longer a duo. The challenge ahead would be difficult and terrifying, a real test of what Brent was made of, but it would be worth it to rescue Jade from the hands of a psycho. He knew, as well, that if he didn't do it he would have her disappearance on his soul like an ugly scar, something he would have to take to the grave in shame, something that would keep him awake at night.

Colin may be able to deal with that, but Brent couldn't.

Brent left the motel for about and hour or so, got a bite to eat, drove by Brisko's liquor store thinking about the strange meeting with the redneck vigilante. What was it his hat had said? Don't tread on me with a rattlesnake coiled and ready to strike. Brent could see Brisko as a rattlesnake, a man one should fear to reckon with. Brent feared him there for a moment last night, until the guy softened up to him.

Sure would be better to have Brisko on my side instead of Colin. Brisko would probably try to save Jade even though he doesn't even know her.

Brent couldn't believe he was thinking about his best friend in such a dim light, but what else was he supposed to do? Colin really chickened out this time, worse than ever before. Brent knew Colin was a bit of a puss who tried to belittle people in order to appear tough, knew he had a sort of affliction to the dark, but never thought he would write Jade off so heartlessly.

As Brent drove around he wondered if the captor was watching him as he said he would in the bloody words of the tombstone. If so, he was good at it because Brent sure couldn't detect a tale.

It could be more than one person.

Could be. Not likely though. That was movie plot stuff. Unless a married couple was on a killing spree--also a very abused movie plot--two friends would have a hell of a time getting along together as a serial murderer duo. Yeah, Henry Lee Lucas pulled it off with his bucktoothed pal Otis, but how long did that last? Generally, serial killers are lone wolves, acting out from some internal struggle they would not wish to share with a comrade. If anything, a serial killer couple would probably end up killing each other.

Brent returned to the motel half expecting Colin to be there, but he wasn't. As the day washed away in a cloak of darkness, Brent felt apprehensive, antsy. Time moved with the urgency of a snail slithering onto sun-streaked concrete, every minute its own millennia, each quarter of an hour an eternity, each hour bringing him closer to the witching hour.

He knew where the cemetery was, having driven by it when he went out for a bite to eat. It would take him a half an hour to get there, a drive that would be as tense as the slow clicking climb of a roller coaster approaching a steep drop.

The bottle of Wild Turkey was looking at him, asking him to indulge himself, and he couldn't refuse the offer. He took a pull straight from the bottle before capping it and placing it in the backpack that formerly concealed the severed hand.

The hand was now wrapped in a bag just in case a maid ignored the 'do not disturb' sign he left on the door before leaving for the cemetery. He knew the hand belonged to Harry Grady's wife, knew the man he was going to face off with had killed her.

He thought of turning the car around and driving back to San Diego as if nothing had happened, do the cowardly thing, but he couldn't, nor did he want to. Colin may have taken the easy road in all his muscular jock façade, but Brent had to do what was right, no matter how dangerous it may be.

In his car he looked at the motel room, at the 'do not disturb' sign, wondering if he was going to make it back here tonight or if he would be surrounded by police in an investigation over the murder of a murderer, explaining the hand. How could he ever explain the hand?

He didn't want to think about the police. They would wonder why Colin and he didn't contact them sooner, and for all he knows Colin has done just that. Maybe he'll see a brigade of police cars at the cemetery when he gets there, their cover blown, Jade likely dismembered and strewn across the graveyard, her hand saved to be placed in someone else's unsuspecting backpack.

Seeing no one else in the parking lot, Brent pulled the bottle out of the backpack and took another drink. He was going to need the numbing courage alcohol provided if he was going to go through with this, that was for sure.

Brent put the car in reverse, pulled out of his parking stall, onto the road, and headed for the cemetery.

CHAPTER 11

On previous nights Brent had felt excited as his two friends and he drove into the dark parking lots of the cemeteries. It was a treat to be able to frolic in old graveyards being that he had always been a bit of a horror film buff. Old graveyards were as synonymous to horror films as old dark houses with evil pasts.

As Brent drove into the parking lot of the Sacred Memorial Cemetery, he felt his stomach sink, the excitement and joy he had felt the past several nights replaced with dread and fear.

There were no police cars, which added to the mystery of Colin's disappearance. Brent had half expected the police to be there, but he guessed Colin was just a big baby who ran away from his problems rather than dealing with them, which was certainly the end of Jade and he. Brent could see no way Jade would be able to forgive Colin for his cowardice.

Brent couldn't. As far as he was concerned, Colin was dead to him. Their friendship, in his mind, was terminated when he walked out the motel door last night and never returned.

Brent opened the car door and stepped into the cool night air. He was trembling. His shaky hand grabbed the backpack slinging it over his shoulder after taking a drink form the bottle of Wild Turkey. The way he figured it, he could drink the rest of the bottle and still have nerves like a small-breed dog shaved and left in the cold.

There didn't seem to be any action in the cemetery, but that was probably how the madman wanted it. The appearance of another night of rest for the dead was deceiving and though Brent had expected this, he couldn't help but wonder if he was walking into an ambush.

Regardless of his fears (thanks to the Wild Turkey) he began his walk through the graveyard, flashlight pointing the way, another roam over the sleeping dead, the beam of light gliding over random tombstones illuminating dates and final messages for only a second before reaching the next one.

How different this walk was from the former graveyard trips. There was no fascination with the dates people lived and died, no interest in the crumbling of old tombs withered by so many years of weather. Now Brent was more aware of what was hiding behind the tombstones, what may be lurking behind a tree or perhaps inside a mausoleum.

There was someone to fear here, someone unknown to him, and he hoped it was only one person, and he again hoped he wasn't blindly walking into an ambush, which he couldn't help but feel he was.

Nothing is as simple as it seems, and walking into the cemetery and saving Jade from a possible serial killer wouldn't be a walk in the park.

Brent was about halfway through the cemetery when he heard footfalls in the distance.

* * * * *

Colin had no way of telling what time it was since he had been secluded to the motel room of horrors only to be gagged and blindfolded before being stuffed tightly into a trunk and driven somewhere.

Was it nighttime yet?

What did that matter when the pain was so terrible?

Colin found that it did matter, no matter how much his eyes hurt. What had the man done to him? He wasn't sure, but he could swear there was something dangling from his eye, something that bobbed against his face. He supposed it could be his eyeball, but he couldn't see anything to be able to tell.

There were familiar smells in the air, nighttime smells that made Colin uneasy. There was that certain scent the saturated ground gave off after dark like a nearby pond, a scent Colin knew to be of the nighttime.

After the maniac used the knife on Colin's eyes, he seemed to have fled, but Colin couldn't be sure. He may be standing there watching him, loving every minute of his torture, wearing a silent smile, doing everything he could to stifle gleeful laughter, the sadist he was.

And then again he may have gone, leaving Colin to wander in the darkness that was only made worse after his crude surgery.

His eyes hurt, yes, they were aflame and likely gouged out, but the smells and sounds of night was cutting deeper into Colin's ruined sanity.

What could be worse than being all alone in the dark? He asked himself that question from time to time and was unable to come up with a sufficient answer, until now. Only one thing was worse.

Being alone in the dark without eyes.

Colin was handling the situation rather well, but that may be due to his fear that the maniac was still standing there, and the worst part about it was not his fear that the madman would harm him, but showing his fear, allowing the man to see his weakness.

Colin's head ached. Deciding the maniac had since left, he held his hands out before him, the same way he had in the motel room, and took steps trying to feel for something familiar that would identify his location.

His feet stomped the soil like Frankenstein's monster as he walked around confusedly searching for something, anything, and when he grabbed hold of a tree, his mind snapped.

Colin knew he was in the dark, outside in the dark, though he couldn't see now that his eyes were useless. He took a few steps backward further disoriented and then a sound rang out, a pain equal to that of his eye pinching his gut, dropping him to the ground.

* * * * *

Brent's hand trembled violently, his nerves reacting to the fact that he had shot someone with the gun he bought from Brisko on his way to the cemetery. Like the Wild Turkey, he gave Brent the gun, not only because of the circumstances Brent explained to him, but because the gun was a Saturday Night Special six shooter, a hybrid of parts from many guns. Brisko told him it may only fire once, maybe not even that, but he gave Brent enough bullets to fill the chambers just in case he needed them.

Now Brent stood there as the form in the distance went to the ground. He had shot someone, maybe killed him, and even though it may be the madman who abducted Jade, he felt remorseful in his actions.

The cemetery was again silent after the loud interruption he caused when his finger pulled the hair trigger. Brent walked toward the body. He held the gun out like the cops do on television shows. He could never remember seeing the police on the show Cops ever draw their guns like this, but it sure looked good on the fictional shows.

As Brent neared the body, he recognized the clothes. His stomach dropped as he realized his mistake, and no matter how much he had written Colin off only hours ago in his fury, he could never forgive himself for what he had done.

101

Making a dash, he knelt down beside his friend, mind whirling, each thought like a piece of debris in a tornado. The blood was running out of Colin's stomach soaking into the soil beneath him. In the dark it was hard to tell how much blood he had lost, but Brent knew it was a lot. He was gushing like a cow in the slaughterhouse with its neck cut open, and Brent didn't know what to do.

"Jesus!" Brent noticed Colin's destroyed eyes, one of them dangling from the socket. Brent couldn't help but wonder how Colin could have lived through something so painful.

"Kill me," came Colin's weak voice. "Kill me."

He couldn't see Brent, had no idea who it was standing before him, but that was no matter. Whoever it was, Colin had one request: "Kill me!"

Brent looked at the gun, the barrel: shiny blue steel, the body: rusted as if it had been left in the rain. He looked at the gun realizing that he was indeed considering putting Colin out of his misery.

Isn't that what people do to horses that are injured badly during a race? What people do to a dog hurt after a run in with a mountain lion?

What people don't do to other people in this age of medical miracles.

"I couldn't have planned it better myself," said a voice from behind Brent causing him to yelp and jump back, his heart in his throat trying to jump out of his body and lay him dead of sheer fright right there on the sod next to his best friend.

The man he had been pondering all day--the one who has torn three friends apart and caused so much strife and horror for so many people including Harry Grady and the countless others who have family members he has killed--was standing there only steps away from him, but he looked more like something that would have been better left buried.

"A gun, that I didn't expect," said the figure, the skeletal face unmoving as words projected from the mouth beyond the death mask. The voice itself was rather soothing like a shrink or perhaps a magician cooing someone into a hypnotic state. This man could have had a future in radio.

His hands were concealed beneath a black trench coat, which made it impossible for Brent to tell if he was armed, though he had to assume as much.

"I suggest you drop that gun," said the man.

Brent pointed the gun at the man. Below him sounds of agony came from his fallen friend. Could he shoot a man, even and evil beast with a skull-face, being

102

in such close proximity? Was there something about shooting a would-be murderer in the distance that made it easier to do?

"If you kill me, how are you ever going to find your precious gemstone, Jade?"

Brent thought about that for a moment, his finger all but pulling the trigger. This thing before him, this human lower than the scum in the deepest dregs of the sewer, had the advantage, the upper hand. Oh, how Brent wanted to pull that trigger, sent this piece of shit to Hell to be Satan's slave, but he couldn't risk it. Without the man standing before him, so sure of himself, Brent may never find Jade.

He lowered the gun.

"That's what I thought," said the voice behind the skeletal mask.

The mask looked authentic, and probably was the front of a human skull with the cranium cut away, strapped around his head like a hockey mask. If it was a real skull, it must have taken him some time to transform it into a usable mask.

"You will need to follow me," said the madman. "He's on his way to greet the reaper," he said regarding Colin. "I'd leave him be... Wait, I've got a better idea."

The eyes behind the mask looked at Brent, and though he couldn't see the smile, he knew it was there, concealed by the skeleton face yet revealed by the gleeful hint in the vocalization.

"You have a six shooter, and all I heard was one shot."

Brent nodded his head, finding himself far too warped to actually respond.

"Shoot him, just for shits and giggles."

"I..."

"Oh yeah, you can do it, you have to. You want Jade back, don't you? You were considering killing him weren't you, when I walked up?"

Brent looked at his friend, the thought of killing him abominable.

"He was asking you to kill him, wasn't he?"

The thought tickled the back of his mind to turn around and pull the trigger repeatedly until all the bullets--the ones that would actually fire--were lodged in the body of the maniac asking such atrocities of him. But, again, he couldn't do that, couldn't jeopardize Jade's life that way.

But could he fire the remaining bullets into Colin's body? He had asked for death, hadn't he?

"Do it. If you don't, you'll never know where Jade is."

Hesitation, repulsion, gnawing at Brent's conscience as he had only moments to make a decision no one should ever have to face, a decision a lifetime couldn't begin to prepare someone for.

"She'll die, you know, if you don't hurry. Time isn't on your side."

Brent pointed the gun at Colin. He couldn't decide whether to shoot him in the head or the heart, but if he was going to go through with it, he was going to kill Colin with the first shot, that way he wouldn't feel the other four.

"Can't I just empty the rounds into the ground?" asked Brent, heartbeat pounding rhythmic beats in his chest.

"Now that wouldn't be fun, would it? No, I'm afraid I cannot allow that. You must shoot him. All five rounds. Wherever you want. Now."

After more hesitation, the masked man said, "I'm going to walk away, and if I don't hear four gunshots before I reach my car, I will leave, and you will never find Jade, and I can guarantee that you will be blamed for the murders, all of them. Even the ones you have no idea about."

"The hand," said Brent just above a whisper.

"Oh, there's more than just the hand. A whole lot more. Your friend there, he had himself a bloody good time back at the motel. His prints are every where, and, of course, since you have been with him, been seen with him, you will be associated with the crime once the body is discovered.

"I'm walking away. You'd better shoot fast if you want to see Jade again, otherwise her blood will be on your hands."

Before the masked man had taken three steps, two shots rang out after which the trigger clicked as the final rounds were jammed or duds.

"That's it," said Brent. "The last rounds won't fire, they're jammed."

The man looked upon Colin's body, satisfied with the hole in his head that assured his death. "Drop the gun and follow me."

Brent did just that.

They were headed for a mausoleum.

CHAPTER 12

The mausoleum looked just like Brent had seen in the movies. It stood tall, made of cinder block and mortar as well as stone, mold creeping from the top of the structure downward as if searching for the ground. Vines grew wild creeping upward meeting the mold halfway as if the two would one day rile the mausoleum and bring down its crumbling walls.

The door was ajar, just enough to slide in. Brent followed the skeletal-faced madman expecting to find Jade tied up all raped and abused, but there were large stone tombs within which were caskets holding dead bodies. No sign of Jade.

The interior of the crypt was illuminated with candles and a lantern leaving the corners dark and forgiving as hiding places for anything.

"It's really quite simple," said the masked man. "She's back here, but don't get any ideas. If you try anything, I'll drop you like a stone." The man revealed a rather large knife he had been hiding beneath the folds of his trench coat. "You walk ahead of me, that way I can keep track of your movements." He pointed down the mausoleum toward the rear where it was considerably darker. "That way."

Brent walked on, fearful of the man behind him, of the knife. He could feel the knife at his throat, but he was quite sure the maniac was several paces behind him, it was just the kind of feeling one gets when they know there's a malicious murderer wielding a deadly weapon behind them.

As he neared the darker side of the crypt, a stone tomb sat open, a glow of candlelight shining from within. At closer inspection, Brent saw Jade lying therein, her eyes wide with terror, mouth closed with a large rectangle of duct tape blocking frantic murmurs from her sealed lips.

"What the fuck did you do to her?"

Jade was awash in blood, stab wounds all over her body, the knife sticking out of her leg, buried deep, almost to the handle.

Rage grew inside Brent, visible with the change of his breathing pattern, his face becoming red with anger as he felt there was nothing he could do but attack the man behind him and hope the blade didn't inflict too much damage as he was stabbed.

"It's quite simple you know," said the man's smooth voice like butter, near enough for Brent to feel his breath on the back of his ear. The knife was now resting against his throat, the blade pressing against his flesh so hard all it would take is a fraction of a movement to cut him.

"All you have to do is grab the knife."

"Grab the knife?"

"The handle's been wiped. You did this after all. You need to grab it so everyone knows you did this."

"Everyone?"

"The police, the investigators--everyone."

"What, then you'll let us go?"

"Not quite, but you'll both live. You can be assured I have taken all the precautions. Even that bastard Harry Grady seen all of you together back at that cemetery, the one you came to the night I was burying Grady's wife.

"You ruined my perfect scheme, my true love in life. So now I have to give up my former life of depravities and disappear. No one has seen my face, and my voice will never be heard around these parts for you to recognize, but I need you alive. I need you as a scapegoat. I need you to grab the knife and pull it out of her leg, now."

For a moment, Brent contemplated what was being requested of him, trying to consider the maniac's plan, but it seemed too simple and he couldn't imagine that he would be let free as long as he grabbed the knife. There had to be a catch.

Brent grabbed the knife. Tears rolled down Jade's face. He realized that the slight friction from him grabbing the knife was hurting her, so he tried to pull it out delicately, but it wouldn't budge and he was quite restrained by the knife the masked man held that was being acquainted with his neck.

Her voice was nothing but muffled whimpers, but her quivering told him that he was hurting her.

"The blood has begun to dry," said the calm voice behind him. "You'll have to yank it."

Brent grimaced at the thought of yanking the knife out, at the thought of all the pain she would feel as it opened a wound that had sealed itself around the steel blade.

But what could he do?

He yanked on the knife freeing it from her leg, her screams, though muted, like an ice pick in Brent's heart. The wound bled freshly over the dried crust of blood that had formed there.

"Now," said the masked man as he withdrew the knife he held to Brent's neck. "I want you to place the knife you are holding against your neck."

"What? Why?"

"Don't ask stupid questions. Just do as I say. Did I not tell you that you would see Jade alive?"

Brent held the bloody knife as if it were a fresh dog turd. Bringing it to his neck was a strange request, but what was the difference? He had a knife to his neck just a moment ago.

Brent played the game, fearful of where it was leading. He placed the knife, sticky with Jade's blood, against his throat.

The nameless horror walked around Brent, his skull mask quite eerie from the illumination of the candles within the tomb. He placed the knife that had previously been to Brent's neck against Jade's. Her eyes were once again wide and wet, brimming with tears.

The eyes that peered out of the dark, empty skeletal sockets were grave. Brent wondered what the face looked like, wondered if the eyes would have the same damning effect if not hidden behind such a frightening mask.

"Now, I want you to cut your own throat," said the voice behind the skull.

"What? I can't do that!"

"You must. It's the only way. Or she dies. Then you die. Either way, you did it. The blood's on your hands."

They locked eyes creating intensity as both of them waited for the other to act. Brent couldn't slit his own throat, nor could he let Jade die, and it appeared that there was going to be a throat slit no matter how he looked at it.

"What is it?" asked the maniac. "I haven't got all night. It's getting late, you know, and I've got a lot of ground to cover before dawn. I'm giving you an opportunity for her to live, but I could just as easily kill the both of you and wash my hands of all this mayhem you caused when you decided to traipse around the graveyard the other night. You're lucky I'm even letting her live, but what do I have to lose? No one will ever believe her ravings, and she never saw my face. They'll think she's gone mad, and probably she has. Now, you had better pull that knife across your neck, or I'll pull mine across hers. Either way, you die."

Brent's grip on the knife was slippery with sweat, his knuckles whitening as he clenched his fist around the handle, his mind telling him to leap for the freak and hope he gets him before the bastard can slash Jade's throat, but could he? This kind of lunatic would be trigger-happy and likely pull his knife across her neck at the slightest threatening movement.

Eyes behind the mask glistened from the reflection of the candle flame, orbs burning like the Hell that awaits this madman.

Brent gripped the knife as tight as he could, the blade quivering in his nervous grip, the razor edge cutting the preliminary layers of his flesh bringing forth only traces of blood that could not be felt in his state of shock.

107

He began pulling the knife across his neck, the cut strangely numbed, perhaps not even deep enough to kill, when a shout came from the entrance to the Mausoleum.

"Get down!" yelled the voice, ceasing Brent's suicide cut. "Get down damnit!"

It was a split second after the warning was issued before the bullets were flying. Brent dropped like a man whose legs have turned to boneless fatty tissue, the sounds of gunfire jolting him as fragments of stone flew this way and that, the walls and tomb being hit by stray bullets.

It was a moment that seemed like forever before the gunfire stopped, leaving an echo that lingered in Brent's ears like the ringing after a loud concert. There was pain in his gut that he thought was a bullet wound--he later found out he had inadvertently impaled himself on the knife he was holding when he hit the floor.

Footsteps rushed toward him, but he was far too shocked to move.

"Are you alright?" asked a voice that was vaguely familiar. "I didn't getcha, did I?"

Brent looked up at the figure standing above him. His face looked like a vision of demons, or a member of the Hell's Angels, and for a moment Brent feared the gun wielding man until he recognized him as Brisko from the liquor store.

"The gun didn't work so well, did it?" said Brisko. "What the fuck was going on in here?"

Brent was speechless. Brisko moved away from him, checking the livelihood of the psycho he gunned down, the one wearing a human skull to conceal his identity.

"He's dead," said Brisko in a voice that wasn't new to the admission of actually killing a person.

Brent rolled over, his hand gliding over the knife embedded into his gut.

"Don't move," said Brisko, a cell phone up to his ear, "I'm calling the police."

CHAPTER 13

"No!" Brent's voice was frantic, as if calling the police was a tragedy to end all tragedies.

Brisko halted his dialing of 911 knowing damn well that the police weren't always a welcome sight, though he assumed, in this situation, that Brent would be more than happy to see them.

"He set me up," said Brent. "The police'll think I did it. My prints are on the knife and the gun he made me shoot Colin with."

"He made you shoot someone?" Brisko looked comical standing there with a semi-automatic machine gun strapped over his shoulder, clutched in his hand like a commando ready for action.

Brent nodded, grabbing the knife that stuck out of his gut.

"I wouldn't do that, you could injure yourself worse pulling that thing out. That's why I thought you'd like the police here, so you could get medical attention, and I think you need it." He pointed to Jade still resting in the coffin. "Her, too."

"It was Him," said Brent, his voice dry and worn out from the battle.

"Who?"

"Him, the one who killed the Grady woman."

"In Colorado?"

Brent nodded.

"But you think he's set you up enough to have you convicted for his murders?"

Brent nodded.

"Not likely, but I can't stick around and wait for the police. This," he raised the sub-machine gun, "isn't legal in the states. I'm not even sure why I came out here, but what you told me, well, it sort of stuck with me, and If I saw a bloodbath on the news that happened at the old cemetery and I saw your face as one of the deceased, I wouldn't have been able to sleep at night knowing I could have done something to help."

Brisko regarded the young man lying on the floor below him, then the young woman in the coffin, her body resting uncomfortably on the dusty, dried out corpse who previously called that coffin home.

"You're losing an awful lot of blood, man." Brisko took a few steps back. "I can't be involved in this, you know. I've got a wife at home, a couple of rug rats. Hell, I'm on parole. Me and a gun like this--shit, I'm not even supposed to carry a licensed pistol, but I'll tell you one thing, Brent: I'm not going to let you die here. I have to call the police and split. All I ask of you is not to tell them it was me who came in here and shot the place up. Tell them what you want, but don't bring me into this. You got that?"

"But he framed me."

"Look," Brisko's voice grew tired, "the law isn't going to arrest you. Your girl there, she's seen everything and will explain what happened, everything but my part in this. You don't have anything to worry about, just do yourself a favor and wait here for the police. I'll tell them to send two ambulances so you can get medical help right away."

"I'm making the call right now as I walk back to my truck."

Brisko's footfalls echoed as he walked out of the crypt, but they stopped abruptly, then sounded as if they were coming back.

"And, Brent?"

Brent looked up.

Brisko smiled. "Next time you're driving through this part of Kansas, look me up. You owe me one."

Brisko walked away, the sound of his echoing feet resonating within Brent's mind as the silence enfolded him, silence save that for the whimpers of Jade in the casket.

"It'll be alright, Jade," he said, afraid to move, afraid the knife may do further damage. "We're gonna be all right."

About Robert Essig:

*Robert Essig's work has appeared in over 20 publications including **Uncanny Allegories** (Post Mortem Press), **Bards and Sages Quarterly**, **Withersin**, **The Scroll of Anubis** (Library of Horror) and **Everyday Weirdness**. Robert is the author of the chapbook **Pantomime** (Panic Press) and the editor of **Through the Eyes of the Undead** and **Malicious Deviance** (Library of the Living Dead).*

DANIEL PEARLMAN

Mistress of a High Purpose

by Daniel Pearlman

Rosie stooped for another armful of dirty sheets pretending not to notice the gaze of the male guard--on her butt now, alternately on her butt or on her chest. Her shape was hard to hide beneath that shapeless green smock, identical to those in the corner pile that would soon be fed to the septicizers. He had given up trying to induce her with heroin. Three months of detox made any shit that Jimmy the guard could offer look as poisonous to Rosie as his little green eyes. As long as she worked with the other three women she didn't care if he dropped to all fours and followed her with his tongue hanging out: she was as safe here, almost, as inside her own cell. Not that her co-workers--two long-termers like herself, and one lifer--cared one damn for her. Respected her, maybe, for wasting her druggie boyfriend; but eyeballed her like Jimmy, furtively and resentfully, lusting to cut down her piled-up honey-blonde hair and stomp her breasts till they turned into pancakes like theirs. As if it was her fault she was all of nineteen and couldn't help what she looked like or how she sounded when suddenly she would find herself singing--lullabies, mostly, to that last, half-remembered fetus that had almost had a name.

Humming to herself, she brought her armful down the aisle to the steel-gray combo that had just emptied its wash load into its bug killer dryer. "I'm ready for another load, I'm ready for another load!" it chirped like a nestling clamoring to be fed. A detergent cartridge was snapped in place at the beginning of each day so that no chemical weapons would be at hand should a catfight break out. Not that she feared anything physical from these three women she did Fridays with at the laundry. She looked around. Where the hell were they? At the sorter-folder behind the big machines? She heard the door snap shut behind her, turned around, saw no one. Her humming suspended, she could hear only the dirge of the septicizers.

When she turned back around, she stood eye to chin with the big blue uniform that towered well over her own five feet ten. "Here, I'll help you with that." He reached out to grab her laundry, but he grabbed beyond and encircled her in a bear-like grip. "You *know* I've always wanted to help you, Rosie. Why do you resist?" She pushed away, but only far enough

111

for the sheets to fall to the floor; then snapped like a rubber band back into the hardness of his middle. She knew that vocalization would be useless. The other women had soundproofed the room by leaving. The next moment her arms were pinned behind her back and his snout was in her hair and dripping saliva on her neck. "You're my dream-girl, Rosie. I need you. I need to have you." When she tried to kick, he spread her legs around him and dragged her back to the pile of sheets still waiting to be sterilized in the corner.

After convulsing on top of her in a few hot grunts, he eased off her enough to let her pull her smock back down over her twitching legs. "This isn't just a casual thing for me, Rosie, you hear? I'm gonna want you over and over."

"I won't be any fun, you bastard! Go back to all those bimbos who *want* your passionate shit. Leave me the fuck alone."

"This isn't just a one-way deal, Rosie," said Jimmy, zipping up his fly. "You're what *I* need, and I'm giving you something *you* need."

"I needed this? I'd rather have an enema."

"Don't get bitchy, Rosie." He gripped her jaw and squeezed, hurting. "I read your C-file. I know all about you. I know how bad you wanted that last one. That cretin boyfriend pushed you over the edge. Two abortions in a row he forced on you, didn't he?"

"None of your business, asshole," she hissed through her teeth.

"That's *really* why you shot the fucker, isn't it? It wasn't all that bullshit about you having the shakes while he holds back the needle till you can't stand it a second more and off him with his own pistola, *was* it!"

"Is that what you think?"

"That's what I think."

"Don't think, Jimmy," she said, biting her lip against the tears that blurred her eyes. "You think even worse than you fuck."

"Be practical," said Jimmy, releasing her jaw. "You're all here doing hard time. The most violent bitches in New York State all crammed into one tiny hellhole, and you're looking at *fifteen years* in that quarry-- hauling stones to the crusher, filling beanbags with gravel, over and over, winter and summer--unless you make a friend that can help you, get it?"

"I"m not like you. I pay for my crimes."

"It's your whole youth! In fifteen years your tits'll sag like that P.R. Maria out there. They say she was a hot tamale once."

Rosie clenched her lips, looked away, and said nothing.

"You know how I can help?"

"There's nothing you can offer that I want."

"By giving you the baby you want."

"God forbid!"

"Once you're knocked up, you get three years in the Family Center to raise the little bambino. Easy time, Rosie. All easy."

Her hand swung to his face, but he slapped it down hard. "Fucking liar! You know damn well they'll force me to abort."

"Bullshit! I'll get you a copy of the statute. As soon as you're pregnant, they treat you with kid gloves."

"Really! And with a hot buck like you around, how come half of us aren't already in Maternity Ward sucking margaritas instead of you?"

"They're pigs. Forget those stupid broads. You, you're special, Rosie."

"And what'll the warden say when she finds out her favorite hack is expanding the prison population?"

"They won't know who, because you won't tell."

"Why won't I tell?"

"Because they can't force you to tell. And besides, do you know of a single sex-harassment suit that ever got past the toilet here? ... So why make trouble? You'll see, you'll need me in the long run."

"Get out of my face." Glaring at him, Rosie backed away, on her knees.

"Next Friday. Again, Rosie." He got up and buckled his pants. "It shouldn't take long--a month or two maybe--until I fill up that soft little belly of yours."

"Drop dead, you piece of scum!"

It was just after ten-thirty lockdown. Rosie lay in the top left bunk on her stomach. A ceiling-panel night-light cast a diffuse pink glow over her pillow and over the rubber doll propped up on it. She was completely absorbed in diapering it with a section from a pair of torn panties. Its dimpled arms reached upward in a supplicating gesture.

"Baby's made doo-doo agin!" announced Tyrona from the bunk across the aisle from Rosie. "Rosie changin' its diapers."

"Oh, really? I knew I smell *something*," said Juanita from below. "And here I was thinking it's Rosie."

"Come off that, Juanita!" laughed Tyrona. "How it be Rosie? Rosie work in the laundry all day."

"Oh yeah? But they tell me that today was a real dirty day in the laundry for Rosie. Is that right, Rosie?"

"Shut up, Juanita. If you can't go to sleep, I'll put you to sleep." Rosie clenched her teeth while she patted her doll's little arm.

"They tell me you had a hard time with a big blue pair of pants. You couldn't close the zipper."

Thrusting her pajamaed legs over the edge of the bunk, Rosie leaped down to the concrete floor and grabbed blindly for any part of Juanita she could reach. But before she could get a good grip, a strong pair of arms locked over her chest and yanked her backward into the bunk across from Juanita.

"Enough bullshit!" said the stocky Concha, the senior cellee, and the oldest of the four. "You raise a riot, they put the screws on *all* of us!"

"How they *let* a fox like that inside this chicken coop?" Tyrona wondered.

"*Chica*," said Juanita, "Corrections is a Equal Opportunity Employer. That means we all equally entitled to get fucked."

Rosie stopped struggling and Concha let her go. Nobody said anything as she climbed, chest heaving, back up into her bunk. Under the covers, she turned to the wall and pressed her wet cheek against her doll.

On the following Friday she didn't glance once in his direction. She went about her business--loading the machines, unloading, feeding the sorter-folder--speaking to her co-workers only when necessary, registering the presence of Jimmy only as a mote that hovered at the edge of the visual field. She reacted with barely a hitch in her breath when the shadows that were the other women no longer moved about her, and she put up only a token resistance when one big shadow, big and blue, rose to the center of the barren stage they had fled.

All she remembered him saying was, "Oh, so you won't kiss back? You will, Rosie, you will. Just give it a little time." Her growing hatred for him gave all her energy a focus, sustained her through the labor of loading stone at the quarry, filled her head with strategies for denying him the minor pleasures that marked a relationship of "lovers." She looked forward to those moments when his snorts grew the loudest that she would just lie limp and face away from his rooting, slavering chin. At other times, while his foreplay took him far below her neckline, she found herself humming a lullaby. At first he pretended not to notice. The next time he objected to her wandering attention, and she answered, truthfully, that she was already thinking of the baby they were making.

But the following Friday he did not make a move on her at all. She grew nervous as the afternoon waned and he wouldn't look her in the eye. She withered under the ironic glances of the rest of the work detail. He has a new sweetie, she concluded. Not so fast! she thought, touching her stomach. Not till you plant one that takes. And she figured out a plan to rekindle his interest. Two days later she had it all worked out. She spoke to him alone, briefly, in the recreation area.

"It's not *you*," she said. "It's just that I want it to be ... *nicer* between us. I'm a friend of old Wanda, the librarian. She said we can use the sofa there. The library's closed between five and six-thirty. We can have it all to ourselves, if you'd like."

His eyes grew wide with surprise and excitement.

"I'll have taken a shower by then. You'll like it so much better."

"How soon?" he said, tapping his hand with his club.

"Are Wednesdays good for you?"

"Perfect."

"Wednesday, then."

She was planning for what the baby would wear. She took torn scraps from the laundry room and designed little outfits for the doll. She did not yet know her name, but she knew it would be a girl. Her other two had been girls but had not had a chance to have names. She would now be much nicer to Jimmy, make him feel he was wanted. It was a strategy sure to increase his passion, and therefore his sperm-count as well. In an age of plummeting sperm-counts, a woman had to work at getting pregnant.

And didn't she indeed "want" him? Here was a man who was offering her the thing she desired above all else--and it even came with a long vacation from the quarry. After those three years ... why bother to think of afterward? She would take it a step at a time. Through Jimmy's influence, she could work it out with Wanda to have Mondays with him too. Just to think of it made her belly ache with a perverted kind of desire, the kind that ancient Greek woman had who made it with a bull. Disguised herself as a cow to bring out the best in her bull. Who was she? She couldn't remember. She'd look it up in the library. Rosie loved libraries. If she hadn't had to be on the road with that scumbag musician (may he rest in eternal torment, she thought), she'd have gone to college. There was so much she wanted to know!

What Rosie did know was that her own far from legendary life had consisted, so far, mainly in being used by others. Her religious fanatic of a mother, who had long since disowned her, had hoped that when she grew up she'd become a bride of Christ. Her druggie rock-star-wannabe of a boyfriend had expected her to follow him endlessly around the country, forever slim and sexy, and tolerant of the mounting trail of bastards left in his wake. Now Jimmy the hack, married and with kids, had his own sense of a Higher Calling for his sweet little bitch of a Rosie. But little Rosie was sick of being sacrificed to the higher purposes of God and Man. At last she would be able to achieve her own high purpose: selfish, meaningless, and personal, true!--but entirely independent of directives from On High.

So she reeled Jimmy in, first on Wednesdays, then on Mondays, and so good she was at what she did that he resumed their dirty-laundry dive on Fridays as well. Rosie, under the circumstances, couldn't have been happier. Spurning every gift of food or goods or light-duty assignment he could wangle for her, she risked offending him in that way only, in order to avoid, as she reminded him often, provoking the wrath of her peers. Her cellmates marveled at her incomprehensible altruism. As to Rosie, she paid attention only to her stomach. Probed it daily, thought she felt different, that her appetite was different. Exulted when her period was delayed. Then fell into a fit of depression when it came on. And inevitably it came on. Four and five months of wringing him dry, three times a week (and his jokes about bringing nothing home any more to his wife but his salary), yet nothing took root in her secret cavern, nothing yet stirred in her dark chamber of hope.

Out in the quarry one Thursday in March, Rosie stopped shoveling and examined with a sigh the piled up fruits of her labor--fifty-pound sacks of gravel that she and Concha endlessly filled, then loaded onto a dolly. No longer able to conceal her despair, she spilled out all her hopes and fears to her dark-skinned, heavy-hipped cellmate.

Dust-covered Concha dropped the sack to the ground and looked sharply up at Rosie. "How stupid can you be, girl? Every woman in the joint knows that Jimmy shoots blanks. He got a vasectomy who knows how many years ago--to make us all very happy and not to have to worry, he said."

Rosie could barely hold back her breakfast.

"You all right, girl? You turning blue! ... You mean you'd *want* a kid by that *cabrón*?"

All Friday morning, in the laundry room, Rosie avoided his gaze. Lunch she just picked at. She could hardly hold anything down. In the afternoon, when the time came, and her co-workers vanished on cue, the Blue Blur came cockily up to her. In a familiar gesture of cuddling, he extended his arms. Rosie met his right arm with as close to a karate chop as she could remember being taught by some old boyfriend or other. Jimmy winced, pressed his hand to the hurt, then grabbed her hard by the shoulders. "What's gotten into you, bitch?... 'Cause whatever it is, it better come out, 'cause *I'm* comin' in, catch?"

"Get your hands off me, you sterile bastard!"

"You got a problem, Rosie?" He forced her up the aisle and down into a pile of sheets.

"The girls let me know. I've been fucking a mule!"

"And loving it, Rosie, right?" He crushed her chest with his left arm while with his right he undid his pants. "This is exciting. I like resistance. You've been getting dull, Rosie. I been doing you a favor."

"Never again. Never. Get off me, you shit!" She tried to bite his arm, but it was just out of reach. She flailed at him uselessly with her free right hand. He tore at her panties, pulled them down to her ankles, and punched her knees apart.

117

Rosie screamed--a scream that had nothing to do with any physical pain he inflicted. When he shoved himself on top of her, she reached blindly for his groin, dug her nails into his testicles, and tore with all the strength in her toughened body.

Emitting a piteous, inhuman howl, Jimmy fell backwards, his hands clapped to his loins, his body shaking all over. Rosie jumped to her feet, stepped over her attacker, and looked with surprise at her co-workers, all rushing back into the room. With even more surprise, she gazed at her clenched right hand. The bloody scrotal sack bulged out over the ball of her thumb. Lifting the lid of a churning washer, she flung the mess inside and wiped her bloody hand on her smock.

- 2 -

She was confined to the Hole until they decided, they said, on the precise nature and extent of her add-on punishment. At first it was almost a pleasure to have a room to herself--tiny, dank, and poorly lit though it was--and not a lick of work to do. But they allowed her no reading or writing materials, had sequestered her miserably few personal possessions, even her doll, and permitted her only one hour every two days to wander around in the courtyard by herself.

She did miss Mail Call, however. Only once had she ever received a letter--two months after her sentencing, a brief note from her father, remote in tone, obviously censored by her mother. Thereafter she wrote to him every two weeks, unlikely though it was that her mother allowed the crippled old man to see letters from his hellbound daughter--letters that, more and more, the more she wanted to say, turned out to say less and less--*effigy* letters (*everything's fine; food is good; yours,...*), each letter sent like a message in a bottle, Ocean Express, with meager hope of a reply. She had disappointed him terribly. At eighty-three, unlike her mother, he'd been *happy* to hear that his only child was pregnant. Conceived in or out of wedlock, that was no issue for him. He had *dreamed* of dandling a grandchild, had gone out and bought things to set up a nursery, and had been crushed to hear of that second, late-term abortion, nearly as crushed as Rosie herself had felt afterward. The first time she had lied, told them she'd miscarried. The second time, the truth had come out. Her father had told her he'd have murdered her boyfriend himself. "Why did you do it?" he asked her, trembling with indignation.

118

He was not referring to her shooting up, or to her shooting of her partner, but to her wanton destruction of his granddaughter.

Every two days she was led, naked, by a pair of female guards to a shower stall. Aside from the barking of orders, neither exchanged a single spontaneous word with her. She marked time only by the meals that came through the chute, delivered by no human hands, announced by no human voice--only by the shrill of a buzzer. Within a week she had taken to screaming into the chute, and the only conversation she had was a shouting match in the courtyard with her own mournful echo. This, then, was the real add-on punishment, the clueless *waiting* for a decision they might never announce.

On the twelfth day, however, she was manacled and led in a different direction, not toward the courtyard, but up in an elevator, down a corridor of closed doors, and straight to the office of the Warden.

Inside sat Concha.

Reaching out her own cuffed hands to Rosie, she smiled at her old cellee through a black eye and a severely bruised lip. The warden looked at Rosie out of sea-green eyes beneath close-cropped, yellow-dyed hair. The gold rings that ran across her eyebrows did not have the softening effect of retro-hip. To Rosie they looked like a string of tiny handcuffs.

The warden studied a monitor on her desk as she spoke. "You've presented us with a difficult problem, Rosie. You should know that at the very least you've lost all possibility of parole."

"It was worth it," said Rosie.

"I didn't expect you'd be the type to feel remorse."

"For what?" said Rosie.

"You assaulted and did grave bodily harm to a member of the staff who did nothing whatsoever to provoke you."

While Concha hooted, Rosie stared ironically across the desk.

"Normally such violence is met with a stiff penalty applied within our own institution ..."

"You're sending me somewhere else for my spanking?"

"... but the unusual circumstances of the assault are better not put on record, as at a hearing before the Board."

"You mean fucking an inmate might be grounds for a guard's dismissal?"

"Right on!" said Concha.

"Shut up!" said the warden.

"So you've figured out a way to shut everyone up and hide our, uh, dirty laundry. Is that it?" said Rosie.

"There is a place out west for extremely violent women. They love to get headstrong babes like you who are full of piss and vinegar. It's in the middle of the north woods of Idaho, near Montana. It's called the Women's Wilderness Worksite. And they tell me it's not exactly like summer camp."

"It'll seem like summer camp after this place."

"Don't bet on it. If you think New York is tough on cons, wait till you see the Wild West."

"What's this got to do with Concha?"

"Because we're shipping her out too."

"I've been bad," said Concha. "I started a 'Free Rosie!' riot and we took apart half the mess-hall."

"I don't think that can happen where you two are going. I hear they do scientific experiments out there. They use women like you instead of rats, because the public won't tolerate experiments on rats."

"You're lying," said Rosie.

"Plenty of fresh air out in Idaho," said Concha. "Lots better than rottin' in a stinkhole like this."

The warden narrowed her eyes at Concha. "By dumping both of you, we fumigate the whole institution."

"*I* did that for you," said Rosie, "when I put Jimmy off active duty."

"Right on, *hija*!" said Concha.

"Shut up!" said the warden.

- 3 -

That same afternoon they were bundled into a van and flown under guard to Missoula, Montana, then shoved into the back of an unmarked paddy wagon, a sturdy vehicle with giant tires, that wended its way along paved, then graveled, then unpaved, rutted, and cliffhanging roads into the pine-shadowed heart of nowhere. Rosie did her best to remember the route. There were no landmarks. What stood out was the fact that the deeper they got into the woods, the more sites of decay and devastation they passed--a roadside stand of withered trees, glimpses of dead trunks collapsed upon the still healthy, the panorama of a clear-cut hillside gullied out with erosion, the gash of a dried-out stream in the valley below. Aside from birds, only once did she see a living creature.

"A dog!" remarked Concha of the brown-furred animal that lumbered across the dirt road in front of them.

"A bear," Rosie corrected. "A skinny bear. The creature looks to be starving." "Never been this far from civilization," said Concha. "Wonder if those scientists gonna feed us to them bears."

They were outfitted at the commissary in bright orange uniforms, easy to spot if they tried something stupid like running away through the woods. They were housed in a barracks, one of several inside a compound of cinderblock buildings centered in a grassless field and surrounded by a razor-wire fence. At the gate an overhead sign said, simply, "WWW1." Rosie assumed, therefore, that there was at least one other section of the prison in the vicinity, a compound labeled "WWW2." That's where the scientists must be, she figured. Inside the barracks stood facing rows of double bunk-beds, a dozen doubles on each side. Several bunks were free, both upper and lower, at the end of the room that was distant from the toilets and showers. Offered a choice by the female guard who accompanied them, Rosie and Concha chose lowers across from each other.

Rosie looked out of the storm window in the wall of the bay between bunks. The sun, descending through thin cloud-cover, outlined the western hills. Several hundred yards beyond the fence of the compound a high wall rose in silhouette above the scrub-strewn clearing.

"What's over there?" asked Rosie.

"That's compound 3--WWW3," said the guard.

"What's WWW3?"

"That's where no inmate wants to wind up. Get sent there and no one'll ever see your lily-white ass again."

"What do they do to you over there?"

"Don't ask me," said the guard with a shrug.

They had been ushered into the barracks just as the other inmates, recently returned from work details, were taking showers or lounging around waiting for mess-call. Everyone stared at the newcomers, saying nothing, apprehensive of the guard. "Mind your business. Make friends," said the guard. "Keep calm. Don't let a little shit blow your cool. There's micro-sensors all over the place, sensors up the kazoo. Violence will not be tolerated."

"Why?" said Rosie. "What more can they do to us?"

The guard pointed with her thumb out the window at the high, sun-tipped wall in the distance. Rosie nodded. The hole within the hole. She got the idea, more or less.

"Lights-out is ten," said the guard. "Wake-up is five-thirty, breakfast six. After tai-chi you'll be assigned to some work-detail or other."

"I hear they use us for experiments," said Concha.

The guard laughed. "I never heard that one before."

Dinner was green vegetables, potatoes, and roast chicken--a feast after their long day of travel. "We grow our own food," said Toni, Rosie's bunk neighbor, a thin, tough-looking black woman with a long scar aslant her left cheek. She had insisted on bringing up the rear of the mess-line, directly behind Rosie and Concha. "Just makin' sure them servin' bitches don't short-sheet you on the chicken. A game they play on newbies, honey."

After casing out the rec room together, taking note of the pool tables, the ping-pong tables, and the full-motion VR cubicles (one of them "out of order"), Rosie and Concha then toured the library, a room with only a couple of thousand physical books but practically a whole Library of Congress on hyperdense CD. No net-link to the outside world, of course. Anxiously anticipating the day to come, they traced their way back across the flood-lit grounds to their quarters. On entering, Rosie drew lots of attention. "*Qué rubia!*" someone shouted. Someone else whistled.

"They love blondes here too," whispered Concha.

Passing the first bunk bay, Rosie locked eyes with a strange-looking Hispanic woman sprawled out in the first lower bunk next to the showers. Dressed only in pajama bottoms, she was one big colorful scroll of ink: her skin crawled with intertwined tattoos. From her waist, to the tips of her breasts, and on up to her forehead she was a dusky wall on which generations of graffiti had been inscribed. A female Queequeg, thought Rosie. Alpha inmate. She'd met the type before. She avoided the impulse to volunteer a greeting, but after a lag of several seconds, just as Rosie

DANIEL PEARLMAN

dreaded, the Amazon queen came sauntering up behind her, with her hands poised at her hips. A green snake bared its fangs upon the mound of each knuckle. The other inmates had stopped what they were doing. A hush came over the barracks.

"You're in the wrong bunks," said Queequeg, addressing herself to Rosie. A violet bat on her forehead closed its jaws when she frowned.

"Oh, really? You want to switch?" said Rosie, settling herself comfortably upon her mattress.

Queequeg grinned and looked around her. In mute response, two other women slid off their beds and ambled up, with hands on hips, behind her. Rosie exchanged a quick glance with Concha, who sat tense at the edge of her bed.

"Since you're new, I'll explain," said Queequeg. "Fish don't take lowers till they're invited."

"We were invited," said Rosie.

Queequeg glanced around her in mock surprise. "Did anybody here invite these fish to bed down where they wanted?"

"We were invited by the guard."

"We have our own rules in here," said Queequeg, advancing a step. "Take the upper bunk."

Rosie was no stranger to territorial behavior. She knew that the way she met Queequeg's challenge would define her status from that moment on--and Concha's as well. "I'm happy right where I am," she said, batting her eyes mock-innocently.

Her half-naked antagonist lunged for Rosie's foot. Rosie gave her a foot straight to the chest, express-mailing her into the arms of one of her goons, toppling them both to the floor. Instantly, the other hench-bitch threw herself at Rosie, but she too landed short, on her chin, tackled by the vigilant Concha.

"You think you gonna sleep tight tonight?" said Queequeg, picking herself up off the floor.

Rosie's scar-faced bunk neighbor and a short, heavy-set white woman suddenly materialized in front of Rosie and Concha, turning around to face Queequeg and crew. "Enough, Vonda!" said the white woman. "We don't need no trouble!" said Toni.

"Just who do you think you're talking to?" said Vonda, formerly Queequeg.

"We speak for everyone here," said Toni, looking around at all the inmates, whose silence voted their approval. "Ain't nothin' more gonna happen here *to*-night nor no night! ... Unless you aimin' to be disappeared after breakfast."

The last remark gave rise to a wave of dark murmurs.

"We all need to get some sleep," said the white woman. "Most of us got road work tomorrow."

Rosie slept well, feeling protected.

- 4 -

Next day after breakfast she found herself tethered, along with Concha, in a chain-gang of ten in the rear of the second of two trucks. The truck in the lead, canvas-covered and a military green, held the supplies they would need for the day. Rosie found herself retracing the twisting road she had descended just yesterday, rutted at times, at times skirting the edge of a steep slope. The ankle bracelets and ten-foot connecting chains were of a tough, flexible, lightweight plastic that their male detail-guard, who was also the driver, said would not interfere with their activities. On their way to the work area, the trucks bore right at a fork in the road that Rosie had not noticed on the journey in. Gazing out over the side of the truck, she saw a sign that said "WWW2," and underneath, "U.S. Ecological Station." The arrow pointed to the left fork. Down that turn she caught a brief, passing glimpse of a tall wire fence along a tree-shadowed lane.

"What goes on in there?" asked Rosie.

"Science and stuff," answered one of the women.

"I think that's where the greenhouses are where they grow our veggies," said another.

"I thought we grow our own," said Rosie.

"None of us *here* ever worked there," sniffed Toni.

"It's a cushy job," said a third woman. "They say only pregnant women are assigned there."

Rosie looked around in disbelief. Male guards were few and far between--their current driver, the sentries at the gate--and none was posted to the rec areas or barracks. "So how do you get pregnant?" asked Rosie.

Everybody burst out laughing. Even the tattooed Vonda, who sat morosely opposite Rosie at the tail-end of the truck, shook her head and snorted.

"I think married broads get congenital visitin' rights," one of the women suggested.

"Conjugal, stupid," said another.

"Whatever."

"That's ridiculous!" said someone else. "Whose old man would come way the hell out *here* to get laid?"

"My old man," said one of the women, "ain't even sent me a postcard for the two years I been here, nor for the five years before that when he was in the jug next door to me in California."

"You so old and ugly, I can't say I blame your old man," said the woman's neighbor. Everybody laughed again.

"So where do they *keep* all these knocked-up farmer bitches?"

"I don't know. I ain't seen 'em myself."

"Course not!" said Toni. "They too busy, honey. Daytime they plowin', and at night they *gittin'* plowed."

Rosie guessed that the ride to the workplace--over washed-out, precarious logging trails--had taken close to an hour, had followed a northerly direction, and had crossed, about midway, a real, all-gravel road headed west. The worksite was a hillside laid waste by ancient mining operations. By now, however, much of it had been ridged with narrow terraces surfaced with gravel where the women's job was to get on their knees, spade in hand, and plant ground-cover at measured intervals. The object was to reverse the effects of an erosion that hampered road-building and that had almost destroyed the trickle of a stream that peeked through brush far below. That was the explanation that Rosie got gratis from the white woman who had helped to keep the peace the previous night.

"And where did they send all the other work-crews?" asked Rosie.

"Oh, road-repair, deadwood removal, shit like that. They cycle us."

The spadework was tough on knees and wrists. The ground beneath the gravel was hard and flinty, and the guard kept coming around to check on the depths of the holes they were digging. To Rosie it seemed a primitive method to combat soil erosion and a poor allocation of human resources. Not much science here, she thought. She tried to figure how long it would take a team like theirs to plant the rest of the enormous slope, most of which still needed terracing. "Concha," she said, yelling over to her friend who was three tangled cords to her right, "this makes no sense. It'll take us at least a year, eight hours a day, to cover this one single hill!"

"Well, they got about a hundred and forty of us slaves right now, *hijita*," replied Concha.

"If they want to save the whole forest," said Rosie, "they'll need half a million of us on hands and knees for ten years straight."

"It's chickenshit, just to keep us busy," said Toni.

"That's right," said the guard, who had come up behind them, "so you damn well better keep busy!" Rosie glanced at his hard dark eyes, his lined, leathery, middle-aged face, the automatic strapped over his shoulder, and she saw in his demeanor not a hint of erotic interest in his "girls." No Jimmy to contend with here! And even if a woman had wanted to toy with him, where could she go--behind a tree, dragging nine co-conspirators behind her? Even at mid-morning break they were released one at a time to use the port-a-poo, a maximum two minutes each, then snapped back into the line immediately after.

Climbing back up the slope after the bathroom break, Rosie felt tugged from behind. Gray sky and gray stone whirled into one another. She fell over backward in a scraping slide two levels down before the cords of the women on either side of her stopped her. The guard rushed up and examined the abrasions in elbow and hand. Streaks of blood filled the scratches and punctures.

"You'll be all right," said the guard. "Did you think this'd get you out of work?"

The sting in Rosie's cheek hurt more than the sting in her arm. It felt like a slap.

"Some girls are *only* used to workin' on their backs," said Vonda, the last on the chain. The remark raised some cackles.

"First-aid kit's in the truck. I'll be back in a minute. Everybody, shut up and move along, and *you* watch where you're steppin', sister."

As the group reassembled, Concha got up close to Rosie and whispered in her ear. "I saw what happened. The bitch behind you pulled on your rope. She musta got orders from Vonda."

"Do you think we could escape ... if we got rid of the ankle bracelets?" said Rosie.

"Where to? Get lost in these hills? And if we followed the trails, they'd catch us."

"They got hidden sensors all over the woods," said a woman linked to Concha. "They'd sniff out your ass quicker'n the wolves."

"And then?" said Rosie. "What do they do to you then?"

"Compound 3," said scar-cheeked Toni, third down the line to her right.

"That's right," echoed the stocky white woman chained to Toni.

"And what's in Compound 3?" asked Rosie.

Toni shrugged her shoulders. The white woman shook her head and fell back to working.

"Nobody knows dick about shit around here," said Rosie.

"We've all lost good friends to C-3," said the white woman. "One moment they're here, next they're gone. Poof! No one likes to think about it."

For the rest of the day, Rosie kept an eye on the sullen, silent, pinch-faced brunette to her left, a crony of Vonda's. There were times when she could have returned the favor of a quick yank at her tether, but she refrained. Meanwhile, she tried to hide all signs of physical discomfort, even though unable to switch the trowel to her left hand for relief.

- 5 -

One night, three weeks later, Rosie found herself back in the mess-hall an hour after dinner. Attendance was obligatory at the monthly ecology lecture. Prisoners were permitted to sit where they wanted, but, as at mealtimes, only within the section assigned to their barracks. A pair of guards stood by the doors at the rear of the hall.

Rosie glanced to right and left down the length of the metal mess-table. A dozen such tables, riveted to the floor, seated a hundred and forty or so weary, muttering prisoners. Rosie did not share in the general mood. Tired she was, but the novelty of the assembly sparked her curiosity. The cynicism around her--especially that of the sneering, slouching Vonda, who sat too close to her for comfort--did not distract her from the giant 3D monitor or the female lecturer poised beside it in the get-up of a forest ranger more than that of a turnkey. To Rosie the woman's strident, matter-of-fact delivery seemed a response to the hostility of her doubly captive audience.

"You're here to do hard time," she began, "but not just to dig holes and fill them up with the same dirt over and over. Maybe you never thought that some day you'd be doing something valuable for the future of your country--" (she ignored the groans and hisses that evidently she'd come to expect) "--but with every tree you plant, with every road you repair, you are serving a *higher purpose*." At this last phrase Rosie too felt personally insulted, but she bit her lip and listened and watched with varying degrees of interest as the lecturer conjured up images of devastation that the Bitterroot Ecosystem, along with other regions of Idaho and neighboring Montana, had suffered just during the thirty-five years that had passed since the turn of the century. She saw time-phase overlays of vast forested regions being progressively sliced to pieces by road-building and logging trails and mining and oil-company excavations; she saw golf courses take the place of stands of bird-haunted tamaracks; she saw legions of dead animals, from brook trout to deer and bear and elk, either starved out of their blighted habitats or poisoned by pesticides within them. A bear cub reduced to skin and bones and panting in the shadow of an oil rig brought a gasp and two hot tears from Rosie, who leaned across the table as if to rescue it.

"That cub is a brown bear, a baby grizzly," said the lecturer. "The adults are called grizzlies because of the silver-tipped hairs that grow over their brownish coat. That one hardly reached the age of two. Its mother was shot by a poacher who was after the gall bladder and other organs to sell in the Asian market, where many men still believe that eating those things will make them better lovers."

The point elicited a riot of laughter. The lecturer pretended to ignore it. "This happened ten years ago, shortly after Idaho passed a law permitting the on-the-spot execution of any poacher caught red-handed." The next picture showed the body of a man beside the mutilated corpse of a grizzly. "That's the mother bear. But as you can see," said the lecturer, smiling for the first time, "they got the poacher." Cheers and hoots followed this announcement, along with suggestions as to what should have been done with some of the poacher's own organs.

The image of the dying cub returned to the screen. "These little ones take eight to nine months to grow in the mother's womb," said the lecturer. "It takes four months for the embryo even to attach to the womb, which it does when she enters hibernation--"

"Wish *I'd* had that time!" shouted one of the inmates. "I could have changed my mind." While others laughed, Rosie felt like telling the fool to keep her stupidity to herself. Reluctantly, she held her tongue.

"How she know she pregnant?" asked a woman everyone called Simple Sarah. "She keep on screwin' all four mont', jes in case she ain't?"

The lecturer pondered the question carefully. "I don't know," she admitted, giving rise to an even bigger round of laughter.

"The little cubs are born virtually hairless," the lecturer continued, "and weigh about a pound and a half. There's usually two to a litter--but litters are spaced three years apart. A female will usually have only a dozen or so cubs in her lifetime."

"One was enough for me!" came a shout from the audience, accompanied by right-ons.

"Brown bears were put on the Endangered Species list in 1975. Now we don't know if there are enough left in the region to form a viable breeding population. The problem is they just aren't *predatory* enough. Deer are plentiful again, but our bears prefer a vegetarian diet, and the supply of their favorite plant foods has been shrinking drastically over the years. And the main reason for that has been the destruction of their territory--*and you women are a part of the solution* to the problem of the survival of these creatures!"

"Bullshit!" muttered the smirking Vonda, catching Rosie's eye--a tear-filled eye, withdrawn for a moment from the image of the death-bound cub. Still looking at Rosie, the tattooed lady whispered something to her neighbor. It went around the table like wildfire. Several women cast mocking glances at Rosie.

"We are experimenting with hybridizing our brown bear with more carnivorous types," the lecturer went on, ignoring the disturbance. "It may work, but it's a long process, so our immediate task meanwhile is to restore habitat for the species that is still *barely* with us." The lecturer smiled, but no one responded to her pun.

"Littoo Wosie needs a littoo teddy bear," said the inmate to Rosie's left. The table rocked with laughter. Vonda followed up with a wisecrack of her own, but Rosie couldn't catch it for the pounding of blood in her ears. The lecturer fell silent, unwilling to compete with the prisoners. As Rosie lunged out blindly to her left, she felt arms whip around her like clamps and bolt her back into her seat.

"Chill," said Concha, who sat to her right. She always sat close to Rosie. Her bear-hug embrace had come to the rescue again. A guard, rushing forward from the back of the hall, peered up and down their table, then withdrew. The lecturer continued her spiel. Images of endangered wolves now flashed across the screen.

"Thanks, Conch," said Rosie.

"Don't be a sucker for propaganda, Rosie," whispered the woman next to Concha. That was Zinnia, who bunked to Rosie's right.

Tall, dark-haired Zinnia, a woman in her mid-twenties with a perfect olive complexion, often gazed at Rosie out of deep-set, hungry eyes. Word had it that Zinnia had been convicted of killing her son, of putting out of his misery a hopelessly brain-damaged and physically deformed five-year-old, and her punishment was twenty-five minimum. It had taken some time for Rosie to overcome the horror of what the woman had done, to accept her for the wretched, lonely, kind-hearted loser that she was. At lights-out Zinnia would chat with Rosie awhile, then stroke her hair and kiss her on the cheek before slipping back into her own bunk for the night. When Zinnia took to hugging her and kissing her on the lips, Rosie gently resisted at first, then resisted more firmly over the course of several nights, till Zinnia came to understand the boundaries. After one such rejection, Rosie heard Zinnia sob through half the night. She wanted to reach out and embrace the poor woman; she wished they could assuage each other's different emotional needs, but she knew she would be misunderstood.

In the recreation hall, when playing ping-pong or pool, Rosie attracted a growing circle of star-struck observers and kibitzers, Zinnia chief among them. She didn't like to play pool with Zinnia because Zinnia, practised player that she was, seemed to beat everyone but Rosie, and Rosie knew that she herself was lousy at the game. Quarrels would sometimes break out about who had priority to play with Rosie next. Concha hung by too, but always unobtrusively, always willing to bow out of the way, to allow a new moth near the flame.

Rosie found popularity a heavy crown to wear and retreated more and more to the library, where prisoners tended to respect each other's privacy. That first ecology lecture had piqued her curiosity anyway, and she lost herself in multimedia reports on regional wildlife, paying special attention to the big, endangered animals like the elk, and the gray wolves, and the brown or grizzly bears. *Ursus arctos*, she remembered, was the scientific name of the grizzly. She studied also whatever maps she could find of the region--none of which bore a trace of anything called the Women's Wildlife Worksite--but she did develop a sense of the Bitterroot region's geographic relation to Montana.

One evening back at the rec hall, while playing a game of eight-ball, she was startled by a sudden commotion directly behind her. Zinnia was trying to fend off a thick-set, muscular woman, no one from their own barracks, who was pummeling her. Unable to hold her off with her elbows, Zinnia beaned her with the heavy end of a pool stick. The crowd cheered both of them on. The attacker came on more viciously and Zinnia struck again, even harder. It seemed only a matter of seconds before two guards raced to the scene from their office at the end of the hall. The rioting women were cuffed and marched to the office. Zinnia looked back and caught Rosie's eye, as if begging for her help. When lights-out came there was no sign of Zinnia.

"Where's Zinnia?" Rosie asked Toni.

"Compound 3," said Toni.

"Compound 3? Is that it? Is that all you can tell me?"

"Forget Zinnia. Zinnia is history. Some newbie gonna fill that bunk inside of a week."

"And it's all your fault, bitch!" someone shouted out of the dark. "They was fightin' over you, sweetie."

- 6 -

A week later it seemed to Rosie she would not even get the chance to welcome any newcomer to Zinnia's old bunk. They came up to her in the barracks, right after she'd returned from breakfast. One of the two guards was the one who had handcuffed Zinnia.

"Rose Langley and Concha Hernandez, step out in the aisle," she commanded. When they did, she cuffed them together. It was done so fast, neither had time to protest.

"What's going on?" said Rosie. "We didn't *do* anything."

"You're going to see the doctor," the other guard replied.

Rosie was convinced that "the doctor" was code for Compound 3. The previous night there'd been a brief shouting match at the ping-pong table. Rosie and Concha, playing doubles, had disputed a point with two women from another barracks. "We're not sick! Where are you taking us?"

Tattooed Vonda stood by, a big grin flexing the green cobra head on each brown cheek. "Up shit's creek without a paddle," she said.

Rosie went reluctantly. The guard had to shove her. "You're going for your medical," the guard finally explained. "Every new arrival gets checked for crabs."

"Feels great," said Vonda, raising one finger, "even *with* a glove."

Rosie and Concha bounced along in the back of a truck with a dozen other handcuffed women, all fairly new to the camp. This time, on reaching that mysterious fork in the road, instead of trailing off to the right, they rumbled up the lane to the left following the sign that read "WWW2 / U.S. Ecological Station." Finally, she thought, she'd get a peek at this off-limits part of her world that had aroused in her such fantasies, such jealousy, such voluptuous images of big-bellied women tending cabbages. Were the lucky girls, she wondered, behind the tall wire fence with razor-wire canopy that stretched on and on along the left-hand side of this road she had never been privileged to visit before? Behind the fence sprawled dense, dark woods still resisting the morning sun. The air was alive with birdsong. The long-drawn-out, baritone howls of wolves-- hungering for mates, she supposed--rose and died in the depths of the fenced-in pines. They sounded nearer than at night in the barracks, as if commenting upon her passage, as if relaying, all along the line, a single momentous and terribly important message: "Rosie is coming! Make way for Rosie Langley!"

At last, at a guardpost with yellow-and-black-striped crossbar, they entered Compound 2. They piled out of the truck at a receiving area like the entrance to a hospital emergency ward. Two other female guards, in decidedly unmilitary, sporty-looking khakis, replaced the two who had

132

DANIEL PEARLMAN

delivered them. A sandy-haired young man in jeans, already blushing under a barrage of whistles and theatrical moans, greeted the women at the door and ushered them into the large, drab, cinder-block building that bore no identifying inscription. "I'm Doctor Stevens," he said. "I'll be giving you ladies an introduction to the Station while you wait for your examination."

"You mean you ain't zaminin' us?" Simple Sarah cried out, disappointed.

"No, I'm not that sort of doctor. I'm a doctor of biological science. Doctor Schwengel will examine you."

"Zat Doctor *Mizz* or Doctor Mister?"

"That'll be Doctor Herbert Schwengel, but he'll be accompanied, of course, by a female attendant."

"What he need *her* for?"

"'Cause he's afraid you'll misbehave, stupid!" someone answered. Everybody laughed. The replacement guards were watchful but silent. Rosie knew that the original pair would have tolerated no such banter. She already liked it here, and would love to be examined from dawn till dusk, and she wished she could somehow manage to stay on to grow vegetables.

They were herded into a white-walled, windowless space that looked nothing like a hospital waiting room. "Don't hesitate to ask questions about the exhibits," said Dr. Stevens.

"Right," sneered Concha under her breath.

The entire ceiling diffused soft light onto three large tables hosting three-dimensional models of large sections of forest rising into hills and descending into stream-threaded valleys. On closer look, Rosie saw that these were holographic projections. When people stood close to a table, a voice began to explain the hologram, which itself changed its appearance to trace the history of damage and subsequent efforts at repair to the region shown.

"We're gettin' the grand tour," said Concha.

"Why do they bother?" said Rosie.

"They don't want us to be bored."

"Why would they give a shit?"

"They want something from us," said Concha.

"What more can they take?"

133

"Why do you think every month we get a lecture, Rosita?"

"To make us better workers. They want us to believe that our work is for the greater glory of God, as my mother would say."

"Right on. They want us to love being slaves."

They were next ushered into a long, dark, semi-circular gallery. Dr. Stevens flipped a switch and suddenly the whole outer wall turned transparent--became a window upon the forest: the actual, non-hologrammic forest. This long, curving window was divided into segments, each with a door that led into a cage, a cage for people, as soon became clear, and not for animals, a cage through which technicians could interact directly with the animals. "Imagine you are at the center of a pie looking out," said Dr. Stevens. "Each fenced-in section of forest you are seeing fans out far and wide from here, like a slice of a giant pie. Each slice of pie is a section of natural habitat made safe for a specific animal-- the elk, for example, which we are trying to breed and reintroduce, slowly but surely, into regions where they've been wiped out."

Rosie looked through the elk-window but saw no elk.

"Usually you won't see animals except at feeding times," Dr. Stevens explained, "or they'll come around for treats when workers enter these human cages to check up on the animals' condition."

Through one of the windows Rosie saw a gray wolf dash across an open space between two clumps of bushes. There was a label on the door, in Latin only: *Canis Lupus*. She remembered that the species was severely endangered, but this one, at least, had nothing to worry about. The sight of it was somehow thrilling--but also depressing. "The wolf is a prisoner, too," said Rosie.

"And gets better treatment than us," said Concha.

"I'd like to be that wolf," said Rosie, "looking through that window at us in our little cage."

"No such luck," said Concha.

"Do you think," said Rosie, "that on the other side of these slices of pie is the vegetable farm?"

"No, *hija*. Just a big bad wolf that's dyin' to chew your ass."

"I searched for a model of the compound in the holograms. Nothing was labeled. I couldn't find a thing."

"They don't want us knowin' too much, Rosita."

"Dr. Stevens is nice. I could ask him stuff."

"He said it to be polite. Don't stand out, Rosie! They'll make a note in your chrono."

When they came to the pie-wedge devoted to the brown bear, or grizzly--*Ursus Arctos*, said the sign--she saw a mother bear lying near the cage and two underweight cubs standing shakily beside her.

"The mother bear knows they're sick," Dr. Stevens noted, "and she's not doing too well herself. She stays close to the cage because she's learned that humans can be helpful."

Rosie stayed and stayed, feeling a surge of pity, but Concha yanked her onward just as a guard came to prod them. The group streamed swiftly on past the next window-wedge, bored, apparently, by a second section devoted to bears. Rosie caught a glimpse of a cub lumbering off after its mother. A strange-looking cub, she thought, comparing it with all the images of bear-cubs that she'd soaked up from library and lecture. It was long-legged, tall, had a big head and short muzzle--but it was frisky and looked healthy. Dr. Stevens was exhorting the group to step ahead quickly if they wanted to catch sight of a mountain lion. Rosie moved along, looking rearward, catching the inscription upon the door to that bear cage: "Hybrid: Ursus Arctos/Arctodus Simus," it read. What was an "Arctodus"? she wondered. "Dr. Stevens," she blurted, pointing back at the sign, "what's an Arctodus?"

From the sharp look he gave her, he seemed to be taken by surprise.

"Shit!" hissed Concha.

"Interested in bears are you?" Stevens said, ruminating over his reply.

"I used to own a teddy."

"Is that right? ... Well, Arctodus Simus is another species of bear. We've been trying to create strong hybrids that will survive in this fouled-up ecosystem." Stevens stopped talking and just kept staring at Rosie. The women noticed. Stevens's cheeks grew pink and he continued to speak, reluctantly, as if needing to say something to excuse his naked staring: "We've given up on the native bear. Its natural rate of reproduction has been falling, and we can't do much about it. Is that enough of an answer?"

"I guess it'll have to do," said Rosie.

"I guess so. Move on."

She was stung by his change of tone.

Finally they were jammed into a waiting room with plastic benches, a water-cooler, and a plastic table strewn with pamphlets all about regional environmental issues. Not a 3V in sight, only pamphlets in Spanish and English to help them pass the time. One by one examinees were uncuffed from each other. Each then had her own hands cuffed and was led out through a door by a big, pudding-faced female in a blue medical frock, an electronic clipboard dangling at her side. Rosie was one of the few who bothered to pick up pamphlets and read them. They were a mix of information and propaganda--boastful, defiant, and poor-mouthing by turns. There were hints that what the Feds were doing to restore "the Bitterroot Ecosystem" brewed distrust among the locals and raised the hackles of various big-business lobbies. The pamphlets, she guessed, were a slimly disguised appeal for more funding. White slavery, thought Rosie, was one way they'd found to narrow the budget deficit.

Fewer and fewer women remained in the room. Those led off for examination did not rejoin the group. Rosie wondered whether the exam was legit, just that and nothing more. Concha, even more suspicious than Rosie, was getting antsy too. At last, with only four women left, it was Rosie's turn.

"I'll be okay, *mamacita*," said Rosie.

Concha squeezed her hand before she left.

Outside the examination room, Rosie was thrust into a booth, made to strip to her skin and don a white paper smock. A blood sample was taken, then a urine squirt. In the examination room she was greeted by a business-like, blue-coated man with sparse gray hair and glasses--in his fifties, Rosie guessed--with a nametag saying "Dr. Herbert Schwengel." His nose was big and his neck was scrawny. With profuse apologies, citing reasons of safety, the doctor cuffed Rosie's already cuffed hands over her head to a metal post at one end of the recliner, then strapped each ankle to a side-post. She felt totally helpless, as if harnessed for gang-rape.

She noticed how the doctor's lips grew watery and his neck flushed pink as he handled her in strapping her down. His furtive glances kept returning to her face and hair. She understood that he found her attractive, very attractive. His transparent desire excited her and she glanced wide-eyed back at him, seductively rolling her tongue over her lips when the female attendant was distracted. He touched her gently, starting with her

136

ears and nose and throat. When he drew his gloved finger out of her mouth, she pressed her lips around it. He stared back at her, watery-eyed and blinking. When he auscultated her firm, full chest and fingered her ribs, she did her subtle best to feign pleasure. When he spoke to her to announce what he was checking for, or dictated something to the attendant, there was a hitch in his voice, as though his breath and vocal cords were in spasm. He redoubled his efforts to sound formal and professional--to avoid arousing the suspicions of his pie-faced assistant; of that Rosie was sure.

To Rosie it seemed miraculous when, in the middle of the examination, the attendant's cell phone buzzed. "Hello?" she answered, listening for a while, her face grown stern and pinched. Turning to the doctor, she announced bad news. "Big Momma Bear has just given birth, but the cubs may not survive."

"It wasn't the fault of the embryos," said Schwengel. "I make damn good embryos."

"That Big Momma's as inbred as a Tennessee hillbilly."

"She tested fine," said Schwengel, scratching his hair. Rosie could see dandruff flake off. "Just one more proof that the native bear is degenerate."

"Could anything be wrong with the intrauterine regulator?"

"The bioelectronics were monitored daily. The hormone mix has been perfect." Dr. Schwengel shook his head. "I give our lousy indigenous population fifteen years to extinction."

"They want someone down there quick," said the assistant.

"You're better with these problems than I am," said the doctor, "but I guess I'd better go." He tossed up his hands at Rosie--at his patient all cuffed and splayed out--as if to point out the absurdity of leaving her indefinitely suspended.

"No, Herb. You stay and finish. I'll go down and do what I can." She shook her head, barked into the phone, then snapped it angrily shut.

"But," said the doctor, tossing his hand out toward Rosie, "I'm not supposed to be alone with ..."

"Rules are made to be broken," said the attendant. "Finish this one yourself, and I'll help with the rest when I get back." She scurried out of the room.

The doctor turned to Rosie in embarrassment. "Sorry. It's an emergency."

"They shouldn't be treating you like a veterinarian," said Rosie. "You're a doctor, a doctor with a ... wonderful touch."

"Oh, I *am* a veterinarian."

Rosie looked sharply up at him.

And a medical doctor as well," said Schwengel, smiling. His nose looked greasy.

"What do you think of the shape I'm in, Doc? Do you like what you see?"

"I, well, I still have to do a proctological examination, and then a vaginal ..."

Rosie lost no time. Her horticultural dream might yet become reality. Staring him boldly in the eye, she slowly, invitingly parted her knees, drew them together, parted them again beneath the thin paper garment that he would soon have to lift. He would look at her perfect, work-hardened thighs. He would not find it in him to resist. Fumblingly, Schwengel pulled on a latex glove. Avoiding her eyes, he pushed back her smock.

"Take me," whispered Rosie. "I want you. Please, please *take* me."

"Are you ... out of your mind?" croaked Schwengel, his lips trembling.

"I promise, I'll never tell. I'll be yours when you want, whenever you ..."

The doctor's face flushed red. His hands gripped her calves and slid their way up over her knees, coasting along her thighs. *Mushrooms, tomatoes, zucchini leapt forth out of warm, wet soil.* "You're driving me crazy! I want you," she breathed. Schwengel's hand retreated to his fly. *Cornfields and cucumbers multiplied in quivering profusion.*

But Schwengel did not follow through, did not unzip his fly. Instead, he drew himself up in front of her, ramrod straight, crossing his blue-sleeved arms over his chest.

"I can't," he whimpered. "What if I make you pregnant?"

"I *want* you to make me pregnant!"

"So that's it, is it?" His parted lips trembled. His Adam's apple sank and rose like tlhe bulb inside a toilet. "Don't be a fool," he said, finally.

"No one would ever know it was you."

Schwengel hesitated, looked guiltily around.

"She'll be gone for a long enough time," Rosie wheedled.

"I can't ... use you for my personal pleasure." The sentence ended in a squeak as his vocal cords went into spasm. "We are both here to serve a greater end than mere self-indulgence."

"Have you seen a greater end than mine, Doc? Huh?"

"I am committed to serving a higher purpose," he said, leaning forward. "You are too, whether you want to or not."

"Stuff your 'higher purposes,' you limp-prick bastard," shouted Rosie, yanking against her cuffs, swinging her knees in a vain attempt to kick him in the chin.

A bead of sweat trembled at the tip of Dr. Schwengel's hawkish nose. "You don't understand. I would *love* to make you pregnant. You more than anybody."

She spat at him.

"But not now, you little idiot." He avoided her next launch of spittle by ducking under the hem of her smock, where he forced her legs apart and went on with the examination.

"You like what you see, you son of a bitch?... It's now or never, shithead! You'll never again in your life get a treat so sweet." This was a *new* kind of rape! she thought.

Rape for a Higher Purpose.

"So you too have heard about the vegetable gardens, eh? You'll do anything to do easy time, won't you?" As Schwengel's sarcasm rose from under her smock, his finger made rough entrance into her colon.

Tears sprang to her eyes. Hurt, humiliated, powerless, she stifled a cry of pain.

"Little Rosie wants easy time? Who knows, maybe one day she'll get her big chance."

Sobs wracked Rosie's body as Schwengel brusquely continued.

- 7 -

The following evening, after eight full hours of communing with Nature--digging out dirt-filled culverts under old, unusable roadways--Rosie summoned up the energy to do a bit of research at the library. She'd made it a point to remember that name, *Arctodus simus*. That cub had looked so strange! It did not take her long to find a disk with artist's pictures of the animal as it *once* must have looked, both walking and

139

standing. This creature was *extinct*, then! Standing, it looked like King Kong, towering over the largest of the other animals--they too long dead-- depicted in its vicinity. Extinct? Then what was this "hybrid" she'd seen, this odd-looking, long-legged cub? It made no sense! With mounting uneasiness, she read the text accompanying the pictures:

*"**Arctodus simus**, the 'short-faced' or 'bulldog' bear, roamed North and South America as the largest predator during the last Ice Age. With its short, broad muzzle, it looked more like a lion than a bear. This bear, possibly the largest that ever existed--and possibly the largest terrestrial carnivore that lived during the Pleistocene, between 12,000 and 30,000 years ago--was much larger than the Kodiak of Alaska. It disappeared approximately 12,000 years ago in the same period which saw the extinction of mastodons, sabre-toothed cats and so many other 'mega-fauna.'*

"Known also as 'cheetah-bear,' Arctodus simus had unusually long legs adapting it to the swift pursuit of prey. It could easily outrun a race-horse. Although not so stockily built as the brown bear (Ursus arctos), it was much taller--the male nearly five feet high on all fours, and eleven feet tall on his hind legs. This fearsome carnivore, about fifty percent larger than the largest living bears, could reach four feet above a basketball hoop.

"Remains of this animal were first discovered last century in the La Brea tar pits of southern California. In 2015, a completely preserved specimen of a male Arctodus simus was discovered in Alaska's Yukon. Its partially intact DNA has been under study for well over a decade. If alive today, that excellent predator could probably thrive in many of the ravaged habitats that now threaten almost all bear species with extinction."

Rosie knew she knew something she wasn't supposed to know. The Feds had managed to resurrect some form of this Ice-Age giant, and they were secretly using the State of Idaho as their laboratory. Wouldn't Idahoans kick and scream if ever the facts got out? she wondered. Would they tolerate, in the name of wilderness renewal, an Arctodus simus tramping over their lawns?

She remembered the look Dr. Stevens had given her--and his brush-off reply. He had invited questions, but he hadn't expected that *particular* question. He hadn't expected the dumb little bimbos to *notice* anything at all! She decided to keep mum about it; for the moment, just tell Concha.

- 8 -

Two evenings a week was supposed to be Mail Call, but that was a joke. Even on the outside, who wrote paper "letters" any more? Her father had, once. As to prisoners sending letters--apart from herself, Rosie knew no one who bothered, given the censorship of outgoing mail. As pointless as her ritual was, she still felt compelled, every once in a while, to scribble off a perfunctory note to "Dad." As to net-mail, inmates were completely denied access to "one of the chief privileges of *civilian* life," they reminded.

Visitors Day was once a week, for one hour, on a Sunday afternoon. But if "mail" was almost unheard of, the appearance of visitors was no more likely than the arrival of an alien spacecraft. No one in the barracks, as far as Rosie could remember, had ever had a visitor from the "free world." And that was why everyone, especially Rosie, was stunned when over the PA system a hack barked one Sunday, giving Rosie Langley fifteen minutes to appear in the Visitors Room. She was near her bunk, playing cards with a group of friends. They all looked up, more incredulous than jealous. They all shot her the same question: "Who the fuck could that be?" Rosie hadn't the foggiest idea. Her mother? Forget it. Her father? How could he ever stand the trip?... She had no other family she could even remember. Tidying up her hair in the bathroom mirror, she practiced a pleasant smile and proceeded under guard, her lips compressed, her heart pounding, to the Administrative Building, site of the supposed Visitors Room whose very existence some of the prisoners denied.

When she entered the fabled room, the guard stopped discreetly behind, at the door. Ten feet ahead she saw chairs in front of a long table. The table pressed against a clear plastic panel that divided the room in half. Flimsy partitions sectioned the table into separate cubicles that offered no privacy at all. On the other side of the plastic panel she could make out the figure of a man. He was seated in front of the middle cubicle, facing away from her, legs crossed, foot impatiently rocking. When she

141

came near, he turned to her, and his frozen grin stabbed at her gut like a knife.

"Hello, little Rosie. Remember me?" He leaned in above the metal voice grate.

Rosie breathed deeply, trying to regain her composure. "I didn't know rapists were allowed across state lines," she said without sitting.

"Oh, nowadays I've got all the time in the world to travel--anywhere I want," said Jimmy, tugging at the front of his sleeveless green hunting jacket. "I'm retired on disability, you know."

"I'm glad I was able to help," said Rosie, beginning to turn away. "Listen, I may rot in here for the next fifteen years, but I can't afford one minute to talk to a six-foot pile of shit."

"Don't be in such a hurry, Rosie. I'm sure you don't get many visitors."

"I'd rather spend time in the hole."

"Do you know they even tried to keep me out?"

"They have a good sense of smell. I'll see they keep you out *legally* if you ever show up here again."

"I showed them my badge, Rosie. They couldn't turn down one of their own. I don't think they want me to know what easy time you're pullin'."

"Easy time is when you're out of my face."

"Wait, Rosie! I just wanted to tell you ... that I can never forget you."

"Creep back under your rock," she said, not looking at him.

"No one means more to me than you, Rosie."

"Fuck off, Jimmy."

"I'm afraid I'll be hanging around, Rosie, until I fulfill my promise to you."

Half turned away, she nevertheless threw him a glance. His lips were drawn back into a malicious smile.

"You wanna know my promise, Rosie? I promise I'm gonna repay you for everything you did for me." Slaver dripped from a corner of his stretched-out lips.

Rosie spat at the plastic. "Don't come knockin' again, slime!"

"Oh, you're gonna get yours, Rosie. Believe me--when you least expect it."

142

"You don't have the *balls*!" she snapped, hurrying back toward a surprised-looking guard who looked at her watch and muttered something about the time she still had left.

"Can you see to it that he's not allowed to visit me again?" asked Rosie.

The guard gave her a strange look, almost human. "You're shakin' all over, girl," she said.

"*Can* you?"

"Sure. I'll get you some form or other to sign."

Back in the barracks, she was set upon by half a dozen women. The tattooed lady and her gang of cronies disguised their jealousy by pretending indifference.

"You look sick," said Concha. "Who was it? Why you back so soon?"

"Jimmy."

"Jimmy!"

"He's out of his fucking mind," said Rosie.

"He gotta be ... if he come all this way to look *you* up," said Concha.

"He wants to fucking kill me."

"Fat chance!" laughed Concha.

"He'll need a fuckin' sex change if he wanna be close to *you*, honey," said Toni.

"Rosie already give him a sex change," said Concha. "He's halfway inside this joint already!"

"Sound to me like he love you," said Simple Sarah, not intending irony. "When my Pepe cut me open, thas when I know he love me."

"You're lucky you in prison, Sarah," said Concha. "Outside, you dead meat." Everyone laughed. Rosie felt her breathing ratchet back to normal.

- 9 -

A week after Jimmy's visit, Rosie decided to tell Concha about Arctodus simus. The image of the beast had begun to give her nightmares. Sometimes, spotting a swift-moving shadow skittering among trees, she imagined it belonged to some creature of outsize proportions. If it wanted to attack the women as they worked at their shifts in the woods, it could have leaped out like a jaguar, and no one could have fired at it fast enough to stop it. But common sense told her that no animal came *looking* for trouble--and that human flesh would rank low among its dietary

143

preferences. There ought to be plenty of deer, she thought, to assuage its ravening hunger. Such logic, however, did not stop her from feeling exposed, vulnerable, the target of ten-inch claws that could rip apart an elk in one swipe.

Rosie, hooked to Concha in a string of five women coated with dust and sweat, advanced slowly along a bend of roadway pushing an unwieldy, long-handled gravel spreader. Up ahead was another group of five, also flattening mounds of gravel dumped by a bottomless pit of a truck that crunched on ahead of the workers and their guards, one male, one female, who had prejudged them all as malingerers. Except for the dust, it was a beautiful, mid-July, bird-twittery day. The woods that straddled their section of road were dense and splotchy with deep, dark shadows under a bright mid-afternoon sun.

"If you wanna be worryin' about things you can't see, you better look closer to home, Rosita."

"What do you mean, 'closer to home'?"

"Elvira and Bobbie. They ain't out workin' with us today, did you notice?"

"So they got assigned to another crew. So what?"

"Wrong. They had a nasty catfight in the rec hall last night, while you was in the lib'ry. Near scratched each other's eyes out."

"So they're lounging in the infirmary?" said Rosie.

"Uh-uh. ... Compound 3."

"What?"

"Say bye-bye to two lovebirds."

"They were like husband and wife," said Rosie.

"Gone like the wind," said Concha.

"It makes no sense. Sometimes there are horrible fights and *no* one disappears."

"They snatch about two of us up every month," said Concha. "If they nailed everyone who fought, there be no one left to work."

"It's their way of making room for newbies," said Rosie.

"I don't know," said Concha. "The older bitches that raise hell--they never seem to get took. No one over thirty that no one here can remember."

144

Rosie glanced out over Concha's shoulder to her left. She shuddered. "Concha, I just saw something move out there. Second time I saw it. Like some great big animal's out there, watching us."

"You're givin' me the creeps, girl," said Concha. "You think it's one of them super-size grizzlies they grow from that North Pole steak?"

"If people got wind of it, they'd close this slave-camp down in a matter of--"

"More walkin', less talkin'," shouted the female guard behind them.

They bore down for a while on their gravel rakes in silence.

"How can they let the critters loose without nobody knowin'?" said Concha, lowering her voice.

"I guess they figure they're smart enough to stay away from people."

"How big could they be, Rosita? You only saw a baby, you said."

"They've had twenty years to fool around. They've been experimenting since 2015."

"You know what we should do, Rosie? Write a letter to the papers. The libr'y gets the papers."

"Great idea, but how would we mail it?"

"Well ... next time they truck us to work, if we pass a road with civilian traffic--"

Concha was stopped by a loud report. Rosie was startled by an ear-splitting twang. "Drop to the ground!" she yelled to Concha. Goddamn hunters! she thought. But Concha was already falling--ragdoll-style, limbs in every direction. Flat on her face.

"Concha?... Concha!"

"Down on the ground, *everybody*!" yelled the guard behind her.

"Concha's been hit!" screamed Rosie, hugging the road as directed.

"Shut up! Lay flat!" shouted the guard.

Concha lay still. Rosie saw the stain darkening the orange jacket that covered her friend's upper back. "Help her, goddammit! Help her!"

"Shut the fuck up!" said the guard, confusedly swinging her weapon around in the general direction from which the shot had come. Rosie crawled to Concha and turned her face out of the gravel.

"*Mamacita*," murmured Rosie. Blood trickled out of Concha's pebble-plastered mouth.

- 10 -

The circumstances were different but the scene was familiar: an extremely distraught Rosie in a face-to-face with an icy-eyed, unfeeling, suspicious warden. Rosie's big surprise was bumping into Vonda, seated cross-legged, with one unmannerly foot tapping the warden's desk. Vonda barely acknowledged her entrance. Rosie slipped into the only other seat in the yellow-painted room and stared across the desk at a frizzy-haired, sharp-featured woman whom Rosie had never seen full-face before.

Warden Bankhouse cut right to the chase. "So what the hell do I do with you, Rosie? That's my problem."

"What's *she* here for?" said Rosie.

"I'm keeping all inmates off field-work for forty-eight hours." Bankhouse glanced at a pop-up desktop monitor. "The bullet does not match your boyfriend Jimmy's service-issue weapon."

"Of course not. He'd be an idiot to use it."

"We've scoured the woods day and night. No sign of your boyfriend."

"He's not my boyfriend."

"Ex-lover? Whatever."

"How about rapist pile of shit?"

"Bullshit," muttered Vonda.

"What? What's *she* got to do with--"

"Found wheel marks near the site from a 2028 Ford Sportster. That's all. That's a pretty common vehicle. Question is, Do we shut down operations because some nut is on the loose? Answer: no! We lay sensors around every work-perimeter, deploy them in depth."

"That won't stop him, warden. By the time the guards reacted--"

"We'll do the best we can with the resources we have available. ... Other question is: Do I believe your story about this Jimmy and that he was really out gunning for you?"

"I've told you why he has it in for me--why he's out on disability."

"Your ex-warden says no such thing ever happened."

Rosie's ears burned. "And what do you *think* she'd tell you? That she's covering for a rapist?"

"Like I tole you, warden," Vonda chimed in, "it's one big cock-'n-bull story, period!"

"Shut up, Vonda. I'll call on you when I'm ready."

146

"What the hell does Queequeg have to do with this?" demanded Rosie.

"Vonda here has filed a serious accusation against you, Rosie."

"Really?"

"She claims that what happened was a set-up."

"A set-up? What sort of set-up?"

"That you and your boyfriend Jimmy had planned this killing--planned to shoot someone next to you to make it *look* like he was gunning for you-- so as to get you out of doing hard time, to get you out of field-work."

"What a load of--!" Choked with anger, Rosie stared at her smug accuser.

"I assume you are denying the allegation."

Restraining the urge to lunge at Vonda and whack her with her manacled hands, Rosie simply repeated what she had said at an earlier briefing: "It's on record that I did not want to see that visitor ever again. It's on record that I cut that only meeting I did have with him down to less than two minutes."

"That's true. That does seem to corroborate your account," said Bankhouse. "But at the same time, that could all have been an act, couldn't it?"

"Just like I'm sayin'," said Vonda.

"I didn't ask you," said the warden.

"You want proof?" said Rosie. "Send me out there. Let him kill me, and then you won't call me a liar."

The warden scratched her head. "That's like dropping an egg on the floor to see if it's been boiled. ... No, I'll keep you out of the woods. I'll put you on Compound clean-up duties for a while--until I figure something better out."

"You're lettin' her get away with *murder*?" shrilled Vonda. "That bitch is an accomplice to murder! She's foolin' you good!"

"I don't know that, Vonda," said the warden. "Maybe it's you who's trying to fool me."

"So she gets away doin' easy time while we all slave in the fields? Damn!" Vonda kicked the desk for emphasis.

"Easy time for me would be not putting up with any more shit from you, Vonda," said Rosie.

"Keep at it, you two!" The warden smiled slyly at each in turn. "I already see a solution to this problem. *You two* are going to solve it for me."

"You mean like Bobbie and Elvira?" said Rosie.

"No way this bitch'll put *me* in the hole," sniffed Vonda.

"Don't leave it all up to luck, Vonda," said Bankhouse.

- 11 -

Several peaceful days went by--except for Vonda's snide remarks about "poor, overworked Rosie," but few girls paid any attention to Vonda. When no one joined in her jeers anymore, she fell silent and took to brooding. Cleaning up barracks *was* easy time. What a relief to be left unchained for whole days at a stretch! Swabbing floors was lots easier on the knees than planting shrubs in gravel. Being surveilled indoors by hidden camera beat being targeted through crosshairs. She even got a chance to see Compound 2 again--bucket and mop in hand, of course, but her eyes were free to roam.

She was cleaning the floor of the hologram exhibit. A guard stood posted outside, but Rosie was alone in the room. After scrubbing for a while, she noticed someone gawking through a panel in the door to the "zoo," as it was called . She stared boldly back. She could not have mistaken those eyes for anyone else's.

A few moments later, the door opened inward and out stepped Dr. Stevens. He looked smart in his light-blue lab coat. His jeans showed underneath. "Hello, Rose," he said.

"You remember *me*?" She was startled.

"You're the only one who asked any questions."

"I thought you held it against me." He had clean-shaven, angular, manly features, she noted.

"Why did you ask?"

Rosie looked into his eyes and caught on. "I just wanted ... to make you notice me."

He stood silent for a long moment, pondering his next step. "Do you think you could clean up in here?" He pointed back over his shoulder.

"Be glad to, Dr. Stevens." She gathered up her mop, her bucket, and a bag of supplies, and walked past him as he motioned her through the door. It was dim in there, too dim to work. The window-wall was opaque. A pair of overhead tube-lights, running the length of the corridor, afforded sparse illumination. Rosie felt a tingle of excitement. "It's hard to do much cleaning in this light," she said.

"I'm not supposed to do this, but ..." He pressed a panel that turned the wall transparent. Rosie saw trees, bushes, and splotches of sun and shadow. "There's no surveillance in the corridor," he said.

"I'll behave. Trust me, Dr. Stevens."

"I didn't mean it that way," he said, his cheeks flushed.

"I look so much better in civilian clothes," she said. She felt so ugly! Her knees were soaked from the scrubbing.

"I know."

"Do you like me anyway?"

"Yes," he said, swallowing hard. "I'm going into my office. Fifth door on the right."

"The fifth?" she repeated.

"Don't be ... long." He turned away and strode out of sight down the long, curving hall.

Rosie stood still and waited till the echo of his footsteps died away. Did he mean for her to make a stab at cleaning, a pretense for a minute or two, and then ... ? He was so trusting! she thought. Obviously not in the Corrections business. Out there, however, where the sun shone, lay the forest--and beyond the forest, a world full of people living in the lap of freedom. Were there vegetable gardens just beyond the rim of the pie? she wondered. What if the slices of the so-called pie had exit gates at the end? Or what if there were no barriers at all at the ends? What if she were only an inch of see-through plastic away from freedom? The bucket of sudsy water trembled in Rosie's grip. Setting everything down, she sped along the corridor trying first one cage-entrance, then another. Incredibly, one of the doors was unlocked! No, these were not Corrections types, not in Compound 2.

She did not even want to *think* about one hour, one day into the future, about how to survive in the woods, about how she would hide, make her way to civilization. ...

She found herself dashing and stumbling outward, threading her way among enormous tamaracks, pine cones crunching under the soles of her work boots. Looking back, she could no longer see the Ecological Station.

That meant no one could see her. The air smelled rich and pure out here. This portion of the woods was healthy, pruned, cared-for.

Reaching the edge of a clearing, Rosie stopped short and froze. An inhuman noise erupted, from every direction at once, it seemed, shaking the very ground beneath her. It was a growling sound--tremendous, rising and falling in pitch. Opposite her, barely ten yards away, a large-headed, dark-brown bear shouldered out into the brush. Coming to a sudden halt, it stared directly at her. On all fours, it stood almost as tall as she did.

Clutching a tree, not daring to move or breathe, she saw the animal rear--as though it too was frightened. On its long hind legs it reached high up the tree behind it. Rosie had once seen a real live adult male grizzly, but this gangly, great-chested creature seemed twice as tall. This was the beast she had seen on that library disk. It kept watching her, waiting for her to move. Bears had weak eyes ... or did they? she wondered. Move, and it's over! She stood frozen, her own eyes fixed on those of the bear. For several seconds they continued like that, a standoff.

Finally, the huge animal, leaning back against a tree, scratched its great hump against the rugged bark--all the while keeping his eyes on her, waiting for her to run. The measure of time for Rosie was the beat of the blood in her ears.

And then a doe skipped out into the clearing, loping across from Rosie's right diagonally to the right of the bear. Sensing the bear, the doe leaped toward cover. Tracking the doe, the bear sprang after. The scene that ensued Rosie saw not with her eyes but with her ears--a crash, a deep-throated grunt, a short, sharp shriek. The birds went silent. Gulping air, Rosie sprinted blindly back where she'd come from. Fear proved to be a reliable compass.

Safe inside the corridor at last, she shut the door quietly behind her. No one was in sight. She stood still, catching her breath. No way a thing like *that* could weigh a pound and a half at birth! she thought. She could not believe her luck. Not a soul had witnessed her brainless attempt at escape.

She would not tell him she'd seen a thing. She would ask no questions, she thought, approaching his door. This was no time to ask questions. Her heart pounding furiously from the adventure just past, and now from the one she anticipated, she ventured a timid knock.

"Come in."

He had dimmed down the light. He was not wearing a shirt. His chest was a field of golden hair, of flaxen tassels of corn. A pale rose glow suffused the room. It was a fair-sized office, big enough for a desk, for a jumble of equipment, and for the wide cot jammed against the wall.

"You seem extremely nervous," he said. "You don't have to be. Don't worry about a thing." Before she could reply, she was in his arms, lurching against him, feeding his hungry lips. The warmth of his muscular body quieted all her trembling. She closed her eyes, felt him sprout against her body. *Giant squash rose to the lip of her watering can.*

With unhurried grace, he helped her out of her orange jacket and pants. How fine, how gentle he is! she thought. Then it was her turn. Lowering his jeans, she nuzzled his thighs, ran her hands up the smooth expanse of his back. They rolled around the cot for a while, but soon, when Rosie was again on top, she decided to take the initiative.

"No!" he said, wriggling out from under her. "Not like this."

"How?" she said, confused.

He grabbed a condom from the table next to the cot.

"No," said Rosie, "please don't. I want you like this!" *Tomatoes hung, shiny and fat, from a thousand sagging vines.*

"I don't want to take any chances."

"I'm clean," she said. "I swear it."

"I know you're clean. You're perfect. I've seen the report."

"Then why ... ?"

"What if I made you pregnant?"

"I'd love it! I want it! I want you to make me pregnant. Please!"

"I mustn't take that chance."

"You're afraid you'll be fired?"

"That's the least of it."

She saw that he was losing his patience.

"Look, I don't want to talk about it. Do you want to make love?"

Maybe there'd be other times. Maybe she'd get lucky, she thought. Surely, he'd want her again and again. *Birds dropped seeds all over the forest floor.* Heaving a sigh, she went back to kissing and fondling him. It was easy to be sincere. He was so gentle, so fine. She even helped slip on his condom.

- 12 -

After dinner that evening there was the usual barracks roll-call. What was unusual was the announcement that followed:

"Mail Call!"

Everyone knew that Mail Call came right after post-dinner roll-call, officially and theoretically, but in practice, since no one ever got any mail, no one ever used the phrase unless she was being sarcastic. Everyone, therefore, was startled. Rosie expected some kind of joke, but the guards looked perfectly serious. One of them lifted what looked like a letter out of an inside jacket pocket.

"Rose Langley, pick up your mail!"

After waiting a few seconds, someone shouted, "That's all?"

"Yes, that's all."

Rosie could hardly breathe. Her fingers began to tremble and she clapped them against her sides. She knew what it must be: a letter from her father, or a brief note from her mother announcing her father's demise. A hush spread over the barracks as Rosie stepped to the middle of the room for her mail. Everyone's eyes were upon her. She felt as she had when she'd clicked across the stage to snap up her high-school diploma.

"I bet it's from the warden," said Vonda, breaking the silence. "She says, 'Rosie, you workin' too hard, dear, so I'm sendin' you on a two-week vacation to Havana.'"

The remark fell dead without raising one sympathetic echo. Worse yet: "Stuff it, Vonda," said one of her ex best friends.

Rosie paid little attention to the secondary dramas around her. Full of foreboding, she stumbled back to her bunk examining both sides of the as yet unopened envelope. It was hand-addressed. The sender was nameless, the address only a P.O. box in Sandpoint, Idaho. Not from New York, then. Her heart sank. Curling up in her bunk, she carefully tore open the flap. She opened a folded note, hand-written on a half-sheet of regular copy paper. She scanned down at once to the gut-twisting signature at the bottom: "Jimmy."

"Dear Rosie," he wrote, "I can't get you out of my mind. As you can see, I've managed to get real close to you. You don't seem to want me around, but who else do you have to take care of you? Believe me, Rosie,

152

next time I see you, I promise I will really <u>take care</u> of you. Still madly yours, Jimmy."

The last "take care" was underlined. She was overcome with nausea. The best thing to do, she thought, was call for one of the guards and demand to be escorted to the warden. If she still harbored doubts about Rosie, *this*, she was sure, would dispel them. "Look," she would tell her. "See? Killing Concha was only to terrorize me. Now he's clearly saying I'm next." She gazed blankly ahead of her, sick with loathing and fear. When she forced herself out of her daze, she looked up and around. Every eye in the barracks was trained on her. She owed nobody an explanation. No one expected one either. When they saw she had nothing to share, the women began dispersing to the rec hall. She could imagine what they were thinking. Lucky old Rosie! Rosie has a link to the free world. Someone out there *cares* for old Rosie. You bet he cares, she thought. As she crossed the barracks to buzz the guard, she noticed Vonda lying back in her bunk, tracking her.

The warden read the letter, then read it again, then shook her head in bewilderment. "Rosie, *you* say this proves his intent to harm you. But anyone could interpret this as a perfectly ordinary love-letter."

"*Love*-letter!"

"I agree that when he says he 'managed to get close to you,' he's referring to killing Concha. Otherwise, he only says he wants to 'take care' of you. He's 'madly' in love with you."

"Let me see that again," said Rosie. She read it over twice, three times. Biting her lips, she realized that the phrasing was ambiguous. Jimmy had weighed every word, making sure he got his message across without saying a thing that could incriminate him. "If you check, I'm sure you'll find the Sandpoint return address doesn't even exist."

"Oh, I'll check, but I'm sure of it, too." Bankhouse typed the address into the computer. "No doubt in my mind he's a killer. And on the chance that he might kill again, whether you or somebody 'close to you,' as he puts it, I'm still keeping you off field-work for a while. A few days more, that's all. And then I'll assign you to a different crew--with women who don't know you."

"It won't keep me or them any safer."

Bankhouse gave her a long, cold stare.

"You still think it's a set-up?"

"Is it, Rosie?"

Flushed with anger, Rosie got up to leave. Stuffing the letter back in her breast-pocket, she felt more alone than ever before--as helplessly abandoned as during the night after Concha had died. If only she could appeal to that well-mannered, educated, decent Dr. Stevens! If there was anyone who might want to protect her, it would be he. But she couldn't be sure she'd ever *see* him again! He'd said no word about how and when they'd get together again. She knew he would love to, she'd given him as good a time as she'd ever given anybody, but maybe he just didn't yet know how to arrange another meeting. From what she could gather, the scientists and the prison guards had separate lines of authority.

Rosie spent the rest of the evening at the library, brooding, hiding her face in her hands when the tears spilled over. She missed her *mamacita* terribly. If she were given the opportunity, she would attack Concha's killer with her bare hands--tear his eyes out this time! She was beginning to feel like a pariah. How could that tattooed bitch have turned the warden against her? she wondered. Jimmy, she knew, had deliberately targeted Concha. He couldn't have gotten any "closer" to her than Concha.

Eyes still wet from tears, Rosie returned to the barracks just before bedtime. Most of the women were already in pajamas, preparing to turn in. Passing Vonda, she couldn't help noticing the multi-colored dragons writhing around her torso, spiraling up to the hard black pips of her nipples. Vonda stared back. "Sweet dreams, Rosita," she said with a twisted grin.

Only Concha had called her Rosita. She let the cheap-shot pass. Getting into her pajamas, she engaged in small-talk with scar-cheeked Toni, her neighbor. She wanted to sink as quickly as possible into oblivion. Leaning to her right, to the bottom foot-locker of the four that stood stacked against the wall, she reached for her rubber doll--the last of her things from New York. She reached, groped, reached again. Leaping out of her bunk, she probed underneath it.

"Whatcha lookin' for, dear?" asked Toni, concerned.

Fumbling beneath her pillow, Rosie found the doll. In two pieces. Its head torn off.

"Hey, Rosie, what's up?" said Toni.

Her tears were not so thick as to obscure her view of the aisle rushing up under her feet, of the edges of bunks flying by to her right like spikes of a picket fence. She uttered not a sound as she threw herself at the reclining coil of serpents, taking her enemy half by surprise, her forearm connecting with Vonda's jaw.

Rosie gasped as Vonda countered with an elbow to the ribs, but she sank her nails into Vonda's cheek, dug furiously as Vonda howled, while with with the ball of her other hand she bore down on her windpipe. Vonda choked and her eyes grew wide, but before Rosie could shut them forever, there were shouts, and then an intolerable backward drag. She felt like a rubberband ready to snap. Fighting against her restrainers, she bruised one or two of her friends. Finally, she wound up flat on her back, restored to her bunk, with five women sitting or lying on top of her. Hyperventilating, saying nothing, she lay there, exhausted, subdued.

"Lord a mercy," said Toni, the pain in her voice having nothing to do with her bruises, "I hope and pray that no one takes this serious. You're the best bunkie I ever had, and now ..."

No guards rushed in. Murmuring and whispering, everyone at last fell asleep. The following morning Rosie went to breakfast as usual. Catching sight of the perforations her nails had made in Vonda's cheek, she felt an odd mix of satisfaction and remorse. She would like to have apologized, but how could she forget all the pain that bitch had caused her? After breakfast Rosie filed out of the mess hall with the others, wondering whether bad luck would ever again find her on the same work-gang with Vonda. Hardly was she out the door when a guard grabbed her wrist and yanked her out of the line. Cuffs snapped shut around her wrists. "The warden wants to see you," said the guard. Rosie looked wildly around her. Everyone stopped and stared. Their looks were grim. No one said a thing. Shoved toward admin, she caught her last glimpse of Vonda. A broad, self-satisfied grin flattened the heads of the cobras on her cheeks.

- 13 -

Hidden behind the walls of Compound 3, in a grassless field, stood three cement-block buildings similar to those in Compound 1, except smaller. A van and a truck stood idly in front of a squat administration center. The real surprise was to see, behind the main buildings, several long, glassed-in enclosures, lined up parallel to each other. Greenhouses!

This made no sense, thought Rosie. But no one had ever actually seen those mythical veggie farms in the woods near Compound 2.

"I'm the assistant warden," said the woman into whose office Rosie had been prodded. Her voice was a bark. Her nametag read "Dora Fletcher." She was tall, thin, and bony, somewhere in her fifties, Rosie guessed. Above a sun-dried face, patches of gray hair lay scattered over a mangy scalp like tumbleweed adrift in a desert. A dozen silver rectangles pierced the rim of her right ear. They looked like staples. "You guards can go home now," she said. Two of her own goons stood in place outside the door to her office.

"Interesting record, Langley." She scanned her monitor with a frown. "Murder, violence, more violence. You've already spent time in the hole. Everybody who comes to me has already spent time in some hole or other--usually much more time than you. You're kind of young to spend the rest of your life in the hole. What do *you* think, Langley?"

"I've been having a streak of bad luck," Rosie muttered.

Fletcher laughed through a filter of phlegm. "You were shipped to Wildlife as a last-ditch effort to make yourself useful to society. The women sent to Wildlife have virtually no ties to the outside world. Do you have ties, Miss Langley?"

"Yes, a bond of hate. There's a man out there, stalking me, wants to murder me."

"That's more connection than anyone else can claim!" Again she laughed that clotted rattle of a laugh. "Langley, let me put it to you clearly. Though I don't see much attitude coming from you, you've proven that you can't be trusted to work in a team with others. However, we can't afford non-productive inmates at this facility. So what do you suppose we're going to do?"

"Send me to an even shittier hole than this."

Fletcher's laugh was so explosive that phlegm poked out over her thin lower lip. She wiped it away with a tissue. "Sorry. You've come to the very last hole. Solitary, twenty-three hours a day. No books, no nothing. One hour for exercise and showers, that's it. Day after day, year after year. No reprieve. How's it sound? Sound better than roadwork, Langley?"

Rosie sighed deeply and thought for a moment. "None of this has been my fault. None of it!"

"Seems to me I've heard that song before," said Fletcher, scratching a tuft of tumbleweed.

"You said you can't afford to keep non-productive prisoners here. We're supposed to earn our keep, and then some. Why put me in the hole?"

"Well, there *is* an alternative to the hole, Langley, and fortunately it does not require the ability to work in a team."

Rosie eyed her jailor with suspicion.

"You're a young, healthy female, Langley. You have great *biological* potential."

"Biological? What do you mean?... You want to use me for parts?"

After emitting a new cackle, Fletcher waxed serious again. She pressed a button to the outer office. "Have Dr. Crofton come in, please."

In walked a slim brunette in gray jeans and a fancy silk blouse sporting an old-fashioned ad for a five-cent bottle of Coke. Her eyes were inscrutable, sunk behind the ridge of a prominent brow. She looked to be in her forties. "Dr. Crofton," said Fletcher, "this is Rose Langley." The woman nodded, looked Rosie over appraisingly, then sat in a chair on the opposite side of the room. "Miss Langley is in excellent physical shape, Dr. Crofton. I recommend that we offer her the option."

"What option?" asked Rosie, her eyes swiveling from one to the other.

"Surrogate motherhood," said Dr. Crofton.

"What?" For a moment she could not believe her ears. But now ... those greenhouses! It all made sudden sense. "So you want me to carry ... *your child*?"

"Not mine, precisely," said Dr. Crofton. Her cultivated voice was pleasant. "I'm an agent for the interested parties."

"I get it," said Rosie. "Women's Wildlife sells babies at cut-rate prices. I knew this place had financial problems, but I didn't think--"

"Cut it, Rose!" Fletcher intervened. "*Our* business is none of *your* business. ... What'll it be, Langley? Surrogacy or the hole?"

"I guess not too many women choose the hole, do they, warden?"

"Not too many," smiled Fletcher.

"And what do I do while my stomach blows up?"

"You eat well and the work is a lot easier than the roadgang. It's vegetable gardening. We've got greenhouses out back."

157

"I noticed." Was she hearing right? Pregnant, she'd be treated for nine straight months like a person! But *it would not be her child to keep*. She blinked away the burning in her eyes. What other choice did she have? She turned to Dr. Crofton. "How long will I be allowed to nurse it?"

"Not at all, I'm afraid. I'm sorry."

"Not even for a couple of weeks?"

"You heard her!" snapped Fletcher.

"Will I be able to ... hold it for a while."

Fletcher and Crofton exchanged glances.

"No. Not ever!" Crofton was clearly impatient.

"That would be sheer torture!" exclaimed Rosie. "How can you be so goddamn cruel?"

"Yes or no," Fletcher demanded, "and turn off the faucet, Langley!"

Dryly, but not without sympathy, Dr. Crofton said, "It would be far crueller if we did let you hold it for a while, Miss Langley. You'll at least have the satisfaction of knowing that you've made others very happy."

"What choice do I have? I'll do it," said Rosie. She dabbed at her tears with her sleeve. Dr. Crofton got up and silently left the office.

It will be *mine*, she thought, as long as it's inside me. And what if I don't *have* to give it up? Concha's idea, like a nearly forgotten jewel, floated up in her mind. If the local papers got wind of some of the shit going on in here ... She felt mildly hopeful. She had an ace in the hole, if only she could figure how to play it. Out in the real world, people resisted out-of-control government; and they still believed in human rights, even for prisoners, she thought.

At the C-3 commissary she again changed her old clothes for new-- including one-size-fits-all drawstring trousers and a commodious overshirt, again in shrieking orange. Bearing these gifts, she entered the prisoners' barracks (there was only one in C-3, they told her), and discovered here the familiar faces of all the disappeared she had known--Elvira, Bobbie, Zinnia. They all looked relaxed, transformed. It was like descending into Hades and meeting your long-dead battle chums, all of them alive again, vanished the wounds that had killed them! Greetings were prolonged and tearful. Her friends did not *look* pregnant, but they solemnly assured her that they were. Of the two dozen women around her, perhaps half of them did show bulges, and a few seemed big enough to burst. Several bunks were unoccupied, and by luck she was able to cop a crib beside Zinnia again--dark-haired, deep-eyed Zinnia, cheerful-looking, no longer pale and sad.

"The greenhouse work is pleasant," said Zinnia. "You actually see the things you've planted grow beneath your fingers. And you always think of what's growing in you as well."

"Doesn't it agonize you to think ... one day they'll just tear it away?" said Rosie.

"Me? No. I owe the world one. If it turns out normal, that'll be enough."

"It will," Rosie assured her.

"It should. After all, it's not my genetics. Dr. Schwengel said the embryos they implant are all checked for flaws."

"Dr. Schwengel?" said Rosie.

"They're all making a buck off us. But who cares? You'll see, you're gonna like it here."

"Schwengel had a chance to fuck me, but he wouldn't. He was afraid he'd get me pregnant."

"Smart man!" said Zinnia. "Why spoil good merchandise, Rosie?"

She was driven in cuffs in the back of an unmarked electrovan along a route that swerved toward Compound 1 then sharply veered left, northward on the "main" dirt road that led to Compound 2. The driver, a thick-set, sour-looking man with hair just turning gray, was one of a pair of C-3 gate-guards, both of them men. He wore jeans and an ordinary short-sleeved shirt--as though to deceive any casual wanderer through the woods into supposing that what lay behind the great wall they guarded was nothing more than some peculiar private estate. Rosie's blue-suited barracks matron rode shotgun. A broad-bottomed stump of a woman in her thirties, she sported a bulldog chin and cropped, dark hair streaked blonde. She squinted and launched a facial tic whenever she talked to Rosie--and that was too often, as far as Rosie was concerned. The inmates named her, among themselves, either Barren Bertha, Big B, or Bulldog.

On the way to Compound 2, Bulldog turned and spoke to Rosie through the wire mesh that separated their universes. "Think ya got it easy, don't ya, girl? Well, farmwork ain't just liftin' your dainty paws and waterin' a row o' turnips."

"I think I know what hard work is," said Rosie.

"Oh, you do, do you? Well, I'm gonna train your butt like no one trained it before. Don't think carryin' a kid means livin' the life of a civilian. Under my whip, you're a prisoner, and always will be a prisoner, hear?"

"I hear ya talkin'," said Rosie.

"Do I hear sarcasm, little miss?"

"Nope," said Rosie.

"Remember, the real farm ain't the veggies. The real farm is *you*, your belly is a plot of ground. But *you'll* never see or touch what they plant in you."

"I hear ya," said Rosie, smarting.

"Remember," said Big B, "when you girls get to deliver, you ain't no more a mother than a post-office deliverin' a package."

"I'll remember," said Rosie. It hurt even more to hear the driver chuckling to the sound of Barren Bertha's barren wit.

"Don't expect no hospital in there," said Bertha. "It's a fuckin' zoo. And they ain't got no doctors in there neither. They're a bunch of vet'rinarians. When they see a critter without a tail, they don't know what to do."

Big guffaws from the driver. He thought it quite a gas.

"Birthrate ain't high, ya know. Lots of the prisoners don't make it."

"And what happens if you don't?"

"They feed you to the wolves. Wolves is more important than people around here."

"Rosie dear, you are going to make a perfect host-uterus," said Schwengel the following afternoon. "But I could tell that the *first* time I examined you."

"What do you mean? Is that what you examined me for?" Once more she lay restrained on the examining table, hands cuffed to a bar in back of her head, legs held apart by ankle cuffs while two men poked her wherever they pleased.

160

DANIEL PEARLMAN

"We examined you for that possibility, yes, among other things." He exchanged a glance with Dr. Stevens, who had apologized for the restraints but otherwise pretended hardly to know her. *Except for one quick wink!* For the time being, that was enough. That wink she took back with her, nursing it, raising it into a garden of secret flowers. That wink became a long and exquisitely tortured love affair, with Stevens abandoning her for another woman--but leaving her with *his* baby kicking in her womb, a treasure that would compensate for all the wounds she'd suffered, a gift that would be hers to keep forever.

"Fortunately for you, Rose, you are perfectly suited for surrogacy," Dr. Stevens volunteered.

"Otherwise you feed me to the wolves?"

The doctors laughed, not looking her in the eye.

"How lucky I wasn't *already* pregnant," she added ironically. "But I've managed to keep my virtue in spite of every temptation."

"Excellent!" said Schwengel. "And you can still consider yourself virtuous, even after the procedure we are going to do right now."

"What procedure?"

"The embryo transfer, of course."

First they gave her a hormone shot. Then she had to wait in the sterile room alone, suspended a half hour like a pig on a spit until finally the men returned. The embryo transfer was simple and painless. They did it by means of a thin catheter threaded into her uterus. "You will be given special hormone injections once a month for the next four months. We've had a ninety-percent success rate," boasted Schwengel . "So unless we tell you otherwise, assume you're doing fine."

"The guard who brought me over here says most of the women fail to carry to term."

"Nonsense! Don't listen to that fat--" He stopped himself and dismissively threw out his hand.

"What happens to women who do fail?"

"In those special cases," said Schwengel, exchanging quick glances with his colleague, "you are usually given the option of trying again."

Rosie nodded noncommittally. She didn't like the sound of *usually*.

"The corrections staff," said Dr. Stevens, "are highly suspicious of us science types. Don't always believe what you hear."

"They are the tail trying to wag the dog," added Schwengel. "Some of them can't seem to get it through their heads that their main reason for being here is to support the Ecological Station."

"And that's the reason for all your labor, too, Rosie," said Stevens.

- 14 -

The controlled greenhouse environments mimicked artificial seasons and enabled the year-round growing of a variety of fruits and vegetables, from a staple like the lowly potato to a luxury item like grapes. Rosie loved tending to green shoots that curled up out of rich, moist soil. The tedious processes of planting seed or seedlings, watering the beds by hand, erecting vine supports, culling and boxing produce--all of these activities, performed without manacles, seemed like the labors of Eve compared to the prior tortures of the chain-gang. If, now and then, she copped an ear of baby corn or gobbled down a cherry tomato, the guards looked the other way--even Barren Bertha, who found numerous other excuses to be on Rosie's back. Big B's reason for living seemed to be to harass all the women she could.

Things grew in abundance. Rosie was sure that the women's combined labor produced far more than could be consumed within just the three compounds. Upon delivering a box of tomatoes or cabbages to the storage shed near the gate, she would often steal a few seconds of rest on a cot someone had thoughtfully placed there. Gazing out at the sky through a small window in the opposite wall, she would wonder where all this produce could be going--for go it surely did. Every few days there was turnover, the piled-up boxes gone, making room for new ones. Fruit and vegetables were boxed according to three quality grades. One of Barren Bertha's quality control methods was occasionally to stop next to Rosie (even the other women remarked on how often she picked on *Rosie*!) and have her unpack the fruit of her labor--right down to the bottom row of her last two crates or so--just to second-guess Rosie's judgment. Always she'd find a few borderline pieces that didn't come up to snuff. Rendering judgment with a few choice expletives, she would conclude by labeling Rosie "incompetent," "a dreamer," "a goldbrick," leaving her to rebox and fall beneath her day's quota. An inmate's "quota" was subjectively set by Bertha and never made clear to anyone.

"Don't let her get to you," advised Zinnia after Bertha had once again put Rosie through the wringer. "What she really wants to do to girls that make her jealous is cause them to have a miscarriage."

"That'll take a lot more than Big Bertha," said Rosie.

One time Rosie met Zinnia in the storage shed. "Who can *eat* all this?" said Rosie.

"Come on," said Zinnia. "You really don't know?"

"Know what?"

"That bulldog and the gate-guards have a regular truck-farm going? They drive to some town or other and sell off the top grade of everything we grow."

"If the warden were to find out--"

"Everyone covers for everyone. They all live in glass houses."

"I guess it's none of my business," said Rosie.

"And you see that cot you're sitting on, sweetie? That belongs exclusively to Bulldog."

"What do you mean?"

"You'll soon find out."

"It's been three months already," said Rosie, working alongside Zinnia tying tomato vines heavy with fruit to a network of support sticks. "I listen to my belly. I don't hear anything, I don't feel anything except my own indigestion."

"You haven't had your period, have you?"

"Not for three cycles now."

"Then I guarantee you, it took."

If so, thought Rosie, then this time she'd take it to term. No bastard of a boyfriend around her *here* to force her to give it up. "*You're* coming along fine, Zin." She patted Zinnia's slight but noticeable bulge.

"I'm in my fifth, and I'm not sure *I* felt much either--until a few weeks ago."

"You must have been worried as hell."

"Why? Who the hell *wants* to be pregnant?"

"I do."

"So many things could go wrong," said Zinnia, blinking rapidly.

163

"It's a chance I'm glad to be taking," Rosie said softly. She averted her eyes from Zinnia.

"You feel you owe the bastards something?"

"No," said Rosie, playing with a twistie, tying a vine to her finger.

"Then *why*? They'll only be taking it away!"

"Between now and then ... maybe the woman'll change her mind, apply for a divorce."

"Wake up, Rosie! They don't even allow us to *see* them. We feed them and water them, just like these tomatoes, and when they're ripe--"

"Stop it! said Rosie.

"Afterwards," said Zinnia, "they use you for breeding again."

"You aren't the only one who owes the world a child, Zin."

"You're full of shit, Rosie. You aren't indifferent like I am."

"Schwengel's a hard-ass, but if I asked Dr. Stevens to let me hold it, just for a minute--"

"Good cop, bad cop, they're all fucking *cops*, and you're a lowly inmate. You're not even human to them."

"Dr. Stevens is not a cop. He's a biologist." Clutching a ripe tomato, Rosie crushed it in her hand. The juice ran down her wrist. "I have needs too!" she cried.

"Prisoners don't have needs," said Zinnia. "They have complaints."

"You know something, Zin?" said Rosie with sudden resolve. She pointed to her stomach. "What's in here is *mine*. They're not going to get it."

"Don't talk like a nutcase, Rosie! In here you're a piece of meat, and don't you ever forget it."

"They're not going to get it!"

"Shush! Bertha's behind us. She's sizing up the zucchini. I hear she especially likes zucchini." Zinnia nudged Rosie with her elbow, but Rosie was in no mood for jokes.

A moment later Bulldog was standing right behind them, uncomfortably close to Rosie, breathing down her neck. Inhaling deeply, Bulldog smelled her, sucked in her body odor. She often did that, making Rosie shudder. "Who tied this last row?" she demanded.

"I did," said Rosie.

"Untie 'em. Do it over. Tie higher, don't worry about the middle."

164

"Yes, ma'am."

"Zinnia, c'mere, I wanna talk to you." Bertha took Zinnia down to the end of the greenhouse, where no one was working at the moment.

Rosie tied a tomato plant so tight, she cut right through it. She hoped she had not gotten Zinnia in trouble just by *talking* to her! A minute or so later, her friend was back at her side, her face strangely flushed. Bulldog exited the greenhouse, moving on to the next. "What did she say?" asked Rosie. "You look weird."

"I'll be having another adventure tonight. It's been so damn *long* ..."

"What do you mean, 'adventure'?"

"Adventure. You know ..." Zinnia motioned with her palms to her crotch.

"With her? I can't believe you're that desperate, Zin!"

"No, idiot! What's the matter with you? *You* must get more than all of us put together."

"I don't know what the fuck you're talking about."

"C'mon, Rosie. How often has Big B. rewarded *you*--you know, for all your hard work?"

"You mean by dumping out my boxes, then making me repack them?"

"Don't be so damn innocent, Rosie. I mean ... the storage shed."

"What are you talking about, Zinnia?"

"I can't believe this! She really *has* been punishing you, hasn't she?"

"No more than usual. What *about* the goddam shed, Zinnia?"

"I've made it with two different guys already. One came back for me twice."

"Are you bullshitting me?"

"She arranges things for the women she thinks her johns are going to like. Pretty soon I'll be too inflated, but you are prime beef, Rosie."

"Zinnia, I swear I did not have a clue!"

"Either she hates you too much to make money off you--and believe me, honey, you are a potential gold mine--or else she's so obsessed with you she won't let anyone touch you for love nor money."

"Who are the guys? Those drag-ass gate-hacks?"

"God, no! Campers, hunters, locals."

"Locals? There's probably not a town within fifty miles."

"From the towns where they market our veggies."

165

Rosie shook her head, trying to take it all in.

"She manages to be very discreet."

"I can imagine her sales pitch," said Rosie. "'Gentlemen, if you think *these* tomatoes are nice ...'"

Zinnia laughed. "She even lets you 'look before you hook.' You're supposed to meet him in the shed, let's say, at eight-thirty some night. What you do, first, is tiptoe up to the little back window and have a peek in. The night-light inside is enough to show you if he's got two heads or not. Even *that* wouldn't stop some of us."

"She's taking a big chance," said Rosie. "What if one of you caught a bug? What would the doctors do?"

"I think she has them in her pocket too."

Rosie's breath caught in her throat. "You mean her clients include ..."

"You never know, Rosie. You never know."

Rosie's heartbeat quickened. "Imagine ... if you could meet someone you *wanted*!"

"One guy," whispered Zinnia, "the second time ... he came with wine and flowers!"

"Unbelievable," said Rosie.

"I cry whenever I think about it."

"I would too."

"I feel so bad for you, Rosie."

"Don't. It's a blessing in disguise. I'd only agree if it was someone I wanted to see."

"Ain't you the picky one!" said Zinnia with a comical thrust of the shoulder. "How else can you even get to *know* anybody?"

Rosie shrugged. An idea suddenly hit her. "Listen, Zin, you say you meet guys from the outside?"

"So, you *are* interested?"

"Do you think they'd mail a letter for you--I mean something you didn't want censored?"

"Why not? I never thought of it," said Zinnia. "Anyway, who would I write to? What's there to say?"

"Would you do me a favor--a real big favor?"

"I'd do anything I could for you, Rosie. You already know that."

Zinnia returned to her bunk a few minutes before lights-out. Her face glowed with excitement. Rosie sat at the edge of her bunk and looked at her, waiting. Finally, hesitantly, "How did it go?" she asked.

Zinnia bit her lips against an irrepressible grin. She tried hard to look serious. "I'm sorry, Rosie," she said.

"What the hell are you talking about, Zin?"

The older woman reached into her breast pocket. Solemnly, she handed back the sealed, unsigned letter--addressed to the *Idaho Times*-- that Rosie had given her. Rosie's heart sank as she crumpled it in her hand.

"There was no way, Rosie. Believe me, no way."

"You used your judgment. Thank you anyway, Zin. I shouldn't even have tried to involve you."

Zinnia clapped her hand over her mouth, making foolish sputtering noises.

"What the hell is it, Zinnia?"

"Remember ... you were wondering about Big B's clients, you know, about the doctors?"

"No!" said Rosie. Her tongue suddenly stuck to her palate.

"Well, I can now tell you--the answer is yes."

"*Who*, goddammit?"

"Ssh!"

"I'm sorry," Rosie whispered. A big hole seemed to open inside her. "It was Stevens, wasn't it? I knew he'd be attracted to you, Zinnia. Look at you, you're beautiful, why *shouldn't* he want--"

"Schwengel," said Zinnia. "I couldn't believe it."

"Schwengel!"

"Fucks like a jackrabbit, Rosie--like he hadn't got off for a year!"

"Unbelievable," sighed Rosie, breathing normally again. Inexplicably happy, she gave Zinnia a fierce hug.

"He asked about you, Rosie."

"Me?"

"I said to him, 'Why don't you arrange to see her?' I said, 'Her calendar's pretty full, but I'm sure she'd find an opening somewhere for you.'"

Rosie and Zinnia broke out into peals of laughter.

"But he said he wasn't interested."

"Bullshit," said Rosie.

"He called you a ... 'castrating bitch.'"

"He got *that* right!"

At that the two women collapsed into hysterics.

"Shut up, you two!" shouted a woman nearby who was trying to get to sleep.

- 15 -

Several weeks later, at the end of November, something began to stir inside Rosie. Not a gas bubble! That was certain. The timing was just right too, since she had just had her last hormone injection. The downside, however, was that she might not see Dr. Stevens for another four months at least. When strapped to the table under his eyes, she had never felt humiliated. She knew what she aroused in him. When she sought his eyes and he averted his (Schwengel was forever at his side!), the thrill that raced between belly and brain was the knowledge of her feminine power. She knew what he would have *liked* to say and do, and that was what she would feed on during the interminably long intervals between visits.

The barracks population had slowly changed around her. Every month a few of the women were whisked away to Compound 2 and kept in a regular maternity ward--treated like queens, they reported!--for the week or more that it took for them to deliver and then to heal sufficiently before being returned to the barracks. The women were plied with endless questions--about anything and everything *except* about the babies themselves. No one was so insensitive as to commit such a stupid faux pas. Some of the women did not return. They, it was rumored, were judged unfit for further employment as surrogates and were secretly shipped off to serve at a facility in some other remote part of the country. Their bunks did not remain vacant for long. As far as Rosie could see, she was caught in a slow, inexorable cycle, a game of musical beds.

The difference between life here and life in Compound 1 defied every expectation she had had. Her present barracks, modest in size, housed women who were judged the most violent of the violent--and yet fights never, and arguments rarely, broke out. No wonder the life here was kept a secret from the regular inmates, she thought. If they had any idea, they'd split each other's heads open to get transferred to this most dreaded of mythical holes. What had Schwengel once told her? The hormone balance in women who fought like tigers was far more suitable to successful surrogacy than that of the average female. Civilization, he had told her, had gone too far in wiping out the primitive hardiness that mammalian life on this planet needed for survival. (And when Dr. Stevens had made love to her, he had called her an *animal*. But he had meant it in a different way.)

For once, Rosie felt safe. She tried to remember the positive aspects of being on the outside, free. But all she could think of was life as a series of painful intervals between heroin highs. And life in the jug, after detox, was a series of painful intervals between one low of boredom and the next.

Planting seedlings one day in the greenhouse, she spotted the blue bulldog waddling straight toward her in her shiny black boots, her hand, as usual, on the semiautomatic at her hip. What would it be now? Rosie wondered. You've planted them too close together? Pull them out and start all over?... This time Rosie stared her down as Bulldog bore down on her. Those hormones Schwengel admired so much--they were tightening her hands into fists. Control yourself! Rosie said to herself as her eyes narrowed into slits.

Big Bertha's face contorted into a smile, a smile so filled with conflict that the upshot was a smirk. She stopped in front of Rosie. Her fleshy mouth worked soundlessly for a second or two.

"You don't deserve it, Langley," she sniffed. "You're not as respectful as some o' the other girls. But I'm gonna give you a shot at the shed anyway."

"What?"

"You heard me. The fuckin' *shed*! Tonight!"

"What makes you think I'm interested?"

"What? I offer you ... and you give me backtalk?"

"I'm in and out of that shed all day. It stinks in there. It's not what you'd call romantic."

"Look, smartass, the best we can offer is a no-frills fuck. Take it and be glad you could."

"I don't need it that bad."

"Really?"

"I'd be totally frigid with a stranger."

"Well, see? Your problem is solved!" Bulldog broke into a grudging smile.

169

"I'm beginning to show. No one would find me attractive."

"Is that right?" Bulldog looked coolly into Rosie's eyes as she ran her hand over Rosie's belly, then ran it toyingly over her chest, ending with a pinch at her nipple. "This guy'll find you attractive all right. He asked for you."

"Asked for me?"

"Believe me, I offered him better. Asshole's stubborn. Go figure."

That long ago wink, thought Rosie. It was a promise. All this time ... he just had to find a *way.*

"Come on, you and him aren't strangers."

He'll be careful, thought Rosie. He wouldn't do anything to hurt what was growing inside her.

"Be there at nine. In your Sunday best," she snorted.

"You're not going to tell me who?"

"You'll find out soon enough, lucky bitch."

"I'm not anybody's whore!"

"He's in love with you," countered Bertha. Inexplicably, her lips began to tremble. "When someone's in love with you they don't make you *feel* like a whore."

Rosie looked down at her hands. Her fingers were shaking. "And what's in it for you?" she asked.

"Plenty," said Bertha, slapping her back pocket.

At dinner Rosie picked at her food. Zinnia noticed. Unable to conceal her agitation, unable to make up a plausible excuse as to why she would not be playing table tennis with her friend this evening as usual, she told Zinnia no more than that Bulldog, swayed by financial considerations, had at last arranged an assignation for her with some stranger. Rosie showered, scrubbing her skin with a coarse cloth till she positively glowed pink. She examined her belly from every angle, her mind exaggerating its incipient rotundity, but the light in the shed would make her look flatter, she thought. Her panties and bra were threadbare and institutionally boxy. She had been ashamed of them even that first time, even in the dimmed-down light of his office. So she decided to dispense with underwear--and the thought of how that would excite him made her, too, begin to ache with desire.

Zinnia helped her by combing her hair, over and over, till it was as soft and shiny as silk. "If only I had perfume!" she sighed, but Zinnia, hugging her sweetly, said, "You don't need any. You smell naturally like a bouquet of fresh flowers." Her nails irked her. She scoured them until not a particle of dirt remained to bear witness to the way she spent her days. She wanted to laugh over all her fussing and grooming, but couldn't. "Relax," said Zinnia. "You act like you're going to your wedding." It was true, thought Rosie; and Zinnia was mother and father and bridesmaid all rolled into one.

When the time came, about five to nine, she sprang out into the clear, crisp night hardly feeling the ground under her flat-soled, after-work shoes. She tried to appear casual, unhurried, as she walked across the open space that divided the rear of the barracks from the sprawling greenhouse complex. What would he be wearing? And what would he have brought her? she wondered. Flowers? Wine? It made her dizzy just to think of such tokens of gallantry in a setting so ugly and base. No, a bar of chocolate would do! She hadn't tasted chocolate since her first day in a cell, a day she had never dreamt would be redeemed by a night like this. Oh, hell! she thought, it wouldn't matter if he brought her nothing but his own inflamed desire, the searing passion that had caused him to risk so much in arranging to meet her, a devotion she hardly deserved. And what if out of love--or just *pity*--for her, he could arrange for an exception in her case that would allow her to hold and keep for a while the child unfolding in her womb?

Throbbing with anticipation, she stumbled along the path to the left of the parallel lanes of greenhouses, long, peak-roofed, see-through structures that emitted a ghostly glow at night from the energy trapped by solar-panel arrays. Was he, too, a bundle of nerves, she wondered, as he sat there waiting for her arrival? She looked up ahead and could see, under the bright, three-quarter moon, the storage shed past the end of the greenhouse to her right. Approaching the shed, she slowed her pace. She mustn't appear to have hurried, she thought. She did not want to seem out of breath. Should she knock ... or would the door be open and he be standing there waiting to catch her in his arms?

She wanted to *savor* him--wanted everything to proceed in slow motion. The door to the shed loomed ahead of her now. It faced her. It was

171

closed. She could imagine him springing it open as soon as he heard her approach. She was not one hundred feet from it when a horrible thought occurred to her, a thought like a punch to the heart. What if Bulldog, to counter resistance, had tricked her? What if the man lying in wait had not asked for her at all? She slowed her steps even more, tried not to make a sound. The night was filled with intermittent noises. The long, whining howl of wolves was enough to muffle the delicate crunch of shoes on hard-packed earth. On the long wall to the left was the window she could peek through. She circled away, to the left of the shed, then approached it again on tiptoe, at an oblique enough angle so that even if he glanced out the window he couldn't possibly see her. Someone had left a long-handled garden tool leaning against the wall. Somebody's ass would be grass tomorrow! she thought.

Her temples pounding, she sidled up to the oblong window. Its base was at the level of her shoulders. Carefully, she peered inside, her angle permitting her to see only the rear half of the room full of baskets and crates. Positioning herself now with her cheek against the left frame of the window, she took in the whole front end, including the door. The light, dim as it was, exploded like a flashlamp in her brain, revealing a man standing stiff beside the door, hiding, waiting for her to come and push it open. Something glinted in the hand he held to his chest. It was not a bottle. It was a knife.

His eyes suddenly fixed on her, and he pushed open the door. There was nowhere for her to run. Grasping at a straw, she clutched the handle of the hoe that leaned against the wall. Seeing him bound around the corner of the shed, only a few feet away from her, Rosie scampered around the other end of the building, knowing he could easily catch her. She could practically feel his breath down her neck. She did not think; she just acted. Having confronted him once, she would confront him again. Rounding the corner to the right side of the shed, she suddenly stopped and swiveled. He practically fell upon her, grabbing for her arm as she swung down and sliced his forehead with the sharp edge of the hoe. Stunned only for a moment, he struck out and slashed her down the length of her right sleeve. She felt next to nothing, just a pinch. Drawing her arm back, her hand well up toward the front end of the hoe, she chopped down at his knife hand as he lunged toward her again. Cutting him across the knuckles, it knocked

172

the knife from his grip. As he bent to sweep it up again, she brought the hoe-blade down into the bridge of his nose.

Dropping the hoe, and not looking back, she sprinted toward the only safe haven--the barracks. Between her shoulders, in the quivering small of her back, she could feel him swooping, menacing. Her ears, awash in the tidal crash of her blood, drowned out the thud of his longer, faster steps. Any second his blade would sink into her back. She ran blindly, squinting as she imagined the bone-splitting thrust. When she saw herself within shouting distance of the barracks, she gathered her breath and screamed without slowing her stride. Shrieking and running, she came within yards of the back end of the barracks, when suddenly, miraculously, the door popped open. An astonished inmate stepped out of the way as Rosie lunged through. "Shut it! Keep him out!" she screamed.

"Who?" asked the inmate, failing to shut the door as Rosie fell face forward in the aisle. "I don't see no one out there, honey." Within seconds she was surrounded. Hands reached out to help her up. Zinnia grabbed her right arm. "My God, you're bleeding!" she cried. "Get the fucking matron, somebody!.. Look at the slice in this arm!" Zinnia tore off the knife-slashed sleeve and proceeded to twist it into a tourniquet. Rosie noticed the blood, but the arm didn't even seem hers.

- 16 -

"He's been stalking me ever since," said Rosie, winding up her debriefing in Barren Bertha's sterile quarters at the front end of the barracks. She sat in a plastic chair in front of Bertha's barren desk. The matron had cauterized the long slash down Rosie's inner forearm with a burning application of hydrogen peroxide, then applied a salve and a bandage. Her treatment of Rosie was rough, even contemptuous. "He killed my friend Concha, then wrote to me and told me I'd be next. Somehow he knew I was here. His only reason for living is to finish me off."

"You expect me to buy this story, right?"

"Yes."

"What else do you expect?"

"He obviously has ways of getting to me. I have to see the warden."

"Did I hear you right?" Bertha leaned over her desk with an exaggerated cupping of her ear.

"Yes."

"Well, you listen to me now, you trouble-making bitch!" Bulldog's cheeks burnt bright red. "I don't believe a fuckin' word you say."

"Then how do you explain--"

"You sliced *yourself* with that goddamn hoe. You want attention, you're a prima donna."

"That's crazy! I've never asked anyone for favors. I work my ass off like everyone else around here. You've got your *own* sicko reasons for treating me like shit!"

Bertha slapped her hands down on the top of her desk. "You calling *me* sick, you twisted little twat you? *I'll* show you who the fuck's mentally deranged around here. I make my girls happy. If they're good, I get them laid. You bring this up to the warden, and what do you think's gonna happen? Ain't nobody gettin' no jollies no more, and *you'll* wind up getting cut to pieces--and I mean for real!--by all your so-called friends whose dessert you took away."

"I'm not interested in shutting down your little Ida-*ho*-house," said Rosie. "My life is in danger, and you don't give a shit, and that's what my *real* friends'll worry about."

"Look, sweet-tits, *I* know what your game is, and they're *all* gonna know what your game is," said Bulldog, waving out toward the barracks. "You wanna start a mutiny!"

"That's nuts!"

"*You're* nuts. Give me just *normal* violent women, them I can handle. Then they drop you on me! Shit! They shoulda put you in the fuckin' zoo with those weirdo animals in Compound 2, not here."

"You've dumped on me ever since I arrived!" shouted Rosie.

"I *know* what you did out there! You never even *met* the guy. You used that knife-trick to fuck me over."

"And how do I know," Rosie countered, looking Bertha straight in the eye, "that Jimmy didn't pay you to set me up?"

"What *now*, bitch?"

"I'm found mysteriously dead, there's hardly any investigation--because nobody's supposed to *know* what goes on in your little vegetable patch, right?--and life goes on, story over."

174

"This story *better* be over, sweet-meat. If that guy you disappointed goes around telling his buddies that I can't be trusted, that I don't run an honest, responsible trade, and business starts to fall off ... look out!"

"You want to avoid the issue?" said Rosie, standing. "I guess you can. You're the boss."

"You don't leave until I tell you to!"

Rosie continued to stand, clenching her jaws.

"You want that baby to come out alive, you make no trouble, you hear?"

"If I abort because of what happened tonight, you will *have* to take me to Compound 2, and when they start asking questions ..."

"You wanna play hardball, honey? Sure we'll take you over, but what if on the way you break loose, you try to escape?" Bulldog fixed her with an icy grin.

Rosie felt a pain in her gut. Was it the baby kicking, or ... Fearing the worst, she wanted to run immediately to Zinnia. She needed to feel the older woman's comforting arms around her.

"You get my message?" Bulldog concluded. "Good! Now get outta my fuckin' face."

- 17 -

It was a harsh winter. As Rosie's belly swelled, so did the snow beside the paths that crisscrossed the compound. Since the paths needed constant clearing, the snow gave Big B an excellent opportunity to make life harder for the women who became her targets. Women in their last trimester were kept off snow clearance altogether, but all the rest were subject to arbitrary assignment.

Zinnia was one of the lucky ones. In January she was in her ninth month. "Next week they'll be shlepping me to Compound 2," she informed Rosie. It was near lights-out and they were sitting in their facing bunks. "Unless you report complications, it's automatic. Two weeks into your ninth you get sent to C-2."

"How long will you be gone?" asked Rosie, her back aching from another day of shoveling. "I'll hate it even one day without you."

"If everything goes well, and they find you fit to carry again, they pamper you in a maternity ward for a week or two after delivery. Then

175

they send you back here, let you wait a couple of months, and then start the cycle all over."

"How long can it go on?"

"I don't know," said Zinnia. "Carlina, you probably know, is in her fourth round. At least two others are in their third. They seem happy enough."

"I can't believe it!" said Rosie. "They can't even hold, can't even *see*--"

"Cut it!" snapped Zinnia. "You got better things to worry about. "She's got you out shoveling every time it snows. Everybody else takes turns. We all see it, but we can't say a word."

"I can handle it, Zin. Don't worry. I can take all the shit she can dump."

"Look how big *you're* getting, baby! ... She's trying to make you miscarry."

"She won't succeed."

"And when it's *not* snowing, she rides your ass too. Who gets the heaviest details, huh? Carrying crates, shoveling the cowshit out of the pickup ..."

"She's only making me stronger, Zin. I feel like my body is a giant fortress. No one can break in. No one can harm the little prince inside who one day will be king."

"Don't talk that way, baby."

"Why not?"

"Talk like that is gonna harm you more than anything Bulldog can do."

"Thoughts like that are what keep me going."

"If you want to stay healthy, Rosie--"

"I'm only worried about one thing, Zin."

"And what's that?"

"The ride between here and C-2. I worry, will I make it to Compound 2?"

"Now that's ridiculous, Rosie. She can't be that crazy. No one can be that nuts!"

"She tried it using Jimmy."

"You're imagining that, Rosie! You have absolutely no proof that--"

"Whoever finds me will find a letter on me, inside my bra. It'll tell everything I know about this place."

"Rosie--"

"I wouldn't give *you* the letter, Zin. God forbid if they found it on you!"

"My poor dear Rosie ... that bitch is driving you up a fucking tree!"

"Listen, Zinnia, you must ask Dr. *Stevens* to let you see your baby. He's kind, believe me. Beg him."

"Please, Rosie! No more of this shit, please!" Zinnia lay back in her bunk, clapping her hands to her ears.

- 18 -

Spring came early, hot as a hairdryer. Rivers of mud sliced down into choking streams. Word had it that funding of the Ecological Station was in danger of reduction because of the diversion of Federal resources into flood control. In Rosie's view, such rumors suggested that the little prince within her had become an even greater financial asset than ever. She took daily delight in the gourdlike shape and firmness of her belly. She tried not to worry about the forthcoming ride to Compound 2, but for several nights before the appointed day she repeatedly awoke in a sweat. Fragments of horrid dreams, images of dismemberment by wild beasts, stayed lodged in her waking memory, taunting her throughout the day.

Her name was called out after breakfast. She had nothing to pack. Quickly, she hugged the returned and flattened Zinnia. Barren Bertha grabbed her by the arm and cuffed her wrists together. Without a word, she prodded her out of the mess-hall to the unmarked van, black except for a skirt of mud, that waited just outside. In the driver's seat sat the same, heavy-set, sourpussed sentry who laughed at the matron's witticisms and usually accompanied her to market. Shoving Rosie into the back, Bulldog locked the door and joined the driver in front.

Rosie's anxiety mounted as the van ground past the sentry post and lurched over the rutted road that curved away from Compound 3, that halfway house for breeders whose fence she could barely make out through the half-naked pines to her right. She felt as she had that first day she'd spent in solitary. Only now that feeling was mingled with foreboding. Not only did she dread the thought of arriving at Schwengel's clinic, but she suspected her companions might have other ideas regarding her arrival. With cuffed hands, she pressed her right breast, felt paper crinkle against skin.

177

The driver proceeded deliberately, avoiding the deepest ruts. Their progress north, on the road to Compound 2, seemed agonizingly slow--and at the same time life was galloping by, far too fast for the mind to hold, to record. The morning sun filtered through pine boughs up ahead. Steam rose up from parts of the road. Much of the way lay in shade. The pristine mud was devoid of vehicle tracks. The driver, spitting a curse, jammed his foot on the brake. Rosie's arms flew up against the wire mesh in front of her, cushioning the blow to her head.

"Goddamn log!" said the driver. Rosie could see it, a small, dead pine lying oblique across the road.

"Don't just sit there, Bill. Move your ass and drag it away."

Rosie watched the driver. He sat there still as a stone.

"Bill, goddamn it!"

"Shush!" said the driver. "Do you see what I see? Look up ahead."

Rosie looked. They all looked. A bear stood on all fours and looked in their direction about two hundred feet beyond the log. It stood there like a statue, not stirring.

"Holy shit!" said Bulldog. "*Get* it, Bill!"

"What I was thinkin'," he said, slowly turning around and lifting his rifle off the rack behind him. Even more slowly, he inched open his door.

"Don't scare him off!"

"Ain't exactly my first damn bear, ya know."

"I just want the paws. You can keep the rest o' the hide."

Rosie stared through the lozenge pattern of the divider, realizing, to her horror, the implications of what she was seeing. Her guardians were intent on committing a capital offense. Bear-poachers in Idaho could be shot on the spot with impunity. And the fact that her witnessing did not even bother them could mean one thing and one thing only: they did not intend to leave her around to tell tales.

The bear noticed something--smelled something, perhaps. In slow motion, it reared up on its hind legs--reared higher than any normal bear could reach, dangling its paws in front of its enormous chest, its long hind legs ballerina-like by comparison.

"Holy shit!" gasped Bertha. "It's one o' them fuckin' freaks!"

Rosie didn't have to be told. It was a twin of the one she had confronted in the "zoo" up ahead. Maybe even the same one. How many

178

grown-up hybrids could there be? The Ecological Station and the attached slave-camp hadn't been in existence for more than fifteen years.

"If they don't keep those circus pets o' theirs penned up, as far as I'm concerned, they're fair game for anybody," the driver hissed through his teeth.

"They ain't natural. Things that ain't natural shouldn't be allowed," said Bertha.

"When I bagged that big cat with the fangs last year, I didn't think I was one bit out o' line," said the driver.

"Those egghead types," said Bertha with contempt, "they need lessons from us in fence-buildin'!"

The driver nodded. "I better make my move," he said. With painstaking slowness he proceeded to detach himself from the vehicle. He kept down low, crouching behind the jutting limbs of the log as he crawled toward the cover of trees. Again, very slowly, gracefully even, the bear descended to all fours but would not take its eyes off the van. Run, freak! thought Rosie. Get back to your damn cell, where you belong! Scat! You're only fit for a cage! All too slowly, the bear turned away and began to lumber onward, shuffling at a leisurely pace, oblivious of the human advancing through the woods behind it. Rosie wanted to scream.

And that was all she needed--the idea of shrieking at the top of her lungs. The plan came in a rush, in a lucid moment of vision. She screamed, threw herself back in the van, and grabbed her belly. "It's coming! It's coming!" she shouted. She kept up a series of agonized wails.

"Bitch!" answered Bulldog. "Not in my fuckin' van you won't!" Scrambling out of the passenger door, she fished out a key from the ring on her belt and unlocked Rosie's compartment. "Come out o' there, get down on the ground!" Not waiting for Rosie to comply, she pulled her out by the collar and flung her down on her back in the mud. "Get these goddamn pants off and spread your fuckin' legs." As Rosie writhed in the mud, her hands still pressed to her belly, two shots rang out up ahead, then a third.

Leaning over Rosie, supporting her weight with one hand planted in the mud, Bulldog grabbed for the drawstring that held Rosie's pants in place. "I can't take it--can't *take* it any more!" Rosie screamed. And as soon as Bulldog's face hovered over her crotch, Rosie lurched forward and rammed the ball of her right hand up into Bulldog's nose. There was a crunch, and the matron collapsed on top of her. Rosie grabbed for the semiautomatic, pulling it out of its holster.

"Got it!" shouted the driver, whose mud-muffled footsteps rapidly approached. "Big guy's down! What's goin' down with you?"

Help!" Rosie screamed, shifting her legs, jiggling the heavy body, which lay between Rosie's legs as if, finally, she had granted her keeper the thing she most desired. She saw the driver step over the tree, come forward a pace, and then stop short. With manacled hands, Rosie lifted the gun, aimed at his chest, and fired. He looked at her surprised. She fired again. He "got it," finally, and keeled over backward into the twisted arms of the tree.

As if following a printed scenario, she knew exactly what to do next. She tried a few keys until she found the one that unlocked her cuffs. She knew she would need money, *cash* money. She fished two fifties and a ten out of the matron's leather belt-purse. The driver's wallet added two hundred plus to that. The next step? Her clothes! She would have to change her clothes. The driver's jeans made a fairly good fit. The matron's blue shirt, stripped of nametag and epaulets, hung nice and loose over her belly. She worked with utter coolness, as if disrobing department-store dummies. Her own clothes she tossed out of sight into the woods, where she rolled and dragged the two bodies. Her big job now was the tree. The trunk was heavy and thick at the left, so she attacked it from the right. Slowly, grudgingly, it scraped through the mud, giving way like the door to a crypt.

The key was in the ignition. The van came noiselessly to life, and she continued up the road. Passing the dead bear, she noted with satisfaction that the driver had not yet mutilated it. No doubt he'd been distracted by her screams. The giant chimera lay stretched out on its side, its lips curled back into a death-grin.

Rosie focused on one task alone: driving along the muddy road as quickly and as safely as possible. Only the image of the grinning bear pursued her as she slipped around each turn. On reaching the fork with the sign for the Ecological Station, she felt a twinge of fear. Bearing right, she entered a region of calm as, mile by mile, the Station and Dr. Schwengel receded like a nightmare behind her. With luck, she figured, nobody'd miss her jailors or herself for at least an hour or two. She knew this road pretty well. The calluses on her hands and knees bore witness to that. She knew it could be treacherous in spots, even in dry weather, for the next twenty or thirty miles. But sometime after that it would cross a gravel road, the road she would then take roughly east toward Montana.

- 19 -

She had not been driving long--ten miles, perhaps--when she entered upon the first treacherous incline her work crew used to pass on its way to some destination farther north. It was dangerous even dry. To the right, the woods descended into a steeper and steeper ravine. To the left, a wall of rotting trees threatened instantaneous collapse. Up ahead, the road began a sharp upward turn.

At the top of the narrow pass a car blocked her path. It was a red convertible that straddled the road at an angle, its nose facing the trees while its tail covered the ravine-side. The only way around it would be over the edge. As Rosie drew up to within a hundred feet of the vehicle, a figure popped up behind the wheel.

It was Jimmy. He raised his left hand and waved. She saw him smile. Then he raised his right hand and brandished the surprise he was keeping for her. She did not hit the brakes. Jimmy took careful, two-handed aim. The bullet made a clean hole through the windshield. Rosie sank down in her seat until only his head and his gun were visible.

She gripped the wheel as if she wanted to break it. She had no other option. She slammed down on the accelerator. Her wheels spun in the mud. Another hole, then another ... They kept ripping through her windshield. The van lurched forward, fishtailing. The wheels groped for the road while Jimmy's face loomed closer, a gun where his nose should be. He sprayed the windshield with bullets, but suddenly the van found solid purchase and leaped with the spring of a panther.

She saw his eyes grow wide.

She saw him so close that she could even see his mouth pronounce "shit" as he lunged to the right. Her bumper struck the grill of his car and rammed the vehicle backwards, airmailing it over the cliff-edge with driver still inside. Instinctively, she applied her brakes, although the force of the collision was enough to stop her cold. She heard the echo of crashing as the car plunged down the eroded steep into the yawning ravine below. All she really felt was relief as she examined, through her Swiss cheese of a windshield, the open road ahead. Not even her motor had conked out. She put her hands over her stomach and felt an answering thump. It was not only her own heart that was savagely beating; it was not only she who wanted *out*. Lips stretched thin with determination, she pushed on. There were lots of miles to cover. "So long, bastard," she mouthed without glancing behind her.

- 20 -

It was twelve-thirty on the dashboard clock when Rosie hit paved road. The first car that came up behind her frightened her till it had passed well ahead and showed no sign of slowing. She, too, pressed on the accelerator, enjoying the luxury of frictionless speed in a way that had hardly occurred to her when, little more than a year before, she had been driven in the opposite direction. Soon she found herself on a much wider road. A stream followed on the right. It was Route 12, and there was a sign to Missoula, and a sign to the Lolo Pass. Traffic was light, and the splendid, changeless blacktop lulled her into a waking sleep. The approach of an oncoming patrol car threw her senses back into overdrive. The patrol car did not turn around for her, but she could picture a roadblock not far up ahead, just at the Montana border. She swerved off the highway onto a road that wound roughly north. Following muddy backroads for another hour and a half, Rosie was surprised suddenly to find a sign indicating that she was finally entering Montana.

A half hour later, on Interstate 90, she was speeding southeast into Missoula. No need to fear roadblocks any more! She hung a right on Van Buren, another onto Broadway, and headed for the center of town. Not much of a city, she thought. All she knew of cities was New York. Here, not a single building tall enough to hide you from the all-seeing sky. Up ahead lay a busy diner with a large parking lot and wraparound see-through windows. She was hungry as a bear, she thought, the inadvertent image making her shudder. No doubt the diner would have netlinked booths. She would look up the regional news. Maybe she had even gone national! They'd be looking for a tall, unfashionably dressed, and extremely pregnant blonde. She was making herself paranoid! The prison staff, she reasoned, would be likely to fish for her first before broadcasting the embarrassment of her escape. She swung by the diner once, just to see if police were in the half-filled lot, then turned down a side street, abandoning the van in a parking space free of restrictions.

Except for the bulge, she didn't think, upon entering the diner, that she stood out much beyond the other blonde bimbos in the place. As she expected, to the left of the long, semi-circular counter, one of the booths was free. She sat facing the rear so that as few people as possible could get a view of her face. The perky little woman who took her order showed no sign of having bumped into a dangerous convict. Rosie could hardly wait for those two double cheeseburgers and double french fries! This would be her first real taste of freedom, she thought, salivating.

The wall-fastened monitor swung out on an accordion arm. "Local and regional crime news," she said. From Idaho, there was nothing much to report. A woman charged her boyfriend with pimping: she assumed she was having virtual sex with *him*, but he had plugged in his friend instead. A teenager was caught targeting a jetliner with a HIRF, a home-made, but very dangerous, High Intensity Radio Frequency transmitter. ... Too early for news about her, she thought. She would still have time to make tracks, but there wasn't a minute to waste. This was a necessary pit-stop: the body needed recharging.

She next called up the intercity bus schedule. Meanwhile, her burgers and fries arrived, along with a large chocolate shake. She paid on the spot with a twenty, enough for a generous tip. She sipped and munched in ecstasy, mingling both the tastes and sounds of freedom as she studied departure times for strange-sounding places like Bozeman, Butte, and Helena. How much farther should she go? she wondered. The East Coast was out of the question for the moment. The ride would eat up her cash reserve, money she would need till, baby at the breast, she could figure out her next major move. Besides, the baby might come tomorrow. She did not want to give birth on the bus. She called up population stats for the various towns in Montana. Size ought to figure into where she chose to give birth, she decided.

Before Rosie left the diner, she made use of the restroom at the rear. Glancing into the mirror before leaving, she noticed with disgust the mud that streaked her face and the frazzled, mud-caked tresses that scraped her shoulders. Filling the sink with warm water, she soaked her hair and wrung it out repeatedly, bought a comb and a hairband from the vending machine,

183

and walked out with a shiny wet ponytail. She could see through the diner window out to the cabstand at the curb in front of the parking lot. On her way out, Rosie glanced down the wide, curving counter to her left. Near the end, his head bowed over a menu, she saw a man in jeans and a blue blazer who looked exactly like Dr. Stevens! Stumbling from the shock, she recovered quickly. Other people looked at her; he did not. He appeared not to notice her. Could it be Dr. Stevens? she asked herself. She dared not steal a second glance. The doctor only *worked* at Women's Wildlife. Maybe this was where he spent his days off. She steeled herself to walk out the door with no change of gait or facial expression. Safely out the door, she hurried toward a waiting cab.

"I think you forgot something, Miss," said a man just behind her.
Rosie spun around. She faced the muzzle of a revolver.
"There's nowhere to run. Your hands, please."

- 21 -

Rosie remembered the face: he came around occasionally to check on the gate-guards at Compound 1. She'd been told he was the Associate Warden. Out of uniform, in a soft leather jacket, black pants and black boots, he looked like just anybody right now. She watched, drained of feeling, as he one-handedly, skillfully cuffed her. Looking up, she saw Stevens advancing upon them. He hadn't even tried to hide from her! She'd been trapped because she had stopped ... had wanted to taste freedom too soon. She felt like killing herself. There was no point in going on, she thought, raging at her stupidity. Her eyes fixed on Dr. Stevens. His face was cold, expressionless. He would not look her in the eye. There was not a word she could utter without bursting into a shower of tears. They marched her over to an unmarked car spattered all over with mud. Opening the back door, the Associate Warden shoved her into the seat.
"Go easy. She's pregnant, remember?" said Stevens.
"It won't make much difference, will it?" said his partner.
"We don't need a miscarriage either."
"I didn't think you'd find me so soon," said Rosie through the wire-mesh divider as the car took off from the curb.
"Your van is equipped with a transponder," Dr. Stevens answered without looking back. They drove for a while through the city. Houses

soon thinned out; trees took over. They were speeding down a highway through the woods, back toward Idaho. Eventually, the going would be slow, thought Rosie. But she didn't expect a slowdown while they were still on the open road. Nor did it make any sense when the driver swerved left onto a narrow, winding road, followed it for several trafficless minutes, then abandoned even that for a route much worse, bouncing over a rutted path gouged between walls of pine.

"Where are we going?" asked Rosie. This was obviously not the high road back to jail.

"You've been a very bad girl," said the driver. "Hasn't she, Stevens?"

"Very bad indeed."

"You've murdered two of our finest. Your case could take a long time going up through channels. Exposing stuff we'd rather keep to ourselves."

"Like the fact that one of our own killed a very valuable animal," Dr. Stevens chimed in.

"Fuck that!" said the driver. "I mean the fact that we're operating a very peculiar zoo."

"That zoo is why you have your job," said Stevens. "Don't ever forget it."

A thousand alarms went off in Rosie's head. "You can't! You'll be caught!" She did not know what she was saying. "They tried to kill me. I'm having a *baby*, for God's sake!"

"And that's another thing we wouldn't want people to know about, would we, *Doctor* Stevens?"

"No question about that, *Mister* Warden."

All she could see of Dr. Stevens was his jaw working nervously, as if he were grinding his teeth.

"As good a place as any," said the driver, pulling over at a point where the path momentarily widened.

"You would not!" shouted Rosie. "Dr. Stevens, *please!*"

"You can stay in the car, Stevens."

"No, I'm coming with you."

"There's no reason for you--"

"I'm coming."

"Whatever you say." The driver got out and yanked the back door open. Rosie cringed against the seat, placing her hands over her swollen belly. Her head slammed into the doorframe as he pulled her out of the car.

"Walk!" he said, jabbing the nose of his gun into her belly. She walked backwards for a few steps. The driver, annoyed, motioned for her to turn. She saw Dr. Stevens biting his lips, following behind the driver, refusing to look at her. She turned into the pathless carpet of humus between tree-trunks. Death pricked the back of her neck with hot needles. She approached a small clearing. Oblivious birds were singing. Here, she thought, let it be here! *Golden wheatfields withered before her; straw blew over acres of dried, cracked mud.* She leaned up against a tree at the edge of the clearing, then spun around--to look it in the face.

The driver was two paces behind her. He raised his gun. "Put your face against the tree!" he ordered.

She complied. She did not see death. She only heard it. The report echoed through the woods. The birds stopped singing. Rosie turned.

The Associate Warden lay crumpled at her feet. His forehead was a blood-drenched cavity. Behind him stood a trembling Dr. Stevens. Rosie's knees gave way. She slid to the ground with her back against the tree. Paying no attention to her, Dr. Stevens holstered his gun beneath his blazer. Then, reaching down, he tore the unfired weapon out of his ex-partner's fingers. Aiming it at the Associate Warden's side, he fired once, then again.

Finally, he spoke to her. "The bullet through the head did not lodge in the body. I have to make sure they find a slug--in him, from his own gun. You see, *you* killed him, with his own gun. I was not even here." Slowly, methodically, he took tissues from his pocket and wiped off every surface of the Associate Warden's gun. Then he dropped it near the body.

"And now ... you are going to kill me?" whispered Rosie.

"Don't be ridiculous. If I wanted you dead I wouldn't have had to do a thing. I wanted to save you."

"Why? You only fucked me once. I'm nothing to you."

"You're free," said Stevens, still trembling. Starting to retch, he turned away until the fit had passed. "They are not going to want to arrest you again. You've heard how you are much more dangerous to them captured."

"Them? *You* are them! Why did you save me? You *hated* shooting him! Why are you setting me free?"

"Get up. We're getting the hell out of here. Wait." He knelt down and, using a tissue, fished the corpse's wallet out of his pants. Handing it to Rosie, he said, "Steal his cash. Come on, you've done it before. Besides, you'll need it. Don't make any damn faces! Let's go!"

Without counting, she stuffed bills--a thin wad of them--into the pocket holding the rest of her gleanings and tossed the wallet back toward the dead man. "What do I do now?"

"I don't know. Follow your plan. I'm driving you back into town. You were studying bus schedules. I'm driving you straight to the bus station."

"Don't you want to know where I'll be going?" said Rosie, struggling to her feet.

"I don't need to."

"But I want you to know."

"It doesn't matter what you want or don't want."

"You don't sound like someone ... who cares about me at all," she said, shuddering. She trudged behind Dr. Stevens, following him through the trees, toward the car.

"Don't mistake my intentions, little Rosie."

"That's what Dr. Schwengel called me. I hated the son of a bitch."

"Then hate me too. I'm no better nor worse than him."

"I don't believe you," said Rosie, sliding into the passenger's seat. Tears filmed her eyes. She pictured what an ugly sow she must look like *now* to this man sitting beside her. Could he still see her as she must have looked to him *then*, as she hoped she would soon look again? "Why did you save my ... ugly, worthless ass?"

"Just *shut up*, will you?" He frowned and drove on in silence. Why wouldn't he speak about his feelings? she wondered. Had he saved her because his conscience wouldn't allow her to be murdered? Why wouldn't he speak to her? He was in shock, of course. He had just killed a man--a colleague--for *her*! This was no time to demand reasons.

When he let her out at the bus station, he avoided meeting her eye.

She leaned on the open car door. "You know, don't you, that I'll be going back to New York?"

"I wouldn't go too far," he said, still without looking at her. "You'll be due in a day or two. I'd look for a city close by."

"Name one."

"Go where you please. Remember, little Rosie, whatever else happens to you, we are not putting you back in prison."

"Then why do you want them to think I killed him?"

"Would I rather have them think *I* did it? Don't be stupid."

"Will I see you again?" she asked.

"Bear this in mind: when your contractions are ten minutes apart, call a cab and get to a hospital."

"Thanks, but will I see you ag--"

He pulled the passenger door shut and drove away.

"Fuck you!" she yelled after.

Rosie entered the terminal and approached the ticketing counter. He killed for me, she thought. He killed for me! She felt a stirring and rumbling in her stomach, a surge of seismic proportions. Frightened, she studied the monitor showing arrivals and departures. The bus to Butte would leave in three hours. The hell with Butte, she thought; and the hell with Dr. Stevens, that son of a bitch! The next bus to Helena, the capital, would be leaving in half an hour.

- 22 -

The sun had gone down by the time she arrived in Helena. She wished it were already over--the giving birth, the recuperating. How did he know she'd be giving birth so soon? she wondered. If she could count on another week, she'd head straight for New York. How stupid, though! she said to herself. Who would want to see her in New York? Her mother? No. But if her father intervened ... he would overrule her mother, that she knew. Her father wanted her back. And if he knew that his Prodigal Daughter was returning with an offering--ideally, an armful of granddaughter--then eventually even her mother would break down and accept her as human.

She walked out of the station into a well-lit street. The evening was chilly. A cabstand was only yards away, but across the street there were shops. At a clothing store she bought a loose-fitting cardigan. Farther along the street there was a big electronics shop. She would need a watch to time those contractions. In the window she noticed a sale on wristphone watches that included an on-the-spot satellite connection: six-months for only $99.99, crypting and message-download included.

The cabbie dropped her off at a medium-priced nearby motel. The bed was spacious and solid, the colors of the walls programmable, the large commutainment center in good working order. On the downside, it reminded her of a hundred such places all over the country where she and her ex would shoot up. Shooing away the memories, she ordered up candy from a wall-console next to her bed. A chocolate bar--she hadn't had candy for well over a year--popped into the slot. She nibbled at it, filling mind and mouth for a few delicious minutes with nothing but the taste of chocolate. It did wonders to ward off the images of gore and the sounds of gunshots that had plagued her all through her busride.

But now, at last, no one pursued her. This was her first real taste of freedom. She ordered up several more, several different kinds. Baby was hungry! She hadn't fed her little one for hours. When she had gotten over her candy fit, she started to press numbers on her wristphone, then stopped. No, she wasn't ready yet. First she would take a shower. Then she would wrap herself in the luxurious bathroom towel. And only then, scrubbed down from head to toe, would she dare make so fateful a call. ...

She had not forgotten her parents' phone number. She let it ring twice, then wished no one would answer, then thought she had best hang up. But her father's voice, mild and cracked, was already saying hello.

"Hello, *Dad*?" she said. The word sounded strange to her, lifted from a foreign tongue she had spoken only as a child.

The response was silence; then the weak voice continued: "R-Rosie?"

"It's me, Dad, yes. Are you okay?"

"I'm fine. Where you callin' from?"

"Montana. I'm free, Dad. They let me out. The law here ... is different."

"You're free? ... Meghan, it's Rosie. Meghan ..."

"That's okay. I'll talk to you, Dad. Did you get my letters from Idaho?"

"From Idaho? No, not one."

"No?..." The pain closed Rosie's throat. "Well," she said, trying to sound unmoved, "I guess that's why I didn't get any from you."

"What is it you want, Rosie?"

"What do I want?"

"Your mother ... can't speak to you right now."

"Please tell Mom I'm sorry for all the ..." She reached frantically for something to say. "Tell her I have a baby."

"You have a baby?"

"A new-born, healthy, bouncing baby."

"Are you married?"

"No. I had it done in the hospital. I just wanted one on my own."

"It's not easy, you know, being a single mother."

"I know that, Dad. But I can handle it. I thought we'd stop off and see you guys when we hit New York."

"Did you hear that, Meghan? Rosie has a ..."

"Thought we could stay with you a couple of days till I--"

"Meghan? Did you hear that?..."

"Dad, do you have my number? Record my number, okay?"

"Is it a boy or a girl, Rosie? What's it's name?"

"I haven't picked a name yet, Dad. I thought you and Mom would like to--"

"Did you say it was a girl, Rosie?"

"Dad, I thought I'd show up and surprise you."

"I have your number, Rosie. Meghan, don't--"

The wristphone went dead. Rosie could visualize the fight they were having. She ordered more chocolate.

- 23 -

The contractions started around four a.m. The discomfort was nothing compared to the exhilaration. Rosie clapped her hands to her hard round stomach and imagined she was at the beginning of a rollercoaster ride that would get wilder and wilder before coming to its happy ending. She slept fitfully during the initially long intervals between contractions, but at eight a.m. they were sharper and longer and were coming about ten minutes apart. She showered quickly, then called the cab service listed on the motel phone.

"We'll send one over in about fifteen minutes."

"Please hurry," said Rosie. "I don't want to give birth in the cab."

Five minutes later there was a knock at the door. "You called for a cab, Miss?"

"You're so early? How great!"

190

She had paid for the night upon registering. With her money stuffed in her sweater pocket and her phone-watch secured to her wrist, Rosie locked the door behind her and followed the driver to his vehicle. She felt disoriented but happy and paid little attention to the flash and sparkle of sunlit streets going by. She focused only on the mysterious movements within her, thinking only of the magical emergence of butterflies from pupae, and of beauty from ugliness, beauty that justified all she had gone through before.

The cab-ride lasted only three contractions, each about five minutes apart. The suburban hospital was surrounded by greenery. The cabbie parked at the maternity ward and gallantly supported her in.

"You called about this young woman?" said the white-frocked receptionist.

"Yes, ma'm."

Rosie reached into her pocket, but the cabbie waved at her in firm refusal and rapidly exited the lobby. At that very moment Rosie's water broke. A nearby nurse took her in hand and led her to a room where she helped her disrobe, clean up, and slip on a gown for the "Great Event," as she cheerfully called it. Rosie insisted on wearing her wristphone and keeping tight hold on her cardigan.

"Okay," said the stout, businesslike nurse. "Check your watch. When your contractions are one and a half minutes apart, press this buzzer, and we'll do the rest. Are you comfortable? Here, I'll turn on the 3V."

"Why do I need my legs strapped?" she asked the same no-nonsense nurse. She wanted to add, That's how they do things in the Compound, not out here in the civilized world! But she kept the thought to herself.

"Because that's what your obstetrical team has ordered, young lady. And I'm also ordered to administer this sedative." The nurse advanced from a nearby cart with gauze and a syringe in hand.

"I will *not* be sedated!" cried Rosie.

Looking at her in amazement, the nurse backed off. "Have it your way, Miss. I only get paid a salary."

"I want to feel everything, pain, whatever!" Suddenly, even as she spoke, she felt herself bearing down, pushing out a great burden, down, down, out. ... She imagined the wings of a butterfly pushing out from its

191

weakening cocoon. *Apples fell ripe to the ground. Hands lopped bunches of fat, purple grapes off the vine.*

Within seconds another nurse entered the room. Each of them grabbed one of her arms and held tight. "Don't fight! Doctor's orders," said the first nurse.

"It's coming, I feel it coming!" Rosie shouted.

And when the doctors barged into the room, she tried with all her remaining strength to hurl away the nurses whose arms were locked around hers. She screamed in terror, but her arms and legs were restrained as if in vises.

"Try to relax. We are not going to hurt you," said Dr. Schwengel, barely audible above Rosie's shrieks.

"You're doing fine," said Dr. Stevens, lifting Rosie's gown back over her knees. "Go on, shout some more. You're making it happen faster."

- 24 -

"How's it look?" said Dr. Schwengel.

"Perfect. Head first," said Dr. Stevens.

"I'm not going back! I'm not!" screamed Rosie above her pain.

"Of course you're not," said Stevens. "I promised you, remember?"

She looked over her shoulders and tried to make eye contact with the Amazons stationed behind her. "It's mine!" cried Rosie into ice-blue eyes. "*Please* don't let them ..."

"She's carried beautifully!" exulted Dr. Stevens. "This one's healthy as a horse."

"Full size, wouldn't you say?" said Schwengel.

"Damn near close to two pounds, and kicking!"

"These will survive. Definitely," mumbled Schwengel.

"Best damn surrogate we've had in three years!" exclaimed Stevens.

"Show me my baby! Show me!" Rosie demanded.

"Stop shouting, and try to control your breathing," advised one of the relentless pair attached to her arms. Once more Rosie felt an enormous contraction, her whole insides squeezing outward.

"Let me see!" she screamed, her contractions continuing, the rollercoaster ride unending.

"Number three, over and out!" said Stevens, his whole face wrinkled into an idiotic smile. His plastic-gloved, blood-covered fingers raised to his lips, he threw Rosie a kiss.

"Rosie, if the others were as fruitful as you ..." Schwengel said wistfully.

"You can't have them all! You *can't*, you bastards."

"Don't make things harder for yourself, little Rosie," said Stevens.

"The fruit of my own labor, and you won't let me *see* them, you shitbag?" She jerked her head forward but could see nothing under the gown stretched over her knees.

Schwengel nudged Stevens with an elbow and nodded. Stevens gave Rosie a long, searching look. As she stared defiantly back, he raised one of the squirming infants into view. It had long legs and was covered with fine, dark hair right down to its paws.

Rosie opened her mouth. A stifled cry was all that came out as her tongue stuck to her palate.

"He's as close to a perfect little Arctodus simus as we've come," said Stevens, tickling the cub's muzzle. When he put a finger to the cub's mouth, it started aggressively sucking.

"Feeding time," said Schwengel, removing baby-bottles from a case he'd carried in.

Rosie screamed and kept on screaming till the assistant behind her slapped her across the face.

- 25 -

"You can see why we couldn't let you too far out of range, now, can't you?" said Stevens.

"You said I was free, *free* ..." Her voice was hoarse, but her glance was unwavering. She made eye contact with Stevens. Anger filled her swollen breasts as if with poisoned milk. "But you knew, you piece of shit, exactly where I was and when I would give b--"

Stevens raised what looked like a little gold button between bloody thumb and forefinger. "You have this little gizmo to thank," he said. "Without a uterine implant we wouldn't have known where to find you."

"It also controlled your hormone balance," said Schwengel.

"And finally, it induced your contractions," added Stevens.

"Swallow it," said Rosie, "so I'll know where to find you in hell."

The doctors exchanged glances and chuckled. "Got some repair work to do on you, Rosie," said Stevens. "You're going to be perfectly fine."

She felt little pain as he sewed her up. She felt little of anything.

"We've lost very few of you volunteers," said Schwengel.

"Volunteers?"

Schwengel's face reddened. "You ought to feel proud, little Rosie. You're an exceptionally strong young woman."

"Feel proud, Rosie!" Stevens echoed. "Feel proud to be serving a higher purpose, like all the rest of us here."

Rosie burst into tears, hating herself instantly for blubbering. She knew what Pride was: something that everyone took from you at every opportunity they got.

"You're our best surrogate ever," said Schwengel.

"Rosie," said Stevens, "we could put you up ... in some comfortable apartment somewhere ... pay your living expenses ... it wouldn't be much, but if you'd like to work for us again--"

Rosie tried spitting but her mouth was too dry.

Schwengel waited till her breathing returned to normal. "You can release her arms now," he said. The nurses did as ordered, and Rosie covered her face with her hands. With no transition, the nurses wheeled her into an adjoining room. There they unshackled her legs. The room was sunny and curtained, done up in homey pastels.

"The regular hospital staff will take charge of you from here," said the first nurse she had dealt with.

"You can go as soon as you feel strong enough," said the other. "And don't worry about the bill. Everything's been paid for."

They advised her to drink what was on her tray. Rosie could not muster the strength to curse them. Abruptly, and without goodbyes, they left her to herself.

As soon as they had locked the door behind them, Rosie heard the beep of her wristphone. She let it ring until a telco voice invited the caller to leave a message.

"Rosie," said the caller, "this is your father. Your mother and I have talked." Rosie heard unrestrained sobbing in the background. "We never did throw out the nursery stuff, you know, that we got for, uh ... We look forward to seeing you and our new granddaughter, Rosie. Your mother

194

says ... be well." She heard the rhythm of hysterical sobbing long after her father had hung up.

Examining her tray, she lifted the plastic cup with the straw in it. A card lay underneath the cup. Beside the card lay two colorful brochures, one entitled "Breast-Feeding," the other "Bonding." She picked up the card--Dr. Stevens's calling card. She crushed it in her fist. Then she held it to her aching breast.

About Daniel Pearlman:

*Dan Pearlman's fiction has appeared in magazines such as **The Florida Review, Spectrum, New England Review, Quarterly West, The MacGuffin**, and anthologies such as **Semiotext(e), Synergy, Simulations, The Year's Best Fantastic Fiction** (1996), **Going Postal** (1998), **Imaginings** (Pocket Books, 2003), and **XX Eccentric** (MSR Pub. Co., 2009). His books of fiction to date are **The Final Dream & Other Fictions** (Permeable Press, 1995); a novel, **Black Flames** (White Pine Press, 1997); a second collection, **The Best-Known Man in the World & Other Misfits** (Aardwolf Press, 2001); and a second novel, **Memini** (Prime Books, 2003). Forthcoming: **Brain & Breakfast**, a paperback novella (Sam's Dot Publishing, 2011).*

Enslavement
by Nicholas Conley

ONE

Delilah King, 17 years old, had cut too deep this time.

She couldn't breathe. Little beads of sweat indicated her mixture of satisfaction and disgust. She dropped her razorblade and cradled her slashed wrist like a wounded soldier.

There wasn't much pain. Three years of cutting had left more scar tissue than flesh on her wrists. Pain was never the point, anyway, though there was something so satisfying about it. It was a release, an escape from the conflicted feelings waging war in her mind.

She peeked out her bedroom door to make sure her parents were asleep. Content, she sat down on her carpet, as standing up at this point made her feel far too lightheaded. She clenched the injured wrist with her free hand, putting pressure on it and keeping it stable.

The waterfall didn't stop pouring and Delilah realized she had never bled this much; it was as though she'd finally struck some reservoir of blood that had eluded her before. Her fingers were so soaked in the stuff that it actually settled in the pores and made her skin look dyed, the way it does in horror movies. She carefully released her hand.

Immediately, the blood started flowing out like a waterfall. It was dark, almost black. Her hand was going white.

She started crying, just as she'd always cried when she got hurt as a kid. It seemed like a bad joke, given her present state of mind. She hadn't even cried when her uncle raped her three years ago. As the blood continued flowing with seemingly no end in sight, she understood that kids don't cry because of the pain. They cry because they don't understand the pain and they're scared of what could happen to them.

"Oh God, God, God…" she whispered to herself, trying to keep herself from going into shock.

Delilah was becoming frantic. It should've stopped bleeding by now. She couldn't risk waking up her parents or calling the hospital; she'd spent the last three years wearing long sleeves every day to hide the fact that she was a cutter. Her parents would blame themselves and she didn't want that. It wasn't their fault.

Her carpet was soaked in blood. She'd have to find a way to cover that up later. Her school papers were red, as was the arm of the teddy bear she'd had since she was a little girl.

She thought about that little girl for a moment. Cute girl with little brown pigtails, shy but friendly. How horrified would that girl be if she could see the seventeen year old masochist she'd grow up to become?

She ducked under her bed and pulled out the roll of paper towels that she kept underneath. She couldn't feel her hand anymore. Hurriedly, she wrapped her wrist up several dozen times and watched in horror as the blood soaked right through. Not tight enough. She wrapped it up again.

Finally, it halted; at least for now. She continued to grip it tightly.

Delilah rested on her bed again, laying her cold, lifeless hand on her lap. The wound felt itchy. Why had she cut so deeply?

She knew why. The voice had told her to. She'd tried to explain that to her best friend Chelsea before and she'd smugly told her that she might be schizophrenic, but she knew that she wasn't. It wasn't that she was hearing imaginary voices. It was just the one voice; a voice she thought of as the craving, or the bloodlust.

It started out quietly, like it always did. It'd first hit her this morning, while she was peeling off an old scab. "Maybe just a little cut?" it had asked her, like a nudge to the shoulder.

It grew throughout the day. In school, it was relentless. She'd wanted to roll up her long sleeves and expose her scars to the world, right there in class. She'd felt a sick, almost artistic desire to cut a shape into the skin of her wrists and peel off all of the skin inside that shape.

The thought made her nauseous, but it was too compelling to ignore. Finally, that night, she'd given in. She'd cut her wrist open and the sense of release had been amazing, but it wasn't enough. It was never enough. She'd wanted more, like she always did. The release of cutting was like an orgasm. Sometimes, it was even more powerful than that.

Delilah looked down at her arms and felt disgusted. With the rows of scars, X-shapes and little scrawled curse words, they looked more like pieces of chewed up, rotted sausage than arms.

198

She cried again, but the tears held no emotion. It was as if the cutting and the sudden burst of terror in its aftermath had drained all that from her. She was numb to the world, just as she had wanted to be. After all, a blank slate couldn't feel pain; it didn't have to remember the past or relive it, over and over again.

Delilah looked out her bedroom window at the streets of Manhattan Beach, California. When she was a girl, she'd loved all the lights, the tiled blue crosswalks and the beach. God, she used to love the beach, especially with her father and uncle, back when things were simple. Or, well, when they seemed simple. Now, she looked at the beach in the same curious but disinterested way that one watches a dull movie.

While she was looking, a black pickup truck pulled up to the side of the road and parked. This was nothing unusual; most people in the area were stuck using street parking, but she'd never seen this truck before. It was covered in mud, as if it'd just driven across the country. The windows were tinted, obscuring the face of the driver.

Even though she'd never seen the truck, there was something familiar about it. Something that made her deadened mind shudder, as if there was a hidden memory it was trying to cover up. She stared at the truck for a moment until the feeling passed.

Delilah closed her eyes. She was tired. She'd lost a lot of blood that night and she'd done a lot of crying. Sleep would come easily.

As Delilah passed out, the shady man in the pickup truck stepped out of the car.

TWO

The same night, Tyrell Freeman stood outside the Seashell Bar in Santa Monica, watching the cars zoom by. He blew his nose. He was already coming down from his high.

He chuckled quietly to himself. That was the downside about cocaine, wasn't it? It perked you up, but only for an hour. Shit, these days he was lucky if it lasted more than half an hour.

After the high, of course, came the low. The deep, depressing low, as if that white powder that you call your savior has just dropped you off a bottomless cliff. These were the moments that a man either allowed himself to become an addict or fought against it.

ENSLAVEMENT

Back when he was still in med school, Tyrell had fought against it tooth and nail; or, at least, he'd fought against admitting that he was addicted. Coke was been a little pick-me-up when he was studying late at night. The same thing as downing a couple of caffeine pills, nothing more. From an early age, he'd been passionate about helping people and saving lives. His dream was to one day be the best damn doctor he could be and nothing was going to get in the way of that.

Not until the day his little sister died.

He was tired of waiting. He took a seat on the bench outside the bar, and rested his head in his hands. His dealer should've been there by now.

Tyrell Freeman was a tall man. He was young, but the deep lines carved into his face made him look older. He was clean cut and always well-dressed. He did anything he could to keep from looking like a drug addict.

As he sat there, his emotions sank lower and lower, as if caught in a dark whirlpool. He hated to admit his dependency, but he needed his fix. The longer he had to wait, the worse his mood became.

"Tyrell!" a voice said jovially, "It's been too long, my friend! Almost a week now, eh?"

Tyrell looked up anxiously, but it wasn't his dealer. It was Jackson Ubel, or as Tyrell's girlfriend Rita called him, "the local crackpot." Jackson sat down next to him with a giant grin on his face.

Jackson was broad-shouldered. His thick beard and messy long hair had a distinctive salt and pepper coloration. He wore a bright, New England-style orange vest every day over a grey hoodie, no matter what the weather. Tyrell sometimes wondered if Jackson was homeless, but didn't want to ask.

"Hello, Jackson."

Tyrell was like a ticking time bomb of nervous energy, but he bit his tongue. He had to admit, he'd always liked Jackson a great deal; the man's insanely over-the-top conspiracy theories made for interesting conversation, if nothing else. In his current state of mind, though, he was in no mood for conversation.

"So what have you been up to lately?" Jackson asked, "Have you been watching the news carefully, as I told you to?"

"What?" Tyrell mumbled, "News, uh…"

"Ah, Tyrell, you shouldn't take these things so lightly. The Illuminati are always leaving clues about their motives, in all forms of media. I'd hate to see you drown with the rest of the plebeians out there."

Jackson stared at him with an unblinking conviction in his blue eyes. He was completely serious. Though Jackson seemed easygoing on the surface and he was always pretty calm, the truth was that he was an opinionated man of strong, aggressive emotions. Tyrell had learned from many long nights at the bar that Jackson would argue with you all night, confidently smiling the entire time, until you finally either agreed with him or gave up.

He was getting jittery, and he started worrying that his dealer might've stood him up again. He tried to think of a response.

"I just don't really buy it," Tyrell said cautiously, "This whole idea you have about that secret society controlling all of us, it's just--"

"Idea?" Jackson asked, with a decidedly sly smile.

"Yeah?"

"It's not an idea, my friend. Tyrell, you have to realize that. The existence of the Illuminati is a fact! A guaranteed, 100 percent proven fact! This news you choose to listen to, all these government ideas, it's all garbage. I suppose you even buy into that bullshit that the Earth is round?"

"That's bullshit too, now?"

Jackson laughed and shook his head. The strangest thing about Jackson was that he was never manic. He wasn't some drug-addled old hippy; he acted like he knew exactly what he was talking about.

"Oh, please. What makes you think the Earth is round? Because you were always been told that in school? Because you've seen doctored photographs? This planet is clearly a flat disc. Just look around you, it's so obvious that I can't believe the way the government has pulled the wool over people's eyes for so long. They'll do anything, they really will. Just like this whole technological hypnosis thing they're doing now."

"Technological hypnosis?" Tyrell asked.

"You haven't heard about that?"

"I guess not."

"Ah, because it's not on the news! You have to examine the underground news reels more. Here, this is the idea. You remember the whole controversy that happened with our supposedly-elected government officials conducting illegal torture on prisoners, right?"

"Yeah, I remember that."

"Cover-up!"

"It was?"

"Absolutely. The government leaked that information, in order to hide their real objective. Behind the scenes, they were creating a new way of gaining information from prisoners and potential terrorists."

"And by that, you mean this whole, uh, what did you call it? Technological hypnosis? Well, goddamn."

"I'd rather you not use the term 'goddamn' when you're around me, if it's all the same to you. Anyway, you are correct. Technological hypnosis is only the layman's term for it of course, but let me put it this way. Our government now has the ability to plug people's brains into a hard drive and stick them into an illusion from which they can't escape, unless they're disconnected. There's only one downside."

"What's that?"

"From what I can gather from my sources, any injury that is afflicted on the subject who is trapped in the illusion, whether it's mental, emotional or physical, is carried over to them in real life. So if you were stabbed in the illusion, your body reacts as if it was actually stabbed and causes you to die in the same way. If you were hit by lightning in the illusion, your body basically electrocutes itself."

"Crazy stuff."

"You think that's crazy? I've seen worse. I've seen Illuminati agents in New Mexico, wearing long robes and chanting in Latin. In New York City, I once talked to a man covered head to toe in bandages and a trench coat who called himself Gleuvinn. Just last week, I saw a disguised cyborg walking down the Redondo Beach pier. There's no such thing as 'crazy' in this world, Tyrell."

Tyrell shook his head. He'd had about enough of this conversation. It was growing more ridiculous by the second, and his mood was already far too irritable.

"Sounds a little too Freddy Kreuger for me. Hey, man, I hate to be rude but I'm waiting for someone here--"

"Ah," Jackson said, "Out of drugs today, huh? You getting a delivery from Toby?"

"Yeah, I mean, well," Tyrell stammered, "How did you know?"

"C'mon, c'mon. You're always twitchy, always blowing your nose and looking around nervously. I know the type. The nice clothes don't fool me."

Tyrell's self-esteem dropped into his stomach and melted like a bouillon cube. Jackson stood up to leave. Tyrell stopped him and shook Jackson's hand with a grim smile.

"See you around, Jackson."

"You too, my friend, you too. Tell Toby I said hi, by the way. I've gotten some blow from him before. Nasty stuff, glad I stopped. Though hey, if you like it--"

"Not sure if 'like' is the right word. Later."

Jackson walked around the corner and disappeared, to continue his rants at another location. His words shot through Tyrell's skull like a bullet. Was it really getting that bad? He noticed that he was unconsciously biting his fingernails and quickly shoved his hands underneath him.

Eventually, Toby arrived, wearing a heavy black coat and a baseball cap. He didn't offer any excuse for his lateness and Tyrell didn't ask. They made the transaction. Tyrell stuffed the bag of coke in his pocket and started walking home.

As soon as he found a secluded spot in a deserted parking lot, Tyrell took out his bag. He inspected it. He told himself he was doing this to make sure it was genuine. Really, he just wanted to cut it up and do a couple of lines right there on the asphalt.

It was easy to blame the drug and pretend that it wasn't his fault. But Tyrell was a doctor and knew all there was to know about physical dependency. He'd simply been arrogant enough to think he could dive back into coke as a refuge from his sister's death and not get addicted. It was his fault and his alone. Not that he really was an addict, though. No, of course not.

In a sick sense, though, he also blamed his sister. He'd always tried to be there for Tiffany. He'd tried to set an example, to help her with her low sense of self-worth. In the end, he'd even tried to save her life, all for nothing.

The night that she committed suicide was still a vivid memory. Most women who commit suicide do so in the most non-violent and cleanest method possible, but Tiffany had always been different. When she put her mind to something, she didn't hesitate and didn't hold back. He remembered the way she'd wandered into the living room in front of him, their parents and Rita. She'd gouged her throat open. Blood was gushing out.

Despite all the injuries he'd seen in his line of work, Tyrell had never become desensitized to the sight of blood. It was something he took pride in; he imagined one day being recognized as the "people's doctor," because of his compassion and ability to work through that compassion for the good of others. But the sight of that gash in his little sister's throat was more than he could deal with.

He'd done everything he could but the damage was severe. Conventional first aid techniques did nothing except slow the bleeding. Still he tried, knowing that the ambulance would never get there fast enough. By the time it arrived, Tiffany was dead.

His parents went silent at the announcement, too horrified to even cry. They'd never suspected it. Rita tried to comfort him and make him believe he'd done everything he could. But all that mattered to him was that he'd been too late. He was supposed to be a fucking doctor, for crying out loud, and when his own sister needed him the most, he'd failed.

From that point forward, he'd let his old habits take over. Soon enough, he wasn't able to get through the day without at least a couple of lines. His usage got more and more frequent, to the point where he had to leave his apartment and move in with Rita because of how much money he was tossing away. He hated that; he'd wanted the day when they moved in together to be a sign of achievement, not a whimpering plea of desperation. In the end, he'd even had to drop out of med school, leaving behind his lifelong dream.

Nobody knew about the coke. At least, he hid it the best he could. Nobody knew why he'd fallen so low, but everyone was angry at him for it. They didn't understand. They couldn't understand. When he was high, he didn't have to think about anything. As soon as he started coming down, though...

As soon as he started coming down, all he could think about was the way Tiffany's eyes had opened one last time, right before she died. They had bugged out, as she choked on the blood in her throat. In his little sister's eyes, he could see everything; he could see the terror in them, as if someone else had plunged the blade into her neck. She was silently begging him to save her. Then they went blank. Unfocused. Dead. The image of those dead eyes haunted him in his sleep; his skin crawled at the realization that despite the fact that they were open, they weren't looking at him. They weren't looking at anything.

Tyrell pulled his mind away from the dark memories. He looked around the abandoned parking lot. Thinking better of his previous idea, he stuffed the bag of coke back in his pocket.

As soon as he did so, a black pickup truck pulled into the parking lot. The truck entered slowly, its headlights piercing through the darkness like a dagger. It pulled into a parking place and stopped. It was waiting.

Tyrell didn't want to find out what it was waiting for. He'd lived in Los Angeles his entire life and he knew damn well when things were getting too sketchy. He left the scene and started walking back home.

He never realized that the truck was following him.

THREE

David Danelo rolled over in bed. His heartbeat slowly steadied. The woman next to him curled around him lovingly. She walked her fingertips up the dip in his chest. Though the room was dark, the city lights outside illuminated it enough to reveal her smile.

He felt satisfied. Already, though, that satisfaction was drifting away like a gentle breeze. He wanted more.

David ran his fingers through her hair. He shuddered as a lock of hair got snagged on his wedding ring. Guilt pricked his heart like a needle. He pulled away and sat up in bed.

"I'm sorry," he said.

"Don't be," she replied, "You were amazing, man. So...aggressive. So on top of things."

"Thanks. Though you saying that is pretty much the same deal as a pizza boy saying the pizza is good, isn't it?" David said with a self-deprecating smile.

"True," she replied.

"Hey," he said with a shrug, "Money is money. Makes it all go 'round, blah blah blah."

The prostitute, Serena, began to stoke David's naked back. It was fake affection, though after being with Serena so many times in the past he was starting to wonder. After you had sex with anyone enough times, the lines started to blur. Of course, he was blowing so much money on her that he'd actually convinced her to come to his house this time, no small feat in her line of business.

He felt his wedding ring again with a sigh. So this was the way he rewarded Kim for going on vacation with the kids, huh? Hey Kim, it's me, David, your husband. Oh, by the way, while you were on vacation for the week, I had sex with two…no, now it's three different prostitutes.

"Well," David spoke, "Let me go get your money. It's okay if I pay you in pennies, right?"

"What?" Serena asked, with a puzzled look on her face.

"You need it in dimes? Damn, that's going to be hard. No, I'm kidding. Sorta."

David got out of bed and stretched. Instantly, he felt a compulsion to clean himself from the act he'd just performed. Everything about it was suddenly revolting. He walked to the bathroom.

"You keep your money in there?" Serena asked.

"Doesn't everyone?" David replied casually.

He shut the door behind him. He washed himself and then splashed cold water on his face. He'd finished only minutes ago, but despite his disgust, he already felt a horrible craving to go back out there and have sex with Serena again. There was an unsatisfied urge there, screaming out at him. The only thing keeping him from doing it was his wedding ring, now that he'd remembered it.

He sneered miserably at his face in the mirror. Yeah, as if saying no at this point redeemed his past mistakes. As much as he tried to wash the guilt away in bleak humor, it still nibbled away at his character.

David looked at the messy bathroom counter. Hastily, he scrambled to arrange the bar of soap, hairspray, shaving cream and razor in a perfectly neat arrangement, from tallest to smallest. Once he was finished, he neatly blew the dust off the top of the hairspray. It made no logical sense for a construction worker like him to be so obsessive about such things, but he couldn't help it.

As he moved toward the door, he had a strange sensation; a desire, no, a <u>need</u> to look out the window. He shrugged and looked out.

There was nothing unusual going on outside. Maybe the strangest thing was the black pickup truck that was pulling up to the side of the road. He wasn't sure why the pickup truck stuck with him. It was as if something was out of place about it. It didn't belong, as if it were a black and white character inserted into a color movie.

Or, well, it might just be that something as rugged as a pickup truck was a rare sight in this neighborhood of shiny new BMWs and Hondas. David left the bathroom.

"She's a beautiful woman, you know," Serena said.

Serena was sitting upright in bed now, zipping up her leather skirt. David pulled her money out of his pants on the ground and handed it to her.

"Who?" he asked.

"Y'know, your wife."

Serena pointed at the photo on the side of the bed. It was a photo of David and Kim together at the Grand Canyon a few years ago. Kim was in his arms, smiling. The surreal nature of a prostitute looking at the photo made David feel sick to his stomach. He sucked it all in.

"Actually, that's me and my brother in the photo. He might look like a beautiful woman but he's really a rugged guy, works at a coal mine."

"No, really," Serena said, "She's got a really gorgeous Latina look to her."

David took a deep breath. He felt more nauseous by the second. For once, he had trouble forming words.

"I...well, thanks. I think so too."

David walked over and laid the picture face down. He didn't want her to look at it anymore. He didn't want to look at it himself.

ENSLAVEMENT

"You sure you don't want any more time?" Selena said, biting her lip, "It's still early. I mean, we haven't done that much tonight compared to what we usually do. It could be even more fun now. I know your body better every time we do it."

David looked at Selena's figure. She was dressed now, which somehow made her even more appealing. Her bruised legs were still exposed. He remembered the way her naked body had looked a few minutes ago. He remembered the way it had felt against his. But all he could think about was that photo. Instead of picturing Serena naked, he was picturing Kim naked.

"No," he said, shaking his head, "No. I...I want to. But I can't."

"Okay."

Serena got up from the bed. As if it were an invitation for him to sit down, David took her place. He looked up at her longingly.

"Well--" he started.

"If we're off the clock, can I ask you a personal question?" Serena asked.

"Shoot."

"You sure?" she asked.

"No. But hey, we've come this far in the conversation. You might as well ask, and I might as well answer."

"I do this with a lot of married men. I guess that's obvious, but still. But that's what confuses me about you. Most of the other men take off their wedding rings."

David felt his ring again. He felt a strange resentment towards it. He tried to speak, then stopped. It was bad enough judging himself; it only made him feel worse when others did it too.

"I love her," he answered.

"Then why are you doing this? I mean, I know I shouldn't ask that, I mean shit, it practically goes against my whole code of work but...why? You have kids too, right?"

"Two little boys. William and Teddy," David said with a wistful smile.

"I just--"

"I don't know," he said.

"It's like..." she said hesitantly, "You love your wife, your kids. Maybe it isn't working out but, I mean, you don't even need prostitutes.

208

You're such a nice guy, and such a great looking guy, much better looking than all the other guys I see regularly. You're really in shape for someone who's...how old are you, 27?"

"35," David replied.

"35! See, that's what I mean. You have this young personality, I mean, all the band posters up on your walls here make it look like a teenager's room, which is cool, shows you still have a young spirit even though you're a dad, y'know? You could find someone else easily. What's the reason behind it all? Why do you call me up so often? Why do you have that huge pile of porn magazines under the bed?"

David blushed at the thought of her seeing his porn collection. He then looked around at all the band posters up on his wall. A teenager's room?

"I...I don't know. Trust me, I wish I did."

Serena sighed.

"Good luck to you, David. Thanks for the night."

"You too."

David guided her out of the apartment wordlessly. As soon as she was gone, he ran back to bed and picked up the photo of himself and Kim. He looked at it with love. He did love her. He did, he really did. There was nothing wrong with her.

Then he looked down at all the porn magazines on the floor, the pile that she'd always screamed at him about. The desire ached within him. He looked back at Kim's photo, as if pleading for it to bring the same desire out. It didn't. David collapsed his head into his hands.

Just outside the apartment, the pickup truck was still. The driver sat motionlessly, patiently waiting for David to fall asleep. It wouldn't be long now.

FOUR

Eugene L. Krank looked at Dr. Lennox through his horn-rimmed glasses with an earnest expression. The doctor sighed, took his pulse again and shrugged exasperatedly.

"I'm sorry Eugene, but it looks like, well...you're perfectly healthy."

"What? What are you talking about?" Eugene asked in a worried, frenetic voice.

"You're fine," the doctor stated.

"There's no way. I could feel my stomach churning, this stabbing pain in my side that was--"

"Your symptoms are psychosomatic, Eugene."

"Wait. Why did you say that you were sorry?"

"I'm sorry because it seems like you want something to be wrong with you. I mean, to be frank with you, you come here into the emergency room late at night at least twice a month now. You're taking time away from patients that really need help and--"

"You don't understand," Eugene muttered, "Everyone says that. You don't know the amount of different vitamins and medications I have to take every freakin' day just to keep myself healthy."

Dr. Lennox took off his gloves. He was looking for an excuse to leave the room; and he dared to call himself a doctor. They all called themselves doctors, but they could never figure out what was wrong with him, could they? A bunch of overpaid, over-educated imbeciles, that's all they were.

"Have you always been like this?" Dr. Lennox asked, half-heartedly.

"No. Only since I was in the accident that did this to me," Eugene said, pointing to the scarred side of his face.

Eugene was never afraid to point out his scars. He couldn't walk down a sidewalk without people staring at them, so he might as well make a show of it.

The scars had been the first blow to Eugene's ego after the accident. After that, his entire body seemed to systematically break down, as if the open wounds had let in an entire colony of viruses. He had constant aches and pains, severe gastro-intestinal problems and every time he got excited, he felt intense heart palpitations. He had become increasingly obsessive compulsive, to the point where he was petrified by the notion of touching a door handle without a tissue in his hand, or at least spraying it down first with hand sanitizer.

"The scars really aren't that bad," Dr. Lennox said, "I mean sure, they're noticeable, but not disfiguring. It's from a car accident, right? A few years ago?"

"Yes, it was a couple of years ago. I was pulling onto the interstate when some hit-and-run driver smashed into me from my blind spot. If I could go back to that time and change things, somehow keep myself from

210

getting so sick, I swear…what does it matter, though? None of you people even believe that I'm sick in the first place."

"You're not sick, Eugene. I'm pretty sure you're just a hypochondriac, obsessively over-medicating yourself out of some irrational fear that you're sick. As an emergency room doctor, I can say for a fact that you're the healthiest person I regularly treat."

"Very funny," Eugene replied pithily.

He walked out of the room. As he did so, Dr. Lennox smiled and gave him a friendly pat on the back. Eugene appreciated the doctor's sense of humor; he knew a man with his health problems must be a hassle to put up with. Still, he was aggravated that his gastro-intestinal symptoms were apparently so impossible to detect.

Eugene popped a couple vitamins and left the hospital, taking the back roads so as to avoid other cars. He already hated trying to drive on the crowded streets of LA with his bad eyesight, and driving on the living nightmare of traffic known as the 405 made it worse. Every time a car pulled out in front of him or zipped past him on the fast lane, his palpitations started up again.

He drove home, parked his truck in the garage and went to sleep.

FIVE

Delilah King opened her eyes. At first, she thought she was dreaming.

She was lying on the cold floor of a moving subway train, with no exit doors. The fluorescent lights of the train were dim, much like the milk-colored foggy sky outside the windows. The blue plastic seats were covered in obscene graffiti.

Delilah closed her eyes again, in disbelief. This had to be a nightmare. It had to be. She reopened them and was seized by the reality of the moment. Goose bumps popped up on her flesh.

She gasped. Where was she, New York? Oh God, oh God, oh God. She tried to calm down; if she'd been kidnapped in the middle of the night, she had to get a hold of herself and figure out how to handle the situation rationally.

She tried to stand up only to discover that her wrists were tied to the floor with barbed wire. When she yanked at the wire, the barbs cut into her tender, scarred flesh.

She panicked.

"Help me!" she screamed, "Please, somebody help! HELP! What's going on here?!"

There was no answer, except for the rumbling of the train. One of the dim lights fizzled out. The train compartment became even darker.

"HELP!"

Delilah desperately tried to pull herself loose from her barbed wire restraints. The barbs pushed into the skin, breaking through the surface. Delilah yanked her wrist away desperately and the enormous scab from last night's cut popped open.

"Fuck," she whispered.

The cut was gushing blood again, though not as badly as it'd done the night before. Delilah was gripped by a horrible feeling of helplessness; the same feeling she'd had during the rape. Normally, cutting had been a way to take control of her pain. It'd helped her take back control of her own body. Here, she had no control.

No. She couldn't let it be this way. She pulled both hands toward herself with one ferocious thrust. The barbs cut deeply into her skin, spilling her blood all over the floor. The wires dug in even tighter; she couldn't pull free.

Delilah gritted her teeth. If there was one thing in this world that she knew how to handle, it was pain. She just had to be smart about this. She wasn't strong enough to break wire.

She examined her restraints. Maybe, just maybe, she could twist her hands free.

She closed her eyes and started slowly. As she did so, the barbs tore in even deeper. She winced in pain. By the end of this, she'd be lucky to have anything left on her wrists but bone. She kept sliding her hands through until finally, they were free.

Delilah jumped to her feet. Immediately, she felt dizzy and nearly fell down. She looked down at her massacred wrists. She'd lost an enormous amount of blood and it still hadn't clotted.

She stumbled into one of the seats. Her head was spinning. She knew that losing this much blood wasn't healthy, and if she didn't find some way to stop the bleeding then she'd pass out soon. She looked out the window of the train as if it had answers, but all she could see was a thick

212

covering of mist that obscured any kind of landscape. Los Angeles? New York? Fuck that, she could be in China, for all she knew.

There was a closed door separating this compartment of the train from the next. Delilah felt almost as scared of the door as she'd been of the barbed wire. There could be anything on the other side. It could be others like her just as easily as the people who kidnapped her.

It was a risk she had to take. She stood up and walked quickly toward the door. Too quickly; she collapsed onto the floor, her head spinning. She was shaking all over now. Her vision was blurred.

Delilah dragged herself across the door on her hands and knees. She reached up for the handle, threw it open and collapsed onto the ground again. She could hear voices. Excited voices. In terror, she started crawling backwards to get away.

"Hey!" a female voice cried out, "Look, it's another one!"

Delilah closed her eyes. She didn't want to see her captors. She didn't want her wrists tied up in the barbed wire again.

"Please, please, please, not the wires again," she whimpered.

She continued crawling backwards with her eyes closed. She crashed into one of the seats behind her and curled into a ball on the ground. She heard the sound of footsteps. They were coming for her now. Their voices were as out of focus as her hazy vision.

They were going to restrain her with the barbed wires again. They'd do it tighter this time. She knew it. She wasn't going to get out so easily.

Several hands grabbed her and lifted her onto the seat. Finally, she opened her eyes. In front of her were three concerned faces; a pale, bearded man in a grey hood and an orange vest, a skinny, gaunt-looking Italian woman and a tall black man with a very worried look in his warm brown eyes.

"You're not alone," the man with the brown eyes told her quietly.

The hooded man shook his head.

"We're all alone up here, Tyrell," he said, "and there's not a damn thing we can do about it."

SIX

As Tyrell took the girl's bleeding wrists into his hands, he couldn't help but notice the myriad of previous scars already decorating them. She was clearly a cutter. These new wounds, though, weren't from a razor blade. She'd gotten her skin caught in some kind of barbed wire.

"Let me see them," he told her with some determination, "I'm a doctor."

He wasn't sure why he felt the need to lie about his profession, but he quickly reasoned that it was so she'd feel more secure. The truth was that he was too insecure to admit that he was nothing more than a failed medical student.

"Really?" the girl whimpered.

"Yes."

She was dazed, barely conscious. The first thing he had to do was to stop the blood flow and bandage the wounds. Give her time to recover.

"Hey, I need a--what's your name again?" he asked the thin woman who had joined up with them a few compartments back.

"Jordan," she answered, "Jordan Romano."

"Jordan, give me your jacket."

Jordan complied and Tyrell immediately tore the jacket into strips. The makeshift bandage wasn't great, and it didn't do a hell of a lot to guarantee against potential infections. But it'd have to do.

"You're okay now," Tyrell told her softly, "We're your friends. Well, we are now that you've met us, anyway."

The girl strained to smile, her eyes closed. She was so young. She was just a girl, no more than maybe 16 or 17.

Tyrell felt immensely protective of her. Even though she looked nothing like Tiffany, she reminded him of her. She'd also been a cutter. As much as the thought of meeting some alternate version of Tiffany scared him, his instincts automatically kicked into big brother mode.

Thinking of Tiffany made him suddenly realize that being trapped on this train meant he didn't have any way to access his coke. The thought made him jump out the window in a mad panic. For the moment, he pushed it to the back of his mind. Staying calm would make all the difference here.

He took a seat next to her and both Jackson and Jordan sat across from them. Since Tyrell had woken up on this train a couple of hours ago, all he'd done was scramble around. It was time to take a rest.

"So there appears to be four of us now," Jackson said, "I wonder what the link is?"

"I'm just glad you and me are here together, Jackson," Tyrell said, "I mean, it's nice to see at least one familiar face."

"I feel the same, friend."

"Must be peachy," Jordan said with a wry smile, "I've sure as hell never seen either of you before."

"Hey, you never know," Tyrell replied.

He glanced over to the girl at his side. She was shivering, but slowly getting control of herself. The bandages seemed to be doing their job.

Jackson shook his head.

"There's no such thing as coincidences."

"You think this is some kind of setup?"

Jackson chortled cynically. He seemed a bit distressed but was trying not to show it.

"You think we all just accidentally went sleepwalking onto a train in the middle of nowhere?"

"Middle of fucking nowhere is right," Jordan said, crossing her arms and shivering in the cold, "I feel like I'm in that fucking Stephen King book with the living train. We're not even on ground. Look out the window. We're on some kind of monorail. Don't know about you guys, but I wasn't planning on going to some haunted theme park ride today."

The first person Tyrell had found after waking up was Jackson. The two of them had found Jordan Romano shortly afterwards. She had beautiful dark Italian skin and eyes, but her beauty was undermined by her bony, angular frame; she wasn't quite skeletal, but pretty close to it.

"Monorail," Tyrell repeated quietly, "I thought it was just a subway. Fuck."

"A subway with no exit or entrance doors?" she asked.

"What?"

"Look for yourself."

Tyrell noticed for the first time that there were, in fact, no exit doors. She was right. Aside from the doors between compartments, there was no way to get in or out of the train.

"How did they get us on here?" he asked.

ENSLAVEMENT

"Fuckin' A. Let me know if you figure it out. Then I can cheat off your paper for the test," Jordan replied, shrugging.

He looked at the mist outside the window. In the last few hours, he'd been so overwhelmed with horror at his surroundings he hadn't had a chance to think about just how dire the situation was. Despite his efforts to keep a clear head, his mind drifted back to coke. He wasn't quite <u>craving</u> it yet, but he was starting to tingle for it.

"We've been kidnapped," Jackson announced, "That's what's obvious to me. It's an Illuminati scheme. They're trying to test something on us. I knew I was revealing too much to people…"

"Kidnapped…" the girl with the slit wrists slurred.

Everyone looked at her. She still wasn't quite back. She was stirring, though. Coming out of shock.

"I can't figure out how they got me," Jordan said, "I was just fucking sleeping in my own damn bed. I'm a light sleeper, too."

"Me too," Tyrell agreed.

"You don't know what of techniques they can use on us!" Jackson cried out, "They've probably had all of our houses bugged for months now, just soaking in information. This has to be the government at work. I know that I'm the reason for all this, somehow. I know they're trying to target me."

"Holy shit," Jordan interrupted, "You're one of those guys, aren't you?"

"What guys?"

Tyrell managed a smirk; "Yep."

"What, one of the few people who have actually opened their eyes to the evil ways of our over-institutionalized planet?" Jackson sneered, "Oh, I do apologize for not being yet another plebian."

Jordan looked at Tyrell.

"You know this guy, right? Is he always this way?"

"Delilah…" the girl mumbled.

Tyrell looked at her. She lifted up her wrists and examined them, as if in disbelief that she still hadn't woken up from a nightmare. She looked at the group around her and shook her head.

"That's my name," she continued, "My name is Delilah. What am I doing here? What are…what are <u>we</u> doing here?"

Tyrell put his hand on her shoulder. He tried to manage a smile but couldn't. His message was far too negative.

"Delilah, I have no idea."

SEVEN

David Danelo woke up with a jolt. Realizing that he was on the cold floor of a moving train woke him up faster than any espresso drink could ever hope to.

He knew right away that it wasn't a dream but he still couldn't figure out what the fuck was going on. Apparently he wasn't in his "teenager's room" of a bedroom anymore. Had he been drinking the night before? Yeah, two beers, but that sure as hell wouldn't lead to him waking up in a strange place like this.

David pulled himself off the floor. His body was sore, as if he'd been thrown around while he was asleep. He examined his surroundings. It looked like a closed-off compartment of some kind of subway, the kind you'd never see in Cali.

"Hello?" he called out, "It'd be nice to know where the hell I am right now? Please?"

No answer.

David felt a cold breeze escape from the windows and realized that he was completely naked. He immediately crouched next to the seats, as if someone was watching. Well, fuck, just when things couldn't get worse. Wasn't the first time he'd woken up on the floor naked, though.

The room suddenly felt a lot colder than before. David realized that no one was watching him and looked at the misty horizon outside the windows. All right, this was getting way too weird.

He tried to put the pieces together. Somehow, he'd been kidnapped in the middle of the night and thrown on a train. Not to mention he'd gone to sleep in his clothes, so the same sicko had stripped him down too.

David searched the train compartment looking for clues, a key or any kind of hint. He wondered if he'd been put into some kind of torture trap, like the Saw movies. Maybe there was a tape recording that was about to start that would tell him he had 30 seconds to escape the train before a variety of exotic daggers spontaneously grew out of the walls and penetrated him in every orifice. Who knew?

217

Normally this idea would've made him smile, but not today.

David found that his clothes had been carefully rolled up in a ball under a seat, covered in a disgusting sticky substance. Fuck it; he'd just have to stomach it and put them on anyway. He dressed himself in the revolting garments, desperately trying not to puke the entire time. His steel-toe work boots were laid out right underneath.

It was time to move on. David looked at the doors on each side of the train compartment. He chose the door at the back; one door was as good as another.

The next compartment was also empty. There was something fishy about it. Could it be that…no, it couldn't be. Could it?

David went back to the last compartment and double-checked. Both compartments looked exactly the same. The seats. The posters. The graffiti. Everything.

He thought about this for a second and then slapped himself on the head. Of course they both looked the same. When did two compartments look any different? The graffiti probably wasn't <u>exactly</u> the same. He'd just have to keep moving.

He walked into the next compartment. Again, it looked the same. This time, he didn't let it bug him.

He walked into the next compartment, and then the next after that. They really did all look the same. It was like the doorways were just mirrors and he was continually stepping into the same room.

David started feeling like he was on a bad acid trip. He should've found the back of the train by now. It couldn't be that long. There was something wrong here. Was he going insane? He knew it couldn't be a dream. Dreams were hazy and unclear. While this whole situation had all the offbeat illogicality of a dream, it was far too real. Just to be sure, he pinched himself. Nope, it was real.

His head spinning, David looked around the compartment for something unique. There had to be some kind of blotch on the wall, some label, some bit of trash on the floor. The train was unrealistically clean. He imagined an old janitor muttering under his breath as he scrubbed the crevices in the wall with a toothbrush.

Finally, he noticed that one of the seats on the left had a small cut in it. He carefully marked the seat in his mind. If he could find a piece of paper somewhere, he'd have to draw out a map. This compartment would be labeled as "cut seat," the next one maybe something like "dirty window" and so on; then he'd know where the hell he was going. He opened the door to the next compartment.

The seat on the left had the same cut on it.

David panicked. If he knew that he was going insane, could he stop it somehow? Didn't people say that if you still had the ability to question your sanity, it meant you were sane? Fucking bullshit, that's all that was, because he was definitely going insane.

"Hello?" he called out again, "If this is some kind of joke, I'm not laughing. All right, all right, you've convinced me I'm a psycho. Ha ha ha, applause. Joke's over!"

There was no answer.

"Hello?" he tried again, "Please! Hello? Is anyone there? Anyone at all?"

The dim overhead lights started flickering, like the power was about to go out. The room became colder. Then, David got his reply.

He heard a deep, congested moan behind him, as if a whale was gagging on its own mucus. Then there was another moan; angrier, more threatening. David trembled.

He turned around.

EIGHT

Delilah felt okay again. Her wrists felt like they'd gone through a meat grinder, but otherwise she felt normal and healthy. Well, except for the fact the fact that she was still stuck on the train.

"All right, I think I've got an idea," the doctor (what was his name again? Tyrone? Tyrell?) announced.

"Well, an idea would be a wonderful thing right now," Jackson replied.

"We need to get to the front of the train. If we can find the driver, we can question him. Then we'll know what's going on here."

"That's not a bad idea," Jackson mused, "They probably have the front sealed off, but perhaps it's worth trying. We just have to figure out which direction the train is moving in."

Delilah pondered this. That couldn't be that hard to figure out, could it?

"Looking out the windows won't work," Jackson continued, "Can't see anything out there but fog."

"Oh, for Christ's sake," the skinny woman, Jordan, exclaimed, "C'mon, watch this."

She stood up and Delilah saw her point immediately. The forward motion of the train couldn't help but make her body sway a little bit. Though Delilah was a bit of a slacker, she'd managed to retain some information from her science class last year, when the teacher mentioned the effects of physics and why when a car crashed, the people riding in it were propelled forward. Delilah kept this to herself; being in this little group made her feel younger and more vulnerable than ever.

"We're going this way," Jordan said, pointing.

"I guess we have to go that way then," Tyrell said, pointing the other direction with a guarded smile.

The doctor interested her. Probably part of it was that he'd been the first to help her out, but she'd been watching since she came out of her daze, and it was fascinating how he always kept his shields up. He clearly wanted to be a gruff, confident leader type, but he couldn't hide the sensitivity wrapped up inside him. She liked Jordan too and felt a strange kinship with her, though she was somewhat unapproachable. She hadn't made up her mind about Jackson yet. Right now, he gave her the creeps.

"Well, let's get to it then," Jackson said.

They started wandering through the compartments, in the direction of the front of the train. After going through six compartments or so, Delilah noticed uneasily that every compartment looked exactly the same. There was something very unnatural going on here.

The next dozen compartments also looked identical, to the point where Delilah felt dizzy. After what felt like hours, as they were about to walk through the next door, Jackson walked ahead of them and put his ear to it. He looked back at them, shaking his head.

"This is the front compartment," he declared.

"How do you know?" Jordan asked, "Looks just like the other doors to me."

"Lots of experience with trains," he replied, "I was a driver, at one time, which is partly why I know our captors must be targeting me. That door leads to the front of the train. You have to trust me here. We need to proceed very, very carefully or--"

Jordan made a dry jerking motion with her hand, which Jackson responded to with a glare. He was sure of himself. Despite the clear dangerousness of their situation, Delilah felt a wave of relief wash over her when she looked at Jackson's confidence; if he was right and they'd found the front, they were at least making progress.

Unfortunately, her relief was short-lived. Behind her, she heard a distant, congested scream that sounded like a large animal in pain. She turned around quickly. Nothing was there.

The door to the previous compartment was still open, revealing there was nothing in that one either. Had she imagined it? No, she couldn't have--there was something back there. She started shivering in horror, hoping that someone else had also heard it, but too afraid to ask in fear of being shut down.

She looked up at the doctor, who was also shaking. Had he heard it? His shaking seemed different, though. It was the way a person shakes when they have the cold chills from the flu. He quietly blew his nose; he probably just had terrible allergies.

"If you're right, then we need to bust in there or something," Jordan whispered, "We can't give the motherfuckers a chance to pull out a gun."

"They already know that we're here," Jackson said.

"We'll see about that, sunshine."

Jordan threw open the door and walked inside.

"Uh, guys…this isn't good," she said.

"What? What isn't good?" the doctor asked.

"It's…" Jordan stopped to shrug again.

"What?"

"No driver," Jordan said, "Yeah, that's right. No. Fucking. Driver."

The group slowly proceeded into the front compartment of the train. Delilah held back a little bit as she heard the horrible moaning again. It was closer now. How did nobody hear it?

Delilah followed the others and closed the door behind her; crowding all of them in the small compartment was a tight fit, but it'd be unlikely

221

that anyone would want to stand outside. She leaned back against the door to block the horrible noise from getting in, like a child covering his eyes to make the monsters go away.

"There's some...well, there's some monorails that go without a driver, right? It's all electronic?" Tyrell asked.

No one answered. Either they didn't know, or they were too distracted by the front of the train, which was even more bizarre than the other compartments. There was no driver and no controls, but Delilah noticed there was a seat in the place where the driver would sit. The front windshield showed that the landscape was still blanketed by mist. However, the elevated train track itself was visible. Jordan had hit the nail on the head when she'd said they were on some kind of monorail, though she wasn't sure how she'd been able to figure it out so easily.

Tyrell slumped down into the seat. He was shaking more uncontrollably now. Delilah looked at Jackson, who was gazing out the front. He looked grim but unsurprised; it seemed that his outlook on life was so pessimistic, so paranoid, that nothing on this Earth could ever surprise him.

"Hey," Jordan said, "I just found something! Some kind of note, almost like it was left here for us. I can't read this motherfucker's writing for shit, though. Someone else wanna give it a try?"

Tyrell shook his head.

"No thanks," he said, his voice quivering.

"Let me see it," Jackson replied, "I have quite a talent at reading different handwriting styles."

Jordan handed Jackson the note. As he read it to himself, Delilah realized she'd been wrong. The man could be surprised. His eyes had become wide, full of worry.

"What does it say?" Jordan asked.

Jackson cleared his throat.

"It says...well, damn, I'll just read it out loud. It says the following-- Hello, passengers of Train 665 and welcome to the ride of your life! Or, well, <u>life</u> might be the wrong word, since this train is on a collision course with the Lee Grady Mountains--"

"There's no such thing as the Lee Grady Mountains," Tyrell interrupted.

Jackson gave him an indignant look.

"Go on. I guess I'm wrong."

"--on a collision course with the Lee Grady mountains and oops, it looks like there's no driver onboard! In other words, there's no easy way to stop the train. Well, except, there is. If you reach the back of the train in time, we've placed a handy little disable switch right there that'll stop it in its tracks. Easier said than done, since you can't reach the back of the train...not physically, anyway. Consider this train a little psychological examination. You can only reach the back mentally--"

"That makes no sense," Jordan stated abruptly.

Jackson continued reading the note; "--and try to reach it in time, before the train hits the broad side of one of those mountains. PS...try to avoid those pesky Grey-Men."

Jackson gulped. Everyone looked around at each other, as if for support. None could be found. Every face was decorated with a look of terror. It was Jordan who finally asked the question on everyone's mind.

"What the fuck are Grey-Men?"

NINE

David turned around.

The door to the next compartment was still closed but something was behind it. The lights flickered even more intensely, as if the train were going through an electrical surge. An eerie, intangible presence filled the room.

David stepped back from the door anxiously, away from the moaning on the other side of the door. He shrunk back against the wall. The sound of the moaning crept down his ears and stayed there.

The door began to open. David bit his lip. As it slowly creaked open some more, he balled his hands into fists. Whoever was on the other side of the door had hostile intentions; he could feel it.

An impossibly long, grey finger slid out from the opening of the door and beckoned to him.

The finger was no thicker than a normal finger, but it extended nearly three or four feet long, all the way to the floor. It scratched David's side of the door with a dirty yellow fingernail and then crept back to where it had come from.

ENSLAVEMENT

Whatever was attached to the finger uttered another congested moaning sound and slammed the door shut. The sound of its voice made David's head feel stuffy, like his brain was drowning in snot. He steadied himself. His heart was pounding in his chest.

The creature moaned again. What was he supposed to do, pretend he hadn't seen it and move forward? Wait for the damn thing to eat him, or whatever it wanted to do? No, he had to fight back, but just thinking about that finger made him shudder.

David looked at the door. He had to surprise this thing before it knew what was coming. He'd have to throw the door open, slam his weight against the creature and throw it to the floor. If he could get the upper hand for at least a couple seconds, it'd give him time to plan out his next move. Hip-hip-hooray for forward thinking.

He cracked his knuckles and took a deep breath. He closed his eyes. Then, he ran forward, threw the door open and pounced downward, in an attempt to tackle the creature to the ground.

David crashed down on the cold floor of the next compartment. He tried to jump to his feet but it was a strain, as the impact of his fall to ground felt as if he'd flung his body through a brick wall. The thought made him smile knowingly; wouldn't be the first time for that, eh buddy?

Then he thought about the long grey finger again.

He opened his eyes with a great deal of trepidation. There was no creature in the room. Where could it have disappeared to? At some point it must've gone to the next compartment. David's heartbeat sped up and he looked around, to make sure that it hadn't somehow snuck behind him.

It hadn't. However, this compartment was different from all the previous ones he'd walked through. The floor was covered in porn magazines. Not just any porn mags, either. They were the same ones his wife always complained about. The same magazines that he'd been collecting under his bed for years.

It suddenly dawned on him that his kidnapping wasn't some random event. Whoever was responsible knew him, or at least knew about him. These porn magazines were some kind of demented taunt.

David picked up one of the magazines, just to make sure. Sure enough, it was his. Not just the same issue, either, as the corners were dog eared in the same places and the cover had ugly stains in the same spots

224

inconvenient spots as on his copy. To whoever his captor was, his life was apparently nothing more than some kind of ridiculous game. That was assuming, again, that he wasn't just in the middle of some mad hallucination.

David tried to get a hold of himself. Sitting here scared shitless wasn't going to help anything. He needed to keep moving. He needed to find the scary thing with the long fingers again.

He gathered his nerves and charged into the next compartment, but things didn't get any better from there. If the last room had been strange, this one blew it out of the water. David collapsed to his knees in frustration.

A train can only have one front side and one back side. The cars go in one direction. Everyone knows that. But this wasn't an ordinary train.

This train, David realized, was the ultimate proof of his insanity, because the compartment David had stepped into split off in three different directions. He could go left. He could go right. He could continue going straight ahead.

Terrific. Just when it seemed like things couldn't get any worse, logic had jumped out the window and was cackling on its way down.

TEN

Tyrell shook his head.

"I don't know any better than you what these 'Grey-Men' are supposed to be, but we can't worry about that right now. The important thing is to figure what we're doing on this train and how we're going to get off of it."

"It's quite apparent to me," Jackson volunteered.

"Really now?" Jordan snorted, sarcastically.

"Yes, in fact, it is! As I was telling Tyrell last night, I'm aware that the government has been practicing a new technique called technological hypnosis, which basically places human beings into a dream in an attempt to extract answers from them. Call it a modern interrogation technique. I believe that all of us have been placed into technological hypnosis."

"Well, shit, then," Jordan replied, "If this is all a dream, then why don't I just go off and break the window, jump off this cock-sucking train and get it all over with? I hate the way you feel like an idiot when you wake up jumping outta the bed, but I'll take it over this fucking shit."

Jackson lowered his head, shadowing his face beneath his hood. Tyrell knew full well what this meant. The conspiracy theorist was about to launch into debate-mode.

"No, young woman. It wouldn't work that way. You know the old saying that if you die in your dreams, you die in real life? It applies here."

"I remember that," Tyrell answered, "But what's the point? Why would they need to conduct this kind of experiment on us? We're not terrorists."

"Their reasons are always mysterious! My friend, you have to understand that we're only a small cog in the machine of their greater plans."

"Look," Jordan said in her usual biting tone, "I can punch myself in the arm here and I feel it. I don't feel that in a dream. I don't feel that in hypnosis, shit, back in high school the guy couldn't even lock my hands together."

"It's not the same thing," Jackson replied.

As the two debated the matter, Tyrell struggled to hide his twitchiness; Jackson already knew the truth about him, but he couldn't let the others know. Trying to distract himself, he looked back at Delilah. Since they'd entered the front compartment of the train, she'd been cowering in the back. She was scared. She looked as though she was about to burst into tears at any second.

He let the two more aggressive members of the group continue arguing as he went to comfort the girl. She barely noticed him, or at least made no motion to indicate it. That quiet way she tried to avoid things made him uncomfortable, the same way it had when Tiffany used to do it.

"You okay?" Tyrell asked.

"Can't you hear it?" Delilah whispered, "Behind us. Can't you hear it?"

"Hear what?"

"Please tell me I'm not crazy. I swear I'm not imagining it."

The look on her face was dead serious. She really heard something. Or at least she thought she did.

"Maybe I should take a look," he answered.

"No!" she cried, "Just listen. Please. It's like…it's like…some kind of…I don't even want to say it.

"Some kind of what?"

"Some kind of…monster."

Tyrell bit his lip. Maybe she was crazy. Regardless, he put his ear to the door. The least he could do was try to clear up the poor girl's imaginary fears and calm her down.

Then he heard it.

It was real. He jumped back, horrified by the reality of the groans. A sensation crept over him, not unlike that which a nonbeliever would feel if he found himself bathed in the incoming lights of a UFO.

A horrible thought crossed his mind. "<u>Avoid those pesky Grey-Men</u>."

"Hey, guys--" he started.

The overhead lights started fizzling and burnt out. The compartment shook, as if it'd been hit by the kind of mild earthquake anyone in Los Angeles is familiar with. Everyone looked back at Tyrell. The attention made him nervous.

"Guys, listen to the--"

The creature moaned again. Jordan, who was usually so cocky, quivered at the sound of it. Jackson marched toward the door bravely. He reached to open it and looked back at the group.

"Better that we find out the truth about this then sit here in terror, I say."

SLAM.

Something slammed up against the other side of the door. Jackson jumped back. There was sickening gurgling noise coming from the creature's throat.

"Grey-Men…" Tyrell whispered.

SLAM.

SLAM.

SLAM.

SLAM.

The Grey-Man wasn't trying to break in. Its blows were too strong for that; it was clear that it could break in anytime it wanted to. Tyrell listened to the sound of its footsteps shuffling backward. Jackson went to open the door again.

ENSLAVEMENT

"What the fuck are you doing, you nutcase?!" Jordan screamed.

"It stepped back," he said, "This is our only chance. We have to take it!"

Jackson threw open the door. Tyrell shielded his eyes with his hands, frightened by the thought of this Grey-Men myth becoming a reality. Slowly, he brought his hands down and faced the truth.

The Grey-Man stood before them.

The creature was a gross mockery of the human body. It was tall and lanky, so tall that it had to hunch its back just to fit in the train. Its skin was appropriately grey and covered in mold, adorned with a web of protruding veins. Its face was long and gaunt. It had empty black sockets where its eyes should be and its hollow mouth dangled limply.

The most terrifying things about it, though, were its fingers. The Grey-Man's fingers were freakishly long and disproportionate to the rest of its body, like the limbs of a giant daddy-long-legs spider.

Tyrell gasped. Such a unnatural creature couldn't exist in reality. Could it?

He was so blown away that he hadn't even noticed that a dead man clothed in a torn janitor uniform was clutched in the Grey Man's fingers. They'd already lost one of their own, a man that they'd now never have the chance to meet.

Tyrell looked back at the horrified expressions of his companions. All of them were as frozen in shock as he was. He suddenly felt compelled by the need to lead them against the creature. It was the same urge that had made him pursue a career in medicine in the first place. After all these years, he felt strong again.

Tyrell stepped out in front of the others. The Grey-Man shuffled toward him, moving in a jerky manner much like a stop motion model. Tyrell held his ground, even though all the hairs on the back of his neck were standing on end. The terror only made him braver.

Then he looked at the Grey-Man's face. There was no life in it. No joy. There was only sheer, desolate emptiness.

The creature threw the dead man at Tyrell, knocking him down to the floor. He tried to throw the corpse off of him quickly but as he was in the process of doing so, he made the mistake of looking into the Grey-Man's eyes. Those lifeless eyes brought him back to Tiffany, and he pictured her dead eyes once again. 'She's dead,' his mind repeated over and over, 'SHE'S DEAD, SHE'S DEAD, SHE'S FUCKING DEAD.' He remembered her bleeding throat. He remembered what a failure he was.

He tried to be strong but he felt drunk on his own self-hatred and couldn't move. 'No!' he pleaded to himself, 'not in front of them. I have to be the hero. I have to be the leader.'

Tyrell was paralyzed. What kind of idiotic, wannabe savior was he trying to be? He knew he needed to do something. The others were in danger. Hell, he was in danger. But he couldn't look away from the dead eyes. He couldn't move.

The Grey-Man snuck into Tyrell's mind and took control of it; a puppet master dangling the strings. It effortlessly found all the controls and ripped them away like floss. The Grey-Man owned him.

He tried to fight the monster's influence but it was too strong. He was small, weak and defenseless. He was a cringing addict and for the first time, he saw himself clearly, as if through the lens of a camera. He pictured every event of the last few years all over again. He'd been lying to himself, thinking that he was hiding his weak moral fiber from others when they could see right through him. Even Rita probably only stayed with him out of pity.

He began convulsing. He wanted to curl up in a ball and whimper. He wanted to go home. He wanted to escape.

Tyrell collapsed under the weight of his own failures as the Grey-Man reached for his throat.

ELEVEN

Jordan Romano watched in horror as this creature, this fucking "Grey-Man," shuffled toward Tyrell. She looked at the others. A bunch of shaking pussies, that's all they were. Jordan's swaggering attitude may have been a disguise for her deep, inner self-loathing, but she was never one to back down from a fight. Even if she did feel like she was about to piss her pants.

"FUCK YOU!" she screamed.

Jordan charged forward with a furious battle cry. She couldn't let herself worry about things right now. She couldn't allow herself to think. She had to act.

ENSLAVEMENT

The Grey-Man lifted its head methodically and its inexplicably hollow gaze penetrated through her shield, as if it was clawing its way into her mind. She looked away. Something about the monster's empty eyes sockets reminded her of fucking Medusa, or some shit.

She jumped at it, trying to tackle it to the ground. There was no hard impact like she expected; nothing solid to tackle. Instead, she was lost in folds upon folds of loose skin, as if the Grey-Man had no insides.

Jordan couldn't breathe. She couldn't see. She struggled to tear her way out of the Grey-Man's flesh, but her release only came when the Grey-Man coiled its icy, unnervingly long fingers around her like enormous crab legs. It pulled her out its body and held her in the air.

Jordan looked into the Grey-Man's empty eye sockets. There was no sympathy in its face. There was no compassion. The creature stretched its mouth in an agonizing howl, in the process tearing open the weak skin on its cheeks.

The Grey-Man's thoughts slithered into Jordan's brain like a snake. It wasn't just telepathy; it was a complete destruction of the mental safeguards she'd set up all her life. What scared her more, though, was that the Grey-Man's voice was so familiar. It was the voice she'd heard in the back of her head her entire life. It was the voice that always taunted her when she fucked up, the voice that still told her she was fat and ugly. It was her.

The Grey-Man tightened its grasp around her waist. It had already won. It plucked her emotions away like petals on a flower.

"You're nothing, you know that?" it told her, "Nothing but a victim. Yeah, put on that tough girl image. Put on those fucking combat boots and pretend that when it gets late, you're not going to curl up in the corner and fucking cry. Pretend that you're not going to scream at your hideous face in the mirror like the lunatic that you are, cunt. Pretend you're not going to arch over the toilet seat, stick a finger into the back of your goddamn throat and--"

"Please, stop," she whimpered.

She was shocked to hear the begging plea spilling from her lips. It was as if she hadn't said it. It felt like the words had come from a radio; they couldn't have come from her. All the hopes and dreams she'd ever had in life melted away like butter on a frying pan. All that remained was her fears. Her weaknesses. Her self-loathing.

The Grey-Man's guttural voice scoffed, pricking at her brain with a thousand little needles while its touch burned into her flesh like a branding iron. Steam rose into the air. She cringed at the pain but it wasn't enough to tear her from her daze.

Then, the creature lifted one long finger and dangled it in her face. It pushed its dirty yellow fingernail between her lips. She cried out in horror.

"Hell no, fuck that. Anything but that...fuck you! FUCK YOU!"

The Grey-Man pried her lips open. It slid the finger over her tongue, reaching toward the back of her throat. It was over. This was the end, this was--

Something tugged on her leg.

The young cutter, Delilah, grabbed onto Jordan's leg and started yanking it downward. Taking advantage of the moment, Jordan pulled her hands free and grabbed the Grey-Man's sick finger and yanked it out of her throat.

Jordan thrashed around madly. This time, she didn't make the mistake of looking into those Medusa eyes. The Grey-Man dropped her to the floor.

She felt it staring down at her, with that expressionless face. The voice it had planted inside her was still there, laughing sadistically.

"I'm coming back," it said, "Stronger next time. You're too pathetic to ever push me down."

Jordan looked away. She struggled to catch her breath. As much as she wanted to claim victory, her self-esteem had been irreversibly damaged. She hadn't escaped from the Grey-Man. She held no illusions about having escaped from the Grey-Man. It was toying with her.

The lights stopped flickering and burnt out completely. Then, just like that, the Grey-Man disappeared. It was as if it evaporated in the brief moment that she'd looked away. The lights turned back on.

Jordan spat the taste of the Grey-Man's moldy flesh out onto the floor. Tyrell, who was still shaking like a lunatic, looked to be in even worse shape than her. She wondered to herself if the Grey-Man had been speaking to him, too. She pulled herself together. She had to put on a confident show again. She had to make herself look strong in front of the others.

Jackson studied the corpse in the janitor uniform that the Grey-Man had brought to them. He looked appropriately grim, but still as confident as ever. God, that asshole was always so was sure he had it all figured out, wasn't he?

"This was one of us. This man, perhaps he…he must have failed the psychological test mentioned in the note. This could've been one of us, but he was too weak," he said.

Jordan tried to think of a smartass comeback but she was still too worn out. Still scared, too, as ashamed as she might be to admit it.

"That's not blood," Delilah announced.

"What?" Jackson asked.

"The dead man's body. Look at it, that's not blood coming out of the wounds."

Tyrell seemed to come back to life a little and wandered over to peer at the body uneasily before looking away. For a doctor, he sure seemed scared of a little corpse. Weird.

"Look," Delilah continued, "I know blood when I see it. That's not blood, it's…"

Delilah crouched down. She put her finger in the "blood" and tasted it. Jordan noted this with some admiration. Between this and saving her life a few minutes ago, the girl had guts.

"Red wine," she finished, "the guy's bleeding red wine."

Jackson tasted the blood himself. He scratched his chin thoughtfully.

"Yes. You're right, the man is bleeding wine. This further proves my theory that we're in a technological hypnosis experiment."

"I…I don't know," Tyrell started, "I just…I don't know."

Tyrell was a mess. He'd seemed a bit shaky from the beginning but now, he was constantly scratching his arms and fumbling his words.

"What do you mean, my friend?"

"It seems like…" Tyrell said, "Seems impossible, so maybe this is some kind of illusion. Some kind of nightmare. But I don't think it's some tech experiment. Can't believe I'm saying this, but…"

He stopped.

"But what?" Jordan asked.

"It seems like there's something more supernatural going on here."

Tyrell stopped, to let the words sink in. He took a seat on the floor and buried his head in his hands. Jackson raised one eyebrow in a dubious, judgmental manner, but said nothing. Jordan gathered that he and Tyrell had known each other before this whole thing had begun, and that the old conspiracy theorist was too fond of Tyrell to argue with him.

She looked at the dead man and thought about Jackson's words. The man was one of their own, one that they'd never meet, because he'd already failed. Of course, that raised an obvious question.

Who else was on this train?

TWELVE

David still couldn't grasp the unreality before him. It made no sense; one hallway going left, one going right, one down the middle. On a moving train. This was the sort of shit that made a guy go crazy.

Except, well, if he was seeing this, he must already be crazy. David decided to run with that notion, because if he was already bat shit crazy, he might as well live it up. Woo-Hoo. He envisioned himself shooting down the highway on a bicycle, or even a unicycle. Maybe pissing on cop cars he passed while he did it. Why not?

Except to do that, he'd have to get out of this mess of a train. Left, right, center. Left, right, center. He was about ready to try playing rock/paper/scissors with himself, then considered checking his pockets for a coin to flip twice. However, the thought of sticking his hand into those slime-covered pockets made him sick. It'd be like dipping it into a public toilet.

David selected the middle hallway. The other ones were just too out there for him. At least if he stayed on the middle path, he'd know which way he was going.

David continued going through compartment after compartment. Now that he'd imagined scary grey fingers and a train that went three different ways at once, identical compartments didn't seem half bad. Maybe he could even learn to enjoy it. He started whistling.

For the first time since he'd woken up in this crazy dream, he remembered Kim. Thoughts of his boys flooded back to him. He stopped walking.

ENSLAVEMENT

If their father had really gone off the deep end, how would they survive? When David's dear old Dad had ditched the family at an early age, he'd had to grow up fast, without any kind of father figure. When his Mom went insane and started hallucinating (a trait he was starting to think he had inherited), he'd had to step up, take on all the pressures of adulthood and raise himself. He'd promised himself that if he ever had kids, they'd never have to grow up without a father in their lives.

David kept walking. He couldn't worry about William, Teddy and Kim right now. Maybe this whole thing was some kind of mental maze and if he made it out, he'd be sane again. Hey, maybe it was just some kind of experiment being conducted on him by aliens or whoever, like that weird movie he'd seen the other week. What was it called, again? <u>Cube</u>?

There was a distant shouting noise in the next compartment.

David stopped. He put his ear to the door. If this was another one of those scary-ass weirdoes with the long fingers, he was going to run the other way. Another one of those and he'd go nuts for sure.

The noise stopped. He opened the door, just slightly. The voice called out again. It was human.

"Hey!" a nasal male voice yelled, "Is anyone there?! Can someone please help me?! Help!"

David stepped inside. The man was glued to the ceiling by some kind of sticky gunk that looked a lot like sewage. His hands dangled down hopelessly.

"Don't worry," David said, grinning fearlessly, "You're not as alone as you think. But I'll tell you right now, partner, there ain't no room in this town for the two of us."

"What?! Help!"

David's attitude was loosened up by having finally finding another human being. It helped having some form of companionship. At least he wouldn't be the only psycho around.

"It's all good in the neighborhood," David said, "Here, let me help you get down from there."

"Good! Thank you, sir, thank you!"

The man looked every bit the stereotypical nerd, with his puffy blond hair and horn-rimmed glasses. One side of his face was badly scarred; not so bad that he'd have to hide from the public and only go grocery shopping late at night, but noticeable enough that David was sure it probably came up in conversation a lot. He decided not to mention it.

David grabbed the man's arms and pulled him down. He crashed to the floor with a thud. As he picked himself up, he looked at the gunk covering his clothing with disgust.

"Oh my God," he said miserably, "I can't imagine how many parasites are in this…this <u>stuff</u>. I can't imagine what it'll do to my gastro-intestinal problems. Oh dear God, my pills, I don't have my pills…"

David smiled. He liked the guy already.

"Well hey, the name's David Danelo. Welcome to my little pocket of insanity."

He reached his hand out. The man looked at it with disgust, as if it were covered in green mold.

"I'm sorry," the man sputtered out, "I don't do that. Shaking hands, I mean, it's…it's the most common way germs are spread. Very hazardous."

"Sure thing," David replied.

"It's…Eugene. My name, I mean. Eugene L. Krank."

David and Eugene looked each other up and down, Eugene doing so with such a baffled expression that David wondered if he'd ever seen a human being before. He figured that either the guy didn't get out much, or he'd been hanging from that ceiling for a long time.

"Hey now," David said, "Staring at my chest there, buddy? My eyes are up here."

"I…I'm not, if you think--"

"I'm kidding. How long were you up there, Eugene?"

"I don't know," Eugene said wretchedly, "Forever. I can't believe how sickening it was. I don't know what I'm going to do here without all my pills. All these airborne viruses…"

"In here?" David said, stopping him, "Wait actually, that's what I want to ask you. Where are we? What's going on here? I almost went crazy back there, thinking I was imagining the whole thing. Well, unless you're just another figment of my imagination, but for the sake of argument let's pretend that you're real."

Eugene responded to this comment with a very indignant glare. David shrugged.

"Sorry. But really, where are we?"

ENSLAVEMENT

Eugene shook his head.

"I don't know, sir. I…I haven't the slightest idea. All I know is it's some kind of train."

David's heart dropped. He'd hoped this guy might have some answers. If they were both lost, it only made things more confusing. David pointed in the direction that he'd been going before.

"Well, Eugene, I'm going this-a-way. This train's got some twisted physics going on and I figure if I keep going the same direction, I'm bound to run into something sooner or later. Hopefully. Care to follow? This place gets creepy at night, or so the stories say."

"What stories?" Eugene asked nervously.

"Joke. Sorry, I do that a lot. But I'm as serious as a heart attack about the creepiness. I'll explain as we walk."

David and Eugene walked forward. Every time they entered a new compartment, David checked carefully to make sure there were no long fingers waiting for them. He didn't want to be caught off-guard again. They were waiting for the right moment. Sooner or later, they'd be coming back.

For some reason, he had a feeling it'd be sooner.

THIRTEEN

Delilah felt justifiably proud of herself. Not only had she saved Jordan's life, she'd pointed out that the dead man's blood was red wine. Whatever that meant, it had to be significant. She'd proven her place in the group.

So why had they ignored the red wine and instead gone on to talk about hypnosis and illusions? It was always that way; even when she tried, people walked all over her. There was no way to win.

"The important thing to focus on here," Jordan said, "Is that we need to get to the ass end of this train, and fast. We gotta reach that motherfucking disable switch before we slam into the mountain."

"No kidding," Tyrell agreed.

Tyrell looked like a nervous wreck. He'd transformed completely from the strong leader/doctor that he'd seemed to be before. To see him collapse this quickly and easily made Delilah nervous.

They started walking back through the compartments. Jordan was right; they had to reach the disable switch fast. But the longer they walked, the more impossible that goal seemed to be. Delilah felt as though her mind been sucked into a vortex. They'd walked through nearly 20 compartments now, each one exactly like the last.

"Wait," Jackson suddenly exclaimed, "I do believe that I may have found a way out of this."

Delilah sighed with relief. She'd felt weirded out by Jackson at first but the more she got to know him, the more likeable he was. Maybe he was a little over the top with all of his conspiracy theory babble, but when it came to everything else he definitely knew what the hell he was talking about.

"What now?" Jordan asked.

Jackson pointed to a door on the side of the wall. They'd been walking so fast that Delilah hadn't even seen it.

"This is the first compartment with an exit door."

This was different; as she'd noticed earlier on, even though the train resembled a subway, none of the previous compartments had the exit doors you'd normally expect to see on one. But seeing one now didn't help, considering they were on a moving elevated train. Opening the door would accomplish nothing but making it easier to commit suicide.

"So this is your big master plan?" Jordan asked, "We're all going to kill ourselves?"

Jackson scratched his beard thoughtfully.

"Jordan, Jordan, Jordan. You have to let go of real world logic. We're in a state of technological hypnosis here. We have to throw logic, physics and all of the rules you know out the window."

"Yeah right," she snickered, "Fuck that. If I'm gonna be jumping out a moving train, you're jumping first. What, you think in this 'hypnosis' we're all gonna fly or something?"

"No," Jackson said, "I'm saying that this door might not necessarily lead outside. We've been wandering through what is essentially the same room in a train over and over again; what if we've only been in one room this whole time, and this door is our only chance to leave it behind? Perhaps we need to think outside the box."

"…and jump out of a train?"

"We have no idea where this door leads. What if it leads to another train? Maybe it leads to another world, where the hypnosis computers will no longer be able to torture us. Isn't that worth investigating?"

Tyrell looked up; "Maybe. Though I kind of doubt that the 'designers' of this place were reading that much Harlan Ellison."

"Whatever," Jordan interjected, "You wanna know an easy way to see what's behind the door? Here. Let me look at this through the window and I'll show ya."

Jordan walked to the door and peeked out the window next to it. Delilah followed her curiously. Sure enough, the door led outside; its other side was clearly visible.

Jackson cleared his throat. He was tired of waiting and apparently unconvinced. He opened the door.

Delilah waited for a sudden rush of wind that never came, because the door didn't lead outside. Behind it was another identical compartment.

Delilah looked out the window again, everyone else following her lead. Outside the window was the side of the train, with its closed door. It was like the inside of the door was some kind of gateway to another plane of reality.

Jackson stepped inside the newly revealed compartment. She half-expected him to disappear, or fall through the floor of the hologram. Instead, he stood there and crossed his arms, with a big grin on his face. He liked being right.

"See?"

Delilah and the others followed him inside. She walked through it again a few times before she was convinced. Denial was pointless. That whole technological hypnosis theory was looking more and more likely by the second.

"It's a maze," Jackson observed.

"I guess you're right," Jordan said, "My bad, man."

"There's some sort of secret explanation for how this all works, I can feel it," Jackson continued excitedly, "There's some giant goal at the end of this. Some kind of revelation. Just imagine! I thought we were being tested as some kind of torture experiment, but what if, instead, we're actually being trained?"

"Trained for what?" Tyrell asked.

"Actually, well…I have no idea! But picture it; what if all the secrets to the world as we know it are at the back of this train, and will be revealed when we flip that disable switch? The truth about Roswell. UFOs. The Kennedy assassination. It could all be here!"

"You creaming your pants over there, Jackson?" Jordan asked sardonically.

"No, I'm terrified," Jackson said, "But the possibilities here are endless. This is the question we must ask ourselves, though. With his compartment revealed, we now have two different options. We could take our chances and march forward on this new route, or we could go back and continue the previous one instead. What do you guys say?"

Everyone shrugged; Delilah was still too confused to even consider the question. Jackson pointed forward.

"I say we continue in this new direction. It's more interesting that way."

"All right," Jordan said.

"Might as well," Tyrell agreed.

Somehow, Delilah noted, Jackson had become the leader. As much as she liked him, this worried her a bit. Knowledgeable or not, this was the kind of dude who she saw standing on street corners with big signs, or walking around town screaming at people about how the government was going to kill them, or spending money on an underground shelter in fear of a zombie outbreak. The idea of him becoming their leader made her uncomfortable, but it seemed like he was the only one confident enough to take the position.

Jackson marched forward. Everyone else followed.

FOURTEEN

David and Eugene were making a great deal more progress than they realized.

Originally, David had been happy just to find another human being. He'd liked Eugene quite a bit, at least at first. Despite David's less sanitary habits, he had some OCD tendencies himself, so he'd immediately related to Eugene as an ally in the eternal fight against disorganization and germs.

Unfortunately, Eugene took it to another level. As they progressed through the compartments, the guy couldn't so much as touch a door

239

without first rolling his hand up in his sleeve. Every five seconds he had to say something about his gastro-something-or-other or how bad his heart palpitations were getting. He had to admit, he missed how quiet it'd been when he was alone.

But every time he remembered the grey fingers, he quickly changed his mind. He needed the company. No matter how annoying that company was.

"How do you survive, man?" he asked Eugene, as they were walking.

"What...what do you mean?"

"In this hostile world that's apparently out to get you. Seriously, how do you do it?"

"It's not out to get me. It's out to get all of us. Other people are just ignorant and don't suffer the same disabilities that I do, which makes it even worse. If only you knew how fast my heart was going right now, you'd appreciate how close I may be to my last legs. If only--"

"What, you have more than two?"

Eugene looked at him blankly.

"Really, though," David said, "Is every day a struggle?"

"Yes."

"All right then."

They continued walking. Eugene sighed. David turned around to look at him.

"What?" David asked.

"Every day since the accident, that is. The accident...the accident that gave me this scar."

"Actually, I've been wondering, well..." David paused, "never mind. What kind of accident was it?"

"Car accident. I was pulling onto the interstate when some idiot smashed into my car and drove away. Nothing was the same after that day. Right after, all my systems seemed to collapse."

"Wow, that's awful, Eugene," David said.

"Yes, you have no idea, sir, how many times I've wanted to go back. Gosh, I'd do anything to go back. Things would be so different if that fucking black pickup truck hadn't crashed into me."

David stopped walking. Had Eugene just said what he thought he'd said?

"Can you repeat that?" David asked.

"I said, if I could go back and--"

"No, not that part. What kind of car hit you?"

"A black pickup truck. Covered in dirt. Disgusts me to think about it now, ugh."

David struggled to remember the previous night. After all the wandering that he'd done on this damn train today, it felt like weeks ago. Last night, he'd looked out the window and seen a black pickup truck.

"You live in LA, right?" he asked Eugene.

"For the last five years, yes, yes I have."

The whole idea was ridiculous. There had to be a thousand trucks just like it in a city as big as Los Angeles. But something about the one he'd seen the night before had unnerved him in a way he couldn't explain. Something about it stuck with him.

There's a difference between accepting an answer because you're hopeless and coming to a conclusion that you intuitively know to be correct. It felt psychic. David was sure that it was the same truck. This wasn't random. For the first time all day, he felt sane again.

Then he laughed at himself. Sane, huh? Sane for assuming that out of the millions of pickup trucks in the world, you and this other guy must've seen the same one? Yeah, good going David. Apparently the bar for sanity was getting lower all the time.

"What are you laughing about? I don't think my accident is very funny," Eugene stated.

"Sorry. I felt one of my ribs tickling the bottom of my stomach. It's my most ticklish spot."

"That's disgusting."

"Eh, I guess. It's just—"

"Sir, stop."

"What? I--"

"Really, David, stop. Look."

David looked ahead. The door to the next compartment was wide open. What lay before them, though, wasn't just another room.

They'd reached the back of the train. David rushed forward in disbelief. The monotony was over.

However, the back of the train revealed very little. The room was wide and empty, the back wall little more than a giant, curved window. David pressed his face to the cold glass and looked down. It was still too misty to see anything other than the elevated train tracks below him. They were falling away behind the train, bit by bit. David nearly jumped out of his skin in fright.

He looked again. The tracks were collapsing, but the train was still moving forward. Somehow, its sheer momentum was carrying it forward; the tracks only fell apart right after the train had passed over them, implying that the weight of the train must have been pushing the tracks down. It didn't make a lot of sense, but given the rest of his psychotic hallucination, David was unsurprised by this.

Apparently there was no going back from wherever this joyride was headed. At least, not any easy way back. David suddenly felt annoyed that he'd reached the back of the train instead of the front. At least up there he'd be sure to find a driver, who could maybe give them some kind of explanation. He and Eugene would have to turn around and go backward. He looked around, hoping for some kind of clue.

At the bottom of the window was a red lever.

The red lever had the word "DISABLE" written across it. This seemed unusual; like something out of a cartoon. He'd ridden a couple trains in his time and never heard about or seen a red lever in the back. Of course, this was hardly a normal train.

David placed his hand on the lever. What did it do? Apparently it disabled something, but he couldn't be sure what and this didn't seem like the most opportune moment to be taking chances. Placing his hand on it, he felt a strange energy pulsing through him.

He had a forceful compulsion to push the lever down and see what it did. It wasn't just curiosity. His fingers were twitching, as if they knew something his brain didn't.

He remembered the way he'd felt when he'd seen the black truck. He remembered his ridiculous notion a few minutes ago that he and Eugene had seen the same truck. But he shook these notions away; coincidences were just coincidences. The idea that he was somehow meant to pull this lever and disable something was just his overactive imagination. He couldn't live on guesses here. Sure, in a computer game you can save your game but here, he only had one shot.

He took his hand off the lever.

David shuddered. How crazy <u>was</u> he, now? He was pretty sure that yesterday he wouldn't have been even remotely tempted to push random buttons in a car or airplane cockpit. He started to turn around.

"Hey, Eugene, you wouldn't believe--"

Eugene was gone. David peered out the door. He must've gone back a compartment or two.

The lights flickered.

He jumped. The last time the lights flickered, the fingers had come out. He whipped his head around. He looked in front of him, behind him, to his sides. There were no monsters in sight. He was safe.

Then, Eugene screamed.

FIFTEEN

Delilah was sick of compartments. Even in this new direction, it was still the same fucking room over and over again. After yet another long, dizzying hour, they finally stopped to rest.

"This is like walking through a fucking desert," Jordan spat out.

"It's the desert of our mutual subconscious," Jackson said, "We are wandering the alleyways of our own minds."

'Whatever that's supposed to mean, Jackson,' Delilah thought to herself. She looked over at Tyrell. Since Jackson had taken the initiative, she'd been waiting for Tyrell to step up too. He'd seemed like the leader at first.

Now, he barely said more than a few words at a time. He was intensely fidgety, to the point where she wondered if he had some kind of disorder. He acted just like some of the major druggies at school.

Delilah considered trying to talk to him, but she wasn't sure what she could say to him, or how to say it. 'Hey, Tyrell, are you okay?' wouldn't cut it. Just imagining the look he might give her in response made her feel uncomfortable.

She leaned back against the window. Besides, if he was a druggie, he might go crazy any second now. She knew all too well what addiction was like.

"Yes," said the voice inside her head, "Things are getting pretty stressful, aren't they? Wouldn't it be nice to carve a little zigzag pattern into your arm? Escape the pain. Control it. Make it yours."

Delilah started breathing heavily. The back of her neck felt cold. Something was watching her. She looked out the window.

It was the face of a Grey-Man.

The creature was hanging upside down, staring at her with its empty eye sockets. A long strand of saliva dripped from the corner of its mouth and stuck to the glass. Delilah screamed.

The Grey-Man smashed its fist against the window. Shattered glass violently flew against her. A jagged shard sliced right through her cheek like butter. The Grey-Man reached inside and tried to grab Delilah's throat. It wanted to pull her outside. Delilah continued screaming, battering her fists against the Grey-Man's thin fingers.

One finger snapped. The Grey-Man pulled its hands away, popped the joint back into place and reached for her again. Furiously, she punched what was left of the window, breaking the remaining glass in the Grey-Man's direction. It moaned in agony. Delilah stepped back.

Her hands and wrists were even more cut up than before. The bandages were torn apart and shards were stuck in the already-open wounds like the spines of a porcupine.

Cold air from the moving train rushed into the room. The Grey-Man pulled itself back onto the roof. It was waiting. Waiting and watching for the right moment to strike.

Tyrell stood up. He was still wavering, but he seemed alive again. He looked out the window, gulped and made eye contact with the others, like he was about to deliver a speech.

"I'm going after it."

SIXTEEN

Eugene hadn't been particularly interested in finding the back of the train. He also wasn't very interested in hearing anything else that this David character had to say. He didn't like David and he didn't trust him; the man was too much of a comedian and Eugene was sure that even though he had a friendly exterior, he was probably secretly making fun of his many illnesses, just like everyone else.

So as soon as David became distracted at the back of the train, Eugene took advantage of the opportunity to slink away. He wasn't sure just yet if he wanted to ditch David altogether, but if he slipped away now he'd have the opportunity to make a choice without causing any kind of fuss or argument. He hated conflict.

He snuck back one compartment, rolled his hand in his sleeve and quietly closed the door behind him. The lights were flickering by this point, but he didn't think anything of it. He was too distracted by the fact that a little bit of his finger had touched the door handle, which made him nervous. God knows who had touched that handle before him.

He dug into his pockets, trying to find his bottle of hand sanitizer. It was gone; he should've remembered that by now, considering how many times he'd reached for it, but it was hard to break a well-learned habit. At some point in the kidnapping process they must've taken it from him. He panicked. If his heart started beating any faster, he'd have a heart attack.

Then he heard an atrocious moaning noise behind him. He whipped his head around. A horrible grey monster stood behind him, a living nightmare from another world that had torn its way into real life.

The monster walked toward him, leaving a slimy trail behind it. Eugene rolled his hand back into his sleeve and desperately tried to open the door. It wouldn't budge, even though it had no lock on it. It was as though the creature in the room had locked it telepathically.

A peculiar phrase began echoing inside Eugene's head, for no explainable reason. Grey-Man. Grey-Man. Grey-Man. He'd never heard of a Grey-Man before, but he knew immediately what it was.

Eugene again scrambled to open the door. The Grey-Man clutched his shoulders and effortlessly flipped him around.

Standing this close to the creature, Eugene was forced to examine it. Its skin was covered in mold, mildew and mud, like it hadn't bathed in 20 years. The Grey-Man lowered its face to be level with Eugene's. It tilted its head and examined him curiously with its vacant eye sockets. Then, something crawled out of the Grey-Man's eye sockets and mouth.

A swarm of insects.

The insects crawled down the Grey-Man's flesh and jumped onto Eugene's body. He squirmed in anguish, trying to get away. The Grey-Man held him in place. It was at this point that Eugene screamed.

ENSLAVEMENT

It was more than just insects now. Maggots, cockroaches, spiders and earthworms emerged and crawled under Eugene's clothing, clinging onto his flesh with their tiny little pincers, legs and slithering bodies. An especially long centipede crept up the leg of his pants. Desperately, he tried to kick it away but the centipede continued climbing toward his crotch, its friends following closely behind.

"OH GOD, GET THEM OFF ME!"

The door handle was moving behind Eugene's back. David heard him screaming. The door still wouldn't open. Eugene felt like his heart was about to burst.

"I'm coming, Eugene!" David cried from the other side.

"Hurry! It's--"

Eugene cut off his exclamation due to the tingly sensation of a mosquito fluttering around in his mouth. The mosquito flew to the back of his throat and he gagged on it. Anxious tears poured down his face.

The Grey-Man lifted its head and thrust its chest up against Eugene's face. Suddenly, the monster's skin split open in a tiger-stripe pattern down its torso. The cuts were festering and infected; a mixture of blood and pus sprayed out. Giant leeches emerged from the wounds and wasted no time in crawling onto him. The leeches were laughing hysterically. They were mocking his afflictions, torturing him.

The Grey-Man slowly tore open the scar on Eugene's face. The weak skin broke easily enough and as the Grey-Man dropped it to the floor, the scrap of skin became a surreal, separate entity from Eugene's body. The pain was immense. The vermin began crawling rapidly toward the fresh open wound like moths to a flame.

The pain and nausea was so intense that Eugene felt his mind go blank. Shock hit first, and then he drifted into a trance state. He was driving his truck, a red Toyota Tacoma, down the interstate. Even though it was his current car, though, the vision seemed to be taking place before the accident. He was confident. He was happy. He wasn't worried about his health. Not yet.

Suddenly, the black pickup truck pulled out in front of him. Eugene crashed into it. His truck was smashed to pieces. He crawled out of the wreckage and was assaulted by the bright sunlight. He could barely make out a thing. But he could see the black pickup truck just fine.

246

It didn't even have a scratch on it.

The driver emerged from the truck. It was a red silhouette in the sunlight, so blurry it could've been either male or female. The driver waved at him, chuckling in an innocent manner.

"You brought yourself here, Eugene," the driver said in a voice so indistinct it was barely audible, "How does suicide feel? Hmm?"

"No," Eugene coughed out, "It's this…this Grey-Man! I never did a thing! I'm innocent!"

The red silhouette shrugged playfully.

SEVENTEEN

Tyrell looked at the broken window. He looked at the others. Sure, he was still a nervous wreck; the Grey-Man that had just bounded onto the roof hadn't helped things. But this was his chance to prove himself. This was his chance to be a hero.

"I'm going after it," he announced.

Everyone stared at him with shocked expressions. Delilah rewrapped her bandages. Jordan was the first to speak.

"Dude, are you fucking crazy?!"

"Don't do it," Delilah pleaded, "Please. You don't need to do this."

Tyrell wanted to scratch his arms, but stopped himself. Fidgeting like that stamped the word DRUGGIE on his forehead. He walked up to the window.

"I'm not crazy," he said, "We can't keep waiting around for this Grey-Man to kill us. I don't know what kind of dream this is, but we can't play by the regular rules. This is our chance to follow this asshole onto his own turf."

"And do what?" Jordan sneered, "Beat him up? You're going to fall off the fucking train! We know you're a good guy, you don't need to prove yourself. You don't need to be some kinda superhero. What can you do to him if you do find him?"

That one stung. Tyrell stopped. He was overwhelmed with nervous energy.

"I don't know. I'll push him off the train, even if it means I go down with him. If I can't get him, though, I can at least try to find the back of the train."

"Tyrell!" Delilah cried.

Tyrell looked back at the girl. Again, he was reminded of his sister. This made his motivation stronger. He looked at Jordan, who was fuming, then finally glanced over at good old Jackson Ubel. The so-called "local crackpot" nodded at him solemnly. He was the only one who understood.

"Do you want me to go with you, Tyrell?" Jackson asked.

"No. If I'm…if I'm killed, you guys need as many people still down here as you can get."

This was the first point where the fear of death prickled against Tyrell's stomach like a cat's claws. He hoisted himself out the window, fast and fluidly, not giving himself any time to chicken out.

As he pulled his body to the rooftop, he suddenly realized that running around on the top of a <u>moving</u> train wasn't as easy as it was in the movies. The rushing wind bit into his face like a swarm of tiny locusts. He slowly stood up on the roof, digging his heels in.

Immediately, he was almost knocked over by the force of the wind. The mist was so thick he couldn't see more than 20 feet below him. He crouched down to maintain his balance.

The entirety of the train was visible from on top, but calling it a train was no longer a reasonable description. Different segments of the train were constantly splitting off and zigzagging in multiple directions. The entirety of the thing resembled a pit of moving snakes, coiling around each other as they all rushed in one direction. Only the front of the train stayed in place.

Tyrell suddenly felt hopeless. In this moving mass of squirming train segments, there was no way they'd ever find the back. Not only that, but the Grey-Man had somehow gotten away. He wanted to go back inside the train. He'd been an idiot to think he was good at anything but running away. An escape, that's what he needed, a good snort of…

"Cocaine," a lustful voice murmured, "<u>Go on, you little piece of shit druggie. Run away from your problems. Just like you've always done since you killed your sister, you</u>--"

"Who the fuck is that?!" he yelled.

No one was there. Tyrell felt a strange cold chill swirling around somewhere inside the fleshy grey matter of his brain. The voice had come from inside him. He crawled forward, trying to escape the voice.

"MURDERER! Oh, that's too nice, isn't it? A murderer has intent. A murderer has skill. You're just someone who accidentally failed at your job. Always trying to be the one everyone looks up to, aren't you?"

"Shut up!"

A loud bellowing noise called out up ahead. The voice rushed back into his mind, laughing at his failures. It was a feeling akin to finding out someone had been reading all your personal emails, tapping your phone and looking into your window at night. Except the voice was his. It was the voice he'd always pretended didn't exist. The voice that he fought away with cocaine. Except this time, there was no coke to fight it away with.

"You're a sham. Pretending to be a good person. Pretending to a doctor, instead of the failed medical student you really are. Pretending to someone in control of his life, instead of just a vermin controlled by an addictive substance. Bet your nose is itching for some blow right now, isn't it?"

It was. Tyrell stood up and forced himself to walk forward. He could deal with the bellowing. Anything was better than the penetrating voice.

A Grey-Man stood before him. It was moving fast; too fast for a creature its size.

"Tyrell, Tyrell...such a failure."

Another Grey-Man walked out from behind, followed by a third, then a fourth. Four Grey-Men advanced on him in a dreamlike fashion. Tyrell tried to put his thoughts together but the voices hammered in his brain like a migraine headache.

"Failure, failure, FAILURE."

The Grey-Man in the front looked different than the others. Its nose was missing, the cartilage torn away. As horrifying as the onslaught of four Grey-Men was, it was the one in front that made him feel like something had dug under his skin and made his bones rattle.

"Grey-Man. Grey-Man."

Tyrell's head felt like it had split open. The lead Grey-Man beckoned to him. He lost control of his mind again, and his body moved against his will in the direction of the Grey-Man.

EIGHTEEN

David couldn't figure out how to open the door as the sound of Eugene's screams pierced the air. The whole thing jiggled like a motherfucker, but wouldn't open. It was as if the handle was free but the door itself was glued in place.

"GET THEM OFF ME!" Eugene screamed.

"I'm coming, Eugene!" David shouted back.

"Hurry! It's--"

Eugene's torturous screams were cut off suddenly. David remembered how earlier he'd thrown the door open, when he'd caught a glimpse of those fingers behind it. Maybe it was time to pull a Schwarzenegger again.

He stepped back and put all his strength into opening the door, in one quick motion. It didn't budge. His shoulder exploded in pain. Well, another fantasy down the drain. Apparently he hadn't had eaten enough Flintstones vitamins.

David grabbed the door handle again. He had to keep trying, no matter how futile his efforts were. This time, it opened as easy as pie.

The grey monolith that David had feared all this time was standing right in front of him. It groaned loudly and dropped Eugene's emaciated body onto the floor. The man's face was torn open, his body mutilated and a swarm of insects crawled from the wounds on his body. David swallowed his own vomit.

"I'm guessing we can't be friends, then?" David asked.

The monster moaned in response. Despite its size, the its motions were startlingly fluid. It was unreal. Yep, he'd definitely taken the train right to Crazy-Town.

David turned and darted to the back of the train. He stopped in his tracks. Another monster was glowering behind him. It glared into his eyes.

"It's too late, David. You already missed your chance."

Missed his chance at what? Fuck, now he was even hearing voices in his head. What was that called again, schizophrenia? David suddenly felt some kind of telepathic claws digging into his brain and twisting it around like silly putty. It reminded him of arguing with his wife; the way she'd always turn all his points around and make him look like the bad guy.

250

He had to get out of here, fast. He looked for an escape. The monsters had him cornered on both sides now. In baseball terms, this situation was called a "pickle."

David felt his resolve weakening, like it was a lemon being psychically squeezed out of him. The grey monoliths stood motionlessly, was if letting him decide which one got to rip him limb from limb. He looked at Eugene's wasted body and realized how easily that could be him in a couple moments. He thought about his kids. They needed their father to come home.

"You might as well forget all your guilt now. You're on this train. You've already failed your children."

David stopped. Whether he'd gone crazy or not, he had to keep his mind as stable as possible. This voice was powerful. It could talk a man into shooting himself.

"Oh c'mon now, that's like telling a kid he's got an F- before he takes the test. I'm not dead yet."

David wasn't sure whether he was talking to the monsters or if he was talking to himself. It didn't matter. If he didn't keep the jokes coming, he was a goner.

David knew that he wasn't going to have any luck running run past these things. They were too fast and they'd already proven how easy it was for them to mutilate a human's body. He looked at the window.

That was it.

David took off his steel-toe boot and smashed it through. He cleared away any remaining glass. As he put the shoe back on, he glanced over his shoulder quickly; the long-fingered creatures were now running towards him.

"Tally-ho!"

David climbed onto the roof of the train.

NINETEEN

Tyrell was shattered out his daze by the sight of a Grey-Man's enormous fist plunging right at him.

Tyrell leapt away and it smashed against the roof of the train. The surface vibrated with earthquake-like tremors and Tyrell fell to his knees to avoid being flung off.

ENSLAVEMENT

Two of the four Grey-Men whisked behind him like ghosts. He jumped back to his feet and looked around. They'd stopped moving. Despite their sullen expressions, they were laughing. He was just a rat in a cage.

"Taking the fight to us? Confusing heroism with pompous, self-aggrandizing suicide, aren't we?"

"Call it whatever you want!" Tyrell yelled.

He remembered his plan. Maybe it had depended on the idea that there was one Grey-Man up here instead of four but if he was careful, he could make it work. He looked at the Grey-Man with no nose, teetering just inches away from the edge.

Tyrell jumped at it.

The Grey-Man effortlessly slid far away. It was faster than he could ever be. Fighting the Grey-Men was hopeless.

Tyrell started toppling over the edge. He was going to die in vain, but at least he'd tried. He wasn't a coward anymore. "Self-aggrandizing suicide," as they called it, he could die happy with. He closed his eyes and let the wind rush against his face.

Something caught him. A long, hard object ran down his bare back like an icicle. A Grey-Man had caught him by the shirt with one finger and dangled him over the edge. They weren't going to let him die unless they were the ones who killed him.

Tyrell struggled to get free. The Grey-Man threw him back onto the roof unceremoniously. The creature reached down and starting carving an image into the roof of the train. The image of was of Tiffany.

Suddenly, the image came to life. Tiffany's face thrust itself from the roof. Her throat was cut open and bleeding again. She was gagging. Crying.

"Ss..ss.." she sputtered out weakly.

Tyrell struggled not to fall victim to the obvious manipulation. He couldn't help it. Tiffany's crying face was breaking him down. The memories flooded back into him, with no way to stop them.

Then, Tyrell realized someone else was on top of the train.

252

TWENTY

David couldn't believe it. He'd actually climbed onto the roof of a fucking moving train to get away from those grey monsters and the second he got on top, there was four more waiting right there.

What really caught his attention was that all of them had crowded around some other guy.

David looked back. Great. Two monsters had been better odds than four. He was only mildly shocked to discover that the back of the train was no longer right behind him; it was as if it'd slithered away in a different direction and left him behind, which considering all the weird things that had already happened wasn't so surprising. He was now somewhere in the middle.

David made eye contact with the other guy. Oh, terrific. Now his conscience would never let him run away.

David crouched down and signaled to the other guy. He was trying to make some kind of signal back without being obvious. David almost yelled out to him but thought better of it.

Not that it mattered, since all four monsters suddenly turned around anyway. David froze in his tracks as all of them shambled toward him at an alarming speed. David started running backwards to get away. The creatures were faster. Sweat poured down his forehead. This time, he had no roof to jump to.

His foot slipped. David struggled to maintain his balance but the force of the wind was too strong. He was flung off the side of the train. Two of his fingers caught onto the railing at the last second. There was an audible crack.

Fantastic. He was holding on for dear life with two broken fingers. Just when he thought things couldn't get--

One of the creatures peered over the edge at him. His heart stopped.

"Not yet."

The creature turned away and disappeared. David's relief was short-lived. His fingers cracked again. He couldn't hold on much longer.

David tried to throw the weight of his body upwards so he could climb back on top of the train. It was useless. The more he moved, the more his fingers slipped.

ENSLAVEMENT

David had never believed that will was everything. That was all just a bunch of psychobabble to pretend we didn't have limitations. However, as his fingers cracked a third time, he suddenly wished that he did believe in the power of will. If this 'will' thing allowed his fingers to hold on a second longer, it'd be great.

His fingers slipped again. Only the barest tips of them were still holding on. They cracked again. Both fingers burned with blistering pain.

'Please hold on,' he begged himself, 'as long as it takes. It's all about will. It's all about will.'

His fingers almost slipped off, showing off the dynamic contrast between the slight strength of his grip and the powerful pull of gravity beneath him.

He tried to keep his legs from dangling too much in the wind. It was this distraction that made him lose his focus. His finger slipped off completely and he began to fall.

Suddenly, someone caught his hand.

It was the same man as before. David laughed. The guy was repaying the favor for distracting those grey monoliths; you scratch my back, I scratch yours. He looked down on David with an intensely caring expression in his dark brown eyes. This was the kind of man who would let himself fall before he ever let go of you. In the man's strong, though shaky grip, he felt calm.

"I got you," the man said.

"Never thought I'd be so happy to hear that," David panted.

His legs waved in the air. Gravity was still strong. David used the man's grip as leverage to pull himself back onto the roof of the train. Once he'd landed, he collapsed onto his back and laid there. The monsters were gone.

"Thank you," David said.

The man didn't respond; he was too tired. He fell down next to David and looked up at the grey skies. There was an interesting smile in the corner of his mouth. Somewhere in this nightmare, the guy was actually amazed by something.

"I actually did it," he said quietly.

"That's the same thing I said when I lost my virginity," David quipped "Great day. Seriously though, man, thank you. Holy shit, thank you. I'd be dead."

"You're...you're welcome. C'mon, we need to join up with the others. Well, assuming we can even find the room I came from at this point, considering how warped this train is."

"Others?"

"There's four of us. Well, four that are still alive. Five, counting you."

David's mind was boggled. Four other people sounded like an entire civilization at this point. He took a moment to breathe. This ride was about to get a lot more interesting.

"I just wish it was possible to find the back of the train more easily up there," the man stated, "It would've changed everything."

David stood up. He looked back where he had come from. The rear had disappeared somewhere in the mist, or curled underneath the train, or shifted somewhere to the side; hell if he knew. Apparently this train reassembled itself as much as a a kid's lego castle.

"Dammit," David muttered, "I can't see it anymore. What the hell? I mean...well, why were you looking for the back?"

"I'll explain when we get inside. You ready?"

"Wait," David said, "What's your name? I don't want to be walking into this room wearing my sunglasses at night, if you catch my drift."

"Tyrell. Tyrell Freeman."

He shook his hand.

"Name's David. Pleasure to meet you, Tyrell. Now let's get this ball a'rollin'."

TWENTY-ONE

Jordan wanted to explode in anger. How had this David guy made it to the back of the train instead of them? It felt like a ball of spit from God. Or the devil. Or whoever controlled this train.

"God," David said, rubbing his face miserably, "I feel fucking horrible about this, guys. If I'd have just known, I would've...fuck. I'm a fucking screw-up."

"You couldn't have known," Tyrell reassured him, "Don't take it so hard on yourself."

"No, when I was sitting there, I felt this…this urge. Like I was supposed to pull the lever. I can't believe I didn't listen to it. I can't believe it!"

David punched the seat next to him angrily. He then stood up and shook his head. Despite the fact that she was secretly furious at him, Jordan couldn't help but admit, somewhere in the back of her mind, that he was a little cute. He had a nice build and looked much younger than his age.

Apparently reading her mind, he looked up and made eye contact. Jordan quickly glanced away. Even so, she could tell he was analyzing her up and down; a girl knew when she was being checked out.

Despite the fact that he was cute, there was something about him that bugged her. He liked her, that much was obvious, but it was also obvious that he had a wedding ring. What bugged her more, though, was that his gaze wasn't a sympathetic one. He didn't look at her as a person. All she saw in his eyes was lust.

"Well you should've pulled it," she said nastily.

That wasn't fair, but he wasn't being fair to her. He'd been friendly to everyone else. It wasn't fair for him to single her out and objectify her this way.

It almost made her wonder if she was actually attractive, but that couldn't be the case. Her body was grotesque. Her hips were bulged and her stomach was a massive lump. No, David was only checking her out because she was the only woman there, other than the little girl. Didn't matter how ugly she was.

Jackson walked over and patted David on the back. During this, David looked at her again. She suddenly felt immensely self-conscious.

"It's just the way things happen," Jackson said solemnly, "They tempted you because you didn't know. It's all a game to them, and they know everything that's going on in the game. Time is their tool, friends."

"Yeah," Delilah said, "It's not your fault. We've all made mistakes."

Jackson's vague comment annoyed Jordan, but she let it go. She'd come to begrudgingly accept Jackson. For all his flawed views, he was the closest they had to a leader. The only question was whether this was because Jackson was good at it, of it everyone else was just too fucked up to take charge of anything.

David spun his wedding ring around on his finger. He seemed to be trying to restrain himself from cracking a joke to break the tension. She again felt sickened by her own attraction to him. She wanted to take this out on him with a couple jabbing remarks but decided not to. It wasn't his fault.

"So what do you think we should do next, Jackson?" Tyrell asked.

Jackson pondered on this for a moment.

"I say that we keep walking. The clock is still ticking and we must reach the disable switch."

"How much time do you think we have left?" Delilah asked quietly, as if raising her voice would shatter the walls of the room.

Jackson thought about this for a moment and then answered.

"I think our time is running short."

TWENTY-TWO

Tyrell walked next to David, a little ways back from Jackson, Delilah and Jordan. He felt a kinship with him. A cynical part of his brain wondered if it was just because David was the first man he'd saved in years, but for the most part he believed that it was just one of those fast friendships that are all too rare.

"I hate that they could be anywhere," Tyrell said to David, somewhat bluntly, "Those…things, I mean."

"No shit," David replied, "What did you say they're called again? Grey-Men?"

"Grey-Men."

"That's like me calling the sky 'blue sky' instead of calling it the sky. Who comes up with these names?"

Tyrell and David were now lagging a good way behind the others, lending their conversation some privacy. Privacy was a great thing to have again, even if only for a moment.

"Whoever wrote the note, I guess. Whoever that is. I still can't figure out how we were all picked out, though."

"Dude, I'm just shocked that anyone else is on this train," David replied, "I thought I was alone for a while there. You think we're all connected somehow? Sounds like one of your buddy's conspiracy theories."

"Heh, maybe not quite as outlandish way as the sort of shit he might come up with," Tyrell said, smirking, "There has to be something though, don't you think? I mean, you could say we're all normal people and we are...but then again, we're not. We're bound together by some kind of...it's almost like we all have the same scar deep inside our brains, y'know what I mean?"

"I don't have the most artistic brain in the world, so you'll need to be more basic, Mr. Doctor, sir," David said.

"Well--"

"I'm kidding, bro. I get you. We've gone all AA here. In which case-- hello, my name is David and I have a problem."

Tyrell laughed, but pondered this to himself. He actually hadn't figured out what was wrong with David. He seemed so likable and easygoing on the outside.

Tyrell's mother had told him once that sometimes a man wears the most jovial mask he can find when he's deeply hurt inside. David was a good guy, but something was twisted.

"So," David said, interrupting his thought process, "What about you? Where are your scars?"

Tyrell considered answering. No one but David would hear it but in a way, talking about his addiction would be a way of owning up to it. He wasn't ready for that. Part of him still was convinced that he didn't have a problem.

"I have a few," Tyrell finally answered.

"Ah, don't worry about it," David said, "I understand. Keeping them close to your chest. I guess we have that in common."

"I guess so."

"Was it always that way, though? Have you always had...whatever you have going on?"

"No," Tyrell took a deep breath, "I guess...I guess not."

"Really?"

"You remember how I told you that I was a doctor, right? It's not quite that simple."

Tyrell checked to make sure that no one was listening. He lowered his voice. He especially didn't want Delilah to hear, but luckily she was up in front with Jackson. Tyrell liked being a big brother figure again and didn't want her to know that he'd lied.

"I'm not a doctor," he continued, "I failed med school, but not because I couldn't do it. I got so soaked up in my own...tragedy, that all I did was try to escape from the grief."

"Tragedy?" David asked.

Tyrell took another deep breath.

"My little sister killed herself. Slit her own throat. I was the big would-be doctor, the one who was supposed to save her. That's all I ever wanted to do, save people. And then my own sister needed saving and I fucked up."

"Wow. I can't even imagine, that's...I never had any siblings but if anything happened to my wife or kids...I couldn't deal with it. Damn, man."

"I didn't. Not well, anyway."

"Have you dealt with it by now?"

"I don't know. In our first encounter with a Grey-Man, it threw a dead body at us. When I looked in that dead man's eyes, it brought me right back. This whole thing is like some kind of deathtrap to try to make us commit suicide. I swear, if I could just--"

"I know what you mean," David interrupted.

"All right," Jackson announced from the front, "We'll take a five minute break."

Everyone stopped and sat down. Tyrell and David stayed back, so that the others still wouldn't be able to hear them.

"Do you?" Tyrell asked.

"Do I what?"

"Know what I mean. Do you?"

"Yeah. When I was on my own, it was all good. No urges. But now, with everybody else here, I just feel this urge, this urge to..."

He stopped and glanced over at Jordan. Tyrell eyed this suspiciously but didn't ask questions. What did Jordan have to do with this urge?

"To do something," David said, "Something, nothing, all of the above and everything else. Whoopee. It's even worse now that I didn't pull that damn lever. I feel like such an asshole."

"It's not your fault."

ENSLAVEMENT

"I know! But that's two failures in one day. One person's already died because of my mistakes, now all of you guys might die as well."

Tyrell looked at him with alarmed eyes. Had David met the man with the red wine blood? He decided not to ask. He'd tell him sooner or later.

"I guess you're wondering what I'm talking about," David said, "This is just between you and me though, okay? You're the only guy here I trust. I mean, I'm not too into the whole idea of trusting people so fast but you're a good guy, I can tell. If we get out of here alive I'm buying you a beer."

"Shoot," Tyrell said with a smile.

"I met this other guy before I met all of you. His name was Eugene Krank, kind of a nerdy looking guy, really health-obsessed. I don't know how it happened, but...when I reached the back of the train, he disappeared. One of those Grey-Men got him, filled his body up with bugs, maggots, all kinds of shit. That was when I went to the roof."

"I guess we've got a lot in common," Tyrell said.

"I guess so. The thing that really gets me, though, is that Eugene had scars over the side of his face. Big-ass scars, not quite like Two-Face, the Batman villain, but noticeable."

"All right."

"I've got something else to say, but again, it's just between me and you. I'm about to go spouting conspiracy theories like your buddy Jackson over there, so call me crazy if you want but keep it private. I don't want Jacko over there arguing with me about how this whole thing is <u>actually</u> because the Earth is flat, or the government did it, blah blah blah."

"What is it?" Tyrell asked.

"Okay, get this. Eugene told me that his scars were because he'd been in a traffic accident. Okay, big whoop, but here's where the shit gets interesting--either that or I'm as crazy as I think I am, and I'm just pulling connections out of my ass. Anyway, back to the point, Eugene collided with a black pickup truck."

David had emphasized the words 'black pickup truck' in a way that made Tyrell shiver. It felt like finding out that the monster in the bed had been real all these years. He nodded and let his friend go on.

David continued; "So, maybe a black pickup truck isn't the most unusual thing in the world. But it got me thinking. Last night, before I fell asleep, I saw a black pickup truck out the window. What's weird to me is that I <u>remember</u> it. Normally, I don't remember what car is parked next to mine in a parking garage. That truck last night though creeped me out, though. I dunno why."

"So you think this truck has something to do with it?"

"Did you see one?" David inquired.

Tyrell remembered how the previous night. He remembered having his bag of coke open in the parking lot when a black pickup truck pulled in. Three people seeing the same truck. Could it be a coincidence? He looked out the window quickly, as if expecting a Grey-Man to be peering in at just that moment. There was nothing but mist.

"Yeah," Tyrell answered, "I saw one last night."

Tyrell shook his head in disbelief. Either he was going crazy himself, or David was right. Either possibility seemed equally likely at this point. Tyrell tried to remember the driver of the truck and found that he infuriatingly drew a blank. It was as if the windows had been tinted solid black.

Something was going on here. Something that had been planned for a long time. Tyrell realized that he was thinking like Jackson but for once, he saw he logic in that way of thinking. The idea of this all being random seemed as illogical as the physics of this train.

Somehow, it was all connected and that black pickup truck was at the center of it.

TWENTY-THREE

As they went back to walking, David couldn't restrain his urge to continually ogle Jordan. Fuck, she was beautiful…though, well, actually she wasn't. Not really. She was far too skinny; almost a walking skeleton, with sunken-in features. Not really his type.

She pulled it off, though, with her strong, outspoken attitude. She was a fighter. But she was also a woman, which was the thing that held his attention most. Heaven forbid he went a day without fucking another woman. Delilah was way too young for him, but Jordan looked about 23, which wasn't too bad. He'd avoided her so far, desperately hoping to restrain himself before it was too late. Luckily, no one suspected anything.

His wedding ring was like a lead weight. Remembering what the prostitute had told him last night, he twisted the ring around his finger awkwardly. A huge part of him was tempted to throw it away, but he couldn't do it.

His eyes slowly traced the curve of Jordan's figure. She looked back at him quickly and then looked away. She felt it too, he could tell. There was something there, but he needed to resist it. He couldn't succumb to temptation. Not now. Never again.

Never again? Well, maybe just one more time…

"You okay?" Tyrell asked him.

David was so caught up in his thoughts that he'd almost forgotten where he was. He smiled, like he smiled in every situation. He was sick of smiling.

"As peachy as a nectarine," he replied.

Jackson, at the head of the group, stopped walking. He peeked into the next room then looked back at everyone else with a surprised expression. Even though David hadn't known the bearded conspiracy psycho long, he knew his type and if a dude like ol' Jackson was surprised, then it had to be a big deal.

"I think we might be making progress!" Jackson said excitedly, "This is even stranger than the door in the side that we found earlier!"

"What? Really? Holy shit, tell me it's not a mirage in the desert," Jordan asked.

David crossed his fingers as the group hurried into the next compartment excitedly. As he entered, he was overwhelmed with the joy of recognition. They'd found the light at the end of their tunnel.

It was compartment that split off in three different directions. The same one he'd seen earlier.

"YES!" David yelled, "Oh, sweet mother of God, this is what I'm talking about?"

"You okay?" Tyrell asked.

"Seems like it," Jordan stated, "Either he's okay as it gets or he just had the most amazing instantaneous orgasm of his life."

David ran into the center and looked down all three tunnels victoriously, with a big grin on his face. They were on the right path, after all. His failure no longer mattered. He was redeemed.

"No, no, no," David said, "Way better than that! I was here before! We're on the right track! As long as we stay down the middle here we'll make it to the end. We're gonna make it!"

David looked at the others. They didn't appear to be as excited as he was. This angered him, until he remembered his own bewildered reaction when he'd come to this fork in the road himself. Oh well. He'd show 'em. It was redemption time, baby.

"God, I hope you're right," Delilah said.

"I'm with you, D., though I'm staying cautious," Tyrell said.

"Follow me!" David called out.

David ran down the center tunnel, just as he had before. He threw open the door and happily marched into the next compartment.

It was a dead end. He stopped. He fell onto his knees as everyone gathered behind him. His blood ran cold.

There was no door to the next compartment, just a wall. The compartments of the train had...moved. They had reassembled. He should've realized this. He'd seen it happening on the top of the train.

"Fuck," Tyrell muttered.

David walked away from the group. Jordan, shockingly, put her hand on his shoulder supportively.

"I'm sorry, David," she said.

He jerked away. He'd failed them again. Some addition to the group he'd turned out to be, huh? He took a seat.

"I think we need to take another quick break," Jackson suggested, "Don't worry, my friends. We're not dead yet."

Dead. They were dead, weren't they? They were in the most ridiculous maze on the planet, trying to disable this weird train they were on before it crashed into a mountain. All they needed now was for those Grey-Men to make another surprise appearance.

"God, I don't wanna fucking die," Jordan said.

Everyone sat down in different corners of the room. David looked at Jordan again. She looked sick, depressed and pissed off; probably pissed off at him, even though she'd been sympathetic a few minutes ago. She wiped tears away from her eyes.

Jackson walked up and put his arm around her. A perverse feeling of jealousy coiled around David's stomach like a snake. He should be the one comforting her. He should hug her, kiss her, wrap his body around hers and…

No. He couldn't. He was a married man. His thoughts weren't loving; they were purely sexual. He knew that. Didn't he?

Jordan hugged Jackson, as if thanking him. Again, David felt jealous. His heart was racing. He had to distract himself. He nudged Tyrell.

"Hey, dude, did you ever hear the one about the golfer and--" David started.

"Thanks," Jordan said to Jackson, "I can't believe I thought you were a fucking asshole at first. My bad, man. I don't believe your theories and shit, but you're a good guy."

"Everyone makes mistakes," Jackson said, "I mean, I used to not believe in the Illuminati either."

"Heh," Jordan said, smiling to herself.

It was a cute smile, but not a flirty one. She wasn't going for Jackson. David was sickened by the thought of how much this observation pleased him. Wow, he was pathetic.

"What was that?" Tyrell asked him.

"What?" David responded, blankly.

"You were about to say something about a golfer?"

"Bad joke, I guess. Just another bad joke. Never enough of them."

Jordan walked away from the others, leaving the compartment. David was suddenly alarmed. 'Don't leave,' he wanted to yell out, 'Stay here, I can be there for you, I can…I can…'

"Hey guys, I need to…I need to get my fucking thoughts together," Jordan said, "I'm just going to go back one room, okay? You'll see me when you come back this way."

"Yes, yes, of course," Jackson replied, "Perhaps it is a good idea that we take a moment to ponder everything."

"Thanks."

Jordan left the room. David's heart thumped with every step she took. He wanted her. He wanted her now.

"Hey, David? Yo, you there?" Tyrell asked.

He barely heard him. The animal inside was taking over. He looked at his wedding ring. Again, he remembered the prostitute's words. Leaving the ring on all those times he'd cheated had made a mockery of its significance, hadn't it? His wedding ring symbolized a promise. It symbolized commitment, a long life with his family. It meant something.

Jordan coughed in the distance.

"David?" Tyrell asked again.

The ring started to feel like some kind of torture device. It was cutting off his blood flow. It was restricting him. He was only 35 years old. Not 40 yet. Why should he have to be so weighed down? It was bullshit! He'd spend his whole youth planning for adulthood, never getting the chance to cut loose…

"David?"

He clasped his other hand around the ring. He closed his eyes and saw Kim. He saw his boys. He imagined what they must think of him. They all saw a man's man, a family man, a strong man. It was a fake image.

"Sorry Tyrell," David muttered, "I was distracted."

"Damn, man, I was worried about you for a second there."

He looked back to where Jordan had walked off. He wouldn't have another chance like this. Maybe a little guilt was worth it. Wasn't it?

"Hey," David said, "I'm going to make sure she's okay. Keep my seat warm, okay? Hot and toasty, if you can manage."

"Sure thing," Tyrell said.

David stood up and left the compartment. As he closed the door behind him, he took a moment to consider his actions. He knew it was the wrong decision; if one of the boys asked him what to do in this situation, he'd tell him to follow his conscience. But hell, sometimes it's hard to listen to your own advice.

"Sorry, Kim," he muttered.

David took off his wedding ring and shoved it deep into his pocket. He followed Jordan's trail.

TWENTY-FOUR

As soon as Jordan Romano left the room, she let the tears spill. Fuck it, they weren't looking anymore. No one could be tough all the time.

She walked back through the tunnel and went one more compartment down, far enough away that no one would be able to hear her. Once she was confident no one had followed her, she sat down on the bench and cried. She hadn't cried in so long; anytime she cried, all she remembered was her mother's fists. She'd always blamed her mother for all the problems in her life.

Maybe that wasn't fair, but maybe it was. It was dear old Mom who'd first told her to watch her weight. She was the one who had berated her anytime she'd eaten as much as a slice of cake.

As Jordan drowned in her tears, she remembered the first time she'd purged herself. She'd been 14 years old, with no fucking clue of the addiction she was plunging into. At first, it didn't even work; she'd had to stick a toothbrush down her throat the first few times, until she learned how to get her fingers down there.

She told herself then that she just wanted to make her mother happy. But it was more than that, wasn't it? She wanted to look better. She wanted to like herself better. She thought it'd make her happy, so she could stop being the spiteful, "fuck the world" girl she'd grown up as. As much as she wanted to blame Mom, she was the one gagging herself. No one forced her to do it.

Jordan opened her eyes. A basket of chocolate-covered doughnuts had appeared on the seat next to her. She looked around sharply; no one else was in the room. What were the doughnuts doing here? They hadn't been there before…

Had they?

Eating a basket of doughnuts on this train was suicide, but holy shit were they tempting. She hadn't eaten all day and her stomach was growing like an animal. Food sounded amazing, but on this train?

Then again, on this train, she was going to die anyway. Fuck it all. There was nothing left to lose. She took a big bite out of the biggest doughnut in there. After going this long without eating, it was the best doughnut she'd ever had.

Once the first doughnut was done, she found herself unable to stop. As any bulimic knows, purging is only half the problem; binging is the rest. She wolfed down one doughnut after another, hating herself more and more with every bite.

'Fatass,' she heard her mom's voice tell her, 'look at what you're doing to your body!' She ignored it, as much as it hurt. It was her choice. The basket of doughnuts disappeared as if it had been vacuumed up and Jordan's small little stomach felt cramped and bloated.

She had to let it out. Leave it to her dumb ass to choose the one eating disorder that lets you stuff your face, huh? She leaned over the floor. Her stomach rumbled. Her throat felt dry.

It wouldn't take much. Just a poke. Then it'd all spill out. It would be as if she'd eaten nothing, nothing at all.

Just a poke.

Jordan bent forward. She opened her mouth. She'd done this a million times but for some reason, her fingers were shaking. She stopped. Then, without understanding why, she cried again. Something was different. Something was hurting her, deep on the inside. It was if some other personality, a positive one, was struggling to pull her back on track.

"Are you okay?" David asked.

David. Goddamn, out of anyone that could've followed her, it just had to be him. She jumped up defensively as he came near her.

"You didn't see any of this," she said angrily.

"Sure, my bad. I didn't see a thing, I swear."

His voice was so soft, unlike its usual tone. So sweet. He sat down next to her and put one arm around her. Despite her apprehensions, she didn't pull away, though she was still breathing uneasily. It felt nice to be comforted by a man like him. Maybe she'd been wrong about him.

"We're all in this boat together," he said, "sinking like the Titanic on a bad day."

"It had a good day?" she asked.

"Good point," he replied, grinning.

"I..." she hesitated, "I just don't want to die."

"Trust me, this wasn't how I wanted to wake up this morning either," he replied.

She laughed. David was looking into her eyes now. There was something behind those green irises of his. The look in them wasn't as shallow as she'd thought it was. Was it?

"I know," she said.

He took a deep breath. She started feeling self-conscious again. David leaned in close.

"What?" she asked.

"Me? What? Oh, I'm just trying to think of some kind of smartass comment," he said.

"Well--" Jordan started.

David kissed her, cutting her off midsentence. Surprising herself, she embraced the kiss. She put her arms around him. There was a moment that she almost could've called romantic. Maybe this guy really liked her. Maybe he actually cared; no one else on this godforsaken train did. Tyrell was protective of Delilah and liked both David and Jackson, but he didn't care about her. Delilah was only focused on herself. Jackson took pity on her, but he was the same as Delilah. David, though...maybe David actually cared about her.

His fingers crept up the back of her dress. She shuddered and pushed his hands down. Oncoming death or not, he was going too fast. They'd barely started kissing.

"Slow down," she whispered.

It was as if her words had bounced off against a brick wall. His kissing became more passionate. His hands reached up around her bra. She started panicking. He didn't care. He wanted her. That was all he cared about. He was just like all the rest.

"Stop," she said.

He kissed her again. Sweat was pouring off him. Jordan was terrified by the sheer intensity coming off him, as if he were radioactive.

"No!" she cried.

She pushed him away and David fell back into a seat. The lust-filled expression on his face changed to anger...then morphed into guilt. He backed away, digging his hand into his pocket as if looking for something. The horribly guilty look on his face made Jordan feel guilty too, even though she'd done nothing wrong.

"Oh my god, fuck, fuck fuck," he sputtered out, "I'm so sorry, I don't know what came over me--"

"Fuck this," she said, "Fuck you! I'm gone."

David looked at her with a sullen expression. His eyes were filled with tears. What a fucking pussy.

"I'm sorry," he said, "I have a problem, I--"

"Damn straight you have a fucking problem. Sorry. Too late, sunshine."

Jordan's words bit into her as much as they bit into him. She left the train compartment, slamming the door behind her. She put her back against the door and started panting. She felt sick. Weak. Violated.

There was a silver exit door on the side of the wall, just like the one Jackson had found earlier, except that one had been grey. She walked up to it. The door was a mirror.

She considered telling the others, but decided against it. This was her discovery. It was time for her to make her mark. She threw open the door.

Behind it was a dark room, filled with a maze of even more mirrors. Jordan stepped in cautiously. She hesitated, just as she with the doughnuts. Then, regaining her stubbornness, she marched forward. No one was going to scare Jordan Romano. Fuck the rest of them. Fuck the Grey-Men. Fuck this train. She was going to do it her way.

The mirrors were of the funhouse variety. Her image was distorted, warped. In one mirror, she looked short and wide. In another, her torso was tiny but with fat, enormous legs. She kept walking.

Then, the door closed behind her. She whipped her head around. "David?"

David didn't respond, but the voice did. The same sickening voice from before crawled back into her mind and stuck its razor-tipped fingers into her brain. She shook her head, trying to get rid of it. It was too late.

"No. It's not David."

Jordan ran back to the silver door and tried to open it. It was stuck. She looked at her distorted image in the mirrors again; now, her skin had become pale green. Her eyes were drooping down her face. What the hell?

"Let it out," the voice commanded.

"Let what out?" she asked, trembling.

Jordan ran to the other side of the room, looking for a door. There were none. She was lost in some kind of closet of mirrors. There was a cold breeze behind her and she turned around.

A Grey-Man walked out of the shadows. This creature, unlike the others, had long rolls of excess fat and loose skin hanging from its body. It moaned as it stretched out its finger and pointed downward.

"LET IT OUT," the voice repeated.

"Let what out? What?! Fucking A, if--"

ENSLAVEMENT

Jordan heard the distinctly uncomfortable sound of her own voice cackling behind her. She looked in the mirror again. Her reflection was laughing insanely.

"Jordan! You know exactly what it fucking means!" her reflection told her.

Jordan kicked the mirror, leaving a small crack. She kicked it again and again, until it shattered. The Grey-Man continued pointing downward.

"LET IT OUT."

Her reflections in all the other mirrors in the room exploded in laughter. Jordan screamed out furiously. There had to an escape.

"C'mon, bitch," her reflections chanted simultaneously, "Stick those fingers down there. End this."

"No!" she cried.

"LET IT OUT."

No. No. No. The Grey-Man stepped closer, as if it was gaining more power. Jordan slammed her fists up against the next nearest mirror, again cracking it. The reflection wouldn't stop laughing; its teeth became enlarged, like some kind of mutated cartoon character.

"LET IT OU--"

"Fine!" she shrieked.

Fuck this. Fuck all of it. Jordan stuck her fingers down her throat. At first, nothing happened. She shoved them down further and held them there. Her gag reflex finally kicked in and the doughnuts came up in a disgusting acidic wave. The vomit spilled over her shirt.

Jordan wiped her lip. She looked up with a proud look on her face.

The Grey-Man was unimpressed as it walked up her. It threw its long rolls of skinny fat on top of her and wrapped her up in them. Jordan screamed, unable to move. Her cries were cut off by the Grey-Man again penetrating her mouth with its horrible long finger. Its flesh tasted like rotten meat.

"N..ngghh..." she gagged.

The finger went deeper. Deeper. It went to the back of her throat and then stopped momentarily. Jordan could've sighed with relief, until she realized that not even half of the finger was in her mouth.

She tried to bite down. The Grey-Man's skin tore, but it didn't react. Tears poured from Jordan's eyes as the monster pushed its finger all the way down her throat and into her chest. Deeper. It pushed into her stomach, puncturing through the lining. She shook violently. The organs that the finger was touching were never meant to be touched.

"N...nnn!!!" she tried to spit out.

She bit down as hard as she could. She couldn't bite through the bone. She struggled for freedom and finally pulled away. The Grey-Man's finger slid out of her throat like a doctor's instrument.

She stepped back and so did the Grey-Man. In her desperation, she saw this as the creature's admission of defeat. She spat at it.

"Yeah that's right, you cocksucker! Thought you had me, huh? Thought you knew who you were fucking with, huh?!"

She stopped. Something rose up in her throat. Her saliva tasted salty. Her ribcage felt like it was being thrust up through her neck. She buckled onto the ground.

"No. Fuck, no..."

"LET IT OUT."

Jordan threw up a giant glob of sticky black blood, with bits of doughnut mixed in. She threw up again. This time, there were little chunks of raw, pink meat. She was a vegetarian.

"Fuck you, you fucking--" she started.

She threw up again. This time, the lumps of meat were bigger. Bits of muscle. She threw up again. Her stomach plopped out on the ground in front of her, drenched in blood.

She vomited her liver, her lungs and her intestines. Every internal organ splattered out on the ground. Jordan was horrified by the realization of what was happening to her and looked up, so she could spit on the face of the Grey-Man one last time.

But the Grey-Man was gone. In its place was another distorted mirror. This one, though, showed the woman that Jordan had never known existed.

It was her, though. It was beautiful woman with a stunning smile, a curvy figure, her age; a woman who looked a great deal like her. It was the Jordan Romano who could've been.

As soon as she saw the figure in the mirror, she reached out to it longingly but as she did so, the mirror shattered into pieces. Jordan threw up blood again.

It was too late.

TWENTY-FIVE

Tyrell was getting worried. While most of the group was still in the dead end room, both David and Jordan had been gone far too long. Even though he'd agreed to watch David's seat, it seemed to him like a terrible idea to start splitting up this way.

Delilah was sitting next to him, but both of them were too worried to exchange any words. The only person who seemed calm was Jackson. It was like the man had it figured out to a science.

"You think we should check up on David and Jordan?" Tyrell asked him.

Jackson stroked his beard in thought. He pulled his hood back on again, as if it was a thinking cap.

"No, I think we should wait a little longer."

Tyrell accepted this answer. Jackson was the only one able to keep a clear head in all this madness, maybe because his regular life was filled with so many wild conspiracy theories that a day like this was almost mundane to him. Tyrell sighed and got ready to lie back for a couple more minutes.

That's when the alarms went off.

It sounded like a fire alarm, sounding out from speakers strategically placed in the corners of the compartment. Red lights started flashing. A computerized voice spoke from the speakers.

"20 minutes until collision," it said.

"Fuck!" Delilah cried.

Tyrell wanted to panic, but held his ground by clenching his fist into a ball. Running around like a chicken with its head cut off wouldn't do shit. The group needed to stay organized.

"We need to find the others and get moving," Tyrell announced.

"Yes," Jackson agreed, "We're running out of time."

The train started going faster, throwing Tyrell and Delilah up against the wall. Jackson barely maintained his balance by gripping onto one of the poles just in time, the wily bastard.

Tyrell slowly reasserted himself, adapting to the train's new speed. He looked at Jackson. Despite the tenseness of the situation, he was still amused by the man's ability to always stay on top of things.

"Damn, Jackson," he said, "You actually managed to stay on your feet."

Jackson smiled.

"I suppose. I'm used to high speeds, though. You should see the way I drive. My truck practically flies."

Tyrell laughed at the mental image. Then, he stopped. "My truck practically flies." A sickening thought crept up his throat like acid reflux.

He looked at Jackson again. Jackson was staring at him, still smiling, but with a strange intensity in his eyes. Could it be?

"You drive a truck?" Tyrell asked, his voice quivering.

"Of course, my friend. A pickup truck, I've had it for years! Haven't you seen it before?"

Tyrell gulped. No, no, no, this couldn't be happening. He remembered his own encounter with the black pickup truck in the parking lot. He remembered David's conspiracy theory, David's story and the story that this Eugene character had apparently told him.

Sweat ran Tyrell's forehead. Jackson still looked confident as ever. Smiling, even. The alarms were still blaring. How could he feel so comfortable in a moment like this?

"What color is your pickup truck, Jackson?" Tyrell asked.

Hopefully it'd be blue. Green. White. Anything but black. Please, anything but black. The idea that he could've known the man this long and never suspected anything was nauseating.

"Why?" Jackson asked.

"Just curious," Tyrell stated.

He was sweating harder now. He felt anxious. He wanted his coke, more than ever. Jackson remained steady. Delilah grabbed Tyrell's arm.

"C'mon Tyrell, let's go! We've got to find Jordan and David!"

"One second," Tyrell stated.

"Why? We're running out time!" she exclaimed.

"What color is your truck, Jackson?" Tyrell asked again.

Jackson smiled and looked downward, as if he had to fully digest Tyrell's question before answering it. He shrugged again. Finally, he answered.

"What can I say? I like to call it Black Dusty."

273

TWENTY-SIX

David felt as if he'd been buried in an avalanche of guilt. He collapsed his head into his hands and replayed his move on Jordan over and over again in his mind. At first, it'd all been calculated, planned and structured. Suddenly, though, his animal instincts had kicked in, just like they always did. That'd been when things when things had gone awry.

The way she'd pushed him away...there'd been fear in her eyes. A look of betrayal. Maybe that had as much to do with whatever her own issues were as it did with his forcefulness but fuck, what kind of man was he?

Seriously, what kind of man was he?

He didn't know anymore. He'd spent so long structuring an image and trying to hide the inside that he couldn't remember who he was supposed to be. It seemed like all that existed on the inside was that sex-craving beast. There was more than that, locked away somewhere, but he couldn't remember what dark hole it'd crawled into.

He'd have to figure it out on another day. It was time to lick his wounds, move on and get back to business. He had a train to catch, so to speak. David reached into his pocket for his wedding ring. There was just one problem.

The ring was gone.

David reached down into the bottom of his pocket--it had to be there, somewhere. The stickiness from before had dried but both pockets were empty. He pulled both of them out all the way. All that fell out was lint.

At first, David was scared of how Kim would react. Then, his sense of guilt gnawed at him again. Oh, look, he'd failed at this too. He couldn't even hold onto his damn wedding ring.

He desperately searched his back pockets. He got down on his hands and knees and looked at the floor. It had to be there. It had to. He couldn't have lost it so easily.

It was gone. This time, he hadn't just failed himself. He'd failed Kim. He'd finally failed his marriage, in the worst possible way. Not only had he cheated on her a couple zillion times, now he'd even lost the one token of his love to her. After all she'd put up with, he was going to die without even having a ring around his finger.

He stopped as that thought occurred to him. This train was going to crash into the mountain and he was going to die. He'd never see Kim or the boys again.

David gave up. All his effort was worthless. Searching for the ring was grasping at straws. He'd finally fallen so low that there was no ladder tall enough to bring him back up. The ring was gone and that was that. His marriage was over.

The lights started flickering. David looked around anxiously, knowing full well what this meant. He ran down to the next compartment that Jordan had fled to a few minutes ago. She probably hated him now, but if the Grey-Men were coming again, he had to warn her.

As David opened the door, the alarm sounded and the train sped up. The velocity threw him back against the wall. He picked himself up, ran forward and threw open the door again.

"20 minutes until collision."

It looked like they were running out of time. As he entered the compartment, he couldn't see Jordan anywhere. Then, he noticed the silver door on the side of the wall.

David walked up to it. His instincts tried to tear him away; it reminded him of how he'd felt when he'd seen the truck. More than that, it reminded him of how every bone in his body had told him to pull the disable switch, but he hadn't done it. Now, those same instincts wanted him to run away from the silver door.

No, he was done running. He was David Danelo, and it was time to redeem himself. Yep, always trying for redemption.

"David," a female voice said from behind the door, "Come in here, David."

The voice sounded a great deal like Jordan's, though he wasn't sure. He opened the door and stepped into the dark room. The lights switched on, revealing dozens of posters of naked women taped up on the walls. David shuddered. Every woman in the posters looked eerily familiar.

"Hurry," the female voice urged him.

The lights switched off again. David suddenly noticed a long line of candles before him and in the dim light he could see the shape of a naked woman just a little ways ahead. She held her naked breasts close enough to the light that he could see them. Her face was hidden.

"Jordan?" he asked.

"I'm sorry, David. I didn't know what I was doing before. Come back here."

"But…"

"What?" she asked.

"Some kind of alarm went off. Normally, from my experience, alarms going off are bad news. I mean--"

"I don't care right now. Come over here."

Jordan's mysterious outline reached forward and beckoned him. David strained to see more, but couldn't. All he could see was her highlights. It was Jordan, wasn't it?

He walked towards her, feeling his body get more and more hyped up with every step. The candles behind him slowly extinguished one by one, making the room darker and darker. Once he'd made it right up to her, he couldn't see a thing.

"You still there?" he asked.

"Right here," she whispered beneath him.

"Whoa," he said, "Didn't realize you were that close. That's me, always going one step too far, huh? Sorry about earlier, I was--"

"Take me," she said sensually, "Make me yours. Do whatever you want. Let your instincts take over. Be a man…be a real man."

David smiled. Ah, who cared about the wedding ring? He'd find it later. This was too in-his-face to ever pass up.

"Well, if you want me to--" he started.

Then, he heard the moan of a Grey-Man behind him. David looked in the back of the room. The door was closed and the room was too dark to see anything.

"Was that one of them?" he asked anxiously.

"No," Jordan answered, "Get down here and--"

"Fuck, wait one sec," he said, "I heard a Grey-Man. I know I did."

"It almost killed me," Jordan said, "But I cut its head off, though somehow the damn thing is still making noises. It's gone. Dead. C'mon, David. We're going to die in a couple seconds anyway. Let's make our death worthwhile."

David heard the moan again. Jesus, this was crazy. Absolutely fucking insane. No one in their right mind would try to get laid with this kind of death hovering over their shoulders. But was he really in his right mind anymore?

"I can't do this," he said.

Jordan grabbed his crotch. Suddenly, his resolve weakened. He bent down and collapsed onto Jordan's body. He let his instincts take over. He started feeling her body, getting ready for the act. Her skin was strangely cold, but that was okay. This was the way to die. This was...

The woman suddenly reached up and threw a small object across the room, making a ringing metal sound as it bounced off the wall. As David turned around, the lights finally switched on. It was his wedding ring. Lying next to it was Jordan's corpse. Her skinny body had become like a living cartoon, flat and deflated. She was covered in blood.

He closed his eyes and gulped. If Jordan's corpse was on the other side of the room, he didn't want to see who--or what-- was underneath him.

"What?" the female voice asked, "Not warm enough for you, David?"

He fantasized for a moment that if he kept his eyes closed long enough, it'd all go away. He'd wake up in his bed and this would all be a terrible nightmare. After all he'd been through today, it couldn't end like this. Please, not like this.

David opened his eyes. The Grey-Man lying underneath him screamed.

TWENTY-SEVEN

Tyrell tried to form words in his mouth as the alarms blared around him. He couldn't. Jackson. The black pickup truck; Black Dusty, as Jackson called it. All the pieces were coming together in a stomach-turning manner.

"What is it, old friend?" Jackson asked.

"Let's get going, guys!" Delilah said, "We're wasting time!"

"Wait," Tyrell said.

He stared at Jackson. The "local crackpot" now had an increasingly manic grin on his face. It was as if layers of tension were melting off of him. He'd never been scared, though. Sure, he'd faked it a few times. But in reality, he'd spent this entire day in the same confident state of mind as a self-centered millionaire walking through the slums.

"Black Dusty," Tyrell stated.

"Tyrell!" Delilah cried out, growing increasingly frantic.

The alarms continued blaring, like a soundtrack. There were only 10 minutes left. Tyrell glared at Jackson. Jackson returned the glare. Black Dusty.

"What the fuck are you guys doing?" Delilah said, now growing furious.

"Delilah," Tyrell said, never taking his eyes of Jackson, "I've got a question for you."

"Quickly! We only have 10 minutes until this fucking thing crashes, and I don't wanna die!"

"Last night, did you see a black pickup truck?"

"Who cares?" she asked angrily.

"Go on," Jackson stated theatrically, "Answer the man! He seeks the truth!"

"All right! Yes!" she said, "Yes, I saw one."

"Right," Tyrell said, "You saw one. I saw one. David saw one. This...what's his name, this Eugene guy saw one and what'd you know, Jackson happens to own old 'black dusty.' What the fuck is going on here, Jackson?"

Jackson shrugged in an obnoxiously cocky way. He wasn't alarmed at being questioned. He expected it. Tyrell suddenly felt more nerve-wracked being around Jackson than he would in the presence of the Grey-Men.

"I know you've got something going on here!" Tyrell shouted, "What the fuck is going on, Jackson? We're in some kind of dream, right? Is it your little technological hypnosis bullshit? Are you and 'Black Dusty' behind all of this? What kind of messed up experiment do you have us in?"

"Calm down--" Delilah started.

"No! This asshole knows something that he's not telling us. Don't you get it?"

Jackson shrugged again. He looked at Tyrell with a cold stare that contrasted against his horribly genuine smile. The man was practically jumping up and down with joy.

"Well," he said, "Now what if Black Dusty isn't actually black?"

Tyrell stopped. Part of him wanted to believe this. He liked Jackson. He couldn't stand the thought that someone he'd known so long could be capable of torturing all these people in whatever illusion he'd cooked up here. The Jackson in front of him, though, wasn't the same Jackson he'd known before. It was a different person, a man who practically had the word "sadist" written on his forehead. The mask was off.

"Ha!" Jackson laughed, "Just kidding! You got me. Sometimes it's not just the Illuminati that are pulling all the strings!"

Jackson crossed his arms in satisfaction. His smile became ever darker and more twisted. There was no empathy in the man's eyes. No touch of humanity.

"What's going on here?" Delilah demanded.

"You have it right, my friend," Jackson said to Tyrell, "You're in my illusion. I did this, I created it. I created all of it, and I can't imagine how exasperating it must really be to have to sit here and watch an egomaniac like me brag about it. It's as if I'm one of the superhuman, top secret government officials that I've been pretending to believe in all this time!"

"Pretending?" Tyrell asked, his voice quivering.

"Oh, the truth hurts, doesn't it? Hearing about your own gullibility, I mean. The idea that you've known me all this time and never suspected what was going on must be catastrophic for your fragile ego. Then, you, Delilah, thinking of me as your <u>leader</u>? Unbelievable how easy it is, sometimes."

Tyrell wasn't sure what to do. Jackson was explaining himself in the same over-the-top manner as a James Bond villain, but what terrified him was how confident he was about it. The madman was beaming with joy, but not exposing any signs of weakness in the process.

"Wha...why?" Tyrell asked.

"What do you think?" Jackson asked.

The alarms were sounding. Only five minutes now. Tyrell looked at the door.

"Oh, please, don't be so naïve," Jackson said with a cocky smile, "You only have five minutes to go, and you really think you can find a way out of here as long as I'm around? You might as well go running through the woods looking for Bigfoot. This whole place is a mind game and nothing more."

"Fuck you," Tyrell said.

"That attitude is a good start, my friend. You'll have to get rid of my terrible influence if you want to get off this train. Who knows, maybe if you kill me it'll bring you right back to the real world. It's my illusion, right? Maybe it'll die with me."

Tyrell stood back, unsure of what to do. He braced himself for Jackson to attack. He couldn't make the first move, he couldn't--

Before he could do anything, Delilah jumped at Jackson in a furious rage.

"YOU FUCKING ASSHOLE!" she screamed.

Jackson elbowed Delilah in the face, breaking her nose. She fell to the floor with a jolt, blood oozing down her lips. Jackson put his foot over her throat.

"The mass media has such a way of deluding the youth these days, doesn't it, Tyrell?"

This was the cue Tyrell needed. He sucker punched the conspiracy theorist in the face, knocking him against the window. Tyrell grabbed him by the neck and smashed his face against the window again, then threw him to floor.

Jackson leapt on top of his body and pounded his bloody fists into Jackson's face. He beat into it until Jackson's teeth were torn from the gums. Wet smacking sounds filled the air. Jackson chuckled; he wasn't even trying to fight back. Why wasn't he trying?

"Oh, dear Dr. Tyrell Freeman. Could it really be that you're committing your second murder now?"

That was it. Tyrell let his rage take over. He grabbed Jackson by his long hair and smashed his head against the ground. It wasn't hard enough; he smashed it again. Again. Jackson was breathing heavily now, his face a barely recognizable, swollen pulp. Tyrell lifted Jackson's head up higher and smashed it against the ground so hard that he heard a cracking sound. He'd finally split the man's skull.

Warm blood pooled around Jackson's body. Tyrell was sickened by the scent and aroma of it. His conscience started creeping into him, but he had to ignore it for now. Tyrell looked up at Delilah, who was still shell-shocked. He hated that a young girl like her had to witness such a scene, but he knew that blood was something she was used to.

"We have to get out of here," he said.

"What about David and Jordan?" she asked.

Tyrell stopped to catch his breath. Somehow, he was certain that they were already dead. This train had some strange kind of psychic thing going on inside it, and he'd just have to trust it. The alarms were still blaring loudly and the train was moving even faster.

"We'll find them later. Right now, we have a train to stop."

TWENTY-EIGHT

Delilah was tempted to run away. Jackson had clearly been a maniac but she suddenly wasn't so sure that Tyrell wasn't one; they way he'd torn into another human being (if Jackson was a human being, that is, which she wasn't so sure of anymore) was terrifying. Delilah used to think that she'd desensitized herself to violence, but seeing that kind of carnage proved otherwise.

But at this point, following Tyrell was the only choice she had.

They raced through compartment after compartment, just as mindlessly as they had been before. Five minutes. Delilah felt hopeless. She couldn't erase the mental image of Jackson's blood-soaked corpse.

Just as she was about to open the door to another compartment, Tyrell grabbed her hand. Delilah jumped back fearfully. When she looked into Tyrell's brown eyes, though, her fear of him melted away; even if he had just killed a man in front of her, the compassion was still there. He was still the older brother she'd never had.

"Stop," he said.

She didn't want to stop. Sitting down and accepting death was worse than racing against it. She tried to push through him.

"No, we can't stop now," she said.

Tyrell took a deep breath.

"You have to trust me. I'm not giving up. I'm just trying to play by the rules of Jackson's game, illusion, whatever you want to call it."

"What do you mean?" she trembled.

"Think about what he said, in that note. We can't get through his maze in any logical kind of way. It's always changing."

"Tyrell, what's your point?! We need to hurry here!"

"Look. That next room there could be the back of the train, if we believe that it's the back of the train. But we need to both believe it, we need to--"

The lights started flickering.

Delilah turned around in a panic. A Grey-Man had appeared and was walking towards them, its long fingers reaching out. She tried to push through Tyrell again but he stopped her, more aggressively this time.

"Listen to me, Delilah! We need to both believe it, I'm not kidding with you! This illusion, hypnosis, supernatural nightmare or whatever it is all in our heads. If both of us believe that the next room is the back of the train, with no doubt, it will be!"

Delilah trembled. The Grey-Man's voice was crawling into her brain. Two Grey-Men were walking up behind them now.

"Delilaaaaah," said the voice, "You know you don't have the strength to believe in anything…"

"No!" she shouted.

Tyrell grabbed her by the shoulders.

"Don't listen to them! We can do this! Close your eyes. Believe. Please, Delilah, believe…"

Delilah looked back at the Grey-Men. One of them was carrying two corpses now; the bodies of David and Jordan. Delilah closed her eyes.

"You can't do it--" the voice started.

Delilah closed her eyes. She could see the back of the train. She was ready, but they had to move fast. The image was going to shatter if the Grey-Man spoke to her again.

"Go!" she said.

Tyrell opened the door. He was right. They'd made it. They'd reached the back of the train, with two minutes to spare. But they weren't alone.

Jackson stood before them, his arms crossed and a giant grin on his face. He was bathed in blood, but his wounds were completely healed, gone, as if they'd never been inflicted. He leaned up next to the disable switch and chuckled to himself, alive as ever.

"I have to say, I'm amazed that you addicts actually made it this far!" he said, "Especially you two. I had high hopes for Eugene and David, but alas, I suppose it wasn't meant to be."

Jackson looked Delilah in the eyes. It wasn't like looking into a human's eyes; in those, you can't help but feel some kind of connection, no matter how cold the person might be. There was none of that in Jackson. This man was something beyond a serial killer. Now that he'd taken off his mask, his true eyes were like daggers.

Delilah's wrists suddenly started pouring out blood again, as if Jackson's gaze had reopened the wounds. The deep cut she'd made on herself the night before throbbed in pain. Her bandages slid off her arms uselessly. Jackson nodded at her, taking full credit.

"But..." Tyrell started, "No, fuck this. You're dead. I killed you, I--"

"Oh, Dr. Tyrell," Jackson said, shaking his head sympathetically, "You're in my world. It goes by my rules. I can't die."

The train started rumbling as if it'd been hit by an earthquake. The alarms blared even louder; there only one minute remaining now. Delilah watched Tyrell tightening his fists, readying himself for a repeat of the earlier scene. She did the same, though she'd lost so much blood in her arms by now that her hands felt numb. Her and Tyrell had made it so far; they couldn't give up now.

"Oh!" Jackson said, "The gang is all here!"

Jackson pointed behind them. Delilah turned around to see six Grey-Man walking up, moaning. Her heart was beating so fast it felt like it was going to explode.

"Six?" she asked.

"Six Grey-Man to stand in for the six of us," Tyrell stated, "Counting the two guys we never met."

"Not quite," Jackson said, "You think the Grey-Men are merely representative of you? No, no, no. The Grey-Men ARE you. In the case of the other four who died, their Grey-Men are the only thing that's left. Their real bodies are lying in bed right now, mysteriously soaked in blood and primed for the evening news."

Delilah hadn't been counting the seconds down, but she knew there couldn't be many left. Jackson was trying to distract them from hitting the disable switch. She looked at Tyrell. He nodded. They lunged forward.

"Sorry, this game isn't going to be that fair," Jackson said.

Jackson knocked Tyrell back first. Delilah struggled to reach past him. Her hands were on the disable switch for a moment, then torn away. She reached out again desperately. Jackson threw her up against the wall and held her there. She struggled to fight him back. Tyrell lunged for the switch. He was almost able to grab onto it when Delilah heard explosions rocking around the back of the train.

It was too late.

As the explosions continued, Delilah felt the peculiar sensation of the floor beneath her falling away. It felt like a rollercoaster, except a rollercoaster is only a simulation of death. On a rollercoaster, no matter how far you plummet and how scary it might seem, you can always tell yourself that you're going to live.

This wasn't a rollercoaster.

Gravity seemed to change directions, as Delilah was thrown back through the open doors of several compartments. She grabbed onto the side of a door as the train began plummeting down the side of the mountain. She desperately looked around for something that could save her. Tyrell, Jackson and even the Grey-Men had disappeared.

Delilah lost her grip. She tried to cling onto the wall with her long fingernails, but the force of the train's descent tore them right out of her fingers.

"TYRELL!" she screamed.

The craggy cliffs of the Lee Grady mountain range punctured the train's surface. A giant boulder toppled in Delilah's direction. There was no way for her to move out of its way as it crashed against her.

Delilah blacked out.

TWENTY-NINE

Blackness. Nothing but blackness. Blackness and pain. Immense pain. Cold. Horrible, stinging cold.

Tyrell shivered. His entire body felt numb and frost-bitten. He stirred out of his forced sleep. He barely remembered the train wreck. He couldn't tell how long he'd been out.

Tyrell opened his eyes to discover that he was sprawled out on the edge of a snowy cliff. The Lee Grady mountain range, a mountain range that only existed in Jackson's imagination, was below him. Torn bits of steel were strewn about. Snow drifted down from the gray sky.

As consciousness returned to him, Tyrell hurriedly crawled away from the edge. His body screamed out in pain; it was so stiff that it hurt to move.

His skin was covered in frozen blood. Small, sharp pieces of metal were embedded into his stomach, shoulder and elbow.

Delilah was nowhere to be seen. Tyrell attempted to get back on his feet with several jerky motions, but was hit by a jabbing pain in his kneecap. It was broken. He collapsed into the snow again.

Lying down to rest, he examined his surroundings. Behind him was an even higher, almost completely vertical cliff edge that reminded him of the rock walls he used to climb in gym class, towering hundreds of feet into the air. Tyrell slowly got back on his feet, supporting his weight against the wall with both hands.

Tyrell looked up to the top of the mountain; the remainder of the train was teetering over the edge, swaying in the howling wind. From the top, he heard Jackson's laugh echo all the way down to him. Then, he heard another sound from the same location.

Delilah was screaming.

She was alive, but maybe not for much longer. Tyrell examined the rock wall. He'd have to scale up it somehow. His knee was broken but with enough willpower, he could do it. He had to do it. She'd die if he didn't; if not from Jackson, then from the freezing temperatures on the mountain. Tyrell grabbed a sharp piece of rock and got ready to hoist himself up.

"You're a brave man," Jackson said, behind him.

Tyrell turned. Jackson was suddenly standing at the edge of the cliff, appearing out of thin air like a ghost. He had a slightly more reserved smile on his bearded face this time. He was still bathed in blood, as if a bucket of it had been overturned on his head, Carrie-style.

"Wish I could say the same for you, 'old friend.' Wish I could say the same," Tyrell muttered.

Jackson wistfully looked down at the drop, like he was an artist examining his own painting. In a way, he was.

"Ah, snow," Jackson said ponderously, "I would imagine that all this snow reminds you of something, doesn't it? Something...white, perhaps?"

Tyrell twitched. No, not now, he couldn't let that affect him now. He bit his lip, letting Jackson's words disappear into the air.

ENSLAVEMENT

Tyrell heard the moans of the Grey-Men above him. He was running out of time. He had to scale up this cliff fast. He couldn't let Jackson distract him again.

"I'm not arguing this," Tyrell stated, "You're an asshole, Jackson. I'm done with you, and I'm done with your games."

Jackson tried to smile, but looked away with a surprisingly hurt expression. Tyrell tried not to overanalyze this. It made no sense; he and Jackson, the true Jackson anyway, had never actually been friends. The maniac was trying to kill him. How could he be hurt by such a rejection?

"I'm sorry to hear that," Jackson said.

"Too bad. I don't care about this snow, white or not. It's not really snow. It's just an illusion, and I'm going to make it my illusion. I'm scaling to the top of this cliff and rescuing the other person you've thrown into this fucking nightmare."

Jackson scoffed. It wasn't the same, ultra-confident laugh as before, though. He was still hurt by Tyrell's comment. Tyrell felt bewildered by this but again, tried not to think about it. He was sick of Jackson's bullshit.

"How do you plan on doing that?" Jackson asked, "Or even better, what are you going to do when you get up there? Not that you'll ever make it that far. Look at the size of that cliff. Look at your injuries. You even have a broken knee."

Tyrell felt his knee twitch in pain as Jackson looked at it. The local crackpot's eyes had turned into sharp instruments of death. Jackson laughed, somewhat more assuredly again.

"I guess I'll have to make do with the illusion of a broken knee, then," Tyrell said.

"No. No. No, Tyrell, your interpretation of this whole thing is embarrassingly simplistic. This isn't just an illusion that I threw you all in, where all you have to do is blink and you'll return to your everyday life. This is the landscape of your combined minds, Tyrell! This is a battle to the death between you and the forces that try to destroy you from within, on a daily basis, 24/7. I'm only the referee. I'm the writer, casting all of you fun little characters in my personal play."

"Why?" Tyrell demanded, "Why the hell are you doing this? This is all that technological hypnosis shit you were talking about, right?"

Jackson shook his head. He seemed genuinely disappointed in what Tyrell had said. He dug his hands into his pockets, searching for something.

"Oh, there's so much more going on here than a simple technological hypnosis, Tyrell. What a naïve little agnostic you really are."

Tyrell stopped cold. He'd never mentioned his religious beliefs to Jackson before. Jackson looked at him knowingly.

"You know exactly what I'm talking about," Jackson said with a low menace in his voice.

"No. I'm not dealing with this. Fuck you, Jackson. I'm going up this cliff."

Tyrell walked back to the cliff. He didn't turn around. He wouldn't let himself look Jackson in the eyes again. The man was too dangerously charismatic to risk talking to.

"Well," Jackson's voice called out, "I have something you might want to snort a couple lines of first! You know, just for the little bit of extra energy you need."

He heard Jackson pulling a plastic bag from his pocket. He gritted his teeth. No, not that. Not now.

"Maybe more than a few lines?" Jackson asked.

"No..." Tyrell murmured.

Tyrell struggled to fight against the chemical urges in his body. He knew what Jackson was holding. Then, he heard the plastic bag rustling in the wind. It was too much. He turned around, as a violent craving began to pump through his veins.

Jackson held out the cocaine.

THIRTY

Delilah pulled her body out of the shattered rear window of the train. She wasn't sure how long she'd been out, but it didn't really matter. All that mattered was that she was still alive, which was a miracle in and of itself.

She was on top of the mountain, though still a good running distance from the peak. The cold wind bit into any bits of exposed skin like an army of locusts. Her hands and wrists felt completely numb, but the cuts had dried into scabs again; not much skin was left anymore. Though her head felt like it'd been hit with a wrecking ball, she was surprisingly unhurt.

Delilah looked at the other mountains in the distance. The remains of the train lay around her, a heaping wreck. Now what was she going to do? She looked back toward the peak of the mountain.

The dark silhouettes of the six Grey-Men were in the distance, shambling toward her.

There was nowhere to run. She was on the top of a mountain, with no way down. Tyrell was dead by now; the realization of that made her tear up. Jackson was…well, hopefully he was dead too, but she had her doubts.

Delilah wrapped her arms around herself, trying to warm up. The Grey-Man continued their march. They moaned. Her most agonizing memories flooding back into her mind. The rape. The first time she'd cut. All the times she'd cut since then. She had a vision of her parents walking into her bedroom tomorrow, finding the bloody wreckage of their daughter. She knew these memories were the Grey-Men trying to get to her, but they were doing a good job at it.

"I'm not running away," she said, just as much to herself as to them.

"Good," the voice whispered, "We don't want you to run."

She was too frightened to breathe. There was no way out. Of course, there'd never been a way out. Jackson's game had never been a fair one.

One of the Grey-Men strode out in front of the others. She could see its features clearly now. Its arms were a roadmap of open, crisscrossing cuts that put even Delilah's wrists to shame. Long strands of loose flesh hung limply from the creature's wounds, while the cuts themselves were yellow, festering and infected. Blood dripped down its long fingers, leaving a trail in the snow.

Its face had a miserable expression that made Delilah wince. Oily tears poured from its eyes. It wasn't moaning like the other Grey-Men; it was wheezing, painfully.

The Grey-Men formed a circle around Delilah, all of them at least eight feet tall, even with hunched shoulders. After all that happened, she was done trying to find an escape. There was no escape from this mad world. Her problems had overwhelmed her.

"God," she said angrily, "If you want to kill me just do it already."

"No," the voice said, "No, Delilah. We want to release you. You can escape, the same way you've always escaped."

"I'm done running away--" she started.

The lead Grey-Man screamed into the skies, causing Delilah to scream back in terror. She looked around worriedly. The lead Grey-Man grunted, suddenly in a tremendous amount of pain. It looked at her with its empty eyes.

"You just have to do what you've always done, Delilah. Cut deep. Cut deeper than you ever have before. Let the adrenaline flow. Get away from your problems. Cut yourself...or let us cut you."

The lead Grey-Man shook tensely. Large bulges appeared in its flesh. Delilah tried to run away but another Grey-Man picked her up and threw her back to the ground. She started panting.

The creature's bulges split open. Long razor blades tore through its skin, all extended towards her. The creature looked like a porcupine. It grabbed one of the blades, ripped it out of its body and threw it at her. It spun through the air and landed next to her hand.

"The choice is yours."

The Grey-Men moaned into the sky. Delilah screamed again. Coming back to her senses, she quickly tried to figure out an escape. There weren't any. Not this time. Either she was going to cut herself again, just as she'd done a thousand times, or the Grey-Men would do it for her. Just like real life, she felt trapped in a routine she had no control over. Nothing had changed.

Delilah picked up the razor blade.

THIRTY-ONE

Tyrell looked at the coke. He looked up at the cliff from where Delilah had screamed. Jackson smiled at him knowingly.

His body ached for the coke. He just needed a little bit, a pick-me-up. That was all he needed. He'd been a fool to have spent this whole day thinking he could quit; sure, it was easy not to crave it as much when it wasn't available, but nigh-on impossible when it was right there.

"Go ahead!" Jackson said, "Just a pinch of it, then you can go on your suicide run up that cliff."

Tyrell looked at the bag. He tried to resist. He tried looking away and pretending it wasn't there. But the fact was that it was there. It was right in

289

front of him. As much as his conscience screamed at him not to do it, he took the bag into his hands.

Tyrell tried to force himself into a state of denial. It was all going to be okay. Sure, Jackson was a scheming lunatic, but he had also been his friend, just yesterday. This was some kind of reward, maybe, for getting to the end of this whole game. Tyrell emptied the bag into the palm of his hand. A dollar bill was inside, already rolled up into a tube.

"Godammit," Tyrell muttered, "Godammit, Jackson."

"Again, Tyrell, that's not my favorite expression."

The coke, which had already been cut to perfection, eerily spread itself into four lines on Tyrell's palm, as if it'd been guided by an invisible finger. Tyrell looked at Jackson, who shrugged playfully.

"I'll have one with you," Jackson said, "If you don't mind. We should get away from all this."

Tyrell looked at the coke again. He couldn't trust Jackson. Could he? He put one finger in the powder, brought it to his lips and tasted it. It was pure, purer than most of the dirty, cheap stuff he usually snorted.

"Y'know," Tyrell said, "I've known you a long time, Jackson."

"Longer than you think," Jackson said, smiling, "Far longer than you think. All of you are more familiar with me and my...well, all of my friends, than you'll ever realize."

Tyrell considered this comment and then looked back up at the cliff. Delilah could be running out of time, for all he knew. The coke in his hand sung out to him. The voice in his mind demanded for him to stop talking, to stop thinking about Delilah and just do it. Get it over with. Feel the rush. Feel the energy.

"But the thing is," Tyrell continued, "All of these things I found out about you today, well, they obviously weren't what I was expecting. Because you were hiding. You were hiding the whole time. I understand that, though. I understand that, because I guess I've spent a long time hiding too. Not just from you, not just from my girlfriend, but from myself."

Jackson glared, but tried to cover it up with another smile. He walked closer.

"Perhaps."

"You know what's ironic though, 'my friend?' You really wanna know?" Tyrell asked.

"What would that be?"

Tyrell smiled.

"You think you have me figured out. Well, guess what-- you're way off."

Tyrell threw the coke off the side of the mountain. It drifted down, becoming one with the snow. It was gone. Jackson, who'd always been so confident, had a shocked expression on his face. Tyrell almost regretted his decision; he was shaking, craving the coke even more now that he'd denied it, desperately wanting to beg Jackson for a replacement bag. But Tyrell felt redeemed; maybe an addict is never truly cured of his addiction, but all that matters is the confidence to march forward, day by day.

"Seeya later," Tyrell said.

Tyrell walked back to the cliff. With a broken knee, it was going to a bitch trying to scale up this thing, but he had to do it. His new little sister needed him.

"Oh, so you think that you're past it all now, do you?" Jackson called out.

Tyrell didn't answer.

"Fine," Jackson continued, "By the way, though, I just thought you might like to know that Tiffany didn't kill herself."

"What?"

"I killed her. You remember that look in her eyes when she died, the one you spend all your time remembering? The look that's haunted your nightmares and made you quit med school? Her throat was cut, but she was trying to tell you that it wasn't suicide. I cut her throat. Me."

Tyrell stopped. He gritted his teeth. Jackson was in his head, and the bastard knew it. The image of his sister's dying eyes played through his mind. She had seemed like she was trying to say--

No. He couldn't get caught up in that right now. As much as he wanted to jump backward and strangle Jackson to death, he couldn't distract himself with that right now, and he already knew it wouldn't do anything. Whether Jackson was lying through his teeth or revealing the dark truth, all he wanted was a reaction.

Tyrell began scaling the rock wall.

THIRTY-TWO

Delilah held razor blade right up to her wrist. She started pressing it against the skin, but her shaking hands dropped it. She panicked.

"Cut yourself. Get it over with. Escape the pain, escape everything."

The Grey-Men were huddled around her. She picked up the razor blade and dropped it again. Her hands were so numb and frostbitten.

"Fine! Cut me!" she screamed.

Delilah twisted into a contorted figure on the snowy ground. The lead Grey-Men sprouted millions of razorblades out of its flesh again, and reached out one spiked hand toward her. She stuck her neck out. It could cut her for all she cared, just so long as it got the fucking thing over with.

Then, a voice called out from the distance.

"DELILAH! DON'T DO IT?"

"Tyrell?"

Tyrell was a small, dark figure climbing up the edge of the cliff. He started running toward her, limping on one leg.

"No," she said, "wait…"

"The time for waiting is OVER. You can see him after the blood starts flowing. Get the satisfaction. Get the--"

The Grey-Man's razor-covered hand swiped at her neck. She ducked away from it.

"DELILAH!" Tyrell yelled again.

"I'm sorry!" she called out, crying.

She ducked away from another swipe by the Grey-Man. This time, one of the blades left a thin slice on her forehead, that started seeping blood instantly. Two more Grey-Men grabbed her by the shoulders.

"No, 'sorry' ain't gonna cut it today," Tyrell said.

Tyrell jumped into the center of the circle and threw Delilah under his body. She tried to pull him down with her, to protect him, but he wouldn't budge. He grabbed her hand and tried to pull her away from the Grey-Men, fighting their long hands away at every turn.

"You can't beat them, Tyrell! Get away while you still can!"

"Wrong," he said, "Dead wrong. You need to believe that you can beat 'em. If you let them win, we don't have a chance. Remember the train, remember--"

292

A Grey-Man scooped Tyrell off the floor and threw him away. Delilah watched his body fly through the air; he slammed into the ground and began sliding off the icy edge of the cliff.

Delilah threw herself past the arms of the Grey-Man, escaping the circle. She charged toward Tyrell and grabbed his hand right before he slid off. He looked at her, smiling. She smiled back.

"Maybe you're right," she said.

The Grey-Men moaned behind her. Distracted, Delilah's foot slipped on the ice. With all the strength in her small body, she desperately yanked Tyrell toward her until he'd pulled himself off the cliff edge.

"What do we do now?" she asked.

For some reason, Delilah expected an answer. Some detailed psychoanalysis of their situation, maybe. Instead, Tyrell shrugged hopelessly.

"Hell if I know."

Delilah looked back at the six Grey-Men. They were running toward them now. She grabbed Tyrell's hand.

"How about we get the fuck out of here, to start with?"

They took off running, the Grey-Men following in hot pursuit. There was no way down the mountain; they'd never be able to scale the rock walls fast enough to get past them. The only thing they could do was run further up the mountain instead.

Delilah quickly realized that Tyrell was slowing her down immensely with his limp, but she wouldn't abandon him. They'd been there for each other this whole time. If he died, so did she. They were in this together.

"I think we need to go there, to the peak of the mountain," Tyrell said, panting, "Don't ask me why. Gut feeling."

"Better than nothing," she responded.

As they neared the peak, Tyrell collapsed in exhaustion. Delilah desperately tried to pull him up.

"Please, get up! Don't leave me! Get up!"

"I..." Tyrell started.

His voice was raspy. He struggled to pull himself to his feet. He finally managed it, but could barely stand without collapsing again.

"Let's keep going!"

"No need," Tyrell muttered.

293

The Grey-Men had stopped pursuing them. They stood still now, content to form a wall behind them. Delilah's first instinct was to take advantage of the fact that they'd stopped, so she tried to continue their mad dash toward the peak. Tyrell stopped her.

"Look," he said, glaring ahead.

Jackson was standing at the peak of the mountain, the king of his world. He had a satisfied expression on his face and his arms were crossed. He looked down upon them and chuckled.

"End of the line, guys!"

THIRTY-THREE

Tyrell looked at Jackson with disgust. All the times he'd talked to the local crackpot in the bar, he could've never predicted that the man would one day be standing at the peak of a mountain, soaked in blood, so confidently taking control of Tyrell's destiny. Again, he wanted to run up the peak and wipe that smug grin off his face. Even if he didn't realize how useless it was to attack him, though, he was too exhausted to attempt. He could barely stand on two feet without wincing.

"The black man and the troubled teenage girl!" Jackson shouted down, "Since when do you two make it to the end of a horror movie?"

Tyrell stumbled forward and fell to his knees. As Jackson laughed at him, he gritted his teeth and glanced back at the six Grey-Men lined up behind him. It was only a matter of time before they went back into motion and slaughtered him and Delilah.

"So this isn't tech hypnosis, huh?" Tyrell shouted back.

"It isn't?" Delilah asked.

"Of course not!" Jackson responded, "It'd be so much easier for all of you if it was!"

Tyrell stood up again, shakily. Delilah tried to support him by grabbing his shoulder but it wasn't much help. They were at the end of the line; he had to either take down Jackson or take down the Grey-Men, and he didn't see much chance of doing either.

Jackson looked down on them with an inhumanely sadistic expression. It was only then that Tyrell realized that Jackson might actually not be human. He might be…could he be? Was that possible?

"What are you?" Tyrell asked.

"Interesting thing to ponder," Jackson mused.

"I'm not asking so we can 'ponder' it, Jackson! You've been hinting at something. What are you, the devil? Lucifer? Satan?" Tyrell asked sarcastically.

Jackson smiled. It was a sickening smile, the kind that spoke a million words without making a sound. Suddenly, Tyrell felt a giant pit in his stomach at the realization that he might not be all that far off.

In Jackson's smile, though, there was a strange kind of insecurity. Perhaps he was a lesser demon. He felt nauseous at the fact that he was even pondering such an idea.

"Do you want me to be the devil?" Jackson asked, still grinning madly.

Delilah clenched onto his shoulder with a death grip. She was shaking, but so was he. His view of the world was shattering before him.

"There's no way," Tyrell said, "There's just no fucking way."

"Really? Do you think so?" Jackson said, "Or are you just as undereducated as the rest of the world?

"You can't be Satan. He isn't real. It's just not possible..." he said.

"Ah, Tyrell," Jackson interrupted him, "Just keep in mind that Satan was originally a title used for a variety of entities that challenged the religious faith of people in the Hebrew Bible. At least, that's what it says on Wikipedia, isn't it? I think so. Been a while since I've updated the article...oh, wait, now you're curious, aren't you?"

Jackson stopped as the Grey-Men began to roar. Tyrell felt the snow slipping beneath his feet and caught himself before falling over again.

"Why? Why are you doing this to us?!" Delilah screamed.

The Grey-Men were walking again, but taking their time. They were cornering them for a slow, miserable death. As they walked, Jackson suddenly burst into a passionate rage.

"You should be thanking me!" Jackson screamed, "Those of you who have died, especially! I've freed you! I've freed all of you, from the state of enslavement that you put yourselves into!"

"Fuck that," Tyrell said, "You're forcing that logic into what's nothing more than a sick game. It's all for your amusement, not some higher moral standard."

295

Jackson's angry expression subsided. He chuckled. The Grey-Men were coming closer.

"Maybe so. I'll admit that I'm not one for sympathy. You know what I despise the most about you people, though? Your miserable need to find meaning in everything. Chaos happens. Things occur without a reason. If this entire dream were nothing more than a silly little experiment, so what? Remember the Book of Job?"

"Jackson, I--"

"Remember it? Nothing more than a meaningless bet between God and…heh, well, 'Satan.' At least, that's my interpretation, though you people always seem to view it differently. So what if this is random? Let it be random. Let it be chaos. Let your deaths be meaningless!"

The Grey-Men started tearing massive, icy boulders off the ground and hurtling them in Tyrell and Delilah's direction. Tyrell quickly pulled Delilah to the floor. As they stood up, they were greeted by an even worse sight.

The Grey-Men were running.

Tyrell desperately grabbed Delilah and run forward. He tripped over his own leg. Delilah tried to pull him off the ground as the Grey-Men came nearer.

"Ah, six Grey-Men, I love it!" Jackson chanted, "Six, six, six! One for each of you!"

"Missing one, aren't you?" Tyrell yelled.

One of the Grey-Men grabbed Delilah by the leg and threw her to the ground. They didn't want her. Not yet. They wanted Tyrell. They knew full well who Jackson's real target had become.

"Are you kidding?!" Jackson said, "Just because I was on the train, you think I fall prey to the same pitiable addictions that all of you do? HA! I think not!"

The Grey-Man reached towards Tyrell. He somersaulted away from it, catapulting right into the legs of another one. He quickly backed up to get away, but it wasn't fast enough. All he was doing was buying time. A man with a limp and a teenage girl could never escape six of these immortal beings.

Suddenly, Jackson was standing next to him. The demonic man was smiling.

"If only you knew all the time I put into this," Jackson whispered into his ear, "There's something so…satisfying, about watching people like you sow the seeds of your own destruction."

The Grey-Man picked up Tyrell and held him over its head. It wrapped its fingers around his body and squeezed. Tyrell felt the life expiring from him. His vision was darkening. He heard his ribs crack under the strength of the Grey-Man. He closed his eyes.

"TYRELL!" Delilah screamed, "Don't--"

She was cut off. They were getting her too. Winning was hopeless in a no-win scenario. As Jackson had said, they'd done nothing more than sow the seeds of their own destruction. Tyrell couldn't see any way out.

Then, a thought occurred to him.

He quickly replayed Jackson's speeches in his head again. Sowing the seeds of their own destruction. All the time that went into this. Addiction, addiction, addiction. That was the solution.

"Stop!" Tyrell gasped.

The Grey-Man didn't let go. Its grip became tighter. Tyrell tried to wrench himself free but it was no use. Once again, the escape wasn't physical. It was psychological.

"S…stop," he gasped again, "It's not me you want…"

The Grey-Man's grip weakened for only a second, but it was long enough. Tyrell threw himself out of its hand and landed in the cold snow. He looked back at Delilah, who was still being strangled to death. He didn't have time to waste.

Jackson walked up to him, cracking his knuckles like an experience brawler. Wearing all that blood like a new tuxedo, Jackson even looked like a devil. He glared into Tyrell's eyes, making him look down uneasily.

"I think it's you they want," Jackson said, "Well, you and her, if you want to get technical."

Delilah gasped for air. Tyrell took a deep breath and again looked Jackson in the eyes. He summoned all the confidence within him. The Grey-Men weren't reaching for him anymore; Jackson, their master, wanted to kill him with his own hands. Good.

"You put a lot of the effort into this, didn't you?" Tyrell asked.

"Of course."

"A lot of blood, sweat and tears went into this project. Almost like you were obsessed with it. There's a funny thing about obsession, though."

Jackson smiled. But it was a fake smile. He was confused, but he still wanted to appear self-assured. Tyrell was trembling like a little girl on the inside, but stayed confident.

"What's that?" Jackson asked.

Tyrell wanted to look away. He didn't.

"You think you're the center of the universe, Jackson, but face it; spending your life obsesses sing something like this illusion, pouring so much energy into provoking our pain, into creating an exploitation of our misery and torment...sounds a bit like addiction, doesn't it?"

Jackson scoffed; "Not really."

"No?" Tyrell said, now with a big grin, "If we're pathetic, Jackson, then you're the most pathetic one of us all. Because you're not just addicted to a chemical substance or a biological reaction. You're addicted to our pain. You're addicted to us."

Jackson stepped back. His bearded face was suddenly decorated by a shocked expression. Tyrell smiled even wider, following him, then turned around. The Grey-Men turned to look at him with hostile expressions.

"Hey, Grey-Men!" Tyrell shouted, "Put the girl down! You can't exploit our weaknesses anymore, you can't feed off our addictions; we've beat them. There's only one addict left on this mountain and he's standing right behind me!"

Tyrell pointed at Jackson. Jackson had faked a variety of emotions that day, but this time he couldn't hide his sheer terror. He scurried up the peak of the mountain.

"The logic doesn't fit--" Jackson started.

The Grey-Man holding Delilah screamed into the sky. It dropped her to the ground, as Tyrell had told it to. Jackson's eyes nearly bulged out of his skull.

"Stop," Jackson commanded, "Now. Now!"

The Grey-Men took a last look at Tyrell and Delilah, and then walked past them. They started running towards Jackson, long fingers outstretched. Jackson tried to run, but one of them caught him in its hand and held him in the sky.

"Stop them!" Jackson shouted down, "If I die in this illusion, then all of you will die in real life!"

Tyrell looked away.

"I guess we'll just have to take that chance."

The Grey-Men all simultaneously grabbed onto Jackson's limbs and began to pull his body apart. The arms tore loose first, then the legs and finally the head. Jackson's head, even detached, didn't stop screaming. His limbs didn't stop struggling to get away. Even when his intestines fell from his stomach, they twisted all around the Grey-Men like a living snake. Apparently, Jackson couldn't die.

Then something even stranger happened. The Grey-Men's bodies started merging together, like multiple clay figures being pushed into one. They slowly twisted together into a single, enormous Grey-Man, groaning from multiple mouths. Jackson's loose body parts continued fighting for freedom, but were absorbed into the fused creature.

Jackson's right leg cut loose from the amalgamation and tripped the merged Grey-Man. The horrifying creation toppled over the other side of the mountain. The sound of Jackson's scream bellowed into the air, slowly dying away as he dropped further and further. Tyrell limped as quickly as he could to look over the edge, but it was too late. The creature had disappeared into the mist.

Tyrell looked back at Delilah. She was still slumped on the ground, unconscious and not breathing. Suddenly, he was struck by panic. He stumbled back to her, falling multiple times. When he finally reached her, he turned her face upwards and looked under her eyelids. She was completely unconscious.

"Fuck!" he said, "No, no, no! Don't be dead. Wake up!"

He slapped her across the face, to try and wake her up. She didn't stir. He slapped her again. He felt along her side; her ribs hadn't been broken by the Grey-Man, the way his had been. She had to be alive. She just had to be.

"Wake up!"

He had no medical instruments, nothing he could do to help. Tiffany's dead eyes haunted his mind again. As he considering performing CPR, he slapped her across the face again even harder, hoping that more force might wake her up.

ENSLAVEMENT

Delilah stirred.

"I...am I..." she whispered, "Are we...are we..."

"I...I think it's over," he said.

Delilah opened her eyes and smiled. When Tyrell looked at her, he didn't see Delilah's face. He saw Tiffany, alive and well, just as she'd appeared before she'd died. Tears of happiness flowed down his cheeks.

"Hey," he said, "What'dya know. I got it right this time."

Suddenly, the air became shockingly warm. Tyrell felt a surreal feeling of lightheadedness. The snow was gone. The remains of the train were gone. The mountains were gone. Everything was fading away. The dream was ending.

For all he knew, the end of the dream could be the end of his life. But he didn't stress over it. Sometimes, it was nice to just let things happen instead of panicking when you can't control them.

He closed his eyes and waited to see what would happen.

THIRTY-FOUR

Delilah woke up in her own bed.

She almost screamed at the sudden change of scenery. She jumped out of bed hurriedly and was greeted by a horrible soreness in all her joints, as if she'd been in a train crash. Then again, she had just been in a train crash, so that made perfect sense.

At least, she thought she had. Hadn't she?

Delilah let the real world sink back in. She looked at her room. The blood stains were still fresh on the carpet. It was still night outside; she couldn't have been asleep more than an hour. She tried to tell herself that it was all a dream but something in the back of her mind screamed that it wasn't. A little voice...not quite a grey voice, but another voice.

Suddenly, she remembered the black pickup truck out the window. She peeked outside fearfully. The truck was gone. She wondered if it'd ever been there in the first place.

Then, Delilah got up and looked at herself in the mirror. As she looked at her wounds, her fantasies that it had all been nothing more than a dream shattered like a pane of glass. It had been all too real.

Her arms and hands were mutilated almost beyond recognition. The cuts and gashes were all dried up, but completely unexplainable. Her wrists had more scabs than skin.

She started crying. She would've thought she'd be relieved just to be alive, but she wasn't. She was a wreck. She was a disaster. She hadn't deserved to be a survivor.

Delilah curled up in bed, still crying. Her dry, scratchy arms felt like sandpaper against the more tender skin of her legs. She tried to get to sleep but was too terrified of what her dreams might bring out. The last one had been bad enough.

Finally, she gave up on sleep. She reached under the bed and took out her bag of razorblades.

She took out one of the blades and held it, examining it in the glimmer of the Los Angeles city lights outside her window. She'd just spent an entire dream fighting against her urges. But...it was just a dream. Thinking on it, she considered the fact that she'd nearly passed out from the cut she'd made before going to sleep. Maybe all of these wounds had been self-inflicted, and weren't from some crazy hallucination. Maybe she'd been in some kind of daze when she'd done it and her subconscious had explained it away through the dream.

Yes, a dream. Tyrell, the train, that homicidal (or as the case may be, demonic) conspiracy theorist were all just characters in her head. The razor blade in her hands wasn't her enemy, it was an old friend. Maybe it wasn't a good friend, but it had helped her through the years more than of her true friends ever had.

She put the blade away. Not tonight. She needed to get to sleep tonight and after all, the nightmare she'd just survived did make her want to stop cutting. She was too old for that shit now and besides, if a dream was the subconscious mind's way of trying to communicate things, then clearly her inner mind was pissed off and trying to tell her to stop cutting.

No, not tonight. But maybe tomorrow.

THIRTY-FIVE

Tyrell opened his eyes. He was back in his bedroom. He smiled at the sight of his girlfriend Rita lying next to him. If he ever tried to tell her all that happened she wouldn't believe a word of it, the damn practical woman that she was.

301

ENSLAVEMENT

As he got out of bed, he was greeted by an immense pain in his abdomen; his ribs were still cracked. He stood up and his leg limped to the ground. Nice, apparently that was still broken too.

None of that mattered right now, though. Sure, it'd be a bitch to explain it to Rita later on, and she'd never believe him. But the important thing was that he'd made it. He and Delilah had won. As soon as he was fully awake, he'd wake up Rita and get to the hospital. Not yet, though. Right now, he wanted to soak in all the inherent joy of the moment. Tyrell walked over to his desk, still smiling.

As he took a seat, he came to the surreal realization that he'd never see Jackson Ubel again. Whatever Jackson was and wherever he'd gone to, he was gone.

Or was Jackson still there, maybe in another form, waiting for him to fuck up again?

Tyrell opened the front drawer of the desk. His bag of coke was inside, tucked away in the back. He looked at Rita to make sure she was asleep and then took the bag into his hands.

It's funny how something inanimate, like a drug, can have so much power over a man. Tyrell looked at the white powder curiously. Before Jackson's nightmare had sucked him in, Tyrell had usually tried to pretend to himself that he wasn't an addict. Anytime he craved his fix, he'd blamed the evil coke. But a substance itself is never evil. Tyrell hadn't been some poor sucker powerlessly absorbed by the power of addiction; he made the choice to not be in control of his actions.

It was time to turn it all around. He'd get rid of this bag first. He'd go to the hospital and get himself fixed up and then he'd check into rehab. The nightmare had been a horrible event, but that didn't mean he couldn't use the lessons of it to his advantage.

Tyrell walked over the window, wincing at the pain in his leg. He'd have to get the hospital soon, before his wounds became worse, but he had something to take care of something first. He opened the window, the bag of coke in hand.

Then, he heard the mental voice that he recognized all too well. He realized with a heavy heart that no matter what battles he won, the voice would always be there.

302

"Don't waste it. Sure, quit, but have just one last hurrah first. Finish the bag. No reason to waste it…"

Tyrell twitched. On the mountain, he'd chosen to save Delilah's life over his addiction but then, the choice had been easier because of the heightened stakes. Here, his choice could only be self-motivated. This was the choice that would truly decide things.

Tyrell smiled and shook his head. He crumpled up the bag in his fist. He'd already made his decision.

"Fuck you, Jackson."

He threw the bag out the window.

THIRTY-SIX

Up in the Lee Grady Mountains, a mountain range that never existed in reality, it was still snowing. It would always be snowing. Tyrell Freeman and Delilah King would never see those cold peaks again, but there was still one man--if he could even be called a man--that was trapped there.

Jackson Ubel cracked open his frost-covered eyelids. He'd never felt welcome anywhere, but here he was truly alone. He was abandoned and lost, trapped in an ironic punishment of his own design.

He struggled to move, just to prove that he still was capable of motion. No use. His entire body was as frozen stiff as a corpse. Even though he'd managed to reassemble the damned thing after all the Grey-Men had pulled it apart, as Jackson was a man of many dark talents, he was still limited by the rules of his own world, and the warped logic that he'd created for it. He could've laughed at the irony of it if it didn't sicken him so much. He couldn't die, but he could definitely suffer.

Jackson's legs had become frozen in the ice below him; everything from the torso up was free, but he was trapped in place.

This would've been bad enough, but his very own Grey-Man wouldn't let it end there. Oh no, that would go against its very nature. Grey-Men fed off the weaknesses and addictions of others. Tyrell had been right when he'd said Jackson was addicted to the pain of the others, a simple though incredibly irritating twist on logic that Jackson hated himself for overlooking. As a result, though, his Grey-Man was the worst of them all.

Grey-Men always mutated to embody the addictions of their "host," so Jackson's was the worst of them all. His Grey-Men was the combination

303

of all the others, joined together in some sick abomination. It, too, had its legs frozen in the ice behind him and its frozen fingers were wrapped around his waist; it felt as if it and Jackson were attached at the hip. The Grey-Man had three heads, each one with multiple rows of shark-like teeth; while the heads on the left and right swiveled about, constantly moaning (no matter how hard he tried, Jackson could never get used to the persistent moaning) the head in the middle had bit down on Jackson's forehead and was slowly chewing his brain. It would never finish chewing, because there was no end goal in sight; it was only chewing so that Jackson's agony would be never-ending.

Ah, irony. If anyone else was in his place, Jackson would've smiled. But no, it was him. It would always be him, trapped in the ice, with his three-headed Grey-Man chewing on his head until the end of time. Jackson finally wished that he could've gotten the chance to live life as a human being; things were so simple for them, and they didn't even realize it. They could escape from their tortures. They could redeem themselves. If nothing else, they were allowed to die.

Jackson screamed out in anguish at the icy landscape around him. No one answered. Not even the Grey-Man.

There was nothing he could do. There was nothing he could say and nothing left for him to think about but his own pain. He'd sealed his own fate. It was his own personal "death" sentence for having the gall to think he was so powerful.

In the end, Jackson wasn't any stronger than a human being. He too was enslaved by his own addiction but for him, there was nothing and no one that would ever free him.

His punishment was eternal.

About Nicholas Conley:

*Nicholas Conley is a 20 something writer from Los Angeles, who has also resided in Arizona, New Hampshire and North Carolina. He spends his free time exploring the open road in search of inspiration and new experiences. His work has been published in **Uncanny Allegories, The Coffee Shop Chronicles, Vol.1, Dark Moon Digest, Short Story Library, Microhorror,** and **Gravediggings**.*

Made in the USA
Charleston, SC
05 March 2011